You're a poison. And I'm addicted.

# NO GOOD

STEVIE J COLE & LP LOVELL

Copyright © 2020 by Stevie J Cole & LP Lovell

All rights reserved.

No part of this book may be reproduced in any form or by any electronic or mechanical means, including information storage and retrieval systems, without written permission from the author, except for the use of brief quotations in a book review.

Cover Design: Lori Jackson

❀ Created with Vellum

# CHAPTER 1

## DREW

"WET FOR ME, BABY GIRL?"

The neon light flashed through the curtained windows. And it provided just enough glow that I could make out Hot Guy's face as he maneuvered me toward the back of the van. All dark hair and perfect jawline, a smirk that promised to make all my problems disappear—of which I had a list a mile long. One look from him had been nothing short of a siren call to a lonely girl needing to feel wanted for just a few moments. So there I was. In a van. In a bar parking lot, letting his filthy words replay through my head while he grabbed my hips and kissed my throat. *Wet for me, baby girl...*

"You say that to all the girls?" I asked, then felt him smirk against my skin while he worked the strap of my dress from my shoulder.

"Only the ones I wanna fuck..."

No matter how hot his words had me, I was *not* actually going to screw him. Nope—although his lips were extremely persuasive.

My legs bumped the back seat. A moment of doubt

crept in as he lowered me to the bench. Though I was probably one in a long line of girls he'd seduced and brought out to this van, I couldn't quite find the will to care. In my defense, he might have been the hottest guy I'd ever seen, so if I were ever going to have a one-off moment of weakness, he was totally worthy. His hand roamed over my thigh, then beneath my skirt, his pure electric touch tracing me through my underwear. No guy had ever had this effect on me. And I wanted more.

"Damn," he mumbled against my throat before pulling my panties to the side, "you're soaked."

His finger slipped inside me, crooking. The flood of sensation that fired through me took any resolve I had to not bang him and threw it right out the curtained van window.

"I'm not fucking you," I said in a rush, and I wasn't sure if that declaration was meant for him or me.

"*Not* gonna fuck me, huh?" His finger worked deeper.

Arrogant prick. He absolutely thought this was a done deal. Not like I was giving him much reason to think otherwise, but still.

"So, you came out to the van to play a game of 'get to know you?' Because I'd say, this is probably a damn good way to get to know someone." He slipped another finger inside. Pressing. Pushing. Driving me crazy. "Wouldn't you?" His mouth was on my stomach now, working lower and lower.

I was so screwed. "I..."

"Or did you come out here to ask me my name and favorite color?

I hesitated for a minute, trying to form words. "Name," I finally choked out, fully aware I probably should have asked that before now. "What's your name?"

"Bellamy." He spread my legs, then settled between

them, locking eyes with me as he nipped at the inside of my thigh. "What's yours?"

I sure as hell wasn't giving him *my* name, and the first name that sprung to mind was my best friend's. "Genevieve." Okay. That was bad...

"How old are you?"

"Twenty-one," I lied, fighting a moan as his lips worked higher. Okay, I was done talking, or should I say, lying. "Any more questions?"

"Yeah." His gaze locked with mine, and he removed his fingers. "How good do you taste?" Then slipped them between his lips on a groan. And that one dirty move was enough to absolutely, one hundred percent, seal my fate.

Within seconds, my underwear had been thrown somewhere onto the floorboard, and his warm tongue was on me, my hands in his hair, my hips grinding against his face as a wave of bliss crashed over me so hard, I could barely draw in a breath. It wasn't just an orgasm; it was an awakening, one that had my thighs clamped around his head, my body trembling, and my heart slamming against my ribs.

"So soon, baby girl?" He sat up, smirking as he reached for his belt.

Someone banged the outside of the van. "Hey, fucker!" a guy shouted. "We gotta problem...Psycho bitch is on the hunt. I repeat, little eagle. Psycho bitch is on the hunt. Over."

Bellamy groaned, still fiddling with his belt. "Tell her to fuck off!"

A girl was looking for him—one that his friend was keeping a lookout for, while he fooled around with *another* girl in his van? Jesus Christ, I was an idiot. Sitting up, I tugged my skirt back into place, then rummaged through the crumpled papers and music magazines littering the floorboard in search of my underwear.

Another bang sounded over the van door. "Did you hear me?"

"Yeah. Yeah." Bellamy lowered his zipper like an asshole who expected me to still touch his dick. "I heard you!"

"Wow." Forget the underwear. With a shake of my head, I opened the van door and came face to face with the guitarist from the band that had played earlier. His fist was lifted, ready to pound the side of the vehicle again.

"Damn, Bellamy," he said, giving me a quick once over. "This one's hot."

On an annoyed huff, I brushed past him then threw a middle finger over my shoulder, the steady click of my heels bouncing off the beat-up cars surrounding me as I stormed across the parking lot. On my list of recent bad decisions, this had quickly climbed to the top.

I rounded the corner of the bar, stopping at my car when the high-pitched shriek of Bellamy's name echoed through the night. I glanced back just in time to catch a curvy blonde chuck something at him. Too bad she missed, I thought as I sank behind the wheel and cranked the engine. My headlights shined over the silhouettes in the back lot when I peeled off in a squeal of tires. At least, I'd never have to see that guy again. It wasn't that I'd expected anything from a quick hookup—I wasn't stupid—but was it too much to ask that a guy *not* make me the skank he cheats on his girlfriend with?

I maneuvered down the narrow roads, speeding over potholes while the events of the last few weeks played out in my head.

Kicked out of boarding school—sent to this shithole

town to live with a father who was too busy with his business trips to even be bothered by my existence. The only communication I'd had with him since I'd arrived had been a series of emails—the latest of which came through earlier tonight—but I had been too busy getting suckered by Bellamy's smile to read it.

When I pulled into the empty driveway, my stomach sank at the thought of walking into the dark, empty monstrosity and being all alone once again. That was the very thing that had driven me to that bar tonight and right into Bellamy's eager arms. But I still didn't feel any better, so I stalled, braving the email my father had sent as my car idled on the drive.

*Drew,*
*Attached is your new school syllabus. You have orientation on Monday at 4 p.m.. I've already spoken to Eddie, and he's changed your shift.*
*William Morgan*
*CEO Darth Enterprises*

Never mind that I'd received the same sign off as his secretary...or that he'd been oh so accommodating to have changed my schedule at the shitty drive-thru he'd secured me a job at. I clicked on the attachment and opened the syllabus with Dayton High typed in bold at the top. I blinked. No, this was a mistake. I was supposed to go to Barrington Prep. Not the public school. I'd been through the neighboring town of Dayton. Once. Last Easter, when I was here on break, a road had been closed and the diversion led straight through that shit hole. The place was awful. Street after street of run-down motels and pawn shops. Graffitied, boarded-up houses. The ones that weren't boarded up looked like they needed to be condemned. And the high school? Olivia, one of the few girls here I knew, said Dayton was basically a prep school for prison. What the hell was my dad thinking? As the sense of horror crept over me, I imagined how smug my father would be if he could see me now, and I knew then that it definitely wasn't a mistake. This was another one of his punishments.

## CHAPTER 2

## BELLAMY

### TWO DAYS LATER

THE HALLS of Dayton High slowly thinned out. The bang of lockers closing grew quiet.

I took the copies of the history exam I'd stolen earlier from Weaver's class and tucked them into my back pocket before slamming my locker door. Kids paid me ten bucks a copy, and this was Dayton. Crap like this was the only way I survived.

I skirted through a group of students gathered outside the library, catching up with Hendrix and Wolf to head to our routine after-school activity—detention.

"Hey, Bell," Hendrix nudged me. A shit-eating grin spread over his face, and Wolf shook his head. "Check this. Betty Newman—" his words fell short when Nikki strutted past in her cheerleading practice shorts and tank, glaring at me like she'd slit my jugular if she could. "Whoa..." Hendrix's gaze followed her as she rounded the corner. "Pepperoni Nips is looking at you like she wants to hack off your dick and shove it up your asshole."

Wolf chuckled. Nikki acted like a woman scorned, but we'd never dated. Never talked on the phone. It was a random, drunken hookup gone wrong. One I was still paying for.

"No shit," I said. "She followed me out to Nash's van last weekend when I was trying to hook up with some hot-ass girl. And she lost her shit."

"Wait." Hendrix elbowed me. "Who'd you hook up with?"

The hottest girl I'd ever laid eyes on in my life. A girl who still had me thinking of her two days later... "Some rich girl," I said, leaning against the cinder block wall outside the lunchroom.

"A rich girl?" A devious glint sparked to life in Hendrix's eyes. "From Barrington?"

Maybe she'd gone to Barrington, but seeing as how she was twenty-one... "Don't know, man. She's older."

Hendrix punched my shoulder. "I hate you. Hooking up with cougars and shit."

"Twenty-one is not a cougar," Wolf said.

"Whatever, man. Still older. It's fine because, like I was saying...Betty Newman."

Wolf sighed, slapping a palm over his face. "Here we go about Betty...She's in band, Hendrix. She plays the tuba. She's like—"

"Exactly, man. She's *in band*. Haven't you seen that movie about all those band kids that get freaky with their band instruments?" Hendrix flattened himself to the lunchroom doors, crotch-thrusting with a laugh.

Wolf leaned in beside me. "Is he talking about an actual movie or porn or what?"

Hendrix moved away from the doors with a scowl. "*American Pie,* you uncultured cocksucker. Band kids are into some kinky shit." Then he clapped a hand to my shoulder, staring me dead in the eye like he was about to hand over some life-changing revelation. "Betty Newman takes it in the ass instead of the cooch."

I knocked his hand away. "So?"

"So?" Hendrix gaped for a second. His gaze pinged between Wolf and me. "The fact that you just said *so* disappoints me, Bell."

Mrs. Smith parted the sea of students crowding the hallway. "Outta the way." She unlocked the door, chugging a thermos everyone knew was filled with vodka, and students begrudgingly filed in.

"Sit your back ends down and be quiet," she grumbled. "Think about whatever bullshit you did to end up in here." Her purse hit the table with a thud before she sank to a stool, thermos already halfway to her lips. "No talking. Just reflecting."

Reflecting. Half the kids in here had been arrested more than once. No way in hell detention would make any of us reflect on anything. It was Dayton. There wasn't shit to reflect on.

Five minutes into detention, I'd made a quick eighty bucks from the copied tests, and Hendrix had talked some band girl into sending him a picture of her tits, which was why his phone was currently shoved in my face. I slapped his hand away just as the cafeteria doors creaked open and Hendrix let out a catcall.

Still in her short-shorts from cheerleading practice, Nora Locke stood at the door, propping it open with her hip. "And this"—she waved an unenthusiastic hand across the room—"is the cafeteria. The food's disgusting. So, don't expect much. Everything about this school is shit."

When she went to move back into the hall, I noticed a

girl beside her. Dark hair. Hot-pink dress. Sexy as hell. It was just a glimpse, but a girl as hot as Genevieve—all it took was a glance to recognize her.

Nora was the ambassador, and the only reason she ever gave someone a tour was if they were unfortunate enough to be transferred. Twenty-one my ass. If that girl were about to start at Dayton, she was as good as mine, and my dick knew it because he rose to attention.

"Is that fresh meat?" Hendrix stared at the door as it swung closed behind the two girls. "Oh shit. Did you see her, Bell?"

I'd seen her all right. Tits and pussy and all...

"It's like manna from heaven." Hendrix raised his hands in makeshift praise. "Fresh meat *this* late in the school year!"

"Yeah, I saw her," I said, already pushing to my feet and asking to be excused for the restroom.

I followed the sound of their voices to the front of the school, stopping by the lockers as Nora gave a peppy wave. And I could now say, without a reasonable doubt, the girl heading through the front doors of Dayton High was Genevieve. When she exited the building, I was right after her, crossing the parking lot in the sticky Alabama heat.

With each step I took, her steps quickened. Then I caught up. "Twenty-one, huh?"

She whipped around with a startled expression and a can of mace held out in front of her like a gun. Her face shifted into an annoyed scowl when her gaze landed on my face, and I fought a laugh. Poor little rich girl was out of her element. That was for damn sure.

She dropped the mace into her purse with a huff. "What the hell are *you* doing here?" Like she was the one who belonged in this dump?

"I think the one of us who's outta place is you," I said, dragging my gaze over her curves.

"Great. Of course, you go to the shit hole school. Why wouldn't you?" She mumbled about how awful her life was, marching off with a sway of hips. "I'm not in the mood," she said, then gave a flippant wave over her shoulder. "So, run back to your girlfriend and leave me alone."

She was mad about Nikki. That was a definite win.

I started after her again. "Oh, someone's salty as fuck."

"Or—annoyed that her poor choices are coming back to haunt her."

"Poor choices?" I scoffed, staring at her ass as I followed her between two beat-up cars. "Since when has an orgasm been a poor choice?" Because she came faster than NASA could launch a rocket.

She spun around and jabbed a finger against my chest. "Since the guy is clearly cheating on his girlfriend while giving it."

I slapped her hand away. "I don't have a girlfriend."

"Oh? Does she *know* she's not your girlfriend? Or is it just when it's convenient for you?" A condescending smirk cut across her lips. "Because no girl is going to chase a guy into a parking lot like that when he's *not* her boyfriend."

The self-righteous, judgmental glare she shot at me lit my short fuse. It wasn't like she had been Mother Teresa that night, riding my face like she was the Lone Ranger and I, her trusted steed. If this girl wanted to judge my character, then I was absolutely going to judge hers.

I narrowed my gaze. "What kinda girl goes out to a van with a guy who offers her a shitty pick-up line?" Yeah, it was shitty of me...

"That—is not the point." A slight red tinged her cheeks. "I was having a very bad night. And you..."

"From the way it felt when you came on my face," I said, "seems I made that *very bad* night a helluva lot better." With one swift movement, I pinned her against a dirty car window.

And like I knew she would, she reacted. Latching onto my biceps and pushing, pulling. Pushing...like she couldn't decide if she wanted me closer or farther away. Rich pricks weren't as gifted as I was in the arena of vulgarity, so if I had to guess, my ability to make her hot and repulsed at the same time must be a new sensation. So why stop?

"And I'd gladly do it again. Right here." I moved my hands to her waist, then nudged her legs apart with my knee. "Right now. On the hood of this car, if you want."

"I..."

"You what?" I breathed against her lips.

Genevieve's hold on my arm tightened. *That's right, baby girl, try to fight it.* The way her chest rose on uneven swells made my dick harder than concrete, and the thought of slipping my dick between her glossy lips sprung to life. My fingers twitched over her sides, the primitive part of me begging to give in. This girl got me going, unlike anything I'd ever experienced. I contemplated what filthy line I could throw at her next, but a string of chatter broke through the silence. Genevieve went rigid.

The conversation fell quiet, and I glanced over my shoulder at Nikki, surrounded by a group of her annoying friends. "Are you serious right now?" Her arms crossed her chest while her gaze pinged between Genevieve and me.

There was one way to quickly clear up this misunderstanding, both between Genevieve and me and Nikki and me. "Hey, Nikki," I said, my hold on Genevieve tightening. "Since you screwed this up last weekend by being a psycho, can you tell her that you're not my girlfriend?"

Nikki's eyes narrowed to angry slits. "Fuck you, Bellamy." Then she marched off, her troop of mean girls in tow.

"See. Not my girlfriend." I smiled.

With a roll of her eyes, Genevieve shoved me back a step. "You're a dick," she said, brushing past me.

She could call me a dick all day long, but that girl was one hundred percent interested, and I was one hundred percent going to ruin her.

## CHAPTER 3

## BELLAMY

THE SCREEN DOOR slammed closed behind me, doing little to silence my dad's angry shouts mixed with the ruckus of things breaking inside the house. I swiped a hand at my lip, catching a trickle of blood on my knuckle. I had tried to de-escalate the fight and gave the asshole just enough time to get one good swing in on me. And I hated that I'd let him.

Crickets silenced when I hopped over the chain-link fence separating my yard from the one behind us. I cut through the tall weeds to the back door.

"Hey! Nash." I pounded a fist on the rotting siding. "You in there?"

Footsteps came from inside before the click of the deadbolt sounded. Nash opened the door, and his gaze immediately landed on my lip. "Your old man being a dick again?"

"Yeah." I shouldered past him and went straight to the sink to rinse off my mouth.

"Where's Arlo?"

"At a friend's."

Nodding, he grabbed a tattered dish towel and passed it to me. Nash was one of the few people who actually knew how bad it was at home. Partly because he lived right behind me and couldn't ignore it. He glanced at my house, then back at me. "You should lay him out one good time."

The problem was, I had, and it hadn't made a difference. Dad was an angry drunk. And I'd been his whipping post for most of my life—until I could defend myself. Now, I was nothing but a rival. "I'm just pissed he got a hit in," I said.

Nash took a beer from the fridge. "Yeah, but girls dig scars, man." He headed toward his living room, fishing out his wallet before he dropped into the ratty recliner in the corner, then held up a crisp twenty. "You got any on you?"

I pulled a baggie from my pocket and launched it at him before taking the cash. Just like the money I made selling those history tests, this would go into the envelope I kept hidden in my top dresser drawer. An envelope that would eventually have an address scribbled across the front and a stamp placed onto the corner.

Nash grabbed his guitar from the side of the couch, strumming out a chord. "Me and some of the guys from the band are having a party tonight if you want to invite your friends over."

Nash and his friends were wannabe rock stars, and they partied just like they were practicing for fame. Having a night off sounded like a great idea.

Hours later, people crowded into Nash's small living room, bumping in beat with the music, spilling beer, and smoking.

Hendrix skirted around a group of girls in short skirts, his gaze going straight to their asses. "Man, this is awesome." He grabbed at his crotch. "If this is what being in a band is about, we need to start one."

"You can't play an instrument."

"I play pussy, Bell. What else do I need to do? I mean..." He dug his phone from his pocket. His brow knitted as he glanced down at the screen. "No way. Wolf said there's some dickhole named Drew selling weed through Frank's drive-thru." Hendrix cracked his neck to the side. "Oh, yeah. Getting into a fight tonight."

I snatched the phone from his hand, skimming over the text. "Through a drive-thru, really?"

Money had been tight since Hendrix's brother, Zepp, had gone to jail. This was not the crap any of us needed right now. We were already barely scraping by. "Come on," I said, digging into my pocket for my keys. "Let's go down to Frank's."

Hendrix fist-pumped the air. "I'm going on a trip, to beat some dumbass dick," he sang to the tune of the *Little Einstein's* theme song. "Soaring through the sky, he might die..."

"You know, your ability to take any children's song and make it messed up is almost impressive." I patted his back on my way to the door.

Ten minutes later, we idled in a line that wrapped around Frank's Famous Chicken. Hendrix sat in the passenger seat, throwing another practice punch. "Why are we in the drive-thru, anyway? We should just go inside and pummel the assdribble."

"Because for all we know, Drew's from the Northside."

That shut up Hendrix. We were high school kids pedaling a little pot to scrape by, and those guys... Those guys were full-time drug dealers, and I didn't really want a bullet in my head. I'd never heard of a guy named Drew in Dayton.

Static crackled over the speakers when I pulled up to the menu board, placed our order, and waited again.

Hendrix huffed, then snatched the boob-shaped stress ball from my dashboard. "You know, if Pepperoni Nips wasn't such a psycho, you could've asked her who the dickhead is."

"Yeah. Well..."

Asking Nikki anything would be a last resort, even if she did work here. That was for damn sure. One sideways glance from me and she thought I wanted her.

The truck in front of us spit out a black cloud of exhaust as it drove off, and we moved forward.

"I'm telling you, man, if old Salami Tits knew about this Drew thing and she didn't say anything, I'm gonna hate her even more, and I'm gonna—"

The drive-thru window cranked open with a creak of old hinges, and before I faced the window, the scent of perfume that reminded me of having my tongue on an expensive-tasting pussy wafted inside my car.

My dick was already at attention before Genevieve spun away from the register. "Two number ones and—" Her expression went blank before she released a heavy groan. "Really?"

"Two number ones, and you forgot the blowjob."

Hendrix punched my shoulder. "No way, man. She's hot. I called dibs in my head five seconds ago."

My gaze remained trained on Genevieve. "I've already had my tongue in her pussy, Hendrix." I cocked a brow. "So, she's mine." Sure, it was an asshole thing to say, but girls rarely ever went for a nice guy.

"Definitely not, asshole." If looks could kill...

I probably shouldn't have found that homicidal gleam in her eyes so hot, but I totally did.

"See!" Hendrix gave me another whack. "If you haven't pumped your dick in it, it doesn't count."

"Dibs, fuckwad."

Genevieve rolled her eyes. "That's fifteen seventy-five."

I passed over the cash. Then the window slammed. So, Miss Champagne and Caviar was about to start at Dayton *and* she was working a drive-thru? Daddy had *most definitely* lost the money.... No way some Barrington kid would be working a drive-thru in Dayton if he hadn't.

"Seriously, Bell. Why do you have to go licking all the hot pussy?" Hendrix slouched in his seat, crossing his arms over his chest like a sulking toddler. "Dick."

I was still staring at him when a grease-stained bag landed in my lap.

"You can go now. Have a nice night," she said, moving to close the window.

But before it swung shut, I grabbed it. "Come on now, baby girl, you..." My next words were lost when my gaze dropped to her tits, and more importantly, to the plastic name tag pinned to her shirt that read: Drew. No way. No fucking way! "Your name's Drew?" There was no way in hell that girl was a drug dealer. She was too—everything *not* Dayton.

She shrugged one shoulder. "What do you want me to say? I wasn't supposed to see you again." Then she slammed the drive-thru window.

Swiping a hand over my face, I pressed back against the seat. That girl may not be a true threat, but God, this was a problem. Hendrix snatched the bag from my lap. "Good job, asshole." Then chucked a fry at my face. "You had your sick tongue slurping over our competition like a Tootsie Pop!" He shook his head.

"She's not competition, Hendrix. Did you see her?"

"Yeah. She's hot. I'd buy weed off her."

I glared at him. "No way that girl is a drug dealer. She's probably got daddy issues and is trying to do something to get his attention, so she's selling a handful of dime bags."

But the problem was, regardless of how much of a threat I felt she posed, we had a reputation. If we let her get away with this little drive-thru stunt, other assholes would try. And eventually, an asshole who *would* pose a threat would get brave. I had to nip this shit in the bud come Monday morning.

A car horn blared behind us. Hendrix flipped them off, then lowered the window and stuck his head out, shouting, "Go suck a dick. We're having a crisis!"

"Get back in the car." I yanked his crazy ass back inside, then floored the accelerator, watching in my side mirror as Drew handed the next customer their mega gulp drink.

That girl was a liar and a con, and God, did I want to fuck her up, then fuck her for it.

## CHAPTER 4
## DREW

JESUS, I could not get away from the guy. Each time I saw him, he was more of a dick, and each time I remembered that night in the back of that van and exactly what that arrogant mouth was capable of. I absolutely was not getting involved with a guy like that, but the public school playboy might just make my time in this shithole more interesting.

Someone squeezed between me and the fryer, giving me a little shove as they did. Cheap perfume cut through the scent of the grease. Of course, I was on shift with Nikki. The two of them could both screw off and leave me out of whatever shit they had going.

"If you seriously think he wants you," she said, full of attitude, "you're stupid."

"Okay, I'll indulge this for a second." I let out a sigh, then turned to face her. "Not that I give a shit, but for the sake of your dignity, maybe you should stop." I almost pitied the girl. That scene in the school parking lot—he had been awful to her, and yet here she was, still chasing the guy.

"Whatever." She scooped ice into a Styrofoam cup, then shoved it under one of the dispensers with an acidic smile. "Think you're something special if you want. I have no problem making your life hell, rich bitch, because, in Dayton, you're nothing."

I forced my expression to remain impassive. "Thanks for that imaginative, mean-girl warning."

The muscles in her jaw tightened. "Seriously, Barrington. I will cut you." And that might have been the most uncivilized thing I'd ever heard.

I grabbed the headset off the cash register and shoved it over my head. "Clucka-Clucka. Welcome to Frank's Famous Chicken. Home of the Bucka-Bucka."

"Hey, can I, uh..." A guy's voice crackled through the speaker. "Can I get a Big Mac?"

I fidgeted with the microphone while jabbing my employee number over the register's screen. "Did you read the sign on the way in? This isn't McDonald's."

"Jesus. I want some weed, lady."

Weed? Really? This is what I got for living in a place like this. I inhaled a cleansing breath, trying to find patience. "Does it look like a dispensary? Order fried chicken or move along."

The speaker cut off, and a car zoomed around the corner of the building. When I went back to the fryer, Nikki smirked at me like she knew something I didn't. I flipped her off, even though she probably would make good on her promise to cut me, but whatever.

I already anticipated that between her and Bellamy, tomorrow would be absolute hell.

At this point, my life was becoming a joke. After my shift, I didn't even bother going home. What was the point? I was just going to sit in that house alone, watching TV, eating Push-Pops, and feeling sorry for myself. Because after my afternoon at Rockbottom High, I was definitely throwing a pity party.

I pulled up in Olivia Bennett's drive, then knocked on her front door. She was one of the few girls I'd befriended in my brief stays here during holidays. Without Genevieve here to console me, she was the next best thing. It was kind of shitty of me that I hadn't contacted her until now, but I'd been wallowing, mourning.

A huge smile shaped her face when she opened the door. "Drew? What are you doing in town?" Her gaze dropped to my Frank's Famous Chicken shirt. "And why are you in that shirt?"

"I'm back for the rest of the school year. And dad made me get a job." I left out the part about him making me get a job to pay him back. It was too depressing. I'd done the math, and with the eight dollars I made per hour, it would take me three years to pay back the twenty thousand in tuition that Dad said I owed him.

"Ew." She snarled her lip at the shirt as I stepped inside. "So, wait, are you coming to Barrington?"

I let out a sigh. "Do you have wine?"

Two glasses of pinot later, I was sprawled on Olivia's plush bed, surrounded by a mountain of throw pillows while she stared at me like I'd grown two heads.

"Dayton?" She looked repulsed. "Your dad is sending you to Dayton?"

"Yep." I sat up and took another swig of wine, but there wasn't enough wine in the world to drown out the shit show that was my life.

"I..." Her mouth opened, then closed. "You're going from Black Mountain to Dayton?"

I nodded.

And the look on her face told me I was in for a horror show. "Just don't go."

"That's what he wants, Olivia. He wants me to be a brat about it, so he's justified in his bullshit."

"It's your funeral." She sat up, pulling her long, blond hair into a ponytail. "Just stay away from the gangs and the girls. And don't use the bathrooms."

"Gangs? They have gangs?" Dear God, was I going to leave with a teardrop tattoo on my cheek?

"Yeah. It's inner-city, babe. There are drug dealers, and if you piss off the wrong girl, they will absolutely, one hundred percent, come at you with a razor blade. Like, they are going to hate you." Shaking her head, she took the wine bottle and brought it to her lips. "Like *hate*."

I fell back onto the bed, staring at the sparkling chandelier. "Great. Just great." And I wasn't even going to tell her about my slutty little rendezvous with the token bad guy.

"Last semester, there was a rumor that they found a dead body behind some of the lockers at Dayton. And I wouldn't doubt it."

"That's going to be me," I said, fighting back tears. "Killed and shoved into a locker." I needed more wine. "And then I'm going to come back and haunt my dad's ass."

I could have dealt with Barrington for two months, where I at least knew Olivia and her brother, Jackson—I could at least blend in. I knew Dayton was bad, but by the sounds of it, I might not survive two months there. There had to be a way out of this.

---

The next morning I woke to the distinct smell of bacon cooking. I found my father in the kitchen, a frying pan in hand. My gaze trailed from his graying hair to the ridiculous-looking apron covering his dress shirt and slacks.

"Oh, hey. Good of you to show up," I mumbled, then went to the coffee machine and started it. "So, have you actually seen that school you decided to send me to? Do you care if I get shanked in a hallway?" It wasn't even a stretch.

He flipped a piece of meat. "Have you always been this dramatic?"

"Only when my wonderful father sends me to what is basically one step up from reform school."

"As far as I'm concerned, Dayton is a reform school for you before you go to college."

A flash of anger jolted through me. I'd been kicked out of Black Mountain for "cheating" on a test. Which was bullshit. I'd never cheated on anything in my life.

"I already told you I didn't cheat on that test," I snapped.

Not that he believed me, of course. All he saw was his delinquent daughter who'd shamed him by getting kicked out of the expensive school he'd shipped her off to at age eleven—most likely so he could brag about paying the ninety-thousand dollar a year tuition while not having to deal with me. Except now, he did have to deal with me. For the last two months of my school year. The horror.

"I've set up for your paycheck to be directly deposited into my account since you owe me for the last two months of tuition."

Annoyance rippled through me. "You know I can just get mom to pay you."

"I don't need the money, Drucella." He huffed, setting the spatula onto the counter. "It's the principle. It's about you learning a little bit of responsibility for your disastrous behavior."

"Yes, yes, I'm such a disappointment, I know." I was so done with this.

I went upstairs, changed for school, then grabbed my purse. He expected me to refuse to go, and that was exactly why I went, the same reason I suffered through the humiliation of working that drive-through. Because I wouldn't give him the satisfaction. Like any "spoiled brat" would do, I made sure to slam the front door on my way out. It had been seven months since I'd seen him. He'd been here for two minutes and I already preferred being alone, and I hated being alone.

---

Orientation through an almost empty school had been one thing. This—this was another thing entirely.

Students poured into the hallway through an open doorway. Girls wore fishnet tights, crop tops, and shorts their asses hung out of. It was a little shocking for someone whose entire life had been spent in a school with rigid uniform rules. And God, did I feel out of place.

A massive guy shifted past me. My gaze went from his spiked hair to the eyeliner caked around his lashes to the studded dog collar circling his neck. Yep. I was not in Kansas anymore.

"You stupid fuck!" Shouts boomed down the hall, and I jumped when a guy got slammed against the lockers. "I'll kill you and your mother." The one shouting threw a punch, and all hell broke loose. One of them ended up on the dirty tiled floor, the other on top. Students congregated around, pointing and laughing while the smack of fists against cheeks echoed down the hall. And the teachers? They passed by with hardly a second glance.

Blood splattered the tiles, and I turned away. My stomach rolled as I shouldered through the packed hallways to my assigned locker and debated going to the office to see if I would get sent home if I pretended to be ill.

I turned the combination to my lock. Just as it popped open, my phone buzzed with a text from Genevieve:

**Gen: How's public school? Is it like TV???**

I snapped a picture of the guy out cold in the front of the dented lockers and sent it to Genevieve.

**Gen: OMG, that's deplorable.**

**Me: Welcome to my new hell. Let's hope I don't get stabbed by the end of the day.**

**Gen: I'll cry at your funeral and get 'rent a crowd.'**

**Me: Thanks.**

I'd just put away my belongings when the ambassador who'd shown me around last week popped up beside me, all bouncing ponytail and smiles. "Hey, Drew."

"Uh." I closed the locker door, trying to recall her name. "Hey...Nora?"

"If you want to sit with me and some of the other girls at lunch, you're welcome to." She smiled again, and I questioned how genuine it was.

One, because at Black Mountain, everyone was fake and kindness always came with a catch. And two, because Olivia had put the fear of God in me, and I was half waiting on Nora to start wielding a razor blade like she was a guest star on *Orange is the New Black*.

The crowded hallway shifted, students scrambling to get out of the way of whoever was coming their way. I glanced in the direction of the chaos, and there he was.

Bellamy. Two tattoo-covered guys trailed behind him like loyal subjects. From the reaction of everyone in that corridor, it was obvious he ran this shithole school. And from my five minutes here, I'd already surmised it was absolutely awful, so how bad did that make him?

Nora looked over her shoulder, then back to me with a shake of her head. "Okay. I see the way you're looking. And just. *No.*"

My gaze drifted over the tight black shirt that clung to defined muscles, stopping on the delicate script tattoos that circled his wrists. He was absolutely the hottest guy I'd ever seen, and that was annoying.

"And… you're still looking…" She sighed like I was a lost cause. "Yeah. They're hot, but Bellamy, Hendrix, and Wolf are no good. Just trust me on this."

"Oh, I'm aware," I mumbled as Bellamy's gaze crashed into mine.

On a smirk, he headed toward me like a shark tracking blood in the water. I backed up to the lockers and instantly regretted that decision when he caged me against them. The now-familiar smell of his cologne wrapped around me as he towered over me.

"I know you're new, and Daddy must have lost his job or left," he said, his voice low and deep.

My pulse slowly ticked up when I took a quick glance over his shoulder, noticing the entire hallway staring at us.

"And as much as I know how eager girls with daddy issues are to suck dick—" He shot an arrogant glance at his friends beside him, who laughed like I was the butt of a joke.

"Jesus…" Nora huffed. "You're seriously an asshole, Bellamy."

The guy in the letterman jacket snickered. "Rah-rah-shut-the-fuck-up-baa, Nora!"

Bellamy's unnerving gaze held mine, his teeth raking his bottom lip. "But no matter how much I want to see my dick gliding between those pretty lips of yours..." His attention focused on my mouth, his vulgar words making heat creep into my cheeks. "I can't let you get away with stealing our business," he said.

And I frowned. Stealing his business. "What?"

"Come on, Bellamy." Nora groaned somewhere behind him. "She's new. Just leave her alone."

One of the guys mocked Nora. Someone down the hall shouted, "The Barrington slut's already banging Bellamy."

I didn't care what people thought of me for the most part, but I wasn't blind. Bellamy was undoubtedly the kind of guy who girls got loose with, and I knew exactly how this looked—how it was—like he'd already seen me naked. I also had no doubt that was exactly why he was doing this right here in the hallway.

I pressed my palm against his chest, digging my nails into him as my temper spiked. "Would you stop?"

He slapped my hand away. "I know you're dealing weed at Frank's."

Of all the things he could have said, that was the last one I saw coming. "Weed? Are you serious right now?" I laughed, but the expression on his face said he absolutely was not joking. Honestly, I was offended.

His brow lifted. His fingers tapped the locker beside my head. I could have easily denied it; after all, I wasn't dealing weed, but something about the arrogance that oozed from him made the defiant part of me rise like a Phoenix from the ashes.

Bellamy evidently wanted a show in the hallway. I'd give him one, and since I refused to play the submissive little rich girl here...

I leaned in and brushed my lips to his jaw. The air between us thickened with an unrivaled tension. "What if I don't care about your warning?" I said loud enough for people close by to hear. I was playing with fire, but then again, so was he. "What are you going to do, Bellamy?"

The amusement that flickered in his eyes was quickly snuffed out by obvious annoyance. His hand wound around my throat, fingers squeezing over delicate skin as he pressed the hard length of his dick against me. "I'm gonna fuck up your life," he breathed the words against my lips, his hold growing tighter. "And then, I'm gonna fuck you."

And I shouldn't have wanted any part of that, or this right here... But as his fingers threatened to cut off my air, I found a thrill in the danger of it all. My life had been nothing but safe, and this guy, he was about as safe as an atomic bomb.

I trailed a hand down his hard stomach, over his belt, and palmed the substantial bulge in his jeans. His jaw clenched, fingers trailing from my throat to my chest.

"You can try." Then I ducked underneath his arm, meeting the stares of what must have been half the school.

"You better stop, Drew." The boom of his deep voice echoed down the hall. "I'm not even fucking playing with you."

I'd spent my whole life around rich guys who would get daddy to pull some strings if someone pissed them off. Maybe spread a rumor that a girl had screwed the Lacrosse team. But Bellamy was an entirely different animal, and I'd just petted the lion. Worse, I think I liked it.

Nora fell into step beside me, her eyes wide. "What the

hell. Was. That?"

"I don't know," I said, stopping to hold up a finger. "But I did not screw him. And I didn't suck his dick." God, I really wasn't helping myself here. She probably thought I was a slut, regardless.

The look on her face said she didn't believe me for a second.

My day only got worse from there. As expected, Nikki was a bitch. I'd received at least six notes calling me a whore. A guy grabbed my ass, so I maced him and got sent to the principal's office. And from the amount of catty female glares I'd received, I was pretty certain the girls here were plotting my death—well, except Nora and her friends… To top it all off, Bellamy was in my AP biology class. He spent the entire class glaring at me, and by the time the dismissal bell rang, I felt like I'd been in this hell hole for a week rather than a day.

I gathered my books. When I pushed up from my desk, a guy in a letterman jacket blocked my path.

"Hey. If you need help catching up in class, we can totally study together after school." Catching up? Pretty sure I learned this stuff two years ago, but the way his eyes tracked over me said he wasn't planning on studying any books. Still, at least he wasn't glaring at me like I was a piece of Barrington shit on his shoe.

"Uh…"

A hand brushed my hip, and the guy shrunk back.

"Never mind," he said before darting around me.

"Just so you know," Bellamy's deep voice rumbled in my ear, "I can make your life here an absolute hell if I want." Fingers trailed along my side as he brushed past me. "And I think that's exactly what I want to do." Then he walked off while I fought the smile that should absolutely not have been there.

## CHAPTER 5

## BELLAMY

I WATCHED Drew's Armani-clad ass weave between the beaters in the parking lot, waiting to see what kind of luxury car she'd sink behind the wheel of. Her face had been Satan's-asshole red this morning in the hallway, and I'd enjoyed it way too much. Not only did I let it be known that not even hot rich girls could get away with stupid shit, but I had also staked my claim on her before any other prick had a chance to smell her coming.

Nora passed behind Wolf's truck, glaring like she wanted to strangle me. Cute. She'd taken Drew under her wing like that broken little bird we all knew she was.

"Hey, Nora." Hendrix stood up in the bed, motioning toward his crotch. "You wanna suck on my spirit stick?"

She flipped him off before disappearing between a set of pickups. And my attention went straight back to Drew as she opened the door of a shiny, black Audi TT. The adjustment to life in the drive-thru and a school of drive-bys must be tough on Little Miss Entitled. Unfortunately for her, her family's recent financial downfall wasn't my problem, but her attitude sure as hell was.

"Man." Hendrix sat on the edge of the tailgate, passing a joint to Wolf with narrowed eyes. "What the hell? She's got a TT. We should set that shit on fire."

Smoke billowed from Wolf's lips; his stare aimed at the ridiculous car like he was contemplating it.

"We're not setting fire to her car," I said. "Yet."

Hendrix frowned. "I vote, we do it now." He pulled a lighter from his pocket, flicking the lint. "We need retribution, Bell."

The engine to Drew's car revved before she peeled off, swerving around a stalled-out Toyota. Wolf leaned over the bed's edge. "Think she got the message?"

Hell no, she didn't. Instead of backing down, all I saw was a challenge rising in her eyes. This girl was not the type to go down without a fight, and if a fight were what she wanted, well then...I guess that's what she'd get. But I wasn't entirely unreasonable; payback didn't have to start with fires, which was why, later that afternoon, I left a message for Eddie at Frank's Famous Chicken, then I laid on my bed and beat one out to the thought of how pissed she would be. Twice.

I'd just cleaned myself up when Wolf texted that he was pulling onto the street. Grabbing my backpack, I went into the hall, stopping in the kitchen to kiss my mom on the cheek. "Love you, Momma. I'll be back before you leave for work." I had to be home to make sure my piece of shit dad didn't try to take a swing at my little brother, Arlo.

"Love you, too." She leaned back from the stove to peek through the window. "It sure is sweet of you boys to take those foster kids to ride Go-Karts."

I forced a smile before ducking through the door. I hated lying to her, because Wolf and I sure as hell weren't taking underprivileged kids to ride Go-Karts. We *were* the underprivileged kids for Christ's sake. But she and Arlo were the most important people in my life, and the last thing I wanted to do was break her heart by letting her know her oldest son was a car stealing, drug dealing piece of shit.

I had to be. It was Dayton. And all of us had already tried to scrape by with some part-time job. It didn't work, and we had no other choices.

I passed by Arlo, sitting on the couch and watching *SpongeBob*, scrubbing a hand over his messy head. "See you later, buddy."

"K."

The kid couldn't be bothered when he was watching that stupid cartoon. I closed the door behind me and headed toward Wolf's pick-up idling at the end of my drive. I slung my backpack into the back and climbed in. "I gotta be back before midnight."

"No problem." The truck backfired when he pulled off, headlights cutting over the neighbor's overgrown grass. "We taking that old Volvo over at the Pig?"

"That's what Tony said he wanted."

And that Volvo would get us a grand to split between us. Enough for Wolf to help his dad with rent. Enough for me to try to catch up on the mortgage before the bank started to foreclose. Zepp's getting arrested a few months back had fucked us all in the ass.

I stared through the window, thinking how shit Dayton was as we passed by the 7-11 and the hookers standing on the corner by the phone booth. We didn't have the luxury of few responsibilities. Hell, Hendrix didn't even have parents. This city was like toxic sludge that ruined anything and everything it touched.

"The new girl's hot. You gonna bang her?"

I thought about the way Drew moaned in the back of Nash's van and smirked. "Might as well."

She may be a pain in my ass right now, but I'd gladly be a pain in hers once we got our little disagreement straightened out.

The truck rattled over a speed bump when Wolf kicked it into the Piggly Wiggly lot, where the rundown Volvo sat beside the dumpster. Wolf parked beside it, blocking the view from the road, and I climbed out, maneuvering between the truck and the car.

Within a matter of minutes, I had the lock popped and I sat behind the wheel, dismantling the steering column and twisted the wires together. A plume of smoke puffed up before the engine rumbled to life. Wolf gave me a thumbs up and swung his pickup around, speeding out of the parking lot with me behind him.

When I got home, I kissed Mom goodbye again, then checked on Arlo on my way to my room. And the second I closed my bedroom door, I shoved the cash I'd made into the envelope I kept tucked away in my top drawer, then crawled into bed. The familiar lullaby of cop sirens blared in the distant, mixing with the angry shouts from the neighbors, made it hard for me to unwind. So, I rolled onto my back, staring at the ceiling and imagined sinking my dick between Drew's thighs. Because I was going to make that girl hate me, and one thing I knew for sure, girls like her couldn't resist a good hate fuck with the bad boy.

---

I felt like a smug bastard the next afternoon when I strolled into biology because soon enough, shit was going to blow up.

Drew scribbled in her notebook, too focused to notice me when I started down the aisle. But the guy behind her sure as hell did, hiding his face behind his book as he slumped in his seat.

I touched the corner of his desk, and he jumped. "Get up."

He shoved out of the chair so fast the thing bumped against the wall, then he stumbled to the back of the class where I usually sat, while I dropped into the seat behind Drew.

That damn perfume of hers seeped into my nostrils, possessing my mind with thoughts of her thighs wrapped around my head. Gripping the edge of the desktop, I forced the idea of sex out of my head. "What kinda mood are you in today, baby girl?"

"Until right now—" She turned in her seat and judging from the lack of reaction—nothing had transpired from my little complaint. Yet— "It *was* just fine," she said, then with a roll of her eyes, she faced the front again, and I fought a smirk.

That rich girl, look-down-her-nose expression called to the primitive part of me. She may have looked at me like she hated me, but the way her chest rose on uneven swells screamed that she'd still let me bend her over and have a go. Because girls like her wanted nothing more than to be dirtied and tainted by a bad boy. I had every intention of taking that invisible, privileged, princess crown and tarnishing every last gem and fuck if that wasn't bad news for her.

The tardy bell rang just before the classroom door slammed shut, and Mrs. Smith tossed her planner to the desk with an annoyed huff. "You're gonna need a partner for the lab class you'll all most likely fail or get high in. So, find another student you can work with, without killing." She took a swig from her thermos. No one moved. She rolled her eyes, then snapped her fingers. "I said, find a partner."

Desks scraped the floor as students switched seats. Drew didn't budge, and neither did I. She glanced around the room. When the commotion of shuffling desks fell silent, Drew didn't have a partner. One, she was obviously Barrington. And two, no one in this school would come within five inches of her because I'd all but taken a piss on her yesterday in the hall.

I swept her hair from her shoulder, leaned over, and placed my lips beside her ear. "No one wants to play with you. Except for me."

"Oh, no." She placed a hand on her chest. "I might cry."

I grabbed her ponytail, yanking her head back. "Please, fucking cry. Rich girl tears are like black tar heroin."

"Would you get off on it?" The sexy-ass low rasp to her voice immediately had my dick hard.

"All over your pretty, rich-girl face."

"Mr. West!" Mrs. Smith clapped her hands before balling them on her hips. "Please tell me why in the hell, you've got New Girl by the hair?"

"Because she's hot." I nodded toward Drew as I released her ponytail.

"My class ain't no Plenty O' Fish."

"I know. But I heard this girl's gag reflex is practically non-existent."

A boom of laughter echoed around the room before Smith clapped her hands again. "All right, Hugh Hefner. Go see Principal Brown." She pointed at the door. "I ain't got time for your shit today."

With a shrug, I pushed out of the chair, flicking Drew's hair as I passed by. "See you later, baby girl."

Brown's idea of punishment was having me spend the remainder of second block in the office, helping the aide file charts. And honestly, I was patting myself on the back for getting sent to the principal today because the file I had just grabbed was none other than Drucella Morgan's.

Drucella Morgan? What a shit name. On a laugh, I quickly crammed the folder underneath my shirt and went back to filing the rest of the charts. By the time the bell for lunch rang, it felt like the thing was burning a hole into my skin.

I skirted into the hallway, opening the folder as I fell in with the students pouring out of classrooms. I flipped past her Barrington address and phone number to her transcripts —straight *A*s at an out-of-state school called Black Mountain Academy, some dumb rich-kid boarding school. And then I came to her notice of expulsion. I expected the reason to be dealing drugs, screwing a teacher, something worth a little excitement. But no. Little Miss Perfect had been expelled for cheating on a test. What a letdown.

"Cocksucker." Hendrix strode up beside me, his gaze dropping to the open file in my hand. "Drucella?" He stopped outside of the cafeteria and doubled over on a cackle. "That's a shit name."

We went into the lunchroom, skipping to the front of the line. "Where's Wolf?" I asked.

"Smith held him after class." Hendrix reached across the line, scooped a handful of mashed potatoes up with his fingers, and licked them off before passing the tray back to the cafeteria lady and asking for another serving. "She wants him to have an all he can eat on her musty, dusty muff buffet."

"Jesus, Hendrix." I filled my tray with crap food, trying to block the mental image of Smith's muff buffet from my mind when we went to the cashier and swiped our cards.

He spent the first five minutes rattling off his updated "Hit it and Quit it" list while I read over Drew's file. "Here comes Drucella and Scora Nora..." Hendrix snorted a laugh. "They can both be on my list, too."

I glanced toward the front of the noisy cafeteria, and the moment Drew's gaze landed on me, I framed my mouth with my fingers then flicked my tongue through the opening. She shot me the bird.

"She's defected," Hendrix said through a mouthful of food. "Most of those rich girls are like horny little beavers hungry for wood."

"It's defective, you idiot."

"Defected. Defective. Doesn't matter. She's not gonna bang your wang, man." He chucked a fry at me, dragging my attention away from her. "Not gonna go all champion pogo-stick rider on your nub. Not going to..."

My phone vibrated in my pocket, the number to Frank's Famous Chicken flashing over the screen. Ignoring the tirade Hendrix had veered off on, I left the table and headed into the courtyard to take the call. And when I hung up, Drew Morgan was no longer my problem, but I was most definitely hers.

## CHAPTER 6
## DREW

I WAS HALFWAY through my shift at Frank's when Eddie, the manager, rounded the corner, with splotchy red cheeks. "Drew Morgan!" He stopped in front of me, nostrils flaring like a stampeding bull. "You've been selling cannabis from my drive-thru!"

"Me?"

"Yes, you!" His balled fists dug into his waist. "Yesterday evening, I received a phone call from a concerned citizen. He said the"—he made air quotes—"hot brunette with an attitude"—another set of air quotes—"put it in his bag." Eddie glanced around. "Do you see any other brunettes in here, Drew?"

This had to be Bellamy, and this was low. "It's bullshit," I said. "I'm not—"

"Bullshit?" He gave a curt nod. "Bullshit. Do you know the number of people who have come through the drive-thru over the past week, asking for a Big Mac? I Googled what that means. And it means weed!"

Motherfuckers.

"If you weren't William's daughter, I'd have called the cops."

The cops. He would have called the cops when he didn't even have proof? What an asshole.

He shook his head with a disappointed frown. "I'm sorry, Drew. But I have no choice but to fire you. William's daughter or not."

He was firing me. With no proof.

"Whatever." I tossed my cap onto the counter and brushed past Eddie to grab my bag. This was unbelievable. Now my dad was going to crawl even further up my ass because God knew Eddie wouldn't keep this a secret. Just great.

As soon as I got home, I stormed into the kitchen and grabbed a Rainbow Push-Pop from the freezer, then went to the living room and flopped back onto the stuffy couch. With each angry bite I took from that popsicle, my teeth hurt.

My phone buzzed again and again. *Father* flashing over the screen. He'd evidently heard from Eddie, which was why I didn't open any of the messages. I wasn't in the mood for his wannabe-parental lecture right now over something I hadn't even done—just like cheating on that test at Black Mountain.

I took another chunk out of the Push-Pop. My dad was going to be such a dick about this, and that made me hate Bellamy with a passion I rarely felt. The buzzing quieted for a moment before sounding again a few minutes later. But this time, it wasn't my dad.

**Unknown number: Sorry to hear you lost your job.**

**Unknown number: Baby girl.**

Simmering rage shot through my veins as I stamped my fingers over the screen:

Me: How did you get my number?

Unknown number: A magician never reveals his secrets….

I'd had every intention of keeping my head down and getting through the next two months in this hell hole with as little drama as possible. Until now. Now Bellamy West was top of my shit list. He thought I was some spoiled rich girl. Well, he was about to learn *exactly* how rich girls played.

---

The next day at lunch, I watched from across the bustling cafeteria as the token bad boy of Dayton sank to his stool, glaring at me. Anger bubbled beneath my skin. Not because I'd been fired, but for the simple fact that he'd had the audacity to *get* me fired.

Nora unwrapped her sandwich, then lifted a brow as she nodded across the lunchroom. "So, I'm guessing *that* hasn't gotten any better?"

"Define better? He got me fired for 'dealing weed at Franks.'"

"Oh. Yeah." Diane, one of Nora's friends, shoved a forkful of wilted lettuce into her mouth before turning to stare at them. "I heard that…"

"What the…" I threw up my hands. "Do *I* look like the kind of person who deals weed?"

"I mean," Nora shrugged, "what *does* someone who deals weed look like anyway?"

"Them, Nora." I nodded toward the guys. "It looks like

them..." Tattoos and piercings and a dangerous edge that was far too enticing.

"Shit..." Nora mumbled. "You made eye contact, Diane. You whore."

Bellamy pushed up from their table and approached ours, jaw set as he skirted around the corner, then behind me. The intoxicating scent of his cologne swirled around me seconds before his hands landed on my shoulders and warm breath touched my neck.

"Gotta problem?" His rough voice dragged over me like a lover's caress, sending a bolt of adrenaline straight through my chest. There was something wrong with me.

"You know, I do." I twisted on the stool to meet his smirk.

He leaned over, gripping the table behind me and caging me in with his arms. "Do tell, baby girl..."

I hated him for getting me fired, and I hated this ridiculous reaction my body had to him. "You're an asshole. You got me fired."

"To be fair, I did tell you not to mess with me." The slight tilt of his head was annoyingly sexy.

"I wasn't selling weed," I said, but I'd sure as hell make him regret not doing his research.

"Right..." He huffed a laugh. "Just like you're twenty-one and your name's Genevieve, huh?"

Like he gave a shit about my name. Of course, the decision to hook up with a stranger was biting me in the ass. Why wouldn't it? Everything else in my life was a shitshow.

He stroked a finger over my cheek. "Know what I think, Drucella Morgan? That you're a really bad liar."

"You know what I think?" I did not need to find this guy exciting. Or rise to his challenge. But I did. "That I'm about to be the worst thing to happen to you, pretty boy."

Without warning, his hand clamped down on the back of my neck, and with one simple tug, he brought my lips mere centimeters from his. "Try me, baby girl. Try me…"

I found it hard to pull away from him, and the moment I did, I missed the force of his grip.

"See you later, Drew." He patted my cheek—hard—like the condescending prick he was, then he cut back through the cafeteria of students focused on me. Screw him and his perfect face.

I turned back to my tray, and Diane and Nora gaped at me.

"Holy. Shit," Diane breathed. "That was, like, the hottest thing I've ever seen."

I grabbed my sandwich and picked off the brown lettuce. "He's an asshole," I mumbled.

An asshole. And a problem.

One I needed to quit and intended to—in monumental fashion.

## CHAPTER 7

## BELLAMY

MUSIC THUMPED through a busted stereo in some run-down house on the outskirts of Dayton. A couple of the girls had stripped down to their bras and panties while guys pounded back cheap beer. And what was I doing? Typing out a text to Drew.

**Me: So, what was it you were planning to do, baby girl? Use your daddy to get me blocked from Ivy League schools?**

**Baby Girl: A magician never reveals her secrets...**

I fought a smile.

**Me: Just so you know, I'm really fucking scared.**

"Bell!" Hendrix shouted from across the crowded room, grinning like an idiot while he pointed at Betty Newman, topless and dry-humping the arm of the couch. "Guess who's plundering booty tonight?" The guy was an idiot... and for some reason, the girls lined up for it.

I drained the rest of my soda, checked my watch, then

pushed up from the couch. Mom left for her second shift at work in an hour, which meant I had to have my ass back so my little brother wouldn't be alone with my shithead dad. Hendrix rounded the corner, his arm around Betty, who still had her tits out.

"Hell no, man." I grabbed the back of his shirt and yanked him away. "I don't have time for your dick to go on a conquest. I've gotta be home to watch Arlo."

Hendrix shot a smile to the girl waiting by the stairwell. "The way she blows on that tuba, I can be done in five minutes flat, Bell...Come on."

There was no arguing with him. He was like a dog with its dick out, which meant I was wasting time. If I had to leave him, I had to leave him. "I'm going to my car, and If you're not out there by eleven thirty-three, I'm leaving your ass."

Hendrix glanced at his crotch. "Your time has come, my little warrior. We're walking the plank and diving straight into a brown star tonight." Then he made a beeline to Topless Betty waiting by the stairs. Unbelievable.

My phone buzzed.

**Baby Girl: You'll see.**

Typing out a response, I weaved my way through the party, past a kid puking in a potted plant.

**Me: Can't wait. XX**

Drew was cute, like a kitten attempting to sharpen its claws on my jeans. My bet was she would try to spread a rumor that I had a small dick or try to turn the Barrington football team against me—which had been done years ago, but why would she know that?

I made it halfway through the overgrown yard before a patrol car stopped at the drive. The kids loitering outside fled like cockroaches, dropping their beers and shouting

Five-O before they hurtled themselves over chain-link fences. Amateurs.

I shook my head and kept walking. I hadn't drunk a drop, and having a dad who was an ex-cop, I knew the police couldn't do anything without probable cause.

The vehicle squealed to a stop, the flashing lights bouncing off my car as Officer Bivens climbed out. Followed by dickhead Jacobs who'd arrested Zepp.

"'Sup, fuckwads," I mumbled.

Bivens frowned, slipping his thumbs through the belt loops on his uniform. "That silver Civic yours, West?" Bivens had been on the task force with my dad. He knew damn well the car in front of him was mine.

"Why?"

"We're gonna need you to open it." Jacobs grinned.

I threw a smirk back at the arrogant bastard, flipping my keys in my hand. "Got a warrant?"

"No."

"Then fuck off. I have to go home to watch my brother."

Another patrol car marked K-9 Unit pulled up and blocked the drive. A sinking feeling settled low in my stomach when a sniffer dog hopped out of the back, tugging on its leash as it headed straight for my car. Then lost its shit, pawing and barking.

"And I'd call that probable cause." Jacobs held out his hand.

I had no choice but to drop the keys into his waiting palm. My pulse threatened to pick up. I watched the officers walk to my car and shove the key into the lock.

Sure, the car probably reeked of weed, but I wasn't stupid enough to leave shit in there. The adrenaline building in my veins subsided. Jacobs could knock himself out. There was no way anything would—

"Got some dope here, Jacobs." Bivens popped up from the open door and shined his flashlight at the plastic baggie dangling from his fingertips.

Where in the actual hell...I tossed my head back on a groan. If Hendrix had dropped some of his shit in my car, I was going to kill him.

Jacobs shoved me, face down, onto the cruiser's hood, slapping cuffs on so tight that my fingers tingled by the time he forced me into the backseat.

"Zippity-fucking-doo-dah," he laughed, then slammed the car door.

The lights flashed. Sirens sounded. And panic settled in. If I weren't at home, no one would be there to watch Arlo. Mom couldn't afford to miss a shift, plus she'd leave, thinking I would turn up late. Then my kid brother would be stuck with Dad. God, I'd messed up. "Man, I gotta get someone to watch my brother, Jacobs."

"Then I guess you better use that one phone call wisely, huh, shithead?"

I kicked at the back of his chair. "You fucking asshole." Then I slumped against the seat, my heart banging against my ribs like a caged gorilla.

The patrol car pulled away from the curb, picking up speed until it rolled to a stop at the end of the street, where I caught sight of Drew's hourglass shape casually leaned against the side of her shiny TT. She threw up a pageant queen wave, and that was enough to send me into full-on rage. I had no doubt Drew had somehow planted that crap in my car. Then probably called the police. Then came to sit back and watch the entire thing unfold. And that was absolutely not the kind of retaliation I'd expected. It was her fault my brother was about to be stuck with my drunk ass dad, and I wanted to literally wrap my hands around her throat until she choked. My hands were cuffed behind my back, which meant I couldn't flip her off, so instead, I head-butted the glass and shouted, "Fuck you," before the car drove off.

A series of texts buzzed in my pocket while Drew's threat: "I'm about to be the worst thing to happen to you, pretty boy," played on a loop through my head. This was unbelievable.

Earlier in the week, I'd found her comment cute, but now, as Jacob's ushered me through the slums of Dayton, in the backseat of a police cruiser, while I worried that my little brother might catch his first busted lip from my dad, I didn't find it anything but infuriating.

---

Instead of the normal twenty-four hours that most people served for a dime-bag of weed—a rookie mistake on Drew's part—the door to my cell opened after ten. Special treatment since everyone in the Dayton PD knew my father was a piece of shit. Plus, the guy doing the booking asked who had Arlo. Sometimes sympathy could get a guy places, even in Dayton.

The clerk highlighted my court date, then passed the paperwork across the counter and buzzed me through the locked doors.

On my way into the parking lot, I powered on my phone. A string of texts came through. Hendrix. Wolf. Then...

*Beep.*

**Baby Girl: Abracadabra?**

*Beep.*

**Baby Girl: You know, you'd think breaking into a car would cost more than $20**

*Beep.*

**Baby Girl: Guess payback's a bitch**

I froze halfway through the parking lot. My thumb hovered over the letters, itching to type out some smartass response while my jaw tensed. But instead, I texted Hendrix:

**Me: Ready to burn some shit tonight?**

**Hendrix: Hell yeah!**

Most people wouldn't up the ante with me—especially not a girl. Girl or not, she'd fucked with the wrong guy because I would burn her shit to the ground.

A horn blared, and I glanced up from the text to Nash's dented van idling at the crosswalk. I hopped in, dragging a hand through my hair as he pulled off. Because this shit was unbelievable, and the longer I thought about, the angrier I became.

Nash dropped me at the impound. I paid the stupid fee—using the last of my money—then drove back home. I slowed to a stop in front of Nora's house, staring across the street at my dad's truck parked haphazardly in the drive. The front bumper touched the side of the carport.

If I had to guess, he was still half-drunk, passed-out on the couch from the poker game he'd probably lost his unemployment check to the night before.

He was the kind of man who played the villain in most made-for-TV movies, and I hated him.

I killed the engine and made my way up the monkey-grass-lined sidewalk, past the potted plants on the front porch, then I knocked on the door. And waited, staring at the wooden, hand-painted "Welcome" sign. Nora and I didn't exactly get along, but her family was nice, and I'd be lying if I said I didn't envy that.

The door opened with a creak of hinges. When Nora's gaze met mine, she rolled her eyes, then leaned back from the doorframe. "Arlo," she shouted. "Your brother's here."

His excited squeal echoed down the hall. Nora just stood in the doorway, glaring.

"Thanks for grabbing him last night," I said. Being nice to her was pretty much the same as trying to swallow a cactus—painful and awkward. But she'd helped my brother out. I had no choice but to be less of a dick to her now.

"Yeah. It's fine." She brushed her nails on her shirt. "I don't like you, but he's cute."

Arlo shot around her like a canon, then latched onto my leg. "I'm glad they didn't keep you."

"Yeah, me too, buddy." I scrubbed a hand over his messy hair, giving Nora one last, thankful glance before we turned and headed to my car.

"Why'd you park here?"

"Because..." I didn't want to deal with Dad, so I opened the back door, motioning Arlo in. "Wanna grab a Happy Meal and go to Hendrix's to play on his PlayStation?"

His eyes lit up and he hopped right in, buckling himself up with a grin. "Yeah! He's got that game with girls in short dresses."

"You are not playing *Grand Theft Auto*, Arlo."

---

A Happy Meal later, Arlo sprinted across Hendrix's living

room, the paper bag in tow as he snatched the game controller from the coffee table. "This is the best day ever!" He threw himself down onto the ratty couch cushions before fishing out a handful of fries.

Hendrix stood by the kitchen, eyeing the bag. "You didn't ask me if I wanted a Happy Meal, cocksucker."

I flipped him a bird, told Arlo not to play anything other than S*pongeBob*, then followed Hendrix into the kitchen.

He hopped onto the laminate countertop, cracking open a can of soda. "Did they make you get naked and lift up your ball bag?" He grinned before slurping back his drink. "Zepp said that's what they made him do."

"Man, shut up." I grabbed a spatula from the stove and hurled it at him, but he ducked. "Zepp's in prison. I was only there for ten hours."

"Why'd you have weed in the car anyway, dickstench?"

"I didn't." I combed my fingers through my hair, pacing the small space between the kitchen table and the cabinets. Pissed.

Drew may not have been competition, but she was definitely a problem. A big, hot-ass problem. I recalled how smug she looked, leaned against the smooth paint of her expensive car, watching while the cops hauled me off—to jail. She was a used-to-be rich girl, which meant she probably had no idea what the implications of what she'd done actually held—of course, she didn't. Or she would have planted more than a dime bag of weed. But still. Forget the record. Forget the inconvenience. She'd inadvertently put Arlo in danger, and that was enough to make my blood boil white-hot. And the more I thought about it, the more sinister my thoughts of retaliation grew.

Hendrix stared at me. "Fuckface! Why was there weed in your car? That's like the cardinal sin of—"

"The new girl set me up."

His eyes popped wide, and he lowered the soda to his side. "Oh, it's on now, cocksucker." He hopped off the counter. "It's on now. 'Cause she just put her feet all over your rug." He tapped the toe of his sneaker over the kitchen rug. "Just like that."

And *that* was an understatement.

CHAPTER 8

DREW

STEAM BILLOWED out of the enclosed shower when I opened the door. My mood had greatly improved since I'd watched the cops haul Bellamy away in the back of a police car. I knew he wouldn't stay in jail for a dime bag, but that hadn't been my intention.

Last night, the entire point had been to show Bellamy West that he was not screwing with some "wet behind the ears" little rich girl. That I could, in fact, get to him.

I wrapped a towel around me, then wiped a visible patch through the fogged-over mirror to clean up the mascara below my eyes before I headed into my room. I made it two steps over the hardwoods then froze before stumbling into the doorframe on a scream when I noticed Bellamy's tall frame stretched out across my bed.

"You always scream like that when a guy's in your bed?" Bellamy asked. One arm rested behind his head like he belonged here. "Huh, baby girl?" He glanced up from the picture of Genevieve and me he held in his free hand, then tossed it to the foot of the bed. That was when I noticed the metal baseball bat beside him, nestled among my blankets.

Something crashed downstairs, followed by a guy shouting. More things shattered. And I was frozen in place, freaking out completely.

He was *in my* house. And he didn't come alone. Fear shot to the forefront of my mind, full force. An alarm wailed at me to run, or at least try to make it to my dad's room where he kept a gun, but I didn't even know how to use a gun. My heart pounded out a frantic rhythm as I pressed my back to the wall, trying to keep as much space between and the baseball bat-wielding maniac as possible.

"Is this where you murder me?" I whispered.

A deep chuckle crept through his lips as he shoved to his feet, wrapping his fingers around the metal bat. "Couldn't fuck you if I killed you, now could I?" he said, twirling the bat as he took slow steps toward me. "And that is what I promised, isn't it? To fuck up your life. Then fuck you?" He lifted the bat, then swung it at the pictures and figurines on my dresser, sending them crashing against the wall. Then he moved closer.

And I didn't want him anywhere near me.

I edged toward my bedroom door, trying to keep a clear escape route.

"Aw. What's the matter?" A mocking frown settled on his perfect face. "Scared?"

The noise of the house being completely destroyed echoed up the stairwell, and I wondered how many of them there were. "How did you get into my house?" I took a couple more steps, trying to stay calm, trying not to have a complete breakdown and beg him not to hurt me. Because the look on his face said he was about to.

"Well...you see, *Drucella*. I'm a criminal. But you know that." Then his expression shifted, and he rushed me. "Since you got me fucking arrested."

I yelped when his hard body forced me to the wall.

"Still wanna be the worst thing to happen to me?" His finger traced the top of my towel.

When it hooked beneath the edge, my pulse jumped into a frenzy, but I somehow managed to summon the courage to still his hand against my chest. "What are you going to do, Bellamy?"

He focused on his hand now resting over my bare skin, then smirked. And if I had to guess, what had him so amused was the ever-quickening thump of my heart against his palm.

"Where would the fun be if I told you?" His hand slid up my chest until his fingers wound around my throat. "You fucked up, Drew." His body pressed harder to mine until I could feel every ripple, every bulge of muscle tensing and coiling in anger. "You really, really fucked up..."

I closed my eyes while willing my knees not to buckle. He tapped the bat over the floor for a second, then stopped, slipping it underneath my towel and pressing the cold metal between my legs, making me flinch.

"I could fuck you up..." His hot breath washed over my lips. "Real good, baby girl."

These were not the games we played at Black Mountain. This wasn't manipulation or payback. This was crossing a line I was not prepared to go over, but it was too late; Bellamy was right here, like a devil dragging me right over it.

He slipped the bat against my pubic bone, right over my clit, and my body reacted in ways I wished it hadn't. A combination of fear and arousal that made my skin tingle with awareness.

"The thing is, baby girl. Your getting me arrested really fucked some shit up. So, you understand why I have to fuck your shit up, right?" He brushed his lips to mine. "No hard feelings, right?" He dropped the bat back to his side, but his hold on my throat remained.

His eyes searched mine, and a slow smirk pulled at his lips. "You like this shit, don't you?"

I would never, ever admit that to him, though. I didn't like feeling scared, and the fact that I wanted that bat between my legs in this situation had me questioning my sanity. His fingers twitched over my neck. "Someone's got some daddy issues..." He laughed before his grip loosened. He took a step back. "Sweet dreams, baby girl." Then he took a swing at my TV before passing into the hall. His footfalls moved toward the stairwell then down the steps.

The noise of things breaking fell silent, and seconds later, the front door opened and closed. I sagged like a puppet with cut strings and drew in a deep breath. This was insane. *He* was insane... I hurried to throw on clothes before rushing downstairs. It was carnage. The smashed big screen TV hung from the wall. Vases, artwork, furniture, all either smashed or broken. Even the couch looked like someone had sliced open the cushions and tossed the stuffing everywhere. I called the police and told them I'd come home to a break-in. Then I texted Olivia, asking if I could stay the night. Because the last place I wanted to be was here. Alone.

---

Olivia sat across her kitchen island, staring at me, wide-eyed. "He broke into your house? Shit, are you okay?"

Now the adrenaline had worn off, and whatever sick shit had been going on in my mind had left, I was terrified. My hands were shaking, heart racing.

"Yeah. I'll be fine."

"He's Bellamy West, Drew! Those guys go to jail and burn cars and break legs." She spun the barstool around, shaking her head. "Shit. What did he steal?"

"Nothing." Just trashed the place.

Confusion blanketed her face. "Then why the hell did he break into your house?"

To threaten me? To trash it? Make it known that he could get in? "I..." I paused, drawing a line over the condensation on my water glass. "Might have gotten him arrested."

"You—" Pinching the bridge of her nose, she held up her palm. "Girl, you have no idea what you're messing with."

"Look, he got me fired!"

She slapped a hand over the counter and rolled her eyes. "You were working a gross drive-thru. He did you a favor, my God, you—"

"That's not the point! He's an asshole."

"Who's an asshole?" Olivia's brother, Jackson, walked into the kitchen, no shirt, just sweatpants, and his blond hair messy from a shower. He winked at me before opening the refrigerator. "Hey, Drew."

"Jackson!" Olivia huffed, thumbing back at me. "She got Bellamy West. Arrested!"

"Fuck those guys." A grin settled on his face as he grabbed an energy drink and closed the fridge door. Then he held up a hand like he expected me to high-five him. A high-five that Olivia promptly slapped away.

"Uh. No. Jackson! She got him *arrested*—" Her eyes widened. "And he *knows*. That's nothing to celebrate."

Jackson popped the top to the canned drink, then took a sip. "Want me to handle West for you?"

"Uh..." My gaze shifted from him to Olivia.

I liked Olivia, and I didn't want to be responsible for her brother getting his ass beat. Because Jackson was nice and Bellamy broke into my house with a *baseball bat*. Bellamy would slaughter him.

"Don't be stupid, Jackson," Olivia snapped. "It's Bellamy West and his little gang of thugs. He will pummel you."

"Screw you, dog-faced gremlin." He glared at her, then stormed into the living room.

Olivia mumbled about how stupid he was beneath her breath before she turned to face me. "Just…" She clasped my hand. "Tell your dad. He'll pull you out, right? I mean, this isn't even funny…."

That what? That Bellamy had gotten me fired from Frank's, then I'd had him arrested, and now he'd broken into our house and trashed it. No. That would absolutely be my fault in his eyes. I'd spend another two years owing him for all the furniture Bellamy and his friends just ruined.

Her fingers drummed over the counter on a concentrated stare. Then the drumming stopped. "You should just get expelled. That's what you do."

That…wasn't the worst idea.

Olivia went to the fridge, pausing in front of the opened door. "This is like, totally insane. Like binge-worthy Netflix insane."

For her maybe, sitting pretty in Barrington, but for me, I was about to have to walk back into the hell-hole, and I'd pissed off the Devil. "I can't tell him. And I have to go to school with him tomorrow." I groaned.

## CHAPTER 9

## BELLAMY

"SHE WASN'T DEALING WEED!" some kid named Dickey shouted, cowering into the locker to block himself from a punch.

And that right there was absolute shit. The rumor—yes, *rumor*—that some kid had been pushing weed through Frank's had caught on like wildfire. Which meant no one had been selling weed through the drive-thru.

"I mean..." Wolf shrugged his shoulder while Hendrix held the guy to the wall. "No one's said they actually bought any..."

I moved toward the kid, bringing myself eye-level with his ready-to-shit-on-himself expression. "How sure are you?"

"Nikki sucked my dick for me to say it. I'm patient zero." The guy flinched like he expected me to punch him, and when I didn't, the word vomit spewed. "I didn't even know a Drew. I just thought it was some guy Nikki was mad at, and I just figured it was just a lie. I'm sorry. I just really wanted my first blowjob, man."

First blowjob. Jesus Christ. I nodded at Hendrix, and he

reluctantly let the guy go. "Bullshit, Bellamy," he huffed, pointing at the kid slowly creeping along the wall of lockers. "He should've gotten two black eyes. Not just one."

Then the kid shot off, sneakers squeaking over the tiled floor as he rounded the corner.

Wolf clapped a hand onto my shoulder. "And the level of psycho just moved to ten: sucking dick like a crack whore to spread a stupid rumor."

I jerked away from his hold and started down the hall, fuming, even though I'd done what needed to be done to save face. Regardless. If a rumor starts that someone's dealing, we have to handle it. But where most kids shit their pants trying to convince us it's bullshit the second we look at them, Drew had antagonized me. *Then* gotten me arrested and pissed me off to the point that I committed a *fucking felony* by breaking into her house.

Maybe I'd kill her and Nikki both.

"I'll see you guys later." Wolf ducked into a classroom, while Hendrix followed behind me, mumbling about not getting to beat that kid's ass. The farther down the hall I went, that anger dissipated into something else. Jesus Christ —I stopped mid-stride, patting my tightening chest. That was guilt. *Guilt!* Over what? Getting her fired and destroying her house because she wanted to…do whatever it was Drew did. That was bullshit. She brought that on herself.

Hendrix punched me in the gut. "Why are you at her locker?"

Because I put time into messing up her life up when she wasn't doing shit. "Go to class, Hendrix."

His eyes slowly widened. Then he shoved me. "Oh. Hell no, man. Do not go all soft on her because you wanna piece of that ass. She stepped on your rug." He tapped a toe over the tiles. "You can't be hunching the ones that'll step on your rug."

I shoved him. "I'm not going fucking soft. Go to class, would you?"

But of course, he didn't. Instead, he banged his forehead against Drew's locker. "She got you arrested, cumstain. Where's the retaliation? The bloodshed? The war?"

"We broke into her house, dipshit," I said. "And demolished it. What else do you want to do?" I stared down the bustling hallway, searching out Drew's perfect curves. "Burn her car?"

"Well, to start with. Yes..."

I leaned against the locker and shook my head. There was no pleasing Hendrix, especially since his brother was no longer around to rein his ass in. "We're not burning her car—or her house. It's over with, man. We scared the shit outta her, and she wasn't even doing anything."

He grabbed his head like he was trying to hold in a nuclear explosion. "Cocksucker! Who cares? That's even worse! She wasn't doing diddle-fuck-what, and she still—" He hopped up and down, slamming his feet over the floor. "Feet. On. Rug. What are you gonna let her do next? Take your balls and hand-milk them for every precious drop of jizz you've got?"

I just wanted answers, and dipshit here would never get that. "Go to class, asshole."

Huffing, he slowly moved away from the lockers, pointing at me. "Whipped by a pussy you haven't even pounded. That's sick, man." He kept backing down the hall. "Absolutely sick."

When Zepp got out of prison, I was strangling him for beating Hendrix with that wiffleball bat when we were kids.

I waited at Drew's locker, replaying the way her breath

caught when I slammed her against that wall. I was still going to fuck her; that much was for sure. Drew stepped through the crowd, and our eyes locked. The rhythm of her steps faltered for a split second before her shoulders pushed back and her chin lifted. Like she was trying to prove she wasn't scared of me. And when she brushed right past me, she made a point to glare at me.

"What do you want?" she asked, yanking open her locker.

There was no witty dig. No sarcasm. Just a dry, monotone question. And from what I knew of this girl, that was very unlike her. "You weren't dealing weed." That statement should have been followed with, I'm sorry, but those words just weren't ready to come out.

"No shit." Anger rippled across her face as she slammed her locker door. "The Barrington girl who doesn't need money wasn't dealing weed. Did you come to that realization all by your bad self?"

And...she was back, as was my anger. My jaw clenched, my gaze tightened on hers. The girl had no humility, so why I'd even let a seed of guilt take root in my chest was beyond me. "You didn't even try to deny it, Drew."

All she did was roll her eyes, then went to step away, like I would let her. Oh, no, this girl had a thing or two to learn about the hierarchy of Dayton. I grabbed her shoulder and spun her back against the lockers. "What was it you said to me, baby girl?" I brought my face close enough to hers I could smell the strawberry gloss coating her lips. "Something like, 'What if I don't care about your warning?'"

She shoved against my chest, but I didn't budge. Instead, I placed my lips by her ear, unable to resist the temptation to nip at her lobe before mocking her, "What are you gonna do, Bellamy?'" I shifted my position to glare at her. "That was stupid."

"You broke into my freaking house. You're a psycho." She attempted to shake free of my hold, but I held tight. "Let go of me," she said.

The image of her in that towel, hair soaking wet and skin coated in moisture, leaped to the forefront of my mind. Directly followed by the reaction she had when I wrapped my hand around her throat. She'd liked that bit of my breaking and entering. "Don't think I didn't notice the little hitch to your breath when I put that bat between your legs." I lifted a brow. "You like this shit, baby girl."

Her eyes narrowed. Her delicate jawline set. Nothing about her anger should have excited me the way it did.

"Get off me," she said through clenched teeth.

"Want me off of you? Get on your fucking knees and make me get off of you."

She leaned in, her jaw ticcing. "I will *never* suck your dick, Bellamy. Now leave me alone. You see me in the hall, don't talk to me."

"You think you're gonna call the shots?" I smirked as I backed away. "Sure thing, baby girl. Sure fucking thing."

---

"I'm telling you, Bell." Hendrix palmed one of the rubber dodgeballs. "Set some shit on fire."

The coach blew his whistle, and the girls bounded over to center-court in their baggy gym shirts and short-shorts.

"Females," Coach started. "Since one of your counterparts thinks it's funny to tie a tampon to my car antenna, you can run laps. Men. Grab a ball."

The girls groaned on their way to the door. All except

Drew. She stood there in shorts barely past her ass, inspecting her nails. And all I could think about was wrapping my hands around her throat again and making her moan. That would be the hate fuck of the century.

"Miss Morgan," Coach shouted. "Get moving."

"Oh, I'm sorry." She placed a hand on her chest, the fakest smile crossing her face. *"I* can't go on the track. Grass allergy."

And that was bullshit. I'd read her file, and she didn't have one damn allergy.

Coach glanced across the gym at us, a befuddled expression on his face. "Grass aller— Well, are you allergic to plastic?"

She narrowed her eyes. "No."

"Then grab a ball and get in line with the boys."

"You want me to play with *them?*" She waved a prissy hand over the line of guys.

"Is that a problem?"

For her prissy ass, it absolutely would be. The annoyed scowl on her face said I was right. I waited on her to whine, possibly pitch a fit, but she just sighed and took her place across the court from Hendrix.

Hendrix snickered. "Fine. No setting her car on fire. But her ass...I'm tagging her ass with a ball." His eyebrows wiggled before he took his spot behind the start line.

The whistle sounded, and everyone took off. Drew and Hendrix went for the same ball. He snatched it, reared back, and lobbed it straight at her thigh. She yelped and hobbled for a couple of strides.

The red mark it left sent an unsettled feeling stirring in my gut. It was just dodgeball, but I couldn't handle shit like that with girls. Scare the shit out of them, sure. Actually, physically hurt them, no.

"Don't hit her again, man."

Hendrix frowned at me. "What the hell did you just say?"

"Don't hit her."

His eyes went wide, and he shook his head before taking his place back behind the line. "I swear to God, if you let the temptation of a hot piece of ass cloud your judgment..."

The whistle sounded again. Sneakers scuffed the floor. Drew beat Hendrix to the ball this time, threw it, and nailed Hendrix in the balls. He fell to his knees, clutching his crotch while he mumbled, "Motherfucker."

"Miss Morgan," Coach shouted. "No aiming at the penile region."

"Sorry. Bad aim."

Hendrix glared up at me from the fetal position he'd curled himself into. "Scared the shit outta her, huh?" He grunted. "How does setting fire to her car sound to you now?"

## CHAPTER 10
## DREW

I WAS woman enough to admit that he'd scared me, really scared me, and I'd made a vow to myself that I was done with him. Done with his level of crazy because I couldn't compete with that, and I didn't need this in my life.

The dismissal bell rang. I grabbed my backpack from my locker, then went to the library to check out a book on the American Revolution for the project I'd been assigned to work on with Nora.

Dayton's library was deplorable. Nothing was organized. Half the books were missing spines. It took me twenty minutes to finally locate the historical book in the self-help section... By the time I left, the rush of students in the hallway had died down. I made my way down the corridor, typing out a text to Genevieve, when I heard Bellamy's voice. "Seriously, Nikki? You do realize it's psychotic."

I paused, lingering around the corner where the hallways intersected.

"It was a joke, Bellamy."

"Do I look like I find it fucking funny?" His voice was a feral rumble, barely restrained, and it made *me* recoil.

"Why do you even care?" she asked, a slight tremor in her words. "I mean—"

"Are you *that* stupid?" Something banged on a locker. If I had to guess, it was Bellamy's fist.

"Jesus Christ! We hooked up. Once. When I was shit-faced. And you just…" Silence fell over the hall. "Leave her the hell alone, Nikki."

I had to wonder who they were talking about and what exactly Nikki had done to piss him off so much because he sounded livid. I waited until a few more minutes of silence passed before I hooked a left down the hall, then exited the school, heading into the half-deserted parking lot

I joined Nora and Diane, huddled against Nora's car in their cheerleader outfits.

Diane's gaze tracked Bellamy and Hendrix as they crossed the lot. "What is it about them getting arrested that makes them so much hotter?"

"Speak for yourself." Nora opened her car door and tossed her gym bag inside. "I had to give up my bed for his little brother. Bellamy was supposed to take care of him, and he got arrested." Disdain leaked through her voice. "For dealing drugs. Again."

Diane's brows pulled together. "That's random. Why didn't his mom watch him?"

"She works like three jobs or something. His dad's a drunk. Bullshit. Bullshit…"

A lump formed in my throat. I glanced across the parking lot at Bellamy, who was standing behind Wolf's truck. All tattoos and attitude. He didn't look like the kind of guy who would watch a kid.

"Bellamy looks after his little brother?" I asked.

Nora shrugged. "The kid's with him more than not."

A horrible sensation dug into my chest. Guilt. Oh,

screw him. He was the asshole in this situation. Not me. I tried to maintain that, even as I pictured his life with a deadbeat dad, a mom who was never there, and a little brother who relied on him. I didn't want to feel bad for him, but more than that, I didn't want to actually *be* the spoiled bitch I knew he thought I was. Maybe I had taken it too far. I did tend to go big or go home, but unlike at Black Mountain, the consequences for a kid in Dayton were immediate and long-term. Bellamy wasn't some trust-fund guy whose daddy would bail him out of a criminal record. It still didn't excuse him breaking into my damn house, but... he said I'd messed with his family—a kid—and that made me feel like the crappiest person in the world right now.

"Oh. Shit..."

I followed Nora's gaze across the lot. Bellamy stood behind an old Camaro, bat raised. He swung at the back windshield, and it shattered before he rounded the car, smashing out every window, then knocking the side mirrors off.

"Wonder what Nikki did to piss him off?" Diane said.

Nikki ran up, screaming, and he cast a cold stare in her direction. Hendrix met up with Bellamy halfway through the lot.

My pulse ticked up when they stopped at my car. Bellamy loosely swung the bat at his side, and I remembered all too well what he'd done with that bat the last time he'd had it. My thighs pressed together. I was definitely sick. Broken. "See you guys later," I said, then started toward my TT. This couldn't be good.

"Nice car." Bellamy kicked his shoe up onto my front tire, all tight shirt and ripped jeans over taught muscles. Like a psycho.

"Don't you dare," I said, eyeing the bat.

"I'm not doing anything, baby girl." He held up his hands, shifting away from the car.

I stood there for a moment, weighing my options. Like a rabbit caught in the sights of a predator, I didn't know what to do. Run and risk him taking chase or freeze and hope he left me the hell alone. He watched me like a hawk as I opened my car door, and if the small smirk on his face was anything to go by, he was doing something all right.

I eased behind the wheel and cranked the engine. I hated that my hands were shaking because I knew what he wanted was for me to be scared. So instead of gunning it out of there the way I wanted to, I took my time and changed the radio station, then I lowered the roof to my car. Of course, he was still standing there.

"I told you to leave me alone."

He leaned over, folding his arms across my window ledge. "Well, I would. But unfortunately for you, the word around school is, you got me arrested. I'd really hoped that would stay between us, but..."

Three guesses where this was going. Nowhere good, that was for sure.

"You started this. Then you broke into my house and destroyed it."

He swiped a hand over his mouth on an amused laugh. "Yeah, but the problem is. They don't know that." He jerked his chin toward the people staring in the parking lot.

I had no idea what he was going to do, and as that slow smirk cut across his face, I snapped. "Screw you, Bellamy."

A low hiss sounded over the purr of the engine. Hendrix's reflection popped up in my rearview mirror.

I'd forgotten about him and realized how monumentally stupid that was when he flipped a knife in his hand, and the tire pressure sensors flashed on my dashboard.

"You did not…" I said through gritted teeth.

Bellamy leaned into my car, placing his lips close to my ear. "You gonna lie to me again?"

"You really are a psycho. You know that, right?"

"And you really are getting off easy…"

Easy? This guy had to be joking. "You slashed my tires *and* broke into and vandalized my house within twenty-four hours. That's a felony and a misdemeanor. You fucking nut job!"

All he did was smile. And that smile was devastating—because I was evidently a nut job, too. I gripped the steering wheel, trying to focus on something, anything but how hot he looked and how crazy I was.

"You know, I was sane before I met you."

"That makes two of us," he said. Bullshit.

My car rocked, tearing my attention from Bellamy.

"Been saving this all day." Hendrix clambered onto my trunk, immediately whipping out his dick.

"What the hell—" But the rest of that sentence was lost when a stream of piss splattered over my passenger seat. I grabbed the handle to throw open my car door, but Bellamy's massive frame blocked my exit.

"Let me out, right now, Bellamy!"

Piss ricocheted off the leather, droplets splashing my arm. Bellamy just smirked at me, refusing to move. My temper skyrocketed. With a growl, I shoved to my feet, climbing over my seat and onto the trunk. I snatched Hendrix by the ankle. "Get off my car!" I yanked hard enough that he lost balance and toppled off the car on a scream.

Good, I hoped that hurt. With any luck, he'd get road rash on his junk.

"The hell, man!" Hendrix shot up, holding his head,

dick still out. A trickle of blood fell down his temple. "She just cracked my skull." Hendrix rounded the back, still clutching his head when he stopped beside Bellamy. "And *that* is the reason I wanted to set her car on fire!"

Set my car on fire. Oh, that was taking this too far. I slid off the trunk, not even caring that my dress had ridden up around my waist. Then I jabbed Hendrix in the chest. "I hope you get a concussion. Not like you had any brain cells to lose anyway."

Both guys stared at me like I'd just grown two heads with horns.

I stormed off across the parking lot, taking out my phone so I could call someone to come pick up my poor car.

"Holy shit!" Nora ran up beside me, skidding to a stop. "What are you doing? They're insane, Drew you can't egg them on!"

"Nora, he pissed in my car! Not like I was just going to sit there and watch." And I may very well get murdered over it, but what the hell could I do now?

---

Nora offered to take me home. The entire drive, she rambled about how awful Bellamy and Hendrix were, making Hendrix's brother, Zepp, out to be nothing short of a complete monster who belonged behind the bars he'd evidently been placed behind.

I directed her down my street and to my drive, and when she pulled in, she gasped. "Holy. Shit. Your house is massive."

I stared past the manicured lawn to the brick home. Between both my parents, I'd lived in god knows how many big houses. Each time I came to visit them from boarding school, I missed my shared dorm with Genevieve. That was home. This—this was miserable, which was why I had spent more time at Olivia's than my dad's since I'd arrived.

"You wanna come in?" I asked as I climbed out.

Beaming, she hopped out of the car and followed me to the front of the house. Then I remembered that the entire house was still destroyed, and I froze. It was too late now; I'd already invited her in.

"So... The house is a bit of a mess."

"I don't care."

"Yeah, well..." I shoved the key in the lock.

The door swung open to the empty foyer. To the several holes in the wall where artwork once hung. I glanced in the living room, surprised to see that everything was gone. All the broken furniture had been removed, leaving behind only the chandelier and a rug.

"So, we'll have to go up to one of the spare rooms if you want to watch TV." I started toward the stairs, and Nora strayed behind me, mouth agape as she took in the carnage.

"What happened?"

"Break in."

She stopped on the bottom step, her eyes widening. "Holy shit, they took everything."

I didn't have the energy to explain that they had, in fact, taken northing, and now that I thought about it, that was weird. They sold weed. Surely they'd hock a TV? But I had a feeling Bellamy just wanted to send a violent message.

Halfway through an episode of *Sex and the City* that I'd seen a thousand times, my phone dinged.

**Dickhead: Just so you know, I spent my time in the slammer beating one out to the thought of what I was gonna do to you when I got out.**

**Me: You get off on breaking into people's houses and scaring them with a baseball bat?**

**Dickhead: People? Nah... You, fuck yes.**

**Me: You're sick.**

**Dickhead: And you think you aren't?**

**Dickhead: Daddy issues...**

Bad, bad, bad.

I glanced across the bed to Nora, who was still engrossed in the TV.

**Me: We done now?**

**Dickhead: Depends...**

No. I was done with Bellamy West. At least that's what I told myself...

## CHAPTER 11
## DREW

I STOOD in the middle of the crowded hallway, staring at the text on my phone: **Hope you're enjoying the new school, darling. Bisous. - Irina**

My mother.

Who refused to let me call her anything but Irina. And who evidently had no idea what type of school Dayton was, or I'd hope to God she'd have curbed my father. Just as I went to reply, someone smacked the phone from my hands.

"Barrington whore."

A group of girls laughed as they parted around me, Nikki standing pride of place among them with a bitchy smile radiating off her face before they moved on. God, she was pathetic. They couldn't even come up with something more original—*Barrington Whore* had been Sharpied across my locker. Looked like the conversation I'd overheard Bellamy and her having did fuck all.

Sighing, I dropped to a knee to reach for my phone, but just as I did, someone else snatched it up.

"Hey, Drewbie." Hendrix smiled, flicking his finger against my knuckles before straightening.

A crisscross of SpongeBob Band-Aids decorated his forehead, reminding me that I'd almost accidentally knocked him out.

"Hendrix," I groaned as I stood. "Give it back."

"Patience." He started down the hall, fiddling with my phone as he maneuvered around students.

"Hendrix!" I jogged after him.

"Call me Daddy and I'll give it back."

"You're gross." When I made a grab for my phone, he ducked away.

"Oh, come on. You gotta have some titty and beaver shots in here somewhere." On a shake of his head, he chucked the device at me, then headed toward the Men's room. "You disappoint me, rich girl."

I flipped him off before rounding the corner and heading toward history. I took a seat and my phone vibrated in my pocket, probably my mother sending a picture of her new yacht.

**Unknown Number: I'm taking a shit right now. I need moral support. It's a burner.**

I didn't need to ask who it was. I dropped the phone to the desk, refusing to acknowledge how vile Hendrix was. A few seconds later, it buzzed again, and a picture of a curled turd popped up on the screen. And that—was another level entirely.

Mr. Weaver was halfway through a lecture on the American Revolution when the intercom system crackled. "Could Drucella Morgan come to the office, please?"

The class snickered, repeating my godawful first name, and I cursed my parents for the millionth time for apparently loathing me from birth. I pushed up from my seat and made my way through the empty hallways to the office, wondering why I was being called in. Maybe someone had said something about my car getting damaged on school property. Doubtful. Everyone in this school was up Bellamy and Hendrix's ass.

When I stepped through the glass doorway, the secretary looked up. "Miss Morgan?"

"Yeah?"

"Coach Todd told me that you have a grass allergy, but..." She flipped through several pages in a chart while shoving her glasses back up the bridge of her nose. "It's not listed on your medical records. I'll just need you to sign a form so we can add it. And you'll need to bring in an EpiPen as well."

Who knew Dayton High would actually care about their students dying? "Oh, it's not that serious. I just get a rash." That sounded plausible...I thought.

She peered over the rim of her glasses, one pencil-drawn eyebrow quirked. "A rash?"

"Yep."

On a sigh, she pushed up from behind her desk. "Let me get a different form then..."

While I waited, two guys in baggy, *Star Wars* shirts walked in. They slumped into the chairs beside the principal's office, fidgeting and wiping sweat from their brows.

"He's gonna kill us."

"If we don't turn someone in, we'll get expelled."

*Expelled.* I looked away and stared at the printer on the back table, trying not to make it obvious I was eavesdropping on their whispered conversation.

"But if West gets expelled, Hunt will murder us." A small whimper leaked through his lips. "Hunt's crazy."

"But if we give another name, someone else will get

expelled, and they didn't do it." Well, at least they had a conscience.

I should have just minded my own business, but of course, I'd never been able to control my impulses. I turned around, my curiosity more than peaked.

"What did West do?" I asked.

Both guys froze, staring wide-eyed at me like deer in headlights. One of them went to open their mouths, but the other nudged him in the ribs. "Don't, Kyle. She's like...*his*."

Wow. "Uh, definitely not," I scowled at them for a moment. "But I might be able to help you."

The guy to the right shook his head. "Don't do it. Getting expelled is way better than getting murdered."

Bellamy was a dick for sure, but murder sounded extreme. "Did he sell you weed?" I asked.

They looked at each other before the one named Kyle broke. "It was a test."

His friend hit him in the arm.

"He what...sold you a test?"

They both nodded. Bellamy really was into anything and everything bad. But *that* was worthy of expulsion? Screw it, I didn't care about the how, only getting out of this awful school and away from that psycho. The slightest concern whispered in the back of my mind that getting kicked out might jeopardize my college acceptance. Then again, my dad had paid them to keep me after one expulsion, and as important as it was to me, the bragging rights were more important to him.

Principal Brown's door creaked open. An excited thrill shot through my veins. Screw Bellamy and screw this school. I was getting out of here.

I turned to the two guys. "Look," I said, feigning

distress. "Just don't tell Brown I sold you the tests. I'll refund you the money."

Both guy's faces washed white. Principal Brown cleared his throat. When I turned to face him, he had both hands on his meaty hips, his cheap dress shoe tapping the floor.

"Would you like to step into my office, Miss..."

## CHAPTER 12

### BELLAMY

WHEN I CLOSED MY LOCKER, Kyle and Robert, two guys from the computer club, stood a few feet away, staring at me like weirdos. One pushed the other forward a few feet.

"I don't know what happened," he whispered. "We were just sitting there."

I shouldered my backpack on a glare. Nothing good ever started with that kind of defense. "What are you talking about?"

"We got caught with that test..."

The slow throb of my pulse pounded my temple. If one of these dipshits ratted me out... "Go on," I said through a clenched jaw.

"And uh. I mean, we didn't tell on you. We'd never do that. But..." He gnawed at his lip, then inhaled a breath. "That new girl..."

I swear to God, if Drew tried to get me in trouble for that shit, I would go to Wal-E-Mart and buy Hendrix an economy-sized box of matches, and we'd burn her shit to the ground. "What about her?"

"She said she sold them."

"To Brown." Robert blurted. "She said it to Brown! And then she got in trouble."

She'd voluntarily taken the blame. For something she had nothing to do with. What in the hell?

"We didn't drop her in. We were just sitting there, freaking out because we didn't want you to murder us and we didn't want to get expelled, and she overheard us. When Brown opened the door to call us in, she said it was her. And Brown suspended her. We didn't know what to do." He took a deep breath. "Please don't beat us up."

I lifted a brow. As long as I wasn't the one getting in trouble, I didn't care who they accidentally ratted out.

"We know she's kinda your girl or something, and you're probably really mad, but..." The other one's face washed a little white, and he clutched at his stomach like he was going to puke.

"Whatever, man. I don't give a shit." I mumbled, turning to head out of the school.

I made it to the exit before it sunk in. Brown had suspended her. That's why she had done it. She was trying to barter a stolen test for the keys out of hell.

And the devil didn't like that.

---

The sun beat down on me while I leaned against the bumper of my car, staring at my phone.

**Me: Where you at, baby girl?**

Of course, she didn't respond. But thanks to Hendrix snatching her phone in the hall earlier, all I now had to do to find her was swipe to the FindAFriend app. Which I did. That little blue dot still hovered above a house two blocks over, just like it had done for the past hour. I couldn't deny it was genius to have Hendrix add my contact in that stupid app—even if the thought that she was probably at some Barrington prick's house getting pounded right now did piss me off. It was worth it for the simple fact of my being able to pop up like a genie anytime I wanted was guaranteed to aggravate the shit out of her. Because we weren't done until I decided we were.

The little blue dot finally moved, and I took off my shirt then reclined back on the sunbaked hood of my car. I figured her walking up in her drive and finding me sprawled out with my abs tensed would get her flustered, and I'd thoroughly enjoy that.

I watched puffy, white clouds pass by, drifting behind the tree line before a huff came from the end of her drive. Seconds later, a shadow fell over me.

"You're blocking my sun," I said, sitting up and adjusting the cross on my necklace.

Her gaze fell to my stomach, and I flexed a little. Just to be a dick. "I'm surprised you didn't just let yourself in."

I would have, had she not moved the spare key. "I'll be sure to make a copy of the spare next time." I slid off the hood.

Drew backed up a step, then halted like she was forcing herself to stand up to some bully and brought her arms across her chest. "What are you doing here?"

"I texted you." I kept moving toward her, and she didn't budge.

"I was busy."

"Nah..." I swept a hand over her cheek, cupping her jaw for a second. My attention went straight to her parted lips, and dammit if I didn't have to fight the urge to slam my lips to hers. "When it comes to me, you're never busy, baby girl."

Her breath caught, and her gaze slipped to my mouth. The thing about it, she may hate me, but she couldn't hide the fact she was attracted to me. Just like I couldn't hide my attraction to her. Girls like her only followed guys like me out to a van when we measured up to every sordid fantasy they'd had. And the magnetic pull that kept us coming back was nothing short of raw sexual urge. Drew could hate me all she wanted. Hate never kept anyone from fucking, only from falling in love. And that's all I wanted from her—a good fuck and a challenge.

So why did I almost feel high by being near her? Why did it bother me when I thought that the most likely reason why she wanted out of Dayton so bad was so she could get away from me? I moved closer, dragging my thumb over her plump lip and smearing her lipstick. "Stealing my thunder to try to get a little vacation?"

Huffing, she pulled her face out of my hold. "I was trying to get expelled."

"For stealing a history test that wasn't even a final?" I barked out a laugh, slapping a hand over my slick chest. "Jesus Christ."

"Whatever." She started up the sidewalk of her ridiculously oversized, million-dollar house. "It's only two more months."

Armani jeans. Expensive car. Attitude out the ass—and that little tidbit was my Kryptonite. She was getting under my skin in ways I didn't need, and the minute she was out of Dayton, whatever bullshit this was between us would be over. Which I needed.

"What's it worth to you?" I shouted just before she reached her door.

She stopped. "Getting out of Dayton? A lot."

"Good." I started toward her front door. I could help us

both out. Get her the hell away from me and get exactly what I wanted—what we both wanted.

She glared at me. "What are you doing?"

"This is called making a deal, baby girl." I pushed past her, letting myself in and half-rolling my eyes at the new décor. Rich people. Just replacing shit like it was nothing.

She followed me. "What kind of deal?"

"Nice décor..." I rounded the hallway to the kitchen. "And a deal where you get kicked out of Dayton and I get you in a bed."

"What?" Her brows pulled together. "You are not serious."

I took a seat at the massive island, glancing around at the kind of kitchen that would Gordon Ramsey jealous. "It's not like I don't know you want to. Come on... You followed me out to a van, baby girl."

"Before I knew what a dick you are." She backed up to the counter, folding her arms over her chest.

"Like that has anything to do with fucking me." I snorted a laugh. "For that hour of your life, you wouldn't give a shit how much of a dick I'd been."

"Some of us have self-respect."

This shit, huh? "Self-respect?" I pushed up from the seat, and she moved back, gripping the edge of the counter. "Why would you fucking me mean you didn't have self-respect?" I stepped in front of her, gripping her chin and tilting her head back. "Huh, baby girl?"

"Because I hate you."

I grabbed onto her waist and lifted her on the counter, placing myself between her thighs. "Yeah? You hate me, baby girl?"

Her chest rose on ragged swells, her cheeks quickly going pink. "So much."

On a laugh, I leaned in. "Good, it'll be way more fun when you cave."

Then I slammed my mouth over hers, fisting her hair as I parted her lips. And she didn't fight it for a second. Her hands went to my arms, nails digging into my skin while I fucked her mouth with my tongue, imagining it was her pussy. When I felt her legs press into my hips, I pulled away. "Tell me you wouldn't enjoy it..."

She hesitated, anger ripping across her face. Because she wanted it, just like I wanted it, regardless of how much I hated her—or she hated me.

"Fucking is animalistic. Instinctual." I trailed my fingertips over her thigh. "Something out of your control. And I'm not the guy to bullshit with." My gaze flicked between her legs. "You wanna fuck me. I wanna fuck you. This just makes it more fun and a one-time deal with no strings attached."

"I don't want you."

My fingers crept higher on her leg, and not once did she flinch. Not once did she try to stop me. "Admit it, baby girl. You want this disrespect. One fucking time."

And she still didn't stop me. Which was the only reason I kept going. I moved my hand beneath her skirt, then stopped, cocking a brow. "You and I both know, I go an inch farther, and you're going to be wet for me." I smirked. "And then there's no denying you want a little taste of a bad boy."

I didn't need to feel between her legs. The way she labored for each breath, the blush on her cheeks said everything I needed to know.

"Admit it." I brought my lips close to hers. "Tell me you wouldn't give me one dirty fuck, regardless of what of whether I helped you or not."

Her eyes narrowed. "If you help me, I'll fuck you. Once."

"No, baby girl." My fingers played over the soft skin of her thigh. "Tell me you'd fuck me once, even if I *didn't* help you."

Because she would. But this—this made it way more fun.

"I followed you out to that van, didn't I?"

Ex-fucking-actly. I went back to the stool and tapped a hand over the island. "Shall we get down to business, then?"

She hopped down from the counter and opened the freezer, taking out one of those stupid Push-Pops she always grabbed at lunch. On day two of her stint at Dayton, I went to the cafeteria before her, gathered every last one of those things, and hid them under the ice cream sandwiches. She bitched about it all through lunch, so I did it every day afterward. I liked it when she was angry.

Her tongue wrapped around the tip of that popsicle in a way that made my dick hard. Then she slid the Push-Pop between her lips. There was no way she wasn't doing that on purpose, and if she wanted to draw attention to that, well...

"Is that how you suck a dick?" I asked, adjusting myself.

She wiped the corner of her mouth with her finger before licking that too. "So, how are you going to get me expelled?"

"Oh. *I'm* not getting you expelled. I'm more like a consultant on how you can get yourself expelled." I didn't trust her enough not to drag me down with her as a final fuck you, and the last thing I needed was to get sent to the reform school an hour away. "And we've already gone over the fee..." God, I was getting her ass expelled tomorrow.

She glared at me. "Okay, asshole. How do I get expelled?"

"Fighting—"

"I'm not getting in a fight."

"Fucking—which I'm not okay with."

She rolled her eyes. "I'm making a deal for a fuck, not to be owned."

The thing she didn't seem to see, as far as anyone in Dayton was concerned, I already did own her.

"All right. Then you're dealing weed." I said.

"Oh, the irony." She gave a long lick over the length of her popsicle. "Let me guess, I'll get arrested, too."

"Depends on how much weed and Brown's mood that day." I focused on the way her tongue stroked over the rainbow-colored sherbet. Thoughts of her on her knees flipped through my mind like a movie reel full of porn. My dick had never had so many moments of being let down in its life until she came around. I shifted again, trying to give it a little more room in my jeans.

Holding up a finger, she pulled her phone from her pocket, then jabbed over the screen—still sucking on that popsicle. A few seconds later, the device pinged, and Drew smiled. "Okay, it's fine. My mom will sort it."

I felt my brow lift. No way this girl had asked her mom if she would bail her out of jail for selling weed—to get expelled. "Your mom will...sort it?"

"Criminal records are unseemly."

What in the hell did they teach kids at those private schools because so far it seemed real-life logic was not on that curriculum?

"Don't look at me like that. I'm not some spoiled brat."

Like she wasn't. I placed a hand on the cool counter, twisting in the chair to glance around the enormous kitchen.

"Right... Armani jeans. Audi. Mansion. The ability to pay your way out of a prison record. Not spoiled in the slightest."

She glared at me, the Push-Pop halfway in her mouth when she bit it clean in two. That almost made my hard-on disappear. Almost.

"My dad is a dick, okay? He put me in that school, and that's as good as throwing me to the wolves."

"He *sent* you to Dayton?" There wasn't one Barrington prick I knew who would voluntarily send their precious kid to Dayton.

"Dayton is punishment. And I want out."

Dayton was punishment for her and life for me. And if that didn't sum up Barrington, I didn't know what did.

I pushed up from the chair. "I'll bring you some weed."

"Okay."

Then I started toward through the kitchen, stopping at the doorway to glance back at her. "And one more thing. I let you do this, and I'll have to get you back. I have a reputation to uphold..."

CHAPTER 13

DREW

THE DOOR SLAMMED CLOSED, and I stood in the kitchen with my empty Push-Pop, wondering what in the hell I'd just agreed to.

I'd literally just prostituted myself out in exchange for his help getting expelled from Dayton. And the worst thing…I knew I probably didn't need his help. I wanted to get expelled in part to get away from him, but I also wanted the asshole.

This was a have your cake and eat it situation.

For one night, I could have a hit, just one dose of Bellamy, to cure this craving. And then I'd be gone, away from this shithole school, and I'd never have to see him again.

---

Girls glared, cupping hands and whispering as I made my way to Nora's locker. That two-day suspension had not been long enough away from this hell hole.

Nora glanced over her shoulder when I stopped beside

her. "So, I heard you got suspended because you said you stole the tests everyone knows Bellamy took." Her brows pulled together. "I mean, did you voluntarily do that, or did he threaten you into it or what?"

"I saw an opportunity." I didn't belong here, but the situation with Bellamy made things so much worse. I needed to get out of this school and away from him. But I couldn't tell her that without hurting her feelings. "I just need to get kicked out, Nora."

Hurt flashed across her eyes before she covered it, then she shut her locker door. "This school is shit. I'd go to Barrington if I could."

"Speaking of getting kicked out, I'm about to start handing out weed. Wish me luck."

Her brows lifted. "Are you getting expelled or arrested?"

"Maybe both."

"Good luck." Then she shoved through the hall, ducking into her classroom.

I made my way down the hall and stopped at the main intersection. My pulse steadily ticked up as I dug in my backpack for one of the tiny baggies Bellamy had given me.

Was I really trusting the guy I was in a little bit of a war with to get me out of this hellhole? Sex didn't seem like enough of a guarantee. I glanced around at the graffiti-covered lockers, the girls glaring at me like they'd cut me given a chance.

Yeah. I absolutely was.

"Who wants some weed?" I shouted, and silence fell over the hall. "I've got weed!" I shook the baggie, then chucked it at one of the guys who'd stop to stare at me with a furrowed brow like I'd lost my mind. And I pretty much had.

A nervous energy wound through me as the crowd of students continued to grow, even though the whole point of this was to get caught. I had to get out of this school, out from under my dad's stupid punishment.

The congregation of students shifted. The murmur of whispers fell to a hush as people scrambled to get out of the way. I knew it was Bellamy before I laid eyes on him. And yes, I had to do this to get away from him.

The second his gaze landed on me, his jaw set. Wolf and Hendrix moved beside him, staring, and when they started toward me, I tossed a bag at Hendrix. "Have some weed."

"Holy. Shit." He caught it, crammed it inside his pants, then pointed at me. "She's *giving* away weed, man."

If I hadn't planned the whole thing out with him the night before, I'd swear the fury in Bellamy's eyes was real.

On a smirk, he swiped a hand over his chin then stalked toward me. It wasn't like I needed any help being drawn to all things bad, but when he looked at me like he wanted to hurt me, he made dangerous seem more than appealing.

He moved forward, and I moved backward until my spine hit one of the classroom doors. He caged me in, bringing his face in close proximity to mine. My thrumming pulse no longer had anything to do with nerves and everything to do with his warm breaths teasing my lips. "Whatcha doing, baby girl?"

"Oh, you know, not dealing." I swallowed, fighting to look anywhere but his lips. "Not taking any money."

His chin dropped on a smile as his hand went to my thigh. "Not very smart." His fingers teased the hem of my skirt, and I swayed toward him.

"What can I say?" I whispered, finding a little too much excitement in this. "You know I love some payback."

"That a fact?" He angled his face like he was about to kiss me, and my breath caught in my throat.

I knew this was an act, but right now, I wasn't acting, and I wasn't really sure he was. "Whatcha gonna do, Bellamy?"

He wrapped a hand around the back of my neck. Rubbing. Caressing. Then his hold moved around my throat, sending my heart into an elated sprint. "Bringing you to your knees, baby girl." His lips touched mine, the taste of spearmint transferring from his mouth to mine on a heated breath. "And hard."

I bit at my bottom lip before I did something to screw this up—like kiss him. Because enemies didn't kiss, and I needed the reminder for myself just as much as for the audience gathered in the hallway behind us.

"What is going on out here?" A teacher shouted, clapping her hands and breaking up the crowd.

Bellamy's fingers trailed my throat as he took one, slow step back. I held his gaze right up until the teacher's hand landed on my arm, then hauled me toward the principal's office.

She deposited me in front of Brown's desk, then chucked one of the bags of weed on top of his mound of paperwork. "Weed! She was selling weed. In the hallway."

"Actually, I was gifting it," I said. "For medicinal purposes."

Brown's bushy eyebrows pulled together. "Thank you, Mrs. Tate," he dismissed her, his narrowing gaze never leaving mine. The door clicked shut.

"Stealing tests. Giving away illegal substances." The hinges to his chair creaked as he moved forward and clasped his hands on his desk. "Let me guess, you don't like it here at Dayton?"

"Who does?"

"I see." He gave a curt nod before thumbing through the files on his desk. "In that case, I guess I have no choice but to give you another two-day suspension." He scribbled something across a paper. Two days. For distributing weed! This was insane...

"Look," I deadpanned him. "Let's just get this over with. I'm going to get kicked out at some point. You have a school full of reprobate kids, most of who don't want to be here. Why not just make your life easier and expel me now?"

A sly smile pulled at his lips as he tore off my suspension notice and passed it to me. "I think it would be making *your* life easier, Miss Morgan. I'm used to this."

I narrowed my eyes. Why was I surrounded by men who wanted to make my life hell? "Fine." I snatched the piece of paper from him, then stormed out of the office.

When I rounded the corner, the stench of burning rubber hit me. A group of students stood, gathered by the entrance. Faces pressed to the glass while chatter hummed between them. *Shit. Shit. Shit.*

The red flames were visible through the door, bright red and reaching like fingers toward the sky as a thick, black cloud of smoke engulfed my car.

"Asshole," I said, pushing through the doors. Whispers and quiet laughter crept through the crowd of students. I stopped at the end of the walkway, annoyance lancing through my chest. I'd let him set my car on fire as his form of fake retribution, and I didn't even get expelled. This was absolute crap.

Sirens wailed on the highway seconds before police cars and firetrucks took sharp turns into the school's lot.

I spent the next hour talking to the police. Of course, I

could have just said I had no idea who did it, but this was high school. Everyone had enemies, and I figured if I—a Barrington girl in Dayton—couldn't throw out at least one name, I figured it would look super suspicious. So, acting on behalf of karma, I mentioned that Nikki Wright hated me with a passion. As evidenced by the "Barrington Whore" written over my locker in Sharpie. I knew they wouldn't do shit, but I hoped it would inconvenience her. And that little, petty bit of payback made this shit slightly more bearable.

After the cops had left, I stood by the smoldering, charred remains of my car, my fingers angrily stamping out a text to Bellamy. God, this was such bullshit.

**Me: Done**

**Dickhead: Congratulations. I'll pick you up at the Methodist church down the street.**

After walking a mile down the litter-strewn shoulder, I reached the Methodist church. Judging from the discarded syringes on the ground, this was where the druggies hung out. I lingered at the edge of the parking lot, watching the highway for Bellamy's crappy car.

My phone vibrated in my pocket, and I pulled it out, expecting it to be him telling me he was joking about being my getaway ride and to go fuck myself, but instead, it was Nora.

**Nora: So, did you get expelled?**

**Me: No. Suspended again.**

**Nora: My condolences.**

**Me: I'm sorry if I hurt your feelings, Nora. I didn't mean to.**

**Nora: I selfishly don't want you to leave, even though the place is an absolute shithole.**

**Me: I just need to get away from Bellamy.**

It was almost a confession, but not quite. Everyone knew we were enemies. What she didn't know was that hating him was the easy bit. The part that had me running was something very far from hate.

**Nora: Are you sure you haven't fucked him? Because you sound cockstruck right now.**

**Me: I haven't fucked him! And I am not cockstruck.**

**Nora: Maybe you should bang him. In the hallway. Or on Brown's desk. Get him out of your system and get expelled at the same time. LOL.**

**Nora: I'm joking. Do not touch him. He's gross.**

Bellamy was many, many things. Hot, dirty, arrogant. *Gross* was not one of them.

**Me: I won't.**

Until I got expelled, and he collected. And why the hell the idea of that turned me on was very, very concerning.

Bass thumped through the air seconds before Bellamy's car barreled down the highway. He swerved off the road, tires kicking up a cloud of dust as he pulled into the lot in front of me. The door handle almost came off when I opened the door to climb into the passenger seat.

Cigarette burns scarred the cloth seats, and the only thing holding the dashboard together was strips of duct tape. The thing didn't look safe, not to mention, I doubted Bellamy was a safe driver. This may very well be the way I died... He shifted gears. The engine made an unhealthy rattling sound, like an old chain smoke, when it took off. When he fishtailed it back onto the highway, he lowered the volume to the rap music blaring through the busted speakers.

"You aren't allergic to latex, are you?" he laughed a little.

"We're not fucking. I didn't get kicked out." I huffed. The more I thought about it, the more pissed I grew.

"What do you mean, you didn't get kicked out? You were doling out weed—"

"Two-day suspension."

"What the fuck?" He shifted gears again, flooring it through a red light. "You were passing out weed like Willy Wonka. How the hell did you not get expelled? What'd you do, give Brown a handjob or something?"

"No, Brown got this smug-ass look on his face, like he knows I want out." I banged my head against the seat, staring out at the shitty town of Dayton as it whizzed past my window. "Why the hell am I surrounded by men who want to ruin my life?"

"And Jacobs didn't argue with him?"

"Jacobs?"

I glanced at Bellamy, and he shot me a glare before taking a hard left, slinging me against the door.

"Jacobs. The cop... Don't tell me he didn't even call Jacobs in?"

"Uh, no. I was in his office for like, five minutes."

"That's bullshit." He sped toward a red light, and I grabbed onto the door handle because I just knew he was going to run this one, too.

"You know," I said, "you owe me now."

*Then* he slammed on the brakes. My hands hit the dashboard; the seatbelt cut into my chest as the car came to a screeching halt. "You dick!"

"I do not owe you anything. It's not my fault you didn't get expelled for something you absolutely should've been expelled for. That's on you—" His gaze dropped to my exposed thigh. "For being hot or some shit. God, my dick can't take much more of this..."

He thought I was hot. Wait—not the point. "I let you burn my freaking car!"

"Correction. You," he jabbed a finger toward me, "suggested I burn your car."

Only because my handing out weed in the hall one hundred percent looked like I was trying to dick him over. And he'd made it clear he'd have to fake retaliation. Whatever. Hendrix had wanted to burn my car. The smell of piss was never coming out of the seat anyway, so he might as well set fire to it. Not like I wouldn't get a new one with the insurance.

The light turned green, and he somehow floored his little car so fast the backend fishtailed. "You're insane if you think I owe you." He snorted. "I was *trying* to do you a favor."

"You were *trying* to do your dick a favor. Now, I have two suspensions and a burned-out car. Oh, and I've ignored every call and text from my father ever since he heard I got fired for dealing weed." And he was about to hear I was dealing in school. He was going to kill me. Possibly bury me in the yard...

"House so big he texts you to shout at you," he mumbled. "Jesus..."

"You're funny." I groaned. "He's totally going to come back home just to kick my ass."

Bellamy went still, and I noticed his knuckles whiten on

the steering wheel. Long seconds passed, the only sound the hum of tires over the road.

"Does he hit you?" Bellamy stared through the windshield, jaw ticcing.

I realized too late that "kick my ass" sounded bad. In Bellamy's world, that was probably very literal. I instantly felt bad for bitching about my dad like he was some kind of monster. He'd never hurt me physically.

"No. No." I tugged at the hem of my skirt and shook my head. "He's just..." An uncaring asshole

"I get it," he said, then turned the music back up.

I rested my forehead against the window and watched fast-food restaurants and pawn shops whizz past the window until they gave way to well-kept subdivisions and manicured parks. Bellamy's car nearly stalled out when we started up the hill that led into Barrington Estates. My phone buzzed in my pocket then stopped. Then buzzed again. It had to be my dad, and I'd just wait to read those texts when I wasn't in the car with Bellamy.

His car sputtered to a stop outside my house, and I turned to look at him, trying to ignore how good he looked with one hand on the stick-shift, the other casually draped over the steering wheel.

"Well, I guess I'll see you in two days. If I haven't been sent to some reform school." My phone went off again. "Or been buried under the pool deck."

"Yeah." His gaze flicked to my house then back to me. "Sure."

I climbed out and went into my empty house, telling myself that Bellamy didn't really give a shit about me or whether my dad would hit me. Because the last thing I needed was to actually like him.

## CHAPTER 14

## BELLAMY

HAD anyone other than Drew pulled that stunt, they would have absolutely been expelled—and had to deal with Jacob's ass. A two-day suspension? That was bullshit. Whatever crack Brown was smoking today cost me a fuck I was desperate for. And I was tempted to make his life hell for a day or two to ease the pain.

I turned onto my street, taking a heavy breath when I spotted Dad's truck in the drive and Arlo's plastic kiddie pool crushed beneath the tire. The asshole had to be shitfaced already. The earlier he got drunk, the more of a dick he was, and today was not the day for this crap.

I parked behind his pickup, got out of my car, and went to the mailbox, sorting through the pile of overdue notices that came more frequently than not.

"You are the biggest asshole in the history of ever!"

I turned away from the mailbox. Nora stormed across the street, fists balled at her side. I hadn't seen her that angry since I'd hacked off one of her pigtails in third grade.

"What the hell did I do to you?"

"You do realize she's just trying to get expelled?"

No shit. I flipped through the mail, pretending I didn't give a flying rat's ass. Because I shouldn't... "Well, she should probably try to find ways to get expelled that don't step on my toes then." I glanced up. "Huh?"

"You burned her car, Bellamy!"

"She was giving away weed. What else was I supposed to do, chop off her fingers?" I laughed to myself at that.

"Oh my God. You're a dick." She huffed, then spun around, marching back to her front door while I stood, stunned in my drive.

"She's not a martyr, Nora!"

She flipped me a bird before slamming her door. That girl was annoying as hell. I made my way up the drive and around the house to the back porch. The second my foot hit the wooden deck, my twelve-year-old, half-blind hound dog sat up. He stretched and limped over, wagging his tail.

"Hey, Scooter." I knelt to pet him before leading him inside through the kitchen door.

The hinges to Dad's recliner creaked. "You better notta gotten that horseshit bourbon again, Carol," he slurred.

The fact that he expected my mother to wait on him hand and foot when he did nothing but wallow in pools of alcohol and poker chips pissed me off. "It's me," I mumbled. "Not Mom."

Staggered footsteps thudded down the hall. "Well, where the hell's she at?"

I tossed the bills onto the table, glancing up when he slumped against the doorframe. Just looking at him sent a jolt of resentment darting through me. "Try work. You know, since she's the only one who does anything to pay bills."

His bloodshot eyes narrowed. "Fuck you," he said and shuffled toward the fridge.

Scooter hobbled over, and Dad tripped, stumbling into the wall before he swung a boot at the dog, barely missing. "That damn dog of yours shit on the floor. I outta beat him for it. Or maybe I outta beat the shit outta you for it."

His lips twitched, then he pushed up his sleeves—a set of movements I knew all too well. One of my first memories was him putting my mom's face through a china cabinet. By the time I was eight, I'd lost count of the times he'd busted my lip with a quick backhand to the face.

"You're a disrespectful little shit." He took a swing, and I ducked. His fist went clean through the cabinet behind me.

On instinct, I charged at him.

"Little shit." He grabbed the collar of my shirt, then his forehead smashed mine before I wrestled him to the floor. I managed to get a good punch to his nose, then the temple, and he let me go.

"You're a piece of shit!" I swiped my keys from the table, grabbed Scooter, and stormed outside. The sound of things crashing and shattering inside followed me to the front yard. I hated him. And more often than not, I found myself wishing he would die. Mom would never leave him, and she deserved so much better than this shit. We all did.

I loaded Scooter into the back of my car and peeled out of the drive, heading to the bus stop a few blocks over to wait on my little brother. The fight with my dad replayed through my head, creating a river of slow rage that needed to be diverted. I flipped through radio stations. Scrolled through my phone. Then finally, I typed out a text to Drew.

**Me: Next on the list, you have fighting or fucking**

Minutes passed and no dancing dots. Curiosity got the better of me, and I pulled up that stupid app on my phone, waiting for the blue locator dot to pop up. God—I shook my head because I had issues. I really did. I'd put the thing on here to screw with her, and here I was, practically stalking her to satisfy my own morbid curiosity. It shouldn't have mattered that she was at the same house she was the other day. Shouldn't have, but damn, if it didn't.

The yellow bus chugged down the street then rolled to a stop, and when the doors folded back, Scooter howled when Arlo hopped down the steps. A wide grin set on his face as he sprinted over, then yanked open the door.

"You brought Scooter!" He chucked his backpack to the floorboard, then piled in, immediately wrapping his arms around the dog's neck. It was easy to make that kid happy. I scrubbed my brother's head, making it more of a mess than it already was.

"Daddy's mad again, huh?"

"Yeah." I shifted into drive, heading the opposite direction of our house. "Wanna slushie?"

"Yeah!"


Arlo mixed all three flavors together, grinning up at me when the sludge overfilled the lid. "I'mma call this one monster puke."

"Good name."

He started down the aisle, then turned and handed the drink to me. "Can I have a quarter for the claw machine?"

"You know that thing never works."

"Please..."

The kid had some good begging eyes. "Fine." I fished spare change from my pocket and dropped it into his dirty and marker-covered palm. "And wait up there for me. I've gotta get something."

"K." He skipped up to the front, and I hooked it around to the toiletries section, looking for a cheap bottle of jerk-lotion. I'd planned to spend the afternoon with Drew's legs pushed back behind her ears while I fucked every bit of hate right out of her, but here I was. In the 7-11. And seeing as how no other girl would cut it now, this was my only choice.

I settled on some cheap off-brand and made my way to the register. Arlo stood by the claw machine, his face plastered to the 7-11 window. A stuffed unicorn peeked out from under one of his arms and a plastic bag hung from the other.

The kid had a habit of shoplifting things from time to time, even though I'd threatened to take his night-light away if he kept doing it. "Arlo," I said. "Where'd you get the bag?"

"That lady bought me some Rainbow Push-Pops." He pointed through the glass just as Drew climbed into the passenger seat of a bright-red Mercedes. "And she won me the horse with a sword on its head."

"Why?"

"She said she knew you. So, she's not a stranger, right?"

I placed a hand over his head, watching the car back out of the spot. "Not a stranger..."

Something tightened in my chest, and I knew exactly why serial killers didn't want to get to know their victims before they killed them. Because when someone became real, it made everything harder. And that had just made her entirely too real for me to keep hating her.

---

Arlo sat on Hendrix's couch, battling him on the PlayStation. "Bell, your brother's a cheater!"

"Am not."

"Are too. Cheater, cheater pumpkin eater."

"You're an asshole."

Hendrix cackled. "Yes! I love it when kids swear."

Wolf shook his head. Lighting a joint as he took the seat across from me at the kitchen table. "You did hear she only got suspension?"

"Yeah."

"Which is bullshit!" Hendrix shouted from the other room.

I hadn't told the guys about my deal with Drew—only because I didn't want to listen to their crap. And had I told Hendrix that Drew was the one who suggested he set fire to her car, he wouldn't have, on principle.

Wolf blew out a cloud of smoke. "Bet her rich daddy pulled all kinds of strings."

And it was like the lightbulb came on. That had to be exactly why Drew hadn't gotten expelled. Her dad was that big of a dick that he pulled strings to keep her in the shit school just because it was the shit school. That was on a whole new level of rich prick assholeness.

"Wonder if she's got a rich mommy who wants a boytoy?" Wolf chuckled before taking another puff.

"Probably..."

"Dude." Wolf slapped a hand over the rickety table. "Why aren't you more pissed?"

"I am pissed." He had no idea how much because it cost me a night inside Drew's tight little pussy.

"Bullshit. You're staring off into space with this..." His lips curled with a hint of disgust. "This look."

I pushed up from the table, rounding the counter to grab a coke from the fridge. "I don't have a look. I'm thinking."

"About fucking her or fucking her up? Because..." He glared at me for a moment, toking on his joint. "Had anyone else been throwing baggies of weed out like Santa on his Christmas float, you would be pacing the kitchen, mumbling."

He was right, so I started pacing. "I am pacing."

"You like her!"

"Shut up, man. I don't fucking like her."

"Hendrix!" Wolf shouted. "He's pulling a Zepp."

I heard the controller smack the wall before Hendrix barreled into the kitchen. He grabbed me by the shirt, and I shoved him away. "Don't give in to the pull, you cocksucking weakling. These girls are like Medusa, and they suck you into their cold, stone eyes filled with hate and then. *Bam!*" He clapped his hands in front of my face. "They got you by the dick, dragging you around, making you buy them jewelry and getting you sent to jail."

"She already sent him to jail." Wolf lifted a brow.

Hendrix narrowed his eyes at me, a sick smirk covering his lips. "At least Zepp got pussy and some blow jobs before he went to jail."

I grabbed an empty beer can from the counter and chucked it at Hendrix, pinging him in the head before Arlo bolted through the doorway.

"What's a blowjob? And did Zepp take the pussy to jail? I wanna see it! What color is it?" Arlo ducked underneath the table, assumedly looking for the cat he thought Zepp had. "Come here, kitty."

Both of the guys were doubled over, cackling. I grabbed Arlo and pulled him out from under the table. "They don't have a cat, Arlo."

"But, the pussy was definitely orange." Hendrix snickered. "Its name was Red."

I jabbed him in the shoulder, mouthing shut up before I grabbed my brother, threw him over my shoulder, and carted him up the stairs to the bathroom.

"I wanna go back downstairs."

"You gotta take a bath." I took a towel from the hall closet.

"I'm not dirty."

"Yeah. You are." I plugged the drain, then turned the taps, hopping up onto the sink while the tub filled.

Arlo stripped out of his clothes, throwing them all over the place before climbing into the bath. "I wanna sleep with Spike tonight."

"Spike?"

"Yep. Spike. The horse with a sword on its head."

Over his donkey he'd slept with since he was two? That was some serious shit. Evidently, Drew's charm could screw with the head of a six-year-old just as easily as mine.

"You know her, right? Can you send her a thank you text?"

My jaw set. "No."

"Why not?"

"Because."

"It's the nice thing to do, Bubba." He splashed his hands through the water.

Of course, it was. But I wasn't nice, and neither was she.

After the water reached the top, I turned off the taps and went back to the sink. If I didn't stay in the room, Arlo would either not wash himself or drown.

I scrolled through my phone, ignoring the need I felt to send Drew a thank you text until I couldn't any longer.

**Me: Thanks for the Push-Pops and the horse with a horn on its head.**

**Me: That's from my brother.**

**Me: I still hate you. X**

**Baby Girl: He's cute, and his taste in popsicles is outstanding. Hate you too. x**

And the second I smiled at her message, I went into my contacts and changed her name to Medusa.

## CHAPTER 15

## DREW

I MANAGED to make it another day of ignoring my dad's calls, texts, and emails before he inevitably turned up. And holy shit, he was mad. Any other time I would have delighted in it, but the nervous eye twitch made me tread carefully.

"Suspended. Twice! Dealing cannabis. Your car..." He took a deep breath, rubbing a hand over his chest as he paced across the kitchen. Was he having a heart attack?

I sat at the breakfast island, clutching a bottle of water in front of me while I watched him. There were times when I pushed my father and times when I didn't. Had I actually managed to get expelled, I'd be smug as hell right now. But I'd failed, and that meant he still held all the cards.

"My car was vandalized," I said. The same as the house.

He shook his head. "Are you trying to ruin your life, Drucella?"

"Me?" The entire reason I was here was that he wouldn't believe me when I told him I didn't cheat on that test at Black Mountain. Had he just listened to me. Tried to defend me... But no, instead, he decided to punish me.

"You're the one ruining my life, Dad. Do you have any idea what it's like at that school?"

Honestly, the worst part about Dayton High was Bellamy. There were times when I didn't want to get expelled at all, where it felt like the excitement of being around him was the only bright point in my day, and that was exactly why I needed to get away from him. Because that boy was dangerous and so very bad.

One night. I'd get one night. And that's all I needed.

My dad's eye twitched again. My father was many things but rarely ruffled, even in the face of all my crap. "I am trying to teach you to grow the hell up!" His voice boomed around the kitchen. He stood at the end of the counter, glaring. Fists balled, cheeks red, nostrils flared. Definitely verging on a heart attack.

"Do you even care if I'm miserable? Or is your only concern what your buddies at the golf club think? I know it wouldn't look good to have a daughter who got expelled from *Dayton High*."

He smoothed a hand over his tie, his anger dissipating on a single deep breath as he forcibly calmed himself. "Is that what you think? That you are getting yourself expelled?" He laughed humorlessly. "Oh no, Drucella. I can assure you, I have lined Mr. Brown's pocket with enough money that you could light that school on fire and not get kicked out. You are staying there, and that is that. It's two months. Grow up and deal with it, Drucella."

Oh, and that sounded like a challenge. Brown could only let so much slip before people would start asking questions, and a principal being bribed? Even in Dayton, that had to be scandalous.

"And your suspension is cut short. You're going to

school tomorrow." He stalked out of the kitchen, still rubbing at his chest.

"I have no car," I called after him.

"Take mine." Oh, daddy dearest really was determined. "I'll organize a new one for you."

If I had my way, I'd be out of that school by the end of the week. Then my normal life could resume. Money and fake people and boys who would not make me want something bad for me. But since Brown was being bribed, I was going to need help from the very person I was trying to escape.

**Me: I need to see you.**

**Dickhead: Wanna picture of the whole thing or just the tip?**

**Me: See YOU, not your dick.**

**Dickhead: What do you need?**

**Me: To. See. You. Didn't I already say that?**

**Dickhead: W**

**Dickhead: H**

**Dickhead: Y**

**Dickhead: ?**

He was infuriating.

**Me: OMG! You still owe me. That's why.**

**Dickhead: You really want to go down this road?**

**Dickhead: Because the way I see it, you still owe me a blow job…**

**Dickhead: Genevieve.**

He was such a dick.

**Me: Just come get me, you asshole. I have no car since you burned mine.**

**Me: Or you know, I could ask someone else for help. I'm sure Hendrix might help me with the fighting….and fucking.**

Several minutes passed before he finally responded.

**Dickhead: I've got errands to run, so you wanna see me then you have to go with me.**

"Errands." Whatever.

**Me: Fine. See you then.**

Errands.

After he nearly killed me speeding through Dayton's pothole-riddled streets, we pulled into a rundown shopping mall. Grass sprouted from the broken concrete, and abandoned shopping carts lay scattered across the Piggly Wiggly parking lot. What in the hell was it with the names of places around here?

Bellamy drove to the side of the empty building and parked by a dumpster but didn't get out.

This place looked sketchy as hell. "Uh, what are you doing?" I asked, staring through the windshield at a cardboard shelter propped against the cargo bay.

"Don't worry about that. What did you need?"

Sighing, I shifted on the cloth seat, then placed my back to the door to look at him. "I still need out of Dayton."

"I already told you…" His stare remained fixed through the windshield like a predator searching for prey. "Fighting or fucking." His gaze swung to mine on a wicked smirk. "Or both."

"Fine. Let me punch you in the face at school."

"Negative."

I lifted a brow before taking an obvious look at his crotch. "I'm not fucking you in a hallway full of people."

And the smile that crept over his face while he practically undressed me with his eyes had filthy thoughts rushing through my mind. "Nah, baby girl, I wouldn't want you to. I don't like people seeing what's mine."

I pressed my head back to the window like the chilled glass had a prayer of cooling the heat crawling up the back of my neck. "And you haven't held up your end of the deal yet..." I swallowed, wondering why in the hell I kept running my mouth. "Or the threat you made on day one, to fuck up my life first." *I'm gonna fuck up your life, then fuck you.* There was no rational reason that threat should have made me hot for him, but it did.

His teeth sank into his bottom lip. "You believing I haven't, proves just how much I have..." His hand landed on my thigh, creeping up as he leaned over the center console.

The citrus smell of his cologne was everywhere. My skin prickled under the intensity of his stare, and I wondered for a moment why I wanted to get away from him so badly.

"Because there is no damn reason you should want me." His mouth touched mine—almost in a kiss before he grabbed my bottom lip between his teeth. "No reason you should have made that deal..."

I did want him, and he was right; I absolutely shouldn't. This was beyond the simple rebellious draw of a bad boy. I knew the second I gave into him, he would destroy me. Because guys like him and girls like me... Well, that was a disaster waiting to happen. And that was why I made that deal. Black and white. Lines drawn in the sand. One night. He couldn't destroy me in one night. Could he?

"I'll fuck you right here if you want, baby girl..." His

fingers were right there, like he was waiting for permission to touch me again. "Make good on my first promise..." His other hand went to the back of my neck, and everything inside of me ignited.

On a sharp breath, I wrapped my fingers around his wrist, unsure whether I should push him away or pull him closer. Then his forehead pressed to mine, his staggered breaths teasing my lips—like he was fighting to restrain himself just as much as I was. My lungs screamed, body aching for him. I debated it. Screwing him right here in the front seat of his shabby car. Wouldn't be the first time I got naked for him in a parking lot...

The bump of bass broke through the tense silence, and Bellamy shifted away. Like this spell was all too easy to break.

A rusted Trans-Am zoomed around the corner of the Piggly Wiggly and screeched to a halt in front of the dumpster.

Bellamy climbed out of the car, going straight to the driver's side of that car and leaning through the lowered window. I witnessed the exchange of money for drugs, then Bellamy gave some weird handshake before the vehicle sped off.

He had brought me to a drug deal, and I wasn't even surprised or that bothered. Not like I didn't know what he did for money. Although, coming here with him was a bad idea simply because being in a confined space with him was not good. I watched him round the front of his car and reach for the door. Even his walk screamed of sex.

The sooner I got expelled, the better, because, one thing was for sure, that boy would ruin me—just like he promised.

Bellamy sank back behind the wheel, then stuffed the

crumpled bills into his wallet and tossed it back onto the dash.

I swallowed, focusing on what I came here for, and not his lips—or his hands or—other things. "My dad's paying Brown to keep me in school."

"Figured."

"So...come on. What have you got?"

He slid a hand over his steering wheel. "You got a baseball bat, or you wanna borrow mine?"

## CHAPTER 16

## BELLAMY

FRIDAY AFTERNOON, I leaned against Wolf's truck's tailgate, covering a smile while Drew went to town on Brown's SUV.

Glass shattered when she rammed the end of the baseball bat through the back windshield. Then she went straight for the taillight while shouting for Brown to fuck off. And everything about this was turning me on. I was absolutely banging her tonight.

Wolf settled against the side of his truck, tucking his joint behind his ear. "On a level of psycho, I think she's right up there with Nikki, dude."

"Probably."

"All the hot ones are, though…"

Brown eventually shoved his way through the students crowded around the complete shit show, his face puce red. "Miss Morgan!" he stammered. "What on hell's earth do you think you are doing?"

She propped the baseball bat over her shoulder on a smile. "I figured with all that money my daddy is paying you, you can afford a new car anyway."

Then she swung at the other taillight, and I should not have—in any way, shape, or form—found it as hot as I did.

"Damn," Wolf mumbled. "She's savage."

And that, she most definitely was.

Brown attempted to snatch the bat from her, but she yanked it away, taking one more swing before tossing it at his feet with a clatter of metal over the pavement. "And now I'm done."

And now my dick was hard. Again.

"Duuuuude...." Wolf smacked my arm on a chuckle. "Dude! If you're not interested—"

"Shut up, Wolf."

Brown stormed off with Drew in tow. When they passed by Wolf's truck, she winked at me.

Wolf shook his head. "You're one doomed motherfucker."

I watched her ass as they went into the school. "Nah, man. I'm not." Because *that w*ould get her expelled, get me my fuck, and get her out of my life, whether I wanted it to or not.

---

**Medusa: I got suspended again! Not expelled. And now I'm grounded.**

On a groan, I dragged a hand down my face. This was ridiculous.

Arlo sat beside me at Waffle Hut, bouncing up and down as he ate his fries. "You mad, Bubba?"

"No."

Hendrix snorted before shoveling hash browns in his mouth. "Bubba..."

Ignoring him, I went back to the text. No way she didn't expelled.

**Me: You're full of shit.**

She sent through a picture of her suspension slip. Her dad must be paying Brown truckloads. Because the damage she did to his car was pretty damn bad.

**Medusa: No sex for you tonight.**

**Me: Not with you...**

At this point, I was so hard up for her, I couldn't even think about another girl. But she didn't have to know that.

**Medusa: Good to know we aren't making our agreement exclusive.**

**Me: Who are you fucking, Drew?**

**Me: Some Barrington dick?**

I thought about that blue dot that practically stayed at another house.

**Medusa: Who are you fucking?**

**Me: Jealous, baby girl?**

"What are you smiling at?" Hendrix glared across the booth, dumping hot sauce over his hash browns.

"Nothing."

"If you've got some beaver picture over there that you're hoarding..." He lifted a brow before cramming food in his mouth.

"I'm in Waffle-Hut, dick."

Arlo shifted in the seat beside me, sucking down his soda.

Hendrix grinned. "And it's a fine place to look at P-O-R—"

I chucked a fry from my plate at Hendrix. "He can spell."

Hendrix rolled his eyes, mumbling under his breath.

Arlo tugged at my sleeve, holding his crotch and wiggling in the plastic booth. "I gotta tinkle."

"Then go." I thumbed back to the bathroom, and he shot off.

"Don't talk about beavers and porn in front of my kid brother, you dipshit."

Hendrix shrugged a shoulder. "Like he knows what kinda beaver I'm talking about. He thinks it's something that gobbles down wood." He froze with his fork halfway to his mouth, a proud grin taking over his face. "Holy shit. Beavers do gobble down wood." Then he and Wolf burst into laughter.

The bell over the diner door jingled, and a group of Barrington pricks in their letterman jackets stepped in.

Hendrix cracked his head to the side, and Wolf crammed the rest of his patty-melt into his mouth, his stare aimed right at them. The shit between Dayton and Barrington ran deep, and any time one of us could dig a grave for the other, we'd gladly oblige.

Jackson Bennett—the quarterback who replaced Max Harford after Zepp sent him to the hospital earlier in the year—stopped at the end of the booth. His too-clean, rich-boy nails drummed over the table while the rest of his dumbass, yuppie friends formed a letterman and Chino clad line behind him.

"I'm going to tell you one time, West, and one time only..." My blood heated at his unfinished pussy-ass threat. "Leave Drew Morgan alone."

And now there was an inferno. He knew her. Well enough to think he had a right to start a bloodbath over her. And wasn't he just the type she would go for?

"I knew you were stupid, Bennett. But seriously?" My

fingers instinctively pulled into fists. "Stupid enough to threaten me?

Hendrix shot up from the table. Wolf latched onto him like a dog on a leash, then shifted himself to the edge of the booth.

Bennett's jaw set. "I'll beat your poor, white-trash ass right here. Right now."

If I had to guess, he'd only been brave enough to say that because there were about six of them, but even being outnumbered by three, we'd still kick their asses. Rich boys had no idea how to fight with their fists.

The door to the bathroom swung open, and the sound of Arlo singing "SpongeBob SquarePants" echoed over the "Waffle-Hut" theme song playing through the jukebox.

"If my little brother weren't with me," I said. "You'd be fucking dead."

Arlo skirted around the corner, and the Barrington guys backed up. "I did a number two!" Arlo held up two fingers before snatching a fry from his plate and cramming it into his mouth. "And I even washed my hands."

"Good to see you, West. Hope I've made myself clear." Bennett started down the aisle.

"Yeah. I'll tell her you sent your regards."

Hendrix glared at me, one eye twitching. "Tuba-Blowing Betty said there's a party at Bennett's house tomorrow night. She even sent me the directions..."

And I couldn't resist the temptation. "Sounds like a plan, man."

We finished our food, Hendrix glaring at the Barrington assholes most of the time, then I took Arlo to get a Slurpee from the 7-11.

Hendrix texted me the address, and I stared down at it, my blood heating with jealousy. Because Bennett's address was the same one Drew practically stayed at. Arlo jiggled the door handle. "Unlock it, Bubba."

I pressed the button, and Arlo shot out of my car, darting into the 7-11 while I fumed over a girl that wasn't even mine. "This is bullshit." I tossed my phone to the console and got out of my car, heading into the quick mart. I grabbed an energy drink from the cooler, then rounded the corner and abruptly stopped. Drew stood in front of the rubber section, a box of condoms in each hand. Heat crept beneath the collar of my shirt as the thought of her and Bennett screwing catapulted to the forefront of my mind.

She glanced at me, froze, then smiled. "Bellamy." She held up the packages. "Which one?"

Bennett's face flashed to mind—that smug ass grin when he told me to leave her alone…

"Those are too small. Put them back," I said, grabbing a pack of Slim Jim's and trying to control the hot wave of jealousy crashing inside me.

She bit her lip on a smile. Then put one box back.

"I said, put them back."

"Or what?"

Every bit of fear I'd put in her was gone. Either because she liked being scared or because of the fact that I wanted her bad enough to make a deal, gave her a false sense of security.

"I got all three flavors, Bubba!" Arlo skipped down the aisle. "And some Dr. Pepper. This one's called monster poop." Arlo glanced at Drew. "I named my horse with a sword Spike." Then he rushed over and snatched a box of condoms from the shelf, shaking it. "Can we get some rubbers, Bubba?"

Drew's hand went to her mouth, smothering a laugh.

This was Hendrix's fault. Telling Arlo that the damn things were water balloons one time when he was the only option left for a babysitter. "Put those back, Arlo."

"Why! Hendrix always gets rubbers. He said the 7-11 is good for two things." Arlo held up two fingers. "Rubbers and hose. And we already got our hose at home." He grabbed my arm and gave it a tug. "Puh-lease." I was seriously going to kill Hendrix.

She flipped the box of condoms over in her hand, skimming the back as she lifted a slow brow. "I bet you've got hoes lined up around the block."

"Nah-uh." Arlo shook his head. "We just got the hose at our house."

Drew smiled at him. "Oh, is that all?"

Bennett. She was screwing Bennett. She had to be. And God, did I hate her for it.

"Fuck off."

Arlo's eyes widened on a deep frown. "That's not nice."

And now, I felt like shit for being a bad example. "You're right." Taking him by the shoulders, I directed him to the front. "Go get some gum or something."

He skipped off, and I redirected my attention back to Drew and that stupid box of rubbers. Annoyed as hell that she wanted someone who wasn't me. More annoyed that I gave a shit. Before her, I'd never been bothered by a girl at all, yet everything about Drew bothered me and pissed me off because it was every fucking thing about her that made me want her. "Surprised Bennett's two-inch prick doesn't slip out of condoms." I couldn't even manage to keep my mouth shut when it came to her. "Might wanna get the rubbers for the genitally challenged."

"Careful, Bellamy. You almost sound jealous." She

pretended to brush something from my shirt. "And I know how much you care about your reputation..."

God, was there something more than hate? On a growl, I started toward the register, grabbing Arlo on my way. He placed his Slurpee on the counter, along with a pack of bubble gum. That was when I noticed the lump in his newly tucked-in shirt.

I took a breath, not wanting to take my complete and absolute aggravation with this Prada-wearing Medusa out on my little brother. "Anything else we need to pay for?"

"Nah-uh."

Frowning, I knelt beside him and untucked his shirt. Kit-Kats and Crunch bars fell to the dirty convenience store floor. "Dammit, Arlo." I gathered the treats up and tossed them onto the counter. "What have I told you about stealing?"

The toe of his Velcro sneaker scuffed the floor. "That it's not right."

"So, don't do it."

I stole. A lot. Some people would say trying to teach my kid brother morals when I was a complete delinquent was hypocritical, but I stole out of necessity. To give him an out of the same shit hand of cards I'd been dealt.

"But Hendrix said if I hide them in my shirt, it's not stealing," he whispered. "'Cause it's only stealing if you get caught." Hendrix somehow screwed up everything I tried to set right with Arlo. "Yeah. Well. Hendrix is a dickhead, Arlo." I dropped the candy onto the counter, and the clerk rang us up. "A dickhead."

Arlo stared up at me, frowning. "You're best friends with a dickhead?"

Drew laughed. I glared over my shoulder at her

Bennett-dick-riding ass before shoving my money across the counter. Then I grabbed the plastic bag and shot the bird at her on my way out to the car. And what did she do in return? Blew me a kiss. Like the fucking princess that she was.

Arlo stopped by my car's back door. "Why are you being mean to the nice lady, Bubba? She won me things."

"She won you things because you're a cute kid. But what she really is, deep down inside, is what we call a soul-sucking bitch, Arlo." His eyes widened. Shit—that was not what I meant to say, but by now, the image of her spread eagle with Bennett's sloppy ass pounding away at her had been ingrained in my mind.

Arlo poked me in the chest. "That's another not a nice word."

"Exactly." I opened his door. "And she's not a nice person."

"But..." His brow creased. Then he looked up at me like he was thinking harder about this than anything in his life. "She's pretty."

"And the pretty ones are always the worst. Because they're entitled."

"Entitled?"

I picked him up, placing him in his booster seat and buckling him in. "Yep. Entitled, meaning they will shit all over you in a heartbeat."

Hook up with you and leave you with blue balls. Flirt with you. Get you arrested. Then ask you for advice on condoms they intend to use with Barrington's dumbass quarterback.

"Ew. Girls poop!" His nose wrinkled before his tongue stuck out on a gag.

The butt-hurt tidal wave inside of me ebbed, and I shook my head. The kid was six. If he wanted to think pretty girls were nice, what did it hurt? "Don't worry about it, buddy. You'll get it one day."

And he would because he was Dayton, which unfortunately meant, one day he'd see exactly what that meant.

## CHAPTER 17

## DREW

"I'M SO NERVOUS," Nora whispered, staring through the windshield at Olivia's house. The landscape lighting directed at it made it look pretentious as hell.

Nora had told me earlier she was worried about what Barrington kids would think of her. Which shocked me. It was stupid to care what any of these people thought, but then, I'd never been the poor girl, so maybe I was ignorant to her concern.

"It'll be fine. Olivia and Jackson are nice." I cut the engine to Dad's Maserati and got out. Technically, I was instructed to only use his car to go to school and for emergencies, but he'd gone on some golfing trip that even his unruly daughter wouldn't keep him from. So, I was going to a party, and there was no way I was walking the two blocks to Olivia's in these heels—I figured driving it a street over wouldn't hurt.

We made our way across Olivia's cobblestone drive. The tap of Nora's heels came to an abrupt halt before we reached the door. "Do I look okay?"

Everything she had on, from the dress that hugged her

curves just so, to the bright-red heels, I had loaned her—and told her to keep. I had legitimately never seen someone so happy to strap on a pair of Prada heels.

"Of course." With a smile, I swept a curl over her shoulder, then rang the doorbell.

A mixture of god-awful pop music and ruckus laughter greeted us when Olivia opened the door, then dragged me in for a hug. Her gaze swept over Nora as I introduced them, and Nora waved shyly. Olivia barely acknowledged her before taking my elbow and dragging me toward the kitchen.

A mixture of drinks covered the island, and when we stopped at the end of it, a group of girls glared at us.

"Ignore those bitches," Olivia said. "Their Jackson's desperate admirers. It's gross."

"Speaking of admirers..." I opened my clutch and handed over the box of condoms I'd bought from the 7-11 earlier—inadvertently pissing Bellamy off. I couldn't help but smile. Maybe I was a dick, but I enjoyed his jealousy. Wanted it even. Again with that boy inducing the crazy. At this point, I'd kind of just accepted that he made me mental.

"Drew!" She snatched the box, her face going bright red before she opened a random kitchen drawer and shoved them inside. "Oh my God. Jackson will rat me out to Mom and Dad in like, two seconds."

"What will I rat you out for?" Jackson's arm came around my shoulders, and Olivia glared at him.

"Everything."

Ignoring her, Jackson turned to Nora and introduced himself.

Nora turned beet-red, obviously stunned into silence.

"Ugh. God." Olivia snatched a glass of wine from the counter, staring across the room at a group of Dayton girls.

"Of course, Dayton's trash would show up." Then her gaze cut right to Nora. "Cute dress." She pinched the fabric. "What is it, Gucci or Armani?"

"Um..."

"Gucci," I said. "Right? That was what you told me."

Olivia poured a glass of wine for me and one for Nora, divvying them out while her gaze never left Nora. "I haven't seen you at Barrington. Where do you go to school?"

Nora gaped, looking at me, then Jackson, then back to Olivia. "Homeschooled. I was um, kicked out of the Catholic school." It took everything in me not to swing my attention to her. Was she that ashamed of Dayton? And did she care that much what people she didn't know thought of her?

"Oh?" Olivia took a sip. "For what?"

"Sex!" she blurted, and I nearly choked on my wine. "Sex with a boy."

"Screw going to a religious school." Jackson snorted and popped the top to a beer.

"Those Catholics." I coughed again.

"She knows I'm Dayton," Nora whispered in my ear.

"No, she just knows you're not Barrington. Because this town is so small, I'm surprised most of them aren't inbred." I glanced at her. "Sorry. Present company excluded."

Jackson walked over to a blond guy in a letterman jacket, and Olivia shifted back to the drawer, quickly opening it and stuffing the condoms into the top of her dress. "Do me a favor, distract Jackson for like, an hour."

"What?"

"It won't be hard. He thinks you're hot." Then she shouldered her way through the party, leaving me unsure how I felt about Jackson's thinking I was hot.

"Hey, Drew?" Jackson waved Nora and me over, introducing us to the blond guy named Max Harford.

Nora looked star-struck, blushing when Max took her hand and kissed over her knuckles. It made me want to gag.

We followed them to the couch, and for the next fifteen minutes, I listened to the two guys talk about football. Max was apparently off the team since he'd broken his legs last year, though how he did it seemed to be a sore subject.

Olivia absolutely owed me for this...

My phone vibrated in my purse, and when I pulled it out, my heart tripped a little at the sight of Bellamy's message.

**Dickhead: Baby girl...**

**Dickhead: You busy?**

**Me: Right now? Yeah.**

**Dickhead: Didn't I tell you you're never too busy for me?**

I was about to type out a response when—

"What's up fuckfaces?" the voice booming over the music was definitely Hendrix's, and like someone had scratched a needle over a record, everyone's attention in the room snapped toward the foyer.

Hendrix and Wolf stood by the stairwell, chugging beers. Electricity zapped through my veins like a hit because I knew that meant Bellamy was here.

"Great..." Jackson huffed, but my attention was still aimed at the entrance.

Bellamy stepped into the foyer's arched doorway and looked around the room like it was his own personal playground. Then his gaze stopped on me, and the small smirk on his lips shifted into something I didn't like.

"West," Jackson grumbled, draining the rest of his beer and crushing the can. "God, I hate him."

"If you hate them, why don't you just ask them to leave? It's your house."

He huffed out a breath. "It's not as easy as that. I'm not in the mood for a fight." And if I had to guess, Jackson was a little bit scared of them.

"Nah, fuck it, let's beat them. There are enough of us," Max said, anger lacing his voice. "Maybe kill them." Max leaned in front of me to whisper across to Jackson. "Your dad has guns, right?"

Jackson's hand landed on my thigh, and I was so in shock, I didn't even think to move it.

They could not be serious, but the way Max's jaw tightened before he glared back at Bellamy and the rest of the guys said he was.

"What *is* wrong with you?" I snapped, shoving Max away.

"Chill out, Drew." Jackson's gaze went right back to the entrance. "I'm not getting a gun. But after what they did to Max, they'll get what's coming to them."

An uncomfortable feeling settled in my chest, and I slapped Jackson's hand away, then pushed to my feet and snaked my way through the party.

Hendrix had a Barrington girl on the kitchen island, his lips at her neck while he groped her boobs. That was a stinging reminder that every girl—*every girl,* wanted the bad boy, and that was driven home monumentally the moment I glanced through the large floor-to-ceiling window at the back of the house and spotted Bellamy on the pool deck with another girl. The second his eyes met mine, he yanked her into his lap, and my chest went tight. I had the very real urge to shove her into the pool and kick him in the nuts. *Crazy, crazy, crazy.* Screw him.

Jackson stepped behind me as I poured a small glass of wine and tipped it back, and Bellamy watched us like a hawk.

"Let's go outside." Jackson flashed a perfect smile before leading me out onto the pool deck. Closer to Bellamy and that blonde.

I shouldn't care what Bellamy did, so why the hell did I have the intense urge to make him jealous? Why the hell was *I* jealous? Over a guy who literally bartered a deal to fuck me... It was stupid and crazy, but undeniable. So, I kicked off my shoes, pulled my dress over my head, and then jumped right into the pool. A bra and panties weren't much different than a swimsuit after all.

"Damn, Drew." Jackson tore off his shirt and stripped down to his boxers before he did a cannonball into the water.

Other people followed suit, taking off their clothes and leaping in. I glanced back at the deck just as Nora snatched her arm away from Bellamy and stormed to the edge of the pool with a roll of her eyes. "He's such a dick," she said, pulling off her dress before diving into the water.

"What was that about?" I asked.

Max shifted behind her. Nora glanced at him, then shook her head. "I'll tell you about it later."

We hung out in the water, everyone laughing and drinking—except me. Every so often, my gaze would drift to Bellamy. That girl was still on his lap, but there was nothing intimate in the way he held her. It looked more like he might snap her in half any second.

One of the guys jumped into the water with a beer funnel. Another guy started swinging his wet boxers around his head. And that was my cue to leave. I looked at Nora. "I'm getting out."

She glanced back at Max, completely smitten. "I'm gonna stay."

I waded out of the pool, and when I glanced across the deck to where Bellamy had been sitting, he was gone, and so was the slutty blonde who had been on him like a parasite all night.

It was fine. I didn't care what he did with her or to her.

I went to grab my dress, but the chair I'd left it in was empty. "Where the hell did my dress go?"

Of course, everyone was drunk, so no one paid attention. "Seriously? Where's my dress!"

"You can go in my room and grab a T-shirt if you want," Jackson shouted, skimming a hand through his wet hair. "You know where they are." That sounded really bad because I was certain no one here knew the only reason I knew where he kept his shirts was because I'd stayed over with Olivia countless times.

I made my way through the house, dripping water the entire way up to Jackson's bedroom. The image of Bellamy screwing that blonde in a bathroom somewhere sprung to mind, and my nails bit into my palms. I hated her, and I hated him, and I hated myself for letting it bother me at all.

I closed Jackson's door and went straight into the bathroom to grab a towel, staring at my reflection as I rubbed it through my hair. The jealousy whirring inside me grew. Bellamy started out as a one-night stand, and that's all he ever should have been, so why in the hell was I letting this get to me so badly?

Sighing, I wrapped myself in the thick towel and went back to Jackson's room to grab one of his shirts.

I'd barely set one foot out of the bathroom before my

gaze landed on Bellamy closing the door and locking it. "You know where his shirts are, huh?"

Folding my arms over my chest, I glared at him. "I'm surprised you could tear yourself away from your new friend. She seemed very attached."

"Right..." His chin dropped on a not-so-funny laugh before he started across the room. "You look really comfortable in your guy's towel..."

He kept coming closer. And closer. Of course, it crossed my mind to tell him that Jackson was not my guy, but then that blonde popped up like a bad smell, and well, I never pretended to be a rational human being. My ass hit the footboard of Jackson's bed, and Bellamy was right there. In my face.

"And you know what?" he said, his voice deep and rough. "I fucking hate it."

Tension mounted, so thick I could hardly breathe. Then Bellamy grabbed the back of my head and slammed his lips against mine in an angry kiss, shoving me back onto Jackson's bed.

"I hate you so fucking much." He ripped the towel away, and his mouth was all over me—lips and throat and breasts. Hands groping every bit of bare skin I had.

"I hate you more."

"Seems like it." His fingers reached between my legs. There was nothing gentle about the way he touched me. Just fingers reaching until they stole my breath. "Is that why you're so wet for me, baby girl?"

I moaned into his mouth, each stroke of his hand contorting my body like it was his own personal puppet. It felt like there was a bomb waiting to go off, and this bastard had been holding the detonator since the first time I'd met him.

His fingers worked deeper, his tongue teasing my neck before he gripped my waist and rolled me on top of him. One hand went to my throat, the other still pressing into me, teasing and pushing while I straddled him.

"You haven't gotten me expelled yet," I gasped.

"And that's the only reason my dick isn't in you right now." He fingered me so hard, I knew I'd be bruised, but it felt too good to care. "And as pissed as I am, you should probably be thankful."

With no shame, I ground over his hand, loving the way his grip on my throat tightened while I chased something I desperately needed.

Heat built in my body. I was seconds away from absolute bliss before he threw me back on the bed. "And like hell I'm letting you come first this time."

He worked his belt loose, yanking his dick out and tugging on it before he straddled my bare chest. "You remember how I told you I was gonna come all over your pretty rich-girl face?"

I shouldn't have wanted it, but I did. I needed Bellamy to be every bit as unhinged for me as I was for him. My anger bled through me as I raked my nails up his thighs and grabbed his hips. And then I swallowed his dick, almost gagging when he touched the back of my throat.

"Fuck..." His hands went to the back of my head, fingers tangling in my hair as he thrust forward.

I dug my nails into his thighs. Hard, threatening him with a tiny bit of teeth, and he fisted my hair. His abs tensed. His muscles trembled. God, he was beautiful, and the sight of him had my frustrated body strung tight, on the edge.

Right when I knew he was about to come, he pulled away, grabbing his dick and pumping over it. His head fell back on a deep groan that echoed around the room as he came on my chest.

"I always knew that would look good on you, baby girl." He swiped a finger at the corner of my mouth.

The door rattled, breaking the silence before a bang sounded over the wood. "Drew?" Jackson's voice came from the other side.

*Shit, shit, shit.* I had just let Bellamy come on me, in Jackson's bed. I scooped up the towel and wiped myself clean.

"Do *not* answer that door!" I pointed at him. "Give me two minutes," I called.

Bellamy pushed off the bed with a glare. "And the shittiest part of this story: I almost fucking liked you..."

A tiny trace of guilt niggled at me. I should have just said: Jackson was a friend, and it wasn't what it looked like. But then I remembered exactly why I'd let him think I was more than friends with Jackson.

"About as much as you like that blonde downstairs, I'm sure."

I dove for the chest of drawers, taking out a T-shirt and covering myself right as he flipped the lock. He yanked open the door, then tucked himself back into his jeans. "'Sup, Bennett?" Bellamy's massive frame filled the dimly lit doorway, practically dwarfing Jackson. "I'd at least let her clean my come off her first..."

Oh, he was a bastard.

Jackson's arm drew back, but before he even moved to throw a jab, Bellamy knocked him clean out. Holy. Shit.

"Bellamy! What is wrong with you?" I gasped.

He had just knocked the guy out in his own house.

"I told you I was gonna fuck up your life, Drew..." He ducked through the door, disappearing into the hallway. My pulse hammered in my veins like a freight train, and my temper spiked as I dropped to the floor to check that Jackson wasn't dead.

"What the hell?" Olivia popped out of her bedroom, hair disheveled and cheeks sex-flushed. She hurried down the hall, her wide eyes on Jackson. "What happened?"

"Bellamy," I mumbled, completely mortified and livid.

"They're here?" She crouched beside her brother. "I'm calling the police..."

"I'll get rid of them."

"I'm still calling the police!" Olivia shouted as I jogged down the stairs.

It felt like everyone's eyes were on me. The slut of Barrington, in Jackson's T-shirt, and Bellamy's come. This couldn't get any worse.

I stopped in the foyer, spotting Bellamy by the front door, that same blonde beside him once again, staring up at him like she wanted nothing more than to drop to her knees and let him come on her face, just like I had.

Irrational jealousy and hurt lanced through me. Jackson was unconscious, Olivia was pissed, and Bellamy...Bellamy was making me crazy, the same way he always did.

Nora popped up beside me, handing me my bag. "What the hell is going on?"

"Nothing. We're leaving."

I glanced at the dickhead as I dragged Nora to the front door. "I'd leave if I were you," I said to him. Not that I cared if he got arrested. Again.

A cold smirk cut over his lips as he slid an arm around the blonde girl's waist. "Nah, I think I'll stay." Then he kissed her forehead.

Kissed.

Her.

Forehead.

And rage was not the fucking word. I wanted to throw something at his head and drag her out by her hair. Red—that was all I saw as something vicious and ugly twisted in my stomach.

Oh, I was about to do something insane because he drove me to it.

## CHAPTER 18

### BELLAMY

THE SECOND DREW STORMED OUT; I shoved the girl away from me. "Go the fuck away."

She glared at me with a frown before storming across the party, tugging down her skirt.

I was livid as hell. The night had been nothing but a clusterfuck. First, I walked in to see Drew snuggled between Bennett and Harford. Which made me grab some waif-thin Barrington bimbo just to get a rise out of Drew. It was the least I could do since I had to watch that asshole touch Drew all night. Then to top it all off, when I was about to spread Drew's legs and give her the orgasm of her life, Bennett had started banging on the door. I had lost my shit, but any rational guy would at that point...

"He knocked Jackson out!" A blonde stormed around the corner, pointing at me as she glanced around the room.

A few of the Barrington guys reacted to her dog-whistle screech and stood up like they were going to do something.

"Ah, hell yeah!" Hendrix pushed a girl off his lap and jumped to his feet, cracking his neck as Max shoved through the crowd. "Time for a fight."

Wolf rounded the stairwell, fists ready to throw blows. These Barrington assholes never seemed to learn their lesson.

The blonde's palms landed on Max's chest, and while he may have looked like he was ready to go to her, I saw the hesitation, the absolute fear pricking a sweat over his brow.

"Do not start a fight with these Neanderthals," she said. "I already called the Barrington police."

"Oh, come on, Olivia?" Max said. "I'll be done with them long before the cops get here."

That made a smirk dart across my face. I hadn't been there when Zepp went at him, but Zepp had left him alive, which was more than I could say I would do had this shithead pulled the same stunt on Drew.

"You really want another stint in the hospital, Harford?" I said, bowing up. "I'd be more than happy to oblige."

"Do *not* do it." Olivia placed herself in front of him, acting like it was her, and not his fear, keeping him from throwing the first punch. "I don't want you guys accountable."

Hendrix walked behind them, eyeing her up and down. "That's a cute way of saying you don't want their asses to get handed to them."

A loud bang sounded outside. A group of people hurried to the massive floor-to-ceiling window. "Holy crap!" a girl shouted. "Someone's ramming a Maserati into a piece of shit by the drive."

"I think it's Jackson's girlfriend," someone else said.

And now, I was going to kill everyone. Because it was Drew—and people thought she belonged to him. Anger fired through me on my way outside, but I managed to tamp it down and stroll down the steps like I didn't give a shit. Wolf followed behind me, puffing on a joint.

The white glow of the reverse lights shined over the driver's side of my Civic while the Maserati's engine revved. Then the car slammed into mine.

"Psycho level twenty," Wolf mumbled, clapping a hand to my shoulder. "You know how to pick them, don't you, dude?"

I couldn't even deal with Wolf right now. I dragged my hands through my hair. The girl was insane, and while it pissed me off to no end, some masochistic, sick-ass part of me liked it way too much.

Shouts came from the front door I'd left open when I had stormed out. Something shattered. Hendrix must have started a damn fight. I glanced at Wolf, and he ducked his head on a shake.

"I'll go get him."

I started to the drive, and Drew's car came to an abrupt halt. The window lowered. Nora sat completely mortified in the passenger seat, refusing to make eye contact with me while Drew leaned forward, a fake smile in place and her tight little body still in Bennett's fucking shirt.

"I am *so* sorry." She touched a hand to her chest. "I just can't seem to find the right gear. Bad aim and all." The car lurched forward, then reversed again.

Metal crunched. Glass shattered. And the loose thread of control I'd managed to cling to all night unraveled like a cheap ball of yarn. "Are you insane?" I shouted.

"Yes!" She flipped me off, then drove away, the broken taillight of her Maserati swinging against the backend of the car.

I heard Hendrix cussing behind me and turned to see

Wolf dragging him out without his shirt, kicking and screaming.

The distant wail of police sirens sounded, and I snatched my keys from my pocket. "Get in the car, assholes."

Wolf let Hendrix go, and he dove through one of the broken back windows while Wolf went to the passenger side.

When I tugged on the driver's side handle, the door wouldn't budge. Thanks to the hulk-sized dent sealing the damn thing shut. "I may actually kill her," I mumbled, rounding the car. "Fuck her. Then kill her."

I shoved Wolf out of the way, then ducked through the passenger-side door, climbed across the console, and sank to the driver's seat, cranking the engine.

"At least it starts," Wolf said.

I backed out at full speed and floored it down the street. As soon as I got out of Barrington, I texted Drew.

**Me: If your dumbass boyfriend is smart, he'll play by the rules and not press charges.**

**Me: Remind him of that.**

One girl shouldn't be able to make me so mad. So what if she wanted to screw Bennett? So what if she hated Dayton and hated me? So fucking what if she drove her hundred-thousand-dollar car into my 1988 Honda?

**Medusa: Fuck you. I hope you get arrested and bummed in jail.**

My blood pressure had never been so high. Until that very moment, I had no idea that it could actually spot your vision.

I tapped across the screen furiously, watching for the red light to change.

**Me: You realize you have anger issues.**

*Message not delivered.* And then I threw my phone into the floorboard.

## CHAPTER 19

## DREW

EARLY MORNING SUNLIGHT streamed through the window. And I hadn't really slept.

All night I had warred with myself. As much as I wanted to pretend I didn't care about Bellamy, I evidently did. Why else would the boy drive me to the brink of insanity?

He used me, made it known, punched my friend in his own house, and then moved onto another girl, just like that.

And deep down, in a cold little fissure of my black heart, I was hurt because Bellamy made me feel like nothing when I had stupidly thought that maybe, just maybe, I was something to him. Of course, me being me, that came out as blind rage and psychopathic behavior, which resulted in two demolished cars.

The doorbell rang, then rang again. I threw off the covers, slipping into my robe before heading downstairs.

Through the stained-glass on the door, I could make out the outline of a black T-shirt and dark hair, and I knew it was Bellamy. My chest tightened as I lingered in the foyer, ready to turn away because I had nothing to say to him.

He pounded over the thick wood. "If you don't let me in, I'll break into your house again, Drew."

There was a moment where the image of him in my room that night with his hand to my throat cycled through my head, and my body reacted in ways it shouldn't. Growing hot and needy for his touch. But I quickly snuffed out those feelings. "Was driving into your car not clear enough? Go away. And I took the spare key, so good luck not setting off the alarm."

"Unblock my fucking number then."

"No! Get out of my life, Bellamy."

He needed to before we killed one another.

A growl came from the other side of the door. "Fine... You wanna be stupid." He jogged down the steps and disappeared around the bushes.

Unbelievable, I mumbled to myself on my way into the kitchen.

The events from the night before played out in my head as I went about the motions of brewing coffee. Just the thought of him kissing that girl's forehead brought a hint of rage bubbling to the surface. The coffee pot beeped, and I grabbed a mug just as glass shattered in the foyer, followed by the distinct click of a lock. The shrill wail of the alarm pierced my ears. I closed my eyes on a groan because, of course, Bellamy would actually break-in. Why wouldn't he? Not like he hadn't before.

His heavy footsteps came down the hallway. "Where are you?"

"What the hell is wrong with you?" I turned from the counter as he appeared in the doorway. "Oh, didn't bring your baseball bat this time?" Why? Why did I have to have a thing for a psycho?

"Bennett's *friends* with Harford?" Stress lined his face, and I didn't get why.

I mean, that was it? That was his grand revelation? No shit. Jackson and Max played football together, of course, they were friends.

"Get out of my house!" I brushed past him to the alarm keypad in the hallway. The siren silenced.

"How good of friends are they, Drew?"

*This* was why he had broken into my house—I paused for a moment. He'd broken into my house, and I was on my way back into my kitchen for my coffee, like this was completely normal. "Seriously, after everything last night, you broke in to ask me about Jackson? Get out before I throw a knife at you."

"I swear to God, woman."

He started across the kitchen, and I clutched my coffee mug, ready to throw it at him. But something about the desperate look in his eyes made me stop. "Why do you care if they're friends?"

"Because Harford is a piece of shit."

"Of course. He's Barrington, and we're all pieces of shit, aren't we? Get out."

"Goddammit, Drew. He's..." He dragged his hands through his hair. "Fuck, Jackson. Max is a piece of shit, and if you give a shit about Nora, you need to tell her to stay the hell away from him. And so do you. Stay the hell away from him!"

Nora? Since when did he give a shit about Nora? Something twisted in my stomach because this seemed so much more than jealousy. "Really, Bellamy? You hate her."

Frustration was written all over his face. "I don't hate her, but even if I did, no girl deserves the shit they do."

"Great. Well, I have zero interest in Max. I'll be sure to tell Nora."

He stood in the doorway, glaring at me. Jaw ticcing and nostrils flaring. "And I wouldn't trust Bennett, either."

And there it was, the jealousy he couldn't hide. Him, Jackson, that girl... it all had my temper bubbling over. I held up my hand. "I've known Jackson a damn site longer than you. So, if you're done, you can go now."

"I swear to God, they do anything to you—or Nora," he backed into the hall. "I will kill them. And that's a promise, not a threat." Then he stormed off. Seconds later, my front door opened and closed, and I stood there, completely dumbfounded.

How far did his jealousy go?

I was in the living room, watching his car pull off when the house phone rang. The police were checking to see if everything was okay, and while I told them it was, it most definitely was not.

I cleaned the shards of glass from the foyer floor. Of all the things for Bellamy to come over here for—that bullshit. No, "I'm sorry for being a whore and making it known that I used you" Just lies and bullshit. Typical.

I dumped the glass into the garbage, took my coffee to the living room, and turned on morning TV that I paid no attention to. Halfway through an episode, I texted Olivia to apologize for making a scene the night before. She didn't seem bothered, and the only advice she gave me was: Bellamy West is the guy you screw, and as long as I could keep it just that, no harm, no foul.

No problem there... At least that's what I told myself.

I binged watched three hours of *Sex and the City* before the back door clicked open.

"What happened to my car?" my dad yelled before the

door slammed shut. His heavy footsteps echoed through the house, then stopped. "Drucella! What the hell happened to my car?" He stood in the living room doorway, his face blood red.

"Uh, about that..." I bit at my lip.

"I said you could use it for emergencies!"

"You left for three days. I ran out of Push-Pops. What do you want me to do, starve?" I was definitely going to give the man a heart attack before he hit retirement. "And before you ask, someone hit it in the parking lot." Someone being Bellamy's empty car, and parking lot being the street around the corner. Just the thought of it had the burning anger rising again. "Sorry," I said. I did feel a bit bad for trashing his car, but he had insurance that would pay out. That and he'd been an asshole to me ever since he wouldn't believe I hadn't cheated.

"Sorry? Sor—" He rubbed a hand over his chest. "That is not the damage of someone backing into a car at a grocery store, Drucella." His face reddened. "That looks like it was sent to a demolition derby!"

"I don't know what you want me to tell you. I found it like that."

"I'm so sure." he pulled a set of keys from his pocket and tossed them to the sofa. "Your *new* car is in the drive. I made sure to order one that shouldn't cause you issues." He rubbed at his chest again. "Care to tell me why the house got broken into, again?"

"Well, you did send your daughter into a school full of lowlifes. Might as well just broadcast the fact that you have money and they don't. They trashed my car. The house got broken into. Twice. Coincidence?" And it was all Bellamy.

Dad went to the wet bar in the corner of the room, poured a glass of whiskey, downed it, then set his gaze on me. His fists clenched and released before he stopped and inhaled a deep breath. "You will be the death of me…" Probably. He inhaled a deep breath. "I've spoken with the school. You're no longer suspended. You're going back on Monday." And then he left the room, taking the entire bottle of whiskey with him.

This was what my life had come to. I couldn't even get a proper suspension, never mind expelled.

An hour later, I stood in the driveway, my backpack slung over one shoulder as I stared at an old, sun-faded Range Rover with chipped paint. My personalized license plate that read: DrewsTT had been attached to the back, mocking me.

Apparently, my dad was taking the insurance money for the TT and leaving me with this.

Well, everything else had gone to shit, and now I'd be driving a literal representation of my life. Really, I probably should have seen it coming, given that I'd pushed my dad so far. Still didn't soften the blow, though.

The unoiled hinges creaked and groaned when I opened the door and sank behind the wheel. The smell of stale cigarettes and fried chicken lifted from the cracked leather seats. Which gave me horrible flashbacks of my short stint at Frank's.

Lowering the windows, I typed Nora's address into my phone's Sat Nav, then backed out and followed the directions out of Barrington.

I eventually turned into one of the rundown neighborhoods nestled between pawn shops and cash payday loan places, and I followed the street until I saw Nora's car in a driveway at the end of the cul-de-sac.

Flower boxes decorated the windows, the lawn was actually green, and unlike most of the other houses, the siding on hers wasn't faded and rotting.

Nora hadn't exactly seemed thrilled when I suggested working on our project at her house instead of mine. But since my dad was home— No one needed to witness just how much of a crap he didn't give about me. That, and I needed to get out of that house. So bad.

She answered the door, rubbing a hand over her arm. "So... just don't like, judge me or anything. The place isn't the best."

"Will you stop?"

She stepped to the side, ushering me onto the worn carpet in the hallway. We passed a bazillion family portraits, and something uncomfortable stirred in my chest. I'd grown up amongst kids who had entire game arcades in their homes—pools and tennis courts, and as ridiculous as it sounded, I had never considered what it would be like to not live like that. Until recently, people like Nora and I were worlds apart, and that had a sense of guilt winding through me. I noted the crochet blankets on the back of the living room sofa, the board games stacked on the bookshelf, their boxes as worn and dog-eared as the books beside them. I tried to imagine my dad offering to play a board game, and the thought almost made me laugh. He was too busy working to ever do anything so trivial.

She led me up the stairs to her room, where nothing matched—stripes and dots and a mish-mash of colors, and there was a certain charm in it that was absent in my dad's house.

She tossed her textbook onto her bed, then flopped back onto the mattress. "So, have you talked to he who shall not be named?"

"No. I blocked his number."

"Good. He's a dick. You should totally date Jackson." That wasn't going to happen. Bellamy and I weren't talking, but I had a feeling Bellamy might kill him based on the fact that he had broken into my house, *again*, just to warn me off. Whether what he said about Max was true or not... I had to tell her.

I let out a sigh. "Bellamy said something to me. About Max..."

Nora rolled onto her side, snatching a stuffed cat from the foot of her bed. "Okay... What?"

"He said he spoke to you, that Max does some bad shit to girls..." I sat up and propped my back to the wall.

"Yeah, he did. That was the whole conversation I had before I jumped into the pool at Jackson's all pissed. He said Max date rapes girls." She rolled her eyes and tossed the stuffed animal in the air. "He's such an asshole."

He had warned Nora...I drew a pattern over my jeans, thinking. "Don't get me wrong, he is an asshole, but he seemed really mad about it."

Mad enough to break-in. Mad over not just me, but Nora. It seemed out of character for Bellamy.

"Look at those guys, Drew, why the hell would *they* date rape girls?" She shook her head, then pushed up to sit beside me. "There's always rumors going back and forth about Dayton and Barrington. Dayton guys hate when Dayton girls go for Barrington."

"Bellamy said if Max hurts you, he'll kill him." And it was that which made me question if it were in fact true because Bellamy was not a guy to stick his neck out for a girl he barely liked unless it was dire.

Another eye roll, followed by a snort. "Since when does the villain play the knight in shining armor?"

I wasn't sure if Bellamy was a villain or just the villain in my story—he sure felt like it right now.

"He's saying crap to get to you," Nora sighed. "That's how Bellamy works. Just ignore him. I promise, it's bullshit."

Bullshit...I pushed to my feet and moved to the window.

The setting sun cast a warm amber glow over the dilapidated neighborhood. Movement caught my attention. A guy across the street pushed a mower over the lawn, stopping to tug his shirt over his head. He was all abs and cut muscle and tanned skin. Then I noticed the tattoos that wound around his wrists. Bellamy. Of course he lived across the street from Nora, hence why she looked after his brother. Why didn't I remember that?

Nora popped up beside me. "Don't get suckered in by that."

I was a sucker for it, though. And why the hell hadn't she told me she lived in the same neighborhood as him? "You live across the street from him?"

"Yeah."

I narrowed my eyes, pretending like I'd never noticed the boy had all that going on. Like I'd never been in the backseat of that van with my hands up his shirt. Or on Jackson's bed with his dick in my mouth. I thought about the girl he'd been with last night, the way he literally made me insane.

I pushed back from the window, and we started on our project. Halfway through the outline, Olivia texted me.

**Olivia: So I hear that Bellamy asked out who blonde girl that was at the party, Sheridan.**

That fast? My stomach twisted, and I fought the foreign feelings bubbling in my chest. That girl at the party, ... Why did I care? And why did I feel like this? I stamped my fingers over the screen.

**Me: Okay. Good for him?**

**Olivia: Just thought you should know. Wouldn't want you to get screwed over. Sheridan is a ho. So is he.**

**Olivia: You're way too good for Dayton trash, babe.**

I knew she was just trying to make me feel better, but she didn't.

After Nora and I finished our project, I politely declined her mom's offer to stay for dinner, my mood now pitch black. The moment I walked through Nora's front door, I spotted Bellamy, shirtless and covered in sweat with some lawn tool in his hand.

Our gazes locked. Olivia's words rang through my head. *No harm, no foul.* But I was already harmed and fouled. So I promised myself I would not engage because God only knew what in the hell would happen if I did...

## CHAPTER 20
## BELLAMY

ARLO CUT through the freshly mowed lawn, clutching a Mason jar while he attempted to catch fireflies. I tinkered with the edger, finally getting it to start. I hated doing this shit, but Dad wouldn't do it and Mom got embarrassed when the yard looked like shit.

"Bubba?" Arlo shouted over the whir of the engine. "Can I water the flowers?"

"Yeah. Sure. Just not where I'm working."

Movement across the street caught my attention when Drew stepped out of Nora's house. I hated, absolutely hated, that I'd tried texting her several times over the day just to see if she'd unblocked me. Drew Morgan shouldn't matter. She'd gotten me arrested. Given me blue balls the entire time she was evidently screwing around with Bennett, demolished my car, and caused this insane amount of jealousy to erupt in me like an angry volcano. Then she had blocked my number. But damn, if that sundress didn't hug her in all the right places, and the way she walked like some Victoria Secret model on a runway just made it all the worse.

She crossed Nora's yard, her gaze every so often directing toward me. The urge to say something rose its head like an angry serpent, and I tried to fight it. I tried to act like I couldn't give two shits less, but by the time she stepped off the curb, I couldn't stand it any longer. I needed a reaction.

Cutting the engine to the weed-eater, I swiped at the sweat trickling down my stomach. "Didn't get enough to look at last night?" I grabbed the waist of my jeans and tugged them down to my hairline.

No reaction. She completely ignored me, then stopped beside a rundown SUV and opened the driver's side door.

Literally couldn't stand it. "I see Bennett listened to you and didn't press charges." Her ignoring me was doing things to me...

Her chin dropped to her chest, then she slammed the door and marched across the street. "What the hell do you want from me?" She stormed up my drive, coming to halt a few feet in front of me. "You got your blow job."

This was fresh rage, and I seriously doubted it was over sucking my dick. And I wanted to know exactly what it was over. "And it was a decent blow job at best." That was a lie. It was the best damn blow job I had ever had.

"Well, don't worry. It won't be happening again." She narrowed her eyes. "I'm done with you, Bellamy."

And that, I wouldn't stand for. No way in hell would I let this girl be done with me so she could ride off into the sunset with some Barrington prick. Not when she'd put me through pure hell and misery.

"Nah, baby girl." I closed the space between us, pressing my sweaty chest against her folded arms. "You're not done with me."

"Why do you care? I hear you have a new Barrington girl to entertain you."

I fought the smirk that wanted to rip across my face. She'd only care about a girl if she cared about me—but then she was messing around with Bennett, and the little bliss of victory deflated like a popped balloon. The girl was making me crazy.

"Bet it would thrill Bennett to know my conquest of other women has his girl all livid with jealousy," I said as I swept a piece of hair behind her ear. All I could think about was how good her lips felt against mine—how good they felt wrapped around my dick, my hands in her hair. But above all else how much I wanted this—this push and pull between us. I trailed my fingers down the column of her throat, resisting so many things I wanted to do to her. "I guess he's not quite figured out how to make you come as hard as I do, huh?"

She finally slapped my hand away. "I didn't come the second time. Just got used. So, I guess we're even now."

The sting that accompanied that comment was unexpected. Because I didn't *want* her to think I'd used her. Last night, I had been pissed and, as much as I hated to admit it, even to myself, jealous. All night I'd watched Bennett touch her, watched her smile at him with her legs wrapped around his neck in that pool, and I had snapped. Had Bennett not interrupted us by banging on that door—I have no idea what may have happened or how this may be different right now. But he had, and I'd defaulted to the part every girl expected me to play—the part of the non-caring asshole so I didn't look like the one with a weakness.

"Stop with the bullshit, Drew. I wanted to use you just as much as you wanted to use me." That was a vague enough response that she could take it however she wanted. One that was safe, and made it seem like I was no more invested in whatever this shit was than her.

"Like I said, we're even."

Even. Hell no we weren't even, and I sure as hell wasn't done with this. I doubted she was, either. "You think blocking my number's gonna fix this?"

She ducked her chin to her chest. "I think it's best if we stay away from each other."

Best? Probably. But how often in life did anyone do what was best for them when the shit that would kill them was so much damn fun.

The spray of the garden hose shot past me to the half-dead rose bush. "What's the gas station lady doing here?" Arlo ran up beside me.

"Just leaving. Go water the plants by the house." My gaze was homed in on Drew. On every breath, each small tic of her jaw. "Now, Arlo."

"You're a butthole!" he huffed before I heard water spray against the siding.

Drew was still right there because, just like me, I'd bet she hated this just as much as she enjoyed it. There was something about her I couldn't get enough of, and I was pretty sure that made me batshit crazy.

I leaned down and touched my lips to her ear. "You know damn well we won't stay away from each other." I latched onto her arm. "Don't fool yourself, baby girl."

She attempted to pull away, and I yanked her right back, then placed an arm across the small of her back, trapping her small frame against me. "And you know how I know you won't leave me alone? Because you're defiant, and you crave this kind of fucking chaos that your daddy's money can't buy."

Her hands went to my chest. Her lips were close enough that I could taste each uneven breath. Part of me wanted to kiss her while the other part of me wanted to fist her hair and fuck her into willing submission. But before either could happen, a stream of cold water pelted my side.

My muscles tensed, and Drew jumped back on a scream.

"Arlo!" When I spun around, he dropped the hose and scurried back a few steps.

"That's what Daddy does when the neighbor's dogs start wrestling in the yard." His nose wrinkled. "I don't want you to wrestle with that lady. And I'mma tell Hendrix on you. He told me to tell if a lady that looked like one of the girls from Daddy's nudey magazines came over. She looks like one of them. 'Cause she's pretty and got those big ole' lips."

I frowned. How in the hell had Arlo gotten into Dad's stash of *Playboy*, and since when was my little brother selling me out for Hendrix?

I turned around as Drew climbed into that rundown SUV. The brake lights flashed, then the engine rumbled to life.

Arlo drew a line through the grass with his toe, then crossed his arms over his chest on a huff. "Why are you trying to wrestle with her, Bubba. You said she's en-en-en-something. And that they're the ones that poop on you."

I scrubbed a hand over his head, the tension and anger that had been rolling through me quickly disappearing. "Right…"

"I don't want her to poop on you."

I watched her taillights round the corner. "Yeah. Me neither, buddy."

And if there were ever a girl that was going to take a shit

on me, it was that one.

---

**Medusa is at 2112 Barrington Cove.**

The notification came through as I pulled to a stop in front of Arlo's friend's house. And that meant she'd unblocked my number. Because she knew I was right—she craved this madness.

I clicked on the notification, watching that little blue dot move toward Bennett's address. I knew, one hundred percent, I should disable this stupid app, but some sick part of me refused to let the decent part of me win that battle.

"See you later, Bubba!" Arlo threw his arms around my neck before hopping out of the car, backpack already on his shoulder.

"Wait a second!" I climbed over my center console and jogged after him up the sidewalk to the front of his friend's house.

"You're a helicopter brother." He nudged me, then knocked on the door. "That's what Jessie says."

"Jessie's a punk..."

The door cracked, and a woman with round glasses peeked over the chain lock. "Oh, Arlo. It's you." The door closed so she could unfasten the lock. And the second it swung open again, Arlo sprinted inside, tackling his friend to the carpet.

"I'll pick him up at ten tomorrow?"

She nodded. "That's perfect. Have a good night." She went to close the door, but I slapped a palm over it.

"He's allergic to Goldfish snacks. So, no cheese crackers or cheese puffs."

She smiled. "Okay."

Then I went back to the car and checked my phone again. Drew was still at Jackson's. I told myself it didn't matter. That if she was that much of a—whatever—to screw around with me then go back to Jackson, that none of it mattered. She was just like any other girl I'd ever been with.

But by the time I pulled up to Hendrix's house, I knew that was a lie. Because I'd checked that app two more times. And three hours later, Hendrix, Wolf, and I had Jackson hogtied in the back of Wolf's truck, *Special Delivery* scribbled across his face along with a masterpiece of dicks drawn in Sharpie over his cheeks.

CHAPTER 21

DREW

IT WAS after midnight when I stumbled through my backyard and dodged the edge of the pool. I'd snuck out of the house and over to Olivia's for another party—upon her insistence. Besides, what kind of rebel child would I be if I didn't climb out my bedroom window to go and get drunk while I was grounded? I stopped below my bedroom balcony, looking up and debating how easy it would be to scale the trellis with alcohol buzzing through my veins.

I placed my hand through one of the open diamonds, and just when I was about to attempt scaling it, my phone vibrated in my bra.

**Dickhead: Have fun at your boyfriend's house?**

I could practically feel the jealousy oozing through his words, and I liked it far too much. People only got jealous over things they wanted, right? Correction, he was jealous because he wanted to *screw* me, and he thought Jackson already had. *Don't get it twisted, Drew.*

**Me: Fuck you, Bellamy**

I texted him back, which meant he'd now know I had

unblocked him. But whatever. And why had I unblocked him? Because I'd sat in Olivia's house, replaying the previous night on a loop and getting stuck on the same sentence over and over again. *The shittiest part about this story, is that I fucking liked you.* At the time, I couldn't see past that blonde, but tonight I'd seen her, all over another guy. And then I felt guilty for allowing Bellamy to think I was dating Jackson.

Guilt was for pussies, though, because he kissed her freaking forehead! Thankfully, I had remembered that earlier in the night, which was what had kept me from doing something stupid, like messaging him first.

**Dickhead: You looked angry walking home, baby girl. What's the matter? Bennett not doing it for you?**

How did he know I had walked home? I chose to ignore the comment about Bennett.

**Me: Are you stalking me now?**

**Dickhead: Of course.**

**Me: You do realize this is creepy.**

**Dickhead: Abso-fucking-lutely.**

**Me: The first step is admitting you have a problem.**

I tucked the phone away and climbed the trellis, practically falling over my window ledge into my room. After I changed into my pajamas, I took my phone, went downstairs for a late-night Push-Pop, and then settled on the couch to watch TV.

**Dickhead: I left a present for you on your front porch.**

Seconds later, a horn blared from the driveway. I went into the foyer and opened the front door, dropping what was left of my Push-Pop when I found Jackson unconscious and laid out across the porch with dicks drawn all over his face. A nasty bruise marred his cheek, reminding me of last night's shitshow, and to top it off, he was in nothing but watermelon-green bikini bottoms.

My jaw tensed as I pulled my phone from my pocket and dialed the dickhead's number. This was over the line. It hadn't finished ringing the first time before he answered.

"Miss me, baby girl?"

"Why is Jackson on my porch?" I stared down at Jackson, irritation bubbling through my buzz. Hadn't Bellamy done enough to the guy last night? Now, this?

"Don't know, Drew. Why is he on your porch?" A series of cackles rang through the line.

"You can't just kidnap someone."

"Kidnap is a strong word. I simply transported him from his pool deck to your front door."

God, I hated him. "Well, come back and get him."

"Nah. I'm good."

"He's unconscious, and he weighs a ton." I glanced around the dark yard. "What am I supposed to do? Just leave him here?"

"You're asking me like I care what happens to him..."

"You're an asshole," I said, then hung up, my face heating with annoyance.

I knelt beside Jackson and shook him, but he didn't budge, so I shook him again. All he did was suck in a deep breath, then roll onto his side. There was no way I was getting him off my porch. Bellamy wasn't coming back, so I called Olivia.

Noise from the party in the background came over the line before slurred out a "What's up?"

"Your brother is on my porch. In bikini bottoms."

"That's amazing." She snorted. "Take a picture and send it to me."

Like hell I was taking a picture of him in this state. "Are you going to get some people together and come get him? I can't move him."

"Yeah. In a minute. But send me the picture first so I can prepare myself."

"Just come get him." I hung up—without taking a picture. I owed Jackson a little dignity in his hour of need.

I went inside and snagged a throw pillow and blanket from the living room, then covered up Jackson. Then I stood on the porch for a few minutes, staring down the dark street, hoping Olivia would hurry the hell up.

**Me: Are you coming?**

**Olivia: Give me 20 minutes.**

Rolling my eyes, I went back inside. I wasn't waiting on the porch for twenty more minutes. I lay down on the sofa and went back to my movie, passing out well before the guy got the girl.

---

"Drucella!"

I half opened my eyes on a groan. Bright morning sunshine spilled through the living room windows. That, coupled with the taste of Grand Marnier coating my tongue and the way my father glared down at me, made me feel sick.

"Why, in God's name, is there a young man on the porch in women's underwear, with male genitals drawn all over his face, Drew?"

Dammit, Olivia never came and got him? "No idea. Probably a hobo."

His eyes narrowed. "It looks like Nathaniel Bennett's son. Not a hobo."

"Well, did he recently become homeless?" I yanked at the blanket, then attempted to roll over to escape the sunlight.

"Drucella Analise Morgan!" I cringed at my full, godawful name. "Go wake him up. Now."

"Fine." I groaned, then rolled off the couch and staggered to the door. Sure enough, Jackson was right where I'd left him. Curled into the fetal position, snoring, with the blanket tangled around his legs.

I was annoyed as all hell at Bellamy for this. Jackson hadn't done anything to deserve this. The guy was still sporting a bruise from Friday night, for fuck's sake.

I nudged him with my foot, and he choked back a breath before his eyes snapped open. Blinking, he sat up and grabbed his head while he glanced around at my porch, then down at his crotch. "What the... Why am I here?"

"Not sure." I could have just said it was Bellamy, but I didn't need any more bad blood between the three of us than there already was. "I did call Olivia to come to get you..."

With reddening cheeks, he stumbled to his feet. "Did your little fuck buddy do this?" His angry gaze met mine.

"He's not my fuck buddy. Jackson, I'm sorry I—"

"Save it, Drew. I don't give a shit." Then he turned and walked off, crossing the lawn as the sprinklers cut on.

I stood on my porch, hating that this was the state of things. Jackson and Olivia had always been nice to me and were my only friends when I'd been forced to visit Dad over various holidays. And now Jackson hated me.

I had no control over Bellamy, but I knew I was to blame for this—because I had let him believe Jackson was my boyfriend. Not that it should have warranted a reaction. Bellamy and I weren't together, and he was all over some blonde. Then again, said blonde did trigger the homicidal rage that led me to destroy his car. So, I guessed I was a hypocrite. If I made him even half as crazy as he made me, this was a problem.

One I really needed to walk away from.

## CHAPTER 22

## BELLAMY

MONDAY MORNING, students crowded the halls, cramming their backpacks inside their lockers. I stopped in the middle of the hallway when I saw Drew standing at hers. She was supposed to be suspended. For a week. Yet, there she was, yanking books out of her locker before slamming the metal door. I shouldered through the group of cheerleaders trying to sell their stupid spirit ribbons. And she must have felt me coming because I was about two feet behind her when she lifted her middle finger. "Leave me alone," she said.

"So that's where the line is, huh? Not getting you fired. Not ruining your car. But dropping your passed-out boyfriend onto your porch in a bikini?"

She stopped in the middle of the hall and whipped around to face me, forcing students to go around us. "The *line* was about three miles back. Jackson is not my boyfriend, so just leave him out of it, Bellamy."

Not her boyfriend. Right. So, he was just a fuck buddy because she was at his house more than her own. "The guy you're fucking then."

"I just said, he's not my boyfriend!"

"I'm not your boyfriend, either, but I came on your face Friday night, didn't I?" And as shit as I felt for saying that, I wanted her anger because it told me I meant something to her.

"And made sure everyone knew about it." Students poured around us as she glared at me. "Is that what you do to your Barrington whores? Did you come on Blondie later that night, too?"

I bit back the smile, then stoked the flames. "You envision that, baby girl?" I tucked a piece of hair behind her ear, and she jerked away from my touch. "Me coming all over her while her nails raked down my spine?"

She went to walk off, and I grabbed her arm, bringing her to an abrupt halt in the middle of the packed corridor. Her jaw clenched before she slapped her palm against my chest. "Fuck you, Bellamy. Leave Jackson alone."

And the anger in her tone—I didn't like. It was over him, and I only wanted that for me. "I'll leave Bennett alone when *you* leave him alone." Because I didn't trust that he wouldn't hurt her.

The air crackled with static electricity; our gazes locked for long moments before Drew finally yanked free of my hold and stormed off, shoving her way through the crowded hallway.

We ignored each other at lunch and every time we passed in the hall. But when she fell into the chair beside me in biology, her perfume caught in the air, and I couldn't control my thoughts. Her. Me. Bennett's bed. "Let me guess. Daddy got you out of your suspension?"

She refused to look at me. "Right now, I'd love for *you* to get suspended."

I moved toward her, my jaw ticcing. "Figure you get rid of the devil, hell might be more tolerable?"

"Yes, because I hate you."

I glanced around the room at the girls I knew hated her just because she was Barrington—forget that she was hot. Then looked at the guys I knew would be giving her more grief than she could handle if they didn't think she was, in some fashion, mine. "I can assure you," I whispered, "the little dance with the devil you've been doing is the only thing that's kept the demons from ripping you to shreds, baby girl."

Her nostrils flared, the anger of hers I knew so well sparking to life as she placed a palm on my thigh and leaned in. "You think I can't handle myself? Because the way I see it, I handle you just fine."

"Oh, you do, baby girl. But only because I fucking let you."

"You let all your Barrington whores get away with so much, Bellamy?"

She had no idea what line she was toeing. On a smirk, I fisted the hair at the nape of her neck, then yanked her head down to my lap. "You wanna know what all my Barrington whores get away with, baby girl?"

She fought to break free of my hold, nails tearing into my jeans as I tugged harder.

"This is what all girls like Blondie get away with."

Whispers bounced around the room. The students in front of us turned to watch.

"Is that supposed to make me feel special, Bellamy?" She relaxed in my hold, resting her cheek close to my dick.

"Whatever you wanna call it."

Then her teeth sunk into my thigh. Hard.

I bit back a groan, then placed my other hand on the back of her head. "I swear to God, when I fuck you, I'm gonna do it with no mercy, baby girl." Then I pushed her away. Her hair was a tangled mess and her face red as shit. Any minute, I expected her to throw a punch.

"Mr. West!" Mrs. Smith whacked her pointer stick on the board. "I swear to the good Lord above." She shook her head, grabbing her demerit slip pad and writing one out. "All 'do it with no mercy, baby girl.' Lord Jesus, take the wheel," she said, placing the paper on the corner of my desk.

"That's on you!" I pointed to the pink slip. "I swear, you are the one-night stand from hell."

"No, that's on you." She shoved the detention slip across the desktop. "A one-night stand would have fucked you. I never will."

"Bullshit."

The bell sounded, and Mrs. Smith groaned, the hinges of her chair creaking when I assumed she'd stood up to go to the board. She started going over mitochondrial DNA.

Halfway through the lesson, I'd almost nodded off until the PA system beeped: "An intruder has been spotted in the building. An intruder has been spotted in the building."

Mrs. Smith tossed the marker down. "Under the desks." She hurried to the door, locking it before she rushed to the windows to pull the shades. Students clamored underneath the tables and Drew pushed out of her chair, turning to me with a look of panic. "What's happening?"

I snatched her wrist and yanked her down to the floor with me. "Just get down."

"Keep y'alls mouths closed," Mrs. Smith called from the back of the room.

My pulse ticked up, the thought that this could be real ran through my head, creating a whirlwind of anxiety with every hallway door that slammed shut.

"Why are we hiding?" Drew whispered as she settled against the leg of the desk.

"Active shooter drill."

Mrs. Smith shushed us again. The girl on the other side of Drew started crying. These things were always shit because we never knew if they were real or not.

"Oh my God." Drew pulled her knees to her chest, placing her forehead on them. She looked like she was about to completely lose it.

"It's a drill, Drew. Stop panicking." And that—that was the first time I had lied to her. I had no idea if it were a drill or not, but if it were real, it wasn't like there was anything we could do.

"How do you know?" she whispered.

I shrugged a shoulder, and she tugged her legs closer to her chest. Seconds ticked by. The eerie silence in a room that was usually chaotic created a suffocating tension. Images of newsreels played through my head on a loop...the sound of gunshots, kids fleeing buildings with their hands behind their heads. That could be us.

Drew released an uneven breath, focusing on the tile in front of her. "I'm scared," she whispered.

I was, too. I swallowed, then I laid my open palm on the floor between us, and she grabbed it, dropping her head to her knees again.

My stomach kinked and knotted; Drew's hand sweated in mine. I watched the second hand on the clock tick by, waiting for shots to ring out or officers to knock on the door and give us the all-clear, while thoughts of what would happen to my mom and Arlo cycled through my head. By the time the officers finally came around and opened the door, letting us know the drill was over, the tension in the classroom was almost unbearable.

We quietly went back to our desks, pretending that drill couldn't have been our shitty reality. Smith went back to the board, pressing her thermos to her lips with shaking hands. Then she picked up where she had left off, drawing another diagram.

Drew sat beside me, lip gripped between her teeth, tears threatening to spill over. She raised her hand and asked to be excused, already halfway to the door before Mrs. Smith acknowledged her.

The girl had evidently never had one of these drills before, and if they unnerved me, I could guarantee it had put her on the verge of a breakdown.

"I gotta piss," I said on my way out of the class.

I followed the empty hallway to the girl's restroom. Drew stood at the sink, swiping at her smudged mascara, even though the tears kept coming. I had no business following her in here. No business giving a shit if she was scared for the simple fact that she wasn't mine. But yet, here I was, making myself weak for her with every passing second.

"You all right?" I asked, my voice echoing off the grimy tiled walls.

Her gaze met mine in the mirror. On a ragged sigh, she dropped her chin to her chest, the sudden movement covering her face with a curtain of hair.

"Guess you didn't have those drills at your prep school, huh?" I moved behind her, placing a hand on her shoulder as I gathered her hair to the side of her neck. She didn't move. Didn't acknowledge me. "They're shit," I said.

"I don't know what's wrong with me."

"It scared you."

She turned to face me, wiping over her face again. "It's irrational to be crying right now. I didn't die."

"Out of all the things you've done that are irrational, I promise you, baby girl, this is not one of them." I half-smiled and swept a hand over her damp cheek, terrified at how normal this felt. At how right this felt.

Her gaze held mine for a moment before she grabbed my jaw, then pressed a kiss to my lips. The kind of kiss that didn't say she wanted me, the kind that said she needed me. And damn if it didn't make my chest go tight.

I grabbed onto her waist, pulling her close, and for once, I didn't feel the need to bend her over and fuck her. I didn't want to hate her. Just protect her.

"I'm not fucking Jackson."

"And I'm not fucking anyone else."

Because I wanted her. Only her.

Her fingers trailed my cheek as she took a step back, her gaze searching mine like there was something she could figure out about me if she just stared a little bit harder. Then, without another word, she slipped out of the bathroom.

Leaving me feeling more vulnerable than I ever had in my entire life.

## CHAPTER 23
## DREW

THAT AFTERNOON when I got home from school, I was still shaken up. I sat on the couch, feeling numb, and my only thought was Bellamy. He'd seen me cry. And I never, ever let anyone see my cry. He held my hand, kissed me... I could still feel the heat of his lips branded on mine.

Where was the bad guy I was supposed to hate?

I stared at my phone. I was passed caring right now. My walls were down. He'd put a big old crack in them in the space of one class. red

**Me: Thank you. For holding my hand**

It sounded pathetic when I wrote it out like that.

**Dickhead: Yep**

**Dickhead: Hope it didn't ruin the whole you hating me thing we've got going on...**

God, I was so screwed. So absolutely screwed. What was the point in fighting it anymore...?

I typed out the first part of a response, then another text came through.

**Dickhead: Because you all angry at me makes my dick hard AF.**

So, this is where we were going. And this I could handle a lot more readily than the weird emotions that were trying to worm their way through my chest.

**Me: That explains a lot.**

**Dickhead: Don't believe me. Tell me you hate me, and I'll show you what it does.**

A little blossom of excitement took root, and of course, I rose to it because Bellamy may have been the solid rock at my back today, but normally he was a blazing fire licking over my skin, threatening to singe me. This...this is what we did, and I wanted the familiarity of it, as though my sense of self were tied to him being filthy and bad. I pressed the voice-clip button. "I fucking hate you."

Seconds later, a picture came through of his fist wrapped around his bare dick. Heat trickled over my skin, and I caught myself squeezing my thighs together. Of course, I'd seen it, had my lips around it, but seeing his hand around it...that was something else entirely. It seemed so much more brutal, almost angry.

**Me: You gonna stroke it for me?**

**Dickhead: You gonna finger fuck yourself for me?**

God, when it came to him, I was a sick addict.

---

The next day at school, Bellamy wasn't waiting at my locker, and the sinking sense of disappointment that came took me off guard. Everything with him was so complicated, my feelings never the same from one day to the next. I kept waiting for him to show up, but he never did.

I shoved my biology book in my locker at the end of the day and grabbed my backpack. When I turned around, a redhead was leaned against the metal wall, staring at me.

Cleavage spilled out of her shirt, and she had this whole aura of "don't fuck with me." She was exactly the kind of girl who would have a razor blade. She was also the kind of girl any guy would want to screw, so when she said, Bellamy sent me to talk to you, I instantly assumed he'd slept with her. And that had my spine stiffening.

I quietly shut my locker door. "O-kay."

"You should stay the hell away from Max, and don't drink anything you didn't pour yourself around any of those Barrington assholes." She looked me up and down. "Then again, I don't know what Bellamy's worried about; you're probably fine. You aren't Dayton trash, are you?"

"He spiked your drink?"

She gave a curt nod, her expression shuttering. "Just trust me on this. They're not good guys." She took a step back. "I'll be sure to tell your friend the same thing."

"Wait. How do you know Bellamy?" I asked.

Her blood-red lips kicked up in a smirk. "I haven't fucked him." Then she walked off, disappearing into the rapidly thinning crowd in the halls.

I shouldered my bag and made my way to the exit, thoughts whirring through my mind. Max had date-raped that girl.

I wondered if Jackson and Olivia knew. They couldn't. They'd never let the guy in their house, surely? Then again, who were they going to believe? Their friend or a Dayton girl? And that thought had a sick feeling swirling in my gut.

My encounter with the redhead played out in my head

the entire drive home. And when Olivia texted to ask if I wanted to go grab food with her, all I could think about was how the hell I could broach this with her. Surely to God, if what the girl said was true, Olivia wouldn't set one of my friends up with him.

---

Olivia's Mercedes barreled over the road. She talked at a hundred miles an hour about some party this weekend while I stared out the window, watching the streets of Barrington whizz by.

I sent a text to Nora, telling her we needed to talk, though I had no confidence that she would listen. Had the original information come from anyone but Bellamy, maybe... I knew Nora was too blinded by the Barrington glamour and her hatred of Bellamy to listen.

"Anyway, Max will be there," Olivia slowed in a turn lane, putting on her blinker. "So, you should bring your friend."

Seconds passed where I grappled with the best way to say it..."I spoke to this girl at school today." I swept a hand over the leg of my jeans. "She said Max Harford date-raped her. You ever hear anything about that?"

She frowned. "What girl?"

"A redhead. I don't know her name; she just came up to me and—"

"Ugh! A redhead? You spoke to Zepp Hunt's trashy girlfriend? You know, the word is, she got him arrested. I wouldn't believe a word she says."

"But wasn't Zepp the one who beat Max?"

She shrugged. "Men are Neanderthals. Who's to say what she told him. They're Dayton. Beating up the

Barrington quarterback is like gold for them. I mean, they kidnapped Jackson and put him on your porch, Drew!"

"Yeah." But they didn't hurt him and considering they hated him, they absolutely could have... I'd seen the scars on Max's face. That wasn't just a beating; that was punishment. That was a blood debt.

"Forget about it. It's bullshit." I didn't think it was, though, and if it weren't...I could totally see why Dayton would hate Barrington. By association, I could see why Bellamy would hate me.

Olivia pulled into a gravel lot filled with pickups and motorcycles. I stared up at the orange and brown sign with the light to half the letters unlit: Waffle Hut. What the hell kind of name was that?

I followed Olivia inside, and the middle-aged woman behind the counter gestured toward an empty table in the corner. I sank to the plastic booth, my hands sticking to the seat before I took the grease-covered menu and skimmed about twenty-different ways to eat hash browns.

A few minutes later, the bell above the door chimed. Jackson walked in with Max and Nora. I didn't even know she would be here, but there she was, her hand on Max's arm. That horrible feeling settled in my gut again.

"God, I live with you. Leave me alone already." Olivia snorted as she shuffled over to make room.

Jackson glared at me before sliding into the booth next to his sister. He was obviously still annoyed over Bellamy's stunt last weekend. Not that I could blame him.

Max plopped down beside me, practically smooshing me to the wall so Nora could squeeze in. I'd never been more repulsed by being near someone.

We placed our orders, and ten minutes later, a feast of greasy food turned up on the table. From the looks of which I was not sad I'd stuck with ordering just a milkshake.

I plucked the cherry from the thick whipped cream, cringing when Max threw an arm around Nora's shoulders. I wanted to rip it off and drag her out of here. Even before I knew what I now did about Max, I thought she was too good for an arrogant rich boy like him.

Jackson glanced up from the phone he'd been paying attention to for the past five minutes. "Davis said he's down. That makes eight of us."

"We're so gonna beat their asses." Max laughed, rubbing his hands together before he picked up his fork.

God, boys and testosterone. "Whose ass are you beating?" I asked, sucking the milkshake through my straw.

Jackson's typed out a text before he shot a sick grin at me. "West and his boys."

Oh, this was not good. Granted, I could see why they'd feel the need for the backup, but it seemed wrong. Unfair. "That seems kind of barbaric," I said. "I mean, aren't you guys above that?"

Max turned his attention to me. "So, I mean, what's the deal between you and West, Drew?"

"Nothing?"

"Not what I heard."

Jackson shifted, stuffing the rest of his greasy sandwich into his mouth before shoving his plate away. "Whose side are you on, anyway, Drew?"

"No one's. I just think fighting is stupid."

Jackson's phone beeped again, snatching his attention from me. "Davis said he'd meet us over in Paradise Valley at ten. Sheridan said all the losers are over at Hunt's house."

The guys kept talking about beating up the Dayton trash, and with every backhanded comment they made about Bellamy, my agitation grew. After a few minutes, I excused myself to the bathroom. Because this was bullshit.

The minute I closed the door to the grubby stall, I took out my phone. Maybe my loyalty should have been to Olivia and Jackson, but eight on three just seemed shitty. I had no idea who I really trusted anymore, but something always pulled me back to Bellamy, no matter how stupid it might be. I couldn't not warn him.

**Me: Just a heads up...Barrington guys are going to turn up at Hendrix's house later, and I quote, "to beat your ass."**

**Dickhead: Yeah?**

**Dickhead: And how do you know that?**

God, he was a dick. Couldn't just take the warning.

**Me: Does it matter?**

**Dickhead: If you're with him—yeah.**

**Me: I told you I'm not fucking him!**

**Dickhead: Doesn't matter.**

Possessive was not even the word.

**Me: Just be careful.**

**Dickhead: Come on, baby girl. Tell me you don't think he could actually beat my ass.**

**Me: Don't think they're planning one on one, Bellamy.**

When I went back to the table, two more Barrington guys had shown up. I ordered a plate of fries, just to stall Jackson and those guys a little longer, hoping maybe Bellamy's idiot self would change his mind and leave Hendrix's house. Although, really, I knew he wouldn't abandon Hendrix.

I'd just shoved the last of Waffle Hut's godawful fries

into my mouth, feeling like I may puke, when the bell over the door jingled.

"Aw, hell." Max grinned, nodding toward the door. "Looks like we'll get to it earlier."

I glanced over my shoulder at Bellamy, Wolf, and Hendrix standing in the doorway. Fists balled by their sides, and Bellamy's angry gaze homed in on me.

How *the hell* did Bellamy know where we were?

"Heard you gotta problem with me, Bennett?" Bellamy jerked his chin up. "Wanna beat my ass?"

"You told him, Drew?" Jackson shook his head, swearing under his breath.

"Not like that's a secret!" I directed my glare toward Bellamy. I helped him out, and he dropped me in it.

"She doesn't have shit to do with it," Bellamy said, pushing up his sleeves.

Olivia glared at me. "Seriously? You're loyal to the trash you're fucking now, Drew?" Her gaze dragged over me, shifting into the way she looked at everyone from Dayton. Like I was beneath her.

Hendrix took a step forward. "Pissed that Bell face-fucked your girl, Bennett?"

And on that comment, Jackson shot out of the booth, followed by Max. The other two guys moved down the aisle behind them.

"Your dumbass didn't learn your lesson the first time?" Wolf said, glaring at Max.

Hendrix nudged Wolf, bouncing on his feet like a puppy. "They think they're gonna whoop our ass, Wolf. Because we don't have baseball bats this time." He tossed his head back on a cackle. "Dumb shits."

Bellamy moved to the front, drumming his fingers over one of the empty tables. "I tell you what, Bennett. You get on your knees right now like the little bitch you are, and I won't beat your ass for talking to my girl."

That should have pissed me off because I was absolutely *not* his girl. But damn if it didn't turn me on. Because it was possessive and arrogant and everything bad boy.

"Your girl?" Jackson laughed. "You want your ass beat over that bitch, West?" Jackson said.

Bellamy's jaw set. Blind rage blanketed his face. Jackson took a swing. Bellamy didn't even flinch, simply ducked, then popped up and socked Jackson square in the temple.

Jackson's head snapped to the side before he fell to a heap on the tile floor.

"Now, who's the bitch?" Bellamy spat on him, and all hell broke loose.

The rest of the guys went at each other, everyone throwing jabs. Hendrix screamed "cocksuckers" at the top of his lungs before literally leaping into the fray. I couldn't tear my eyes from Bellamy, the way he moved so effortlessly, all coiled muscles with an air of calm that contradicted the violence. I liked to think I was above such things. Turned out, I really wasn't. The way he moved made me crave his scarred hands at my throat, his body over mine, dominating me—sick, twisted, addiction.

Olivia pulled her phone from her purse, swiping her fingers over the screen before placing it to her ear. "Yes. I need to report a fight..."

Shit. I grabbed Nora's arm and dragged her out of the booth, ducking around fallen Barrington guys and swinging fists before I hauled her out the door into the humid Alabama air.

Nora followed me out onto the highway, making it past the pawnshop before she stopped and sighed. "We can't walk home."

"It's fine." I tapped over my phone as we walked down the litter-strewn shoulder. "I'm getting an Uber." Correction, there were none because it was Dayton! Cars rushed by us, and a truck beeped its horn, kicking up a gust of wind. We kept walking, and my mind whirled at a hundred miles an hour. Bellamy, Jackson, Max...Nora turned up with Max. The idea that she might date a guy like that left a horrible sick feeling in my gut.

"You know, I really don't think Max is a good guy, Nora."

"Drew..."

"I spoke to a girl today who was date raped by him. Call it gut instinct, but I believe her."

She huffed and folded her arms over her chest. "Can we not talk about this right now?"

I glanced at her, with her chin dropped to her chest, traipsing along beside me. She looked defeated, and I had a feeling she did, in fact, believe it; she just didn't want to. She wanted the guy to actually like her, and that was understandable. I felt bad for her. "Okay."

We made it halfway down the shittiest block I'd ever walked in my life before a car slowed beside us. The passenger window lowered, and Bellamy leaned around Hendrix. "Get in the car, Drew."

Hendrix glared at me from the passenger seat like I'd stolen his favorite toy.

Nora crossed her arms over her chest. "So what? We can get hauled off to jail when they report your tag, Bellamy. No thanks. We'll walk."

I took one look at the hookers loitering outside the pawnshop across the street. The car idling at the corner with what was one hundred percent a drug deal going down.

Hendrix leaned over the lowered window, grinning. "Aw, Snora Nora is all pissy wissy because her Barrington turd bucket got his ass handed to him. Again."

"I don't give a shit if you wanna get in Nora. But Drew...*You* get the fuck in." Bellamy's voice was authoritative and deep, and it sent white-hot heat crawling into my cheeks.

Hendrix slumped in the seat, rolling his eyes while he mocked Bellamy.

I turned to Nora. "Just get in. It's like five minutes or a half-hour walk through...this shit." For all of Bellamy's shit, I knew he wouldn't actually leave her here.

"Whatever," she said before moving toward the car.

Hendrix climbed out of the front, throwing himself into the back and patting his thigh. "Time to get all cozy, Nora Bora."

The scent that was all Bellamy greeted me the second I sank into the passenger seat. His hand landed on the stick shift, and my attention went to his grazed knuckles before moving to the split in his lip. I told myself that the heat churning in my gut was just a reaction to the violence, but I knew it was more than that. Bellamy was a brand of awful that I wasn't even sure I wanted to escape anymore.

He floored the engine, fishtailing back onto the highway before running a red light. When we reached the interstate, Hendrix popped between the seats.

"You two gonna fuck like stray cats and dogs tonight or what?" He whacked Bellamy on the back of the head. "Meow-fucking-meow." He flopped onto the backseat on a cackle.

"No. I hate him," I said, turning around to face the back of the car.

"Like that means shit. I hate Hora Nora, but I'd still let

her sit on my dick and take a spin. Don't worry, stumpy legs, no one will judge your judgment if you take a ride on my Whorey-Go-Round." He pinched Nora's side, and she slapped him in the face. I gaped for a moment because everyone knew Hendrix was crazy.

"And now you've given him a boner, Nora." Wolf shook his head. "Congratulations. He's gonna hump your leg like a dog with its red rocket out." The guys all laughed while Nora glared at Hendrix like she'd choke him if she could.

The car rolled to a stop at a red light, and I faced the front again, unable to ignore the way the streetlight played over the shadows of Bellamy's face. He turned and caught me staring. "Don't worry, I hate you, too, baby girl." His hand landed on my thigh, rough fingers sweeping over sensitive skin.

I turned my gaze out the window, staring at the boarded-up buildings around us while trying not to react to the heat of Bellamy's palm branding my flesh, promising he would eventually own me. Nora sighed from the backseat. "You know you guys are gonna get arrested?"

The guys barked out laughs. When the light turned green, Bellamy moved his hand from my thigh, shifting into first, and I missed that contact.

"Come on, Hora Nora, that's not how shit works between Dayton and Barrington. You know that."

Bellamy weaved in and out of traffic, eventually taking a hard turn into Barrington and gunning it through the subdivision. The brakes screeched when he slammed to a halt in front of my drive. Nora shouted for Hendrix to move before the back door opened, then slammed it shut.

"Thanks for the text." Bellamy brushed his rough, battered knuckles over my cheek, and my heart fluttered like a dying bird. "It was cute."

I swept my thumb over his split lip. "Put some ice on that," I said, then I got out of the car.

Nora stood in my driveway, glaring at Hendrix, whose face was plastered to the back window. His tongue pressed over the glass before the car sputtered off.

"That..." Nora pointed down the street as the taillights of Bellamy's car disappeared around the corner. She started up my sidewalk, toward my house, stopping at the door to wait on me. "Seriously, Drew, I'm telling you, you keep messing around with Bellamy, and you're gonna get hurt."

That was nothing I didn't already know, but I couldn't stop myself. He was like a tsunami I couldn't outrun, and I knew I'd just chosen him over my friends. He had my loyalty, whether I liked it or not. I was going to drown.

I unlocked the door, then shoved inside the cold foyer. "It's not like that."

"I saw his hand on your thigh, Drew."

"It's..." I dropped my keys to the entranceway table, then we headed through the dark house toward the stairs.

"It was a ride home, Nora. What was he gonna do? Leave us to walk through Dayton..."

"Did you miss the part where he called you his girl? Or where he was willing to leave me while demanding *you* get into his car?"

"He was just saying that to wind Jackson up." And I like it, way too much. I changed out of my clothes, pulling on an oversized T-shirt before I settled on the bed beside her. "And he wouldn't have left you."

"Had it just been me, he wouldn't have stopped in the first place. He's not nice, Drew."

No, he wasn't, but for all the shit between Bellamy and me, he'd never hurt me. Although I now realized how easily he could have; I understood the wide berth people gave them in the hallways. The fear, the reverence. In my world, money was power, but in theirs, violence ruled. And that, they had in spades.

"I'm just trying to warn you. Fuck him all you want, whatever. Just don't fall for him. Okay?"

Nora fell asleep, and though I usually found the sound of another person's breathing comforting—thanks to always sharing a dorm—I couldn't sleep. My mind was a jumbled mess, my body restless—and it was Bellamy's fault. I couldn't get him out of my head. I'd tried to block him out after the party at Jackson's house, told myself he was bad and that I was done, but we weren't done.

**Me: You called me your girl...**
**Dickhead: Yep**

That was it, not "because you are" or "I was just winding Jackson up." Just "yep."

**Dickhead: So, are you going to tell me why you were with him?**

How quickly he moved on, and to such an obvious topic. I didn't owe him an explanation, but after the beating he'd just given Jackson, I could surmise that this was a very sore spot right now. Whereas Jackson had always seemed like the good guy, tonight I saw that he wasn't. He wanted to pit eight against three, was friends with a guy who would date rape girls, and the way Olivia looked at me... I thought maybe they were nice, so long as I fit into the perfect Barrington box. They were no better than my dad. And now, I was no better than the trash I'd "sided" with. I'd sooner be trash than an asshole.

**Me: We were friends. Not after tonight, though.**

I didn't really have any friends here other than them,

but whatever. I'd rather hang out with Dayton kids than fall into the predictable role of the stuck-up rich kid. I didn't get it, the vehemence toward a person simply because they didn't have money.

**Dickhead: Can't say I'm sorry…**

**Me: Pretty sure you're at the top of Barrington's shit list. No more rich girls for you...**

I really needed to let that go, but, yeah, that wasn't happening anytime soon. Yes, I was petty and jealous.

**Dickhead: I'm always at the top of that list. Only one rich girl I like. And you are definitely NOT Barrington.**

I typed out a response, deleted it, typed another. All while those words played through my mind. *The shittiest thing about this story is that I almost fucking liked you.*

**Me: I hate you.**

It was true. No one had ever made me want to kiss them and kill them at the same time the way he did.

**Dickhead: It wouldn't be half as much fun if you didn't.**

**Dickhead: By the way. We're going to a party tomorrow night.**

**Me: Okay… Have fun?**

**Dickhead: You're coming. And that wasn't a question.**

Damn the bit of me that found his commanding bullshit hot.

**Me: Fine, but you're not picking me up.**

If he picked me up, it was like a date. I wasn't sure I was ready to *date* Bellamy West.

**Dickhead: Whatever you want, baby girl.**

## CHAPTER 24

## BELLAMY

I TOSSED my phone onto my bed, then grabbed the bag of ice from the floor and put it back to my lip. Forget that Bennett was trying to jump us; the second I walked into that Waffle Hut and saw him at the table with her, war drums went off in my head, calling some primitive part of me to battle. Because whether she liked it or not, the very animalistic part of me had claimed her as mine.

That was what I'd surrendered to tonight, and her leaving with me meant she'd inadvertently surrendered to it, too.

My bedroom door cracked open. "Bubba!" Arlo slipped inside, then leaped onto my bed. "I'm hungry. Momma went to work early, and there's no Spaghetti-O's."

I tossed the ice-bag onto the floor. "Dad didn't feed you?"

"No."

It was almost ten at night. Before the incident at Waffle Hut, I'd been over at Hendrix's trying to move a car. Mom had messaged me to tell me she'd been called in when I was taking Drew home and said she was leaving a sandwich for

Arlo, which, if I had to guess, Dad ate in the ten minutes Arlo was here without me.

My jaw tightened as I pushed off the bed.

The hum of the television in the living room crept down the hallway, and my blood came to a low simmer.

Dad was worthless. I grabbed my shirt from the floor, pulled it on, then took the envelope filled with cash from my dresser drawer and tucked it into my back pocket. "Come on, you wanna go to McDonald's?"

"Yeah!" He tumbled off my bed and flew to the door, stopping before he bolted out. His brow scrunched when his gaze landed on my busted lip.

"Did Daddy do that?"

"No."

"Then who did?"

I followed him into the hallway. "Busted it with the car door." I hated lying more than anything. But some shit, he just didn't need to know. Like that his big brother had gotten into a brawl over the girl he said would poop on him.

The ding of a bell and roar of a crowd blared from the TV before two oiled-up men went at each other in a ring. Dad sat in the recliner, passed out with a burned-down cigarette in one hand, and a whiskey bottle in the other.

My fingers twitched, the urge to knock his unconscious ass right out of that chair. But it would only cause more problems for Mom, and that was the last thing I wanted to do.

On my way to McDonald's, I stopped by the post office and dropped off the envelope, addressed to my mother, with almost two-thousand dollars in it before driving off.

The late-afternoon sun streamed through the pine trees surrounding Hendrix's backyard. I finished filing off the Chevy's serial number, swatting at the mosquitoes biting the absolute shit out of me. "Come on, man. There'll be plenty of girls there," I said. I wasn't even sure why I was trying to talk Hendrix into coming to the party—all he'd do would be give me grief about Drew. But he and Wolf were my boys. We did everything together.

Hendrix slammed the hood and shook his head. "I'm not going to The Dump party. The ginger's gonna be there." He rounded the car, snatching a wrench from the tall weeds before pointing it at me. "You go to that party, and you're taking a steamer on Zepp."

"Seriously, man?"

"Seriously, dick."

Hendrix hated Zepp's girlfriend's guts because he was one hundred percent sure she was the reason Zepp had gone to prison. But Zepp himself had told me his arrest was all on him. Of course, Hendrix refused to listen because he was Hendrix. "It's the dump, Hendrix," I said. "That's our territory."

"Was! *Was* our territory until the ginger devil came along." He chucked the wrench into his toolbox. "And I already told you, we're going to the Methodist revival."

He'd watched some documentary about cults and convinced himself that church girls were freaks. I wiped off my grease-covered hands on a towel, watching as he tossed the toolbox down then rummaged through one of the coolers on the back porch.

"I am not going to church, man."

He cracked open a Dr. Pep and gave me a disapproving glare. "You're going to The Dump for her. You weakling."

"I'm going to The Dump because your theory about finding freaks at a revival is messed up."

Hendrix snorted. "Come on, Bell. It's a place full of sweet, virginal girls hungry for a little taste of the devil."

And that—that was something I wouldn't even touch. The second Hendrix and Wolf set foot in the place, it was going to go up in flames.

"You've got issues, man."

He slurped back more of his drink on his way to the back door. "Whatever. Like you wouldn't."

"I wouldn't."

He shook his head. "Drew's done gone and fucked you up. Passing up virgins and Jesus..." The screen door slammed closed behind him.

Oh, the girl had fucked me up all right...

---

I left Hendrix's and swung by the house to grab Arlo and take him to a friend's for a sleepover. And when I got back to the house, Dad was already shitfaced. He stood at the open fridge, swaying on his feet as he grabbed another beer.

Mom shuffled into the kitchen, pinning her dark hair away from her face before taking a can of peas from the pantry.

"I don't want no damn peas with my dinner, woman. I want hamburger steak and mashed potatoes."

She froze, then placed the can back on the shelf. "We don't have any fresh potatoes, Dan."

"Well, better go get some."

"I don't have time. I have to be at the Dollar Ser—"

"I don't care what you've gotta do. I want a decent damn dinner."

"Don't fucking talk to her that way!" My heart thumped against my ribs, the sensation hitting the back of my throat. I took the can of peas from the shelf and slammed it down on the worn counter. She worked her ass off, and she loved him when he didn't deserve it. There was no way in hell I could stand by and let him disrespect her. "She's not going to the store."

"Bellamy..." Mom whispered.

Dad was already shoving up his sleeves. "She *will* go to the goddamn store." He staggered toward me. "You think you're a big bad man now, son?"

I thought about all the times I'd seen him hit her, all the times he'd left me with a black eye as a kid. Then I thought about him not feeding Arlo the other night.

"Dan, please," Mom whispered, then he reared back like he was going to smack her, and I just snapped.

Dishes shattered. Sheetrock splintered. After I'd busted his nose and his lip and he'd taken a beer bottle to my head, I grabbed him by the collar of his shirt and shoved him through the screen door. "Get the hell out."

He staggered to his feet, swiping at his bloody nose.

"I swear to God," I said, fighting through my ragged breaths. "You come back in here before you're sober and I'll kill you."

He froze, dragging in deep breaths before he stumbled around the side of the house. The engine to his truck sputtered, tires gripped the gravel, and then silence fell over the house.

Mom stood at the kitchen counter, hands bracing the sink while her chin hung to her chest. I hated that she was upset, but I wouldn't let him hit her. On a hard sigh, I grabbed the broom from the pantry and began sweeping up the shards of glass and Wal-E-Mart china.

"You don't have to clean that up, Bellamy…"

I picked up a few more broken pieces, biting my tongue until I couldn't. When I turned to throw it into the trash, I looked at her. "Leave him, Mom. Leave his ass before I have to kill him."

Sighing, she knelt beside me, grabbing pieces and tossing them into the bag. "I…"

"You can."

And then her chin dropped to her chest. "I love him."

"He's an asshole."

"But he didn't use to be…"

Annoyance lapped at my veins, and I hated it. She was the last person on earth I ever wanted to be annoyed at, but it was so damn hard sometimes. Because she deserved better, and she just wouldn't let herself see it. Mom was still stuck on this idea of who he *used* to be. The man who used to buy her flowers and hold down a job. She clung to that like it was a life raft in this shitty storm, and that notion of love was what I was afraid would either end up as her demise or mine. Because every time he got rough with her, it was harder and harder for me to stop throwing punches at him when I got him down.

Shaking my head, I dropped to my knees to collect more pieces of glass. We went through the motions of cleaning up the destruction, then she grabbed the meat from the fridge and pushed up on her toes to kiss my cheek before she moved to the stove. "I love you, Bellamy."

"And I love you, too." What else was I supposed to say to her?

I helped her with dinner, then sat down beside her to eat. After I'd washed up the dishes, I sent Drew a text: **Can't make it. Sorry.** Because like hell would I leave Mom here alone. And when she went in for her shift at eleven, I grabbed Dad's bottle of half-drunk whiskey from the coffee table, and I went outside to look at the stars because, at times, those little white dots were the only thing that reminded me that some things are born from destruction.

And sometimes, that was the only damn hope I had to cling to.

## CHAPTER 25

## DREW

I SAT on the tailgate of some pickup truck, staring at the people dancing by the bonfire. Alone. I'd tried to talk to Nora about Max on the drive through the woods to this hillbilly party, but of course, she didn't listen. By the time I had parked my car amongst the other rundown SUVs and trucks, she was annoyed. The second I'd stopped the car, she got out and stormed off.

I'd spent the last thirty minutes sitting here, scanning the crowd of drunk kids for Bellamy. He was nowhere to be seen. I checked my phone, and there were no texts from him. Half an hour passed before I spotted Nora stumbling across the field a bottle of vodka dangling from her grip. She collapsed onto the tailgate beside me, swiping dark curls away from her face.

"You okay?" I asked.

She tipped up the bottle, taking a heavy gulp before offering it to me.

"I'm driving." Because I didn't want to get drunk and lose all inhibitions around Bellamy. Not like I had many to begin with. "Nora." I grabbed her arm when I noticed her eyes were glassy. "What's wrong?"

"Monroe came and spoke to me."

"Oh."

"Yep." Another gulp. She was going to get sick.

"Look, you're better than those Barrington pricks anyway."

She gave me a hopeless look. "You're Barrington, Drew."

I laughed. "Yeah, and I'm a prick."

"You are not."

She stared down at the bottle in her lap, picking at the label. "I'm sorry I didn't believe you about Max... It's just Bellamy..."

"I know." Since day one, Nora had warned me off Bellamy. I understood why she wouldn't take his word but on something so serious? "Can I ask why you hate him so much?"

She exhaled, then took another swig of vodka. "It's not hard to hate him, Drew. He's awful." No, it wasn't, but at the same time, it really wasn't hard to want him. "He's not awful to you, though, so you don't see it."

I stared across at the crackling fire, watching the way it danced over the field, casting shadows over the tree trunks. "I'm sorry about Max."

"I thought he liked me." She tipped her bottle up, the liquid glugging against the glass. "Why do we end up liking guys we shouldn't?"

If only I knew the answer to that. "It's some ingrained part of female DNA to go for guys who will inevitably screw us over."

I checked my phone again before typing out a message to Bellamy.

**Me: Where are you?**

Another pickup pulled into the clearing, and I strained to see if it was Wolf's.

"Why do you keep checking your phone?"

"I'm not."

Her eyes narrowed then widened. "You're waiting for him? Oh, no. No, no." She pointed the bottle at me. "I know that look. Don't be falling for that asshole, Drew."

"Calm down, Nora."

My phone vibrated.

**Dickhead: Can't make it. Sorry**

My stomach clenched as something that felt a lot like disappointment settled over me.

Nora leaned over my shoulder, then glanced at me. "And now you look like a kicked puppy. I do not get it."

I put my phone away and shoved the vodka against her chest. "Just get drunk, would you?"

And Nora didn't just get drunk. She got shitfaced.

It was almost midnight when I helped her into my passenger seat while she giggled and hiccuped. "Max is a dick," she slurred.

"Yep."

I fastened her belt while she tried to push me away. "I'm fine."

When I got in the car, I realized I had no idea how to get out of here or where I'd come in. All I saw around me was a wall of trees. I picked a random track, figuring it would come out somewhere. It didn't.

We ended up in the middle of thick woods, my headlights shining out over the edge of a cliff.

"Shit," I mumbled, putting the car in reverse. "How do we get out of here?"

The electric glow from a phone screen lit up the inside

of my car. Nora swiped her fingers over the screen, squinting against the light. "If I use that app, I can find my house." She squinted harder. "Wait. Dickhead?" She tossed the phone at me. "That's your phone." Then she fumbled in the door pocket for her own.

I glanced down at the phone in my lap. A map was on the screen with a pop up at the bottom that read: Friends. And one contact was listed. Dickhead. I stared at the screen, confused as hell because I didn't even know what app this was, so how in the hell had Bellamy's contact ended up in there? "What the..."

"Why are you tracking Bellamy? That's creepy, Drew."

"What? No." *Tracking* him... "I've never even used this app, I don't know how—" Then I remembered that one time when Hendrix had gotten my phone.

That motherfucker.

Suddenly, it all made sense. The slick asshole. Bellamy had been watching me. Which meant this was how he'd known I was at the Waffle Hut, known when I was walking home from Jacksons so he could dump him on my porch. Known every time I was in Jackson and Olivia's house. Well, now his raging jealousy made sense, and I was going to kill him.

"So, *he's* tracking *you*. Okay. That's psychotic, Drew!" She kept fiddling with her phone. "But it's kind of hot. I hate him, but..." She waved a hand around, and I threw the car into drive.

"Just get us out of here, Nora."

---

When I finally pulled up in Nora's driveway, my gaze drifted to Bellamy's house. I could not believe the asshole had actually put a tracker on my phone, but really, it shouldn't have surprised me, seeing as he'd broken into my house. Twice. I rounded my car, stopping midstride when I noticed the figure sprawled on the drive. "Uh," I closed my car door, silencing the chirp of crickets. "Is that Bellamy?"

Nora stumbled through her yard. "Probably."

Probably? Why was he just lying there? Outside. In Dayton. Mug victim was practically stamped on his forehead.

I followed Nora up through the grass, grabbing her shoulder to keep her from veering off into the bushes. "Is he dead?"

"No. He just does that."

"And you don't think that's weird?"

"Well, duh, it's weird." She hiccupped. "He's weird, weird, weird. And bad, bad, bad." She touched her hand to her lips on a giggle. "My lips are all tingly."

"Wow. All right, AA. Just..." I opened her front door, and she staggered into me on her way inside.

Getting her up the stairs was no easy feat. We almost stacked it about three times before we made it to her room, and the second she set foot inside, she faceplanted onto her bed.

"Are you going to throw up?" I asked.

"Nope. Throwing up is for amateurs."

And I'd rarely seen Nora actually drink.

I tugged her shoes off, then put the wastepaper bin by the bed, just in case.

Hopefully, she wouldn't throw up because her mom actually gave a shit if her underage daughter went out drinking, and Nora would get in trouble.

She was already snoring by the time I snuck back downstairs and out the front door. I stood on her porch staring at

Bellamy's form, still lying on the drive like a complete weirdo. Tracker. He had put a tracker on my phone, the asshole.

I cut across the dark street. "You put a tracker on my phone!"

"Actually, I didn't physically put shit on your phone." The soft ember of a cigarette glowed red before dimming. Bellamy didn't smoke...

"You're a dick." I continued up his drive. "There was me thinking you were stalking me, and you were literally next-level stalking me."

"Keep your friends close and your enemies closer..."

I stopped and glared at him for a second. "Did it piss you off? Seeing me at Jackson's house all the time?" I hoped it made him livid. Nothing less than he deserved.

"When I knocked his ass out, I pictured him fucking you all those times you were over there, so yeah. I'd say it pissed me off."

I swear my ovary twitched a little, and the fact that it pissed him off appeased my own temper. "Karma."

"For him..." He took a drag from the cigarette. "Yeah."

My gaze drifted over the exposed strip of skin above his jeans. The streetlight overhead played over the deep V that disappeared beneath his beltline, and I hated that something so simple could cause my body to heat. "Why are you lying on the ground?"

"Why are you standing up?" He turned his head on the pavement, blowing out a thin stream of smoke. I took in the hard set of his jaw, the straight angle of his nose, and through the dim light, I barely noticed his red, swollen cheekbone.

He brought the cigarette back to his lips, his gaze never leaving me as I dropped to the asphalt on a sigh.

"You get in a fight?"

His gaze swung away, and he sat up, lifting a bottle to his lips. "Yep."

"Well, you're just indulging in all the bad things tonight." And I knew a little about indulging in things that were inevitably bad for me.

He might smoke, drink, and fight. And me? I was sitting here because I wanted to indulge in *him*. My own personal vice. I plucked the cigarette from his fingers, and before I could place it to my lips, he stole it back

"That doesn't look right on you. I don't like it."

"*I* don't care what you *don't* like."

He shifted on the pavement, resting his elbow over his knees as he looked at me. "You're a shitty liar."

Maybe I was. I brushed my fingers over his battered cheek and wondered who he had gotten into a fight with, why he hadn't turned up tonight... "You know, getting drunk alone is kinda tragic."

"Yeah. Well. Dayton is fucking tragic."

"It is," I whispered, a sudden tightness forming in my chest. I felt bad for him. This town was my temporary hell, but for him, it was a permanent home, and that sucked. "What are you doing after graduation?"

"Don't know. Maybe go to Alabama State." He paused. "What about you? You going to some rich-kid school?"

"Cornell."

"New York?"

"Yeah."

Silence stretched between us, filled only by the soft chirp of crickets and the hum of traffic on the highway in the distance. My entire body thrummed with awareness in his proximity, and I wanted to just reach out and touch him.

The bottom of the bottle clinked against the pavement,

then Bellamy' shifted, placing his warm palm on my leg. "Did you wear that skirt for me?"

The way his fingers played over my skin was like static teasing over me. "What if I did?"

His hand went to the back of my neck, pulling my face close to his. The hint of clove and whiskey washed over me, and the pull of his lips felt like a magnet, one I didn't even fight. "Then I'd tell you, you look hot," he said, his fingers knotting in my hair.

I wanted everything this boy had to offer, and that was bad. So bad... "And what if I didn't?" I whispered.

"Then, I wouldn't do this." His lips pressed to mine, his grip on my neck tightening as he shifted, lowering my back on the pavement as he settled himself between my thighs.

"Those poor choices still coming back to haunt you, baby girl?" His palm glided up my thigh, bunching my skirt, then stopped.

I gripped his shirt, the heat of his body almost burning me. I could no longer convince myself that Bellamy was a poor choice. "No."

He smiled against my mouth before biting me. "Good." Then his hand sank between my thighs, slipping beneath my panties.

One touch and I was already coming undone. My hands slammed down onto the pavement to steady myself as his fingers worked deeper.

"I've never wanted a girl the way I want you." His lips were at my throat, his free hand gripping my jaw. Everything about the way he touched me was possessive, animalistic, and every part of me craved it. Needed it... "And it pisses me the hell off." His teeth sank into my skin on a deep groan, and that in and of itself nearly sent me spiraling over the edge.

A rock song blared from his phone, and he ignored it, pressing his fingers deeper, harder, driving me closer and closer to losing all control. Then it rang again and again.

"Shit..." He pulled his phone from his pocket, his fingers still in me as he placed it to his ear. The noise of a kid wailing echoed into the night, and he yanked away from me.

Bellamy's brows pulled together. "Okay. I'll be there in...Shit. Just give me like twenty minutes, Arlo. Okay...." More wailing. "Yeah. I know. I'm leaving now. Twenty minutes, buddy."

He knocked the liquor bottle over when he stumbled to his feet. "I've gotta go get my brother."

I stood up, tugging down my skirt. This was so not dignified. "Okay."

Bellamy was already halfway through his yard.

"What are you doing? You're drunk," I called after him. "And it's one in the morning."

He turned around, continuing to walk and nearly tripping over the sidewalk. "That's why I'm walking."

"Really?" I threw out my hands. "Get in my car, you idiot." I turned and stalked across the street to my car, still in Nora's drive, Bellamy staggering behind me.

He directed me through another rundown neighborhood to another rundown house, leaving me in the idling car while he jogged toward the front door. When someone answered the door, I wonder why his little brother had called him instead of their parents.

A tiny shadow emerged, trudging down the drive alongside Bellamy.

Bellamy opened the door, ushering Arlo in and buckling him into the backseat while the kid stared at me, red eyes and wrinkled forehead. "Hey, Gas Station Lady." He crossed his arms over his chest on a huff.

Bellamy closed the door, then climbed back into the front.

"He seems pissed," I whispered as I reversed away from the shitty looking house.

"His friend pissed in the bed." Bellamy scrubbed a hand over his face. "That's why he called me crying like someone had tried to murder him. Cockblock…"

"What's a cock block, Bubba?"

Bellamy face-palmed on a hard sigh. "It's a…Jesus Christ…"

"It's a kid who wets the bed?" I offered.

"Why?"

I frowned and looked at Bellamy, who was no help. He just smiled and waved a hand through the air like I was supposed to magically come up with an explanation. "Well…why is your name Arlo? It just is." I turned onto the highway, driving past the swarm of cop cars at the 7-11.

"My name's Arlo because my mom liked it."

"And I like cockblock." I frowned. I'd literally just told a kid I liked cock block.

"Peehead sounds better than cock block," Arlo mumbled. "Cock block sounds like something you'd call a rooster." He huffed again. "I like peehead."

The kid was exhausting. "Okay, let's change it then. Peehead it is."

We drove through another of Dayton's rundown neighborhoods. I rapidly flipped through radio stations, trying to find something at one am on a Friday night that didn't have lyrics involving hoes and bitches.

"I need to know one thing, Gas Station Lady." Arlo blurted. "Are you gonna poop on my brother?"

Bellamy snorted, covering his mouth as he looked out the window.

I glanced in the rearview at the kid who was now scowling toward the front of the car. "Uh, no."

"You promise?"

"Yeah. It's not my thing."

"Bubba, you said she was gonna poop on you!"

"Arlo...Just leave it alone."

After a couple of minutes of awkward silence, I pulled up to Bellamy's house. An old pickup that wasn't there when we left was parked on the drive, and it was almost impossible to ignore the heavy breath Bellamy dragged in. "Go wait on the porch, okay?" he said, glancing over the headrest at Arlo. "Scooter's out there."

The kid unbuckled himself and hopped out of the car, darting through the dark yard to the side of the house.

"So," I said, lifting a brow at Bellamy. "I'm going to poop on you?"

His chin tucked to his chest on a short laugh. "The kid has to hang around Hendrix... Don't judge him."

"Enough said." I was still scarred from the turd picture he'd sent me.

He stared at me, his gaze dropping to my lips, and I thought, for a minute, he was going to kiss me again, but the front porch light cut on, and his hand shot to the door. "Later, baby girl."

And he was out, jogging across the yard toward the house.

At that moment, Bellamy didn't seem like the bad boy. He was a guy who was willing to walk twenty minutes through the slums of Dayton to get his little brother. Just because his friend had wet the bed.

## CHAPTER 26
## BELLAMY

WOLF BOUNCED a quarter across the table, ringing the cup then telling Hendrix to drink while I shot off a text:
**You're sure Arlo can stay again?**

**Miss Wright: For the third time. Yes. He's begged all day. They're having a good time.**

**Me: Thank you. I'll be there to pick him up at ten.**

"Who you over there texting, Bell?" Hendrix moved behind me, craning his neck to try to catch a glimpse of my screen. "Drewbers?"

"Fuck off, shithead." I closed out of my messages and slipped the device back into my pocket, then bounced a quarter into the cup and told Hendrix to drink.

"Happy Birthday in prison, Zepp." Wolf tipped back his beer.

Hendrix grabbed a Miller Lite from the cooler, cracking it open and pouring it into the sink while humming the birthday song.

This was shit. I bounced the quarter and rang the cup. "Drink, Hendrix."

He chugged his beer, then sank into the chair across from me. "Zepp said they didn't give him a cake. Such bullshit."

"It's a prison, dude," Wolf said.

Hendrix pushed his sleeves up and leaned back in the chair. "I told Zepp when I saw him today that we beat Harford's ass again. He said that was the best birthday present ever." Hendrix cackled, then fell silent, twisting the tab on his beer back and forth until it pulled loose.

We sat in silence for a minute, drinking and thinking. The doorbell rang, and Hendrix shot up to answer it. Girls giggled, and seconds later, Hendrix had them in the kitchen, plying them with cheap vodka. Music cut on in the living room as more people filtered in. And this was what we all needed, a distraction from the shitty reality of Dayton.

"Hey, Bell!" Hendrix shouted, holding a tequila bottle in one hand and whiskey in the other, pouring them both into a Mega Gulp cup. "Mary thinks you're hot." He waggled his eyebrows in the direction of one of the girls he'd escorted in.

"Congratufuckinglations, Mary," I said, barely glancing at her.

Wolf laughed, and Hendrix scowled before putting the liquor down and rushing to Mary's side to wrap his arm around her. "It's all right, Mary. I think you're hot." He shot another glare at me.

"Dude," Wolf slid the quarter across the table to me. "You just passed up a hot girl."

"That?" I thumbed back to the girl I probably would

have thought was hot before Drew. "Nah, man. That's nothing."

He lifted a brow. "That's not nothing? That's a pair of double D tits and a girl who I've heard has a suck like a vacuum."

And nothing about that appealed to me now. I scrolled through my phone, changing Drew's contact back to Baby Girl. Medusa didn't fit her, even if she was most likely going to seduce me, then fuck me up.

I shot off a text: **When are you going to come back over so we can finish what we started?**

More people came into the kitchen. Girls in tight dresses, guys who wanted a piece. The pungent smell of weed filled the air as some people passed a smoldering bowl back and forth.

**Baby girl: I don't know. That's twice you've left me hanging. I expected more, bad boy**

The balls on this girl. I took a sip of my drink, leaning back in the rickety kitchen chair.

**Me: We were already at third base in my head until cock block happened.**

**Baby Girl: Peehead actually**

**Baby girl: And just so you know, getting frisky on a driveway is not my regularly scheduled Friday night activity**

**Me: Yet…**

The thought of having my hand up her skirt, my lips on hers sent a drop of precum rolling to the tip of my hardening dick.

**Baby Girl: Maybe it was a limited time**

**offer. Maybe I only want to fuck you when I really hate you...**

Hate me. Like me. Those words seemed to be interchangeable these days. And I'd take that.

I tossed the quarter into the cup and told Wolf to drink.

**Me: On a scale of 1–10, how much do you hate me right now?**

**Baby Girl: You're sitting at about a 5. You need to up your game**

**Baby Girl: How much do you hate me right now?**

**Me: More than enough**

A girl in a short skirt perched on the table beside me. "Heard you beat up Bennett?"

"Yeah. Fuck off."

She frowned. Another girl took a seat across from Wolf. "Yeah, Nancy. He beat him up over that Barrington girl."

I glanced up just as she rolled her eyes. "Yeah, I did. You got a problem with it?" They both pushed up, shouldering their way into the living room. Girls got on my damn nerves.

**Baby Girl: Good. It wouldn't be half as much fun if you didn't.**

**Me: I want to see you.**

**Baby Girl: When?**

**Me: Now.**

Seconds ticked by. Those little bubbles popping up then disappearing.

**Baby Girl: I'm grounded.**

**Me: And?**

**Me: Rich girl with daddy issues who has a thing for the bad boy of Dayton...**

Bullshit, you'd pay attention to being grounded

**Baby Girl: Who said I have a thing for you?**

**Me: Your wet pussy when I had my fingers in it last night.**

**Baby Girl: And they say romance is dead...**

**Me: You should come to Hendrix's house. It would ruin his night....**

**Baby Girl: Maybe...**

Hendrix whacked me on the back of the head, then shoved a beer at me. "Drink, you hairy sack of balls." Then he wandered off into the living room, grabbing a random girl and grinding against her to the beat of the music.

"What you wanna bet, he pukes before midnight?" Wolf said, nodding to Hendrix, already stripping out of his shirt.

"Probably."

And then I pulled up the FindAFriend app on my phone, smiling when I saw that she hadn't blocked it. Because like I'd told her, she craved this chaos. And, damn, wasn't it shit she was moving to New York for college?

## CHAPTER 27

## DREW

ME: **Maybe...**

I'd texted that because one, a guy like Bellamy West was all too used to getting what he wanted from women, and two, I was terrified of where this was going. In two months' time, I wouldn't even be here. I'd accepted an offer from Cornell weeks ago. In New York. So, whatever it was between Bellamy and me...it couldn't be more than a bit of fun, some hot sex. And him inviting me to his best friend's house for a party, that was more than just "I want to fuck you." Any other party, sure, but amongst his boys. No.

I wasn't going...but I'd already changed into a short dress, lined my eyes with Dior's best eyeliner, and doused myself in Chanel No 5. Because I was an addict, and Bellamy was my sick little addiction. One with zero rationality. I fastened my Tiffany necklace, then checked the last text that had come through on my phone. One offering a plausible excuse to cover my newfound obsession.

**Diane: There's a party at Hendrix's**

tonight. They're always the best. Way better fun than Barrington.

Nora: No. No. No.

Nora: Tell her no, Drew.

Diane: You suck, Nora. Drew, Hendrix's parties are fun.

Diane: And we all know you have a thing for a bad boy.

Diane: AKA Bellamy

Nora: Don't encourage that shit, Diane.

Diane: Nora's just salty because we can't go to Bennett's parties anymore.

I didn't mention the fact that Bellamy had, in fact, already demanded I go to said party. Or that I was already dressed.

Me: Sounds fun. What time?

Nora: Hendrix. Hunt. The guy who licked the window, Drew. No!

I snorted.

Me: I mean, yes, but tell me you wouldn't...

Diane: What window? Is that code word for your va-jay-jay? OMG. NORA!!! Did you let him go down on you????????????

Nora: NO!

Me: We're going. It'll be fun. I'll pick you guys up at ten.

---

"I can't believe you made me come here." Nora sulked in

my passenger seat, staring through the windshield at Hendrix's delipidated house.

"Lighten up, Nora." Diane shoved out of the car, swigging wine from the bottle as she rounded the front.

I grabbed the tequila I'd stolen from my dad's office, then we followed her through the maze of cars scattered over the driveway.

Music thumped from inside, and the second we stepped onto the sagging porch, something inside smashed, followed by a loud cheer. Truly, I expected nothing short of complete chaos from a party at Hendrix's house.

The door swung open, and a very drunk girl wearing shorts and a bra staggered out, thrusting her drink at me.

I glanced at the half-empty cup with lipstick stains along the rim. "I'm good."

She shoved it against my chest, anyway, giving me no choice but to take it unless I wanted it all over the front of my dress. And then she stumbled to the railing and hurled over the porch.

I chucked the drink into the bushes.

Nora looked from her to me to the bottle of tequila in my hand, then she held out her hand. "I'll drive tonight."

I shrugged and dropped my keys into her waiting palm. If she wanted to try to do this sober...by all means. She could have at it.

We shouldered through the packed hallway and into the crowded living room. The place looked half derelict. The carpet was worn and stained, and wallpaper peeled from the corners of the ceilings. The smell of body odor, beer, and weed was repulsive. Did people actually live like this? I couldn't help but wonder if Bellamy did.

Hendrix stood on the coffee table, shirtless and with a Coors Light box on his head.

Several topless girls darted through the room as he performed some rendition of the Macarena.

A guy from my history class reclined back on the couch while a girl gave him a blow job. I'd never seen this kind of debauchery in my life.

On a frown, Nora gestured around the room. "You two wanted to come to this."

"Again." Diane took another swig of wine. "Lighten up, Nora. It's a party."

Hendrix froze mid-hip circle-thrust, wiping a hand over his heavily tattooed chest. "Nora the Explorer!" he cackled, then thrust his hips while singing: "I've gotta a ballsack loaded up with things and knickknacks, too. Anything I might need, I'll find inside of you—ballsack. Ballsack."

I didn't even know what to say.

Diane frowned. "Did he just make Dora the Explorer perverted?"

"Hell yeah, I did!" He grabbed his crotch and gave it a shake before hopping off the table. "Feel free to take a number. I'll make sure you get serviced before the night's over. Free oil checks with my dipstick O' orgasms." He pointed to a red plastic ticket dispenser in the corner, a sign attached to it that read: Take a number. A couple of girls actually went and took a ticket from that thing.

Of all the random shit to have... "Where the hell did you get that?" I asked.

"Stole it from the DMV."

Of course, he did.

"I don't get it. He's gross." Nora shook her head at the girls with their tickets. "I'm going to find some water." Then she walked off.

"Oh, she gets it." Diane laughed, eyeing Hendrix up and down like he was her next snack.

A warm hand landed on my side, sliding around to my stomach and sending a thrill zipping through my veins that only he could elicit.

"Aw, baby girl." Bellamy's breath heated my neck, and my heart leaped into an elated little sprint as he pulled my back to his chest. "Whatcha doing here?"

Diane gave me a knowing glance before slipping into the crowd.

I turned in his arms, meeting those honey-colored eyes. "Changed my mind. Figured I'd come and witness the depravity."

"Nah." He leaned into me, his fingers playing at my hips. "I don't think you changed your mind."

Seconds ticked by, bass thumping in the background while the dancing party goers around us faded into the background. The heat of his skin seeped through the material of my dress, and that intoxicating thrum hummed to life between us.

"Do your friends know you came here just to see me?"

"Is that what you think?"

"It's what I know." His teeth raked across his lip, then he laced his fingers through mine and led me through the crowded party. Not only did I follow without hesitation, but holding his hand felt far too normal, and I hated that I liked it so much.

We passed through the kitchen and onto a back porch decorated with Christmas lights and old street signs.

Wolf sat at a rickety card table surrounded by girls, and the second Bellamy stopped beside it, the attention of every girl there snapped to me.

"We're playing never have I ever," he said, his hand still firmly on mine as he shifted us around the table to an empty chair, promptly pulling me into his lap as though it were the most natural thing in the world. But it wasn't because everyone knew we were enemies, and this was a very public statement that we absolutely weren't.

Only I wasn't sure what we were, so I stiffened, glaring at him. A smirk pulled at his lips, that eyebrow ring hiking in a way that said he knew exactly what he was doing. He took the bottle of tequila from me and set it on the table.

Wolf snatched it, inspecting the bottle. "Holy shit, dude. This is Gran Patron..."

"So?" One of the girls said, shooting daggers in my direction.

"So? It's like four hundred bucks a bottle."

She huffed at that, rolling her eyes as she crossed her arms.

"Still just gets you drunk," I said. And I hated to admit it, but of all the bottles in my dad's liquor collection, this was probably the cheap stuff.

Wolf placed the bottle back on the table. "Rich-people drunk..."

Bellamy popped the cork from the tequila and passed it to me while Wolf's gaze pinged between us. Then he shook his head. "Fuck my life, dude. Just fuck it..."

"Fuck yourself, Wolf." Bellamy settled back in the chair, his hand landing on my bare thigh, burning me. "The rules are, the newest person to the table starts."

The girls glared at me like they'd slit my throat, given a chance.

"Fine." I fought a smile. "Never have I ever been arrested."

Wolf and Bellamy both drank. Bellamy glared at me as he took a swig.

"Never have I ever gotten off to the thought of someone at this table," he said. The bottle was already to his lips before he'd finished his sentence, his gaze boring into mine. "Don't lie, baby girl. I know you have."

I took the bottle from him, my fingers brushing over his before I drank. Because I had gotten off to the thought of him on numerous occasions. And the bastard knew it.

Wolf shook his head. "Never have I ever *fucked* someone at this table." Wolf drank, as did several of the girls, but much to my surprise, Bellamy didn't, and neither did I.

Wolf frowned at Bellamy. "Seriously, dude?" He waved a hand around the table. "No one?"

Bellamy shrugged his shoulder, his gaze aimed solely at me. "I'm picky."

"Jesus Christ. What kind of guy is picky with pussy?" He crushed the empty beer can, then tossed it to the corner of the porch as a group of people made their way into the yard. "There's no way you haven't pounded her." Wolf pointed at me. "No way."

"I mean, finger fucked, tongue fucked... but not fucked-fucked."

Heat engulfed my face, and I feigned a sudden fascination with the label on the tequila bottle as I elbowed Bellamy.

A girl pushed up from the table, disappearing inside.

We kept going through questions until there were only four of us left seated, and I had a slight buzz from the tequila.

After a never have I ever given or received a bathroom blowjob, Wolf glared at me through a drunken haze. "There is no way you're this pure, Paris Hilton." He hiccupped before slamming back against the seat. As much as he drank, he was going to throw up later.

"Or you're just asking the wrong questions," I said.

"Screwing in a Dayton High bathroom. Really? That's just gross."

On a snort, he staggered to his feet, grabbing the arm of the blonde beside him. "Congratu-fucking-lations! You win," he said, leading her into the house.

And then it was just Bellamy and me and the hum of noise from the party inside.

"Wow," I mumbled. "That is..." The words trailed off when Bellamy's eyes dropped to my lips. Something wild coursed through my veins, stirred to life by a combination of tequila and him. His smell, his touch, that devastating smirk that got me every time.

His hand trailed along the inside of my thigh while his lips brushed my neck. I may have only been tipsy, but his touch made me feel absolutely drunk.

"Do you like it when I touch you, baby girl?"

"I shouldn't," I breathed, leaning into his chest as his hand wandered farther.

"You're right." His teeth raked my throat. "You really shouldn't."

Shouldn't and wouldn't were a million miles apart where Bellamy West was concerned. I had hated him, wanted him, reasoned as to why he was a terrible idea, and every time it came back to basic animal instinct that was as natural as breathing.

There was nothing rational about it. He was awful, but the tequila made the voice of reason a muffled whisper I no longer cared for.

His finger skimmed an inch higher. I shifted, spreading my legs just enough to give him access.

"But you're just full of bad decisions, aren't you?" he mumbled against my neck.

"Only when you're involved."

"Good."

His fingertips brushed my cheek, and just when the heat of his lips touched mine, the back door banged open and people stumbled out.

On a groan, Bellamy tugged down my skirt, grabbed the tequila, then led me through the overgrown backyard to a ratty trampoline.

He hoisted himself over the springs, then pulled me up beside him. And the second my back hit the material, he was on top of me, fisting my hair and kissing me. His hands roamed over my body, bunching my skirt before his warm palms slid over my thighs. This was no longer simply me wanting to screw him and get whatever this was out of my system, and I was no longer resisting this because I thought I'd lose all dignity. This was me being terrified of losing all control.

I shifted, rolling on top of him and straddling his lap.

"You know, you never got me expelled."

"But, I did fuck up your life..." His hands grasped my hips, forcing my hips over him on a groan.

I wasn't sure if he had fucked up my life because, really, he'd somehow become a highlight in it.

"Do you know how long I've thought about having you?" His hands went to my ass, squeezing as his mouth worked down my throat to the top of my breasts.

"Since you had me in that van?"

"No. I've wanted to *fuck* you since I had you in that van."

Fuck me—have me. Two different things. One of which I never expected from him.

He flipped me over and shoved my dress up my thighs. With every touch, I melted for him, and that scared me because he already felt like so much more than simple lust to me.

"I've *wanted* you since you got me arrested."

"That's messed up."

"Of course it is..."

## CHAPTER 28

## BELLAMY

THE NOISE from the party had died down to a low hum of music. I stared up at the few stars that managed to break through the electric glow of the city, then sucked the taste of her off my fingers.

As much as I'd wanted to, I didn't try to fuck her. And it had absolutely nothing to do with our agreement. As far as I was concerned, that had been null and void since that party at Bennett's. Since I'd realized this was a hell of a lot more than needing a simple fuck. And that sent anxiety rippling through me because she was going to leave in a few months.

I swept the hair away from her neck, and she caught my hand, pulling it close to her face. "Never forget where you're from; someone will remind you," she read the words of my tattoo.

"DMX knows his shit."

I stared at the script inked on my wrist. That was my first tattoo—at sixteen. With Zepp and Hendrix, we all got the same lyrics. Because being from Dayton...no matter where we ended up in life, someone would remind us, if for nothing other than to kick us down.

"And the other one?"

"It's Linkin Park. 'All I want to do is be more like me and less like you.'" And that one I'd had inked just to remind myself I didn't have to turn out like my dad.

"Great song." Her finger traced over the ink.

"You don't look like the kinda girl who would listen to hard rock."

"No?" She smiled. "What am I supposed to listen to? Taylor Swift?"

"Probably. Or Katy Perry. Maybe Cardi B?" I laughed.

"I got you arrested, Bellamy. If that doesn't scream, In This Moment, then I don't know what does."

It totally did. "You're the black sheep of Barrington, you realize that? Listening to heavy metal. Hanging out with the bad boys from the other side of the tracks."

"I'll tell you a secret." Her fingers drifted along the inside of my arm, a small smile playing over her lips. "Those expensive boarding schools people send their kids to, thinking they'll make them perfect little clones of themselves—they're a breeding ground for daddy issues and rebellion."

"You don't say?"

She swept a hand down her body. "Their finest example. Because I really, *really* like bad boys."

"No, baby girl." I leaned over her and covered her lips with mine. "You only like *this* bad boy." My tongue dipped into her mouth, my body shifting on top of hers.

I thought there may be a round two, until Nora screamed Drew's name from across the yard.

Drew groaned. "Shit," she mumbled against my lips.

Footsteps crunched over the dry grass, then stopped. "Gross!"

Deepening the kiss, I raised my middle finger in the direction of Nora's voice.

"I can't find Diane." Nora huffed, and Drew shoved me off. "She texted telling me to leave her here. And I have a curfew."

"I'm sure she's fine." Drew sat up, shaking the pine straw from her hair, a concerned expression wrinkling her brow. "Where's Hendrix?"

Nora rubbed at her temples. "I swear, between the two of you..."

"Oh, come, Nora," I wrapped an arm around Drew. "Get off your high horse. You lost your V-card to Wolf freshman year."

Drew glanced from me to Nora with wide eyes. "Oh my God. You did not, Nora?"

"She did..." Was it my business to spread? No. But it was obvious that Nora wanted Drew to have nothing to do with me. Which made her a hypocrite, and I was an asshole, so...

Nora flipped me off. "I'm taking your car, Drew. Come on."

I grabbed Drew's wrist, then bit her neck. "Stay here."

"I'm not fucking you in some room of Hendrix's brothel house."

"Fine. You can fuck me out here."

"No fucking in the proximity of Hendrix's gross house."

Nora grumbled. "Are you leaving or staying?"

"She's staying," I said, threading my fingers through Drew's hair and slamming my lips over hers.

She nipped at my lip, then pushed me away. Her gaze bounced between Nora and me. "I'll stay and make sure Diane's okay."

Bullshit.

"No, you're staying because of him. But whatever." Nora turned and made her way toward the house. "Just come get your car from my house tomorrow. If this knight in perverted armor can manage to drop you off..." She disappeared onto the porch.

"She's not wrong," I said, slinging my legs over the side of the trampoline and jumping to the ground. "You're staying because of me."

I held out my hand to help Drew down.

She took it with a roll of her eyes. "I'm not fucking you."

"You already said that." I led her onto the back porch and into the kitchen.

"Do I need to find Diane, open a door, and throw condoms at her head?"

"I don't know. Do you?"

"If she's with Hendrix, yes!"

A couple of girls were asleep on the couch, someone laid passed out on the steps amongst a pile of beer cans. This was how parties usually ended here. But it was better they were here than on the streets.

We made it to the first landing before we heard the squeak of springs and thud of Hendrix's headboard banging the wall. Moans trickled into the hall, followed by the smack of skin against skin.

"Call me, Big Papa."

"Too late." Drew groaned. "She's getting chlamydia and pregnant."

Placing an arm around her shoulder, I dragged her down the hall. "Believe it or not, Hendrix is safe. He's got a fishbowl of condoms on his nightstand. Germs freak him out."

"The guy who sent me a picture of his shit?"

"Yep."

I opened the door to Zepp's room and flipped the light switch. It felt weird coming in here. Not that he would give a shit. The first time I visited Zepp in prison, he told me I could move in if I wanted to. Keep Hendrix in check, get away from my old man, but I couldn't leave mom and Arlo.

It just made everything feel empty when I couldn't ignore that he was gone.

Drew stopped by the nightstand, glancing at the picture of Monroe and Zepp. "Is that Zepp?"

"Yeah."

"He looks so much like Hendrix."

I glanced at the picture. "He's not as insane as him."

"Who the hell is?"

And that was a good question. Not wanting to go down that depressing-ass road, I pushed the thoughts of Zepp away. I pulled my shirt over my head and tossed it at her. "Wanna sleep in that?"

"Can you unzip me?" She gathered her hair to the side.

"You know this is wrong?" I slowly inched the zipper down, exposing the skin of her back while making a point to breathe over her neck.

"What is?" she whispered.

I slid one shoulder off, then the other, and the material fell to a puddle around her high heels. My dick swelled. My balls drew tight. "Making me do this when I can't fuck you." I could. If I really wanted to. I had no doubt I could talk her into it, but I respected her more than that.

"Well, I can't undo my own zipper, can I?" She pressed her naked back to my chest, then turned to face me as she backed away. All curves in nothing but lace underwear and high heels.

I slipped out of my jeans while I stared at her nipples, hard and inviting. It took every damn thing inside me not to grab her by the hips and throw her onto the bed.

"Behave," she said.

I flopped down onto the mattress, thinking about how this girl was going to break my dick. "You've got your tits out, and you're asking me to behave?"

With a smirk, she pulled my shirt over her head, then took off her shoes before hitting the light switch. "Better?"

"No. I liked it better with your tits out."

"Of course you did." She crawled into bed beside me. "Don't sulk."

An awkward silence stretched between us in the darkness. What in the hell was I supposed to do here? Tell her goodnight and roll over?

I swiped a hand down my jaw, then turned on the pillow to look at her. "This is me, not fucking you."

She laughed, and holy shit, she was gorgeous when she smiled like that. "You're doing so good."

I wanted to kiss her. But kissing would make my dick even harder. Then I'd want to touch her. Then I'd need to fuck her.

"Is this a first for you? Having a girl in bed and not screwing her..."

"Having a girl in a *bed* is a first, baby girl." Taking a girl to bed said things; it was too personal, and it gave them every opportunity to try to stay. You get one in the back of a car, a bathroom, a closet—they had no choice but to leave.

"Is this where you confess you're secretly saving yourself for marriage?"

"Yeah—no."

"So, what do you do? Just screw them in a random van? Whose van was that?"

"My neighbor's, and anywhere but a bed."

"We've been on a bed before, so you're full of shit."

"A Barrington prick's bed doesn't count."

"Uh-huh. Don't worry, I won't tell anyone."

She went to kiss me, and I grabbed her throat. Because if she wanted to torture me, I was going to torture her. "If you really don't want me to fuck you, you can't kiss me in this bed."

A slow smile inched over her face. "Not even one kiss?"

I pressed a quick one to her lips, then adjusted my dick. "Now go to sleep, or I'm fucking you."

On a laugh, she threw her leg over mine, then laid her palm on my chest, like it was the most natural thing in the world. And I stared at the ceiling, realizing I was more than officially screwed.

I was in bed.

With a girl.

And I was okay that I wasn't going to fuck her because I liked her that damn much.

## CHAPTER 29

## DREW

THE BANG of pots and pans in the kitchen woke me way too early the next morning.

A heavy arm lay across my waist. The rasp of Bellamy's breath soothed me, and his firm grip on my body was reassuring and protective.

Another loud bang came from downstairs, and Bellamy groaned, tightening his hold on me.

"What is Hendrix doing?" I grumbled, wincing against the bright light spilling through the threadbare curtains.

"Who knows." He pressed a kiss to the back of my neck, and a comforting warmth crawled through my veins. "It's best not to ask, though."

I didn't want to get out of this bed, but I was grounded and had no idea when my dad might pop up. Plus, Nora had my car. "Can you take me home? Nora took my car."

"Yeah. I gotta go get Arlo, anyway." He threw back the covers, then shifted off the bed. My gaze trailed over his broad back and his ass when he leaned over to grab his jeans. "I guess I'll need to take your friend home, too. Hendrix's ass sure can't."

I got dressed, then I did the full-on walk of shame through Hendrix's decaying house. Only I hadn't had a one-night stand.

We'd slept in the same bed, and Bellamy hadn't tried it on once. He'd even told me not to kiss him so he wouldn't try, and I wasn't quite sure what to make of that.

We rounded the corner into the living room. Dishes clattered in the kitchen before something shattered.

"What the hell are you doing, dipshit?" Bellamy shouted.

I followed him into the kitchen, immediately covering my eyes when I saw Diane on her knees in front of Hendrix.

"What the hell, man?" Bellamy turned, pressing my face into his chest and shielding me from the sight of Hendrix face-fucking my friend. "You've got a bedroom," Bellamy said.

"And you've got a house..."

"Seriously?"

"The kitchen's way better," Hendrix said on a cackle. "Can you leave so she can finish?"

Bellamy started pushing me toward the living room.

"She'll be done in five—no two minutes," Hendrix called. "Damn. Where'd you learn *that*..."

---

My stomach dropped when Bellamy pulled up outside my house, and a new Maserati sat in the drive. My dad was back early. And I was supposed to be grounded.

I didn't care about my dad's punishments for the most part, and neither did he, so long as there was at least the perception that I was actually following them.

I tossed my head back against the seat and groaned. "Shit."

Bellamy leaned forward, staring at the driveway. "So, the asshole went with a black one this time?"

"Apparently so. Think I can convince him I went for a morning run?" I asked, attempting to cover up that I was probably about to get put on house arrest.

Bellamy's gaze skimmed over me. "In that dress. Nah. Don't think so, baby girl." He rubbed his thumb over my lip, smearing what little lip stain was probably left. "Shame. You look fucked, even though you weren't."

"Just to add fuel to the fire," I mumbled as I reached for the door. "Pray for me."

He caught my chin between his fingers, slamming his mouth to mine before his teeth sank into my lips. "I don't pray."

I placed a finger on the silver crucifix he always wore. "Could've fooled me." Then I got out, flushed and breathless.

I opened the door to my father sitting on the bottom steps of the stairwell. Lips flat. Dress sleeves rolled up, and hands folded over his slacks. He pushed up without a word and crooked a finger, telling me to follow him as he went into the kitchen.

I was not scared of my father, but at that moment, I was.

I'd been fired for dealing weed, suspended twice, crashed his car, and been grounded. And now, he caught me sneaking back in wearing my clothes from the night before on a Sunday morning. It didn't really get much worse.

He yanked a chair from the island. "Sit." Then rounded the other side.

I took a seat, perching on the edge as tension set my spine ramrod straight.

"Where were you?" he asked.

"At a friend's house."

"A friend's house. That's what we call it these days?" His nostrils flared. "You are grounded, Drucella."

"I was studying late?" Shit, that lie was weak, but what was I going to say? I was at some brothel house in Dayton with Bellamy West.

"Yes. I'm so sure." He looked at me with the usual, loathed disappointment, laced with a healthy dose of disgust. "Where is your car?"

"Nora borrowed it. Hers broke down." Another crappy lie.

"Well, when *Nora* brings it back, you will give the keys to me."

"What? You're taking my car away?"

"Yes."

"How will I get to school?"

"The school bus."

Oh. My. God. I honestly didn't think there was anything left for him to do to make my life worse. Turns out rock bottom has a sewer.

"You will go to school. You will come home." His finger jabbed against the counter. "And you will do nothing else. I've evidently not been hard enough on you, and from your behavior, I can see Black Mountain was nothing but a waste. Not even *they* could manage to instill a sense of decency in you." He went to move away from the counter. "But I sure as hell will, Drucella. If it kills me."

Then he left the room.

I didn't even know what to say. So, I called the one person who could possibly save me from this: my mother.

Irina was nothing if not the typical rich, absent parent,

but she tried to act like she cared by way of material things. Like cars.

An hour later, I heard my dad shouting on the phone from my room. With a smile, I put my headphones in and let her work her magic.

I flopped back onto the bed, and though everything was crap, I couldn't help but think about Bellamy, of waking up wrapped in his arms.

The way he kissed me like I was more than just some girl he wanted to screw, some girl he'd made a deal with. I could no longer pretend that was the case because we'd slept in a bed together and he hadn't even tried to touch me.

I couldn't quite work out when we'd gone from hating each other to this, but I wanted it. And that scared me because the things we really want have the power to break us. And Bellamy West had heartbreak written all over his beautiful body.

## CHAPTER 30

### BELLAMY

NIKKI'S FRIENDS glared at Drew when she climbed out of my car on Monday. I threw my arm around Drew's shoulder as we started toward the school's entrance, falling in step with the other grumbling students. "You got a fan club, baby girl."

"Nikki is totally going to come at me with a razor blade," she mumbled.

"I seriously doubt that." I had laid a claim on Drew. Which meant everyone knew not to mess with her.

We passed by the security guard at the front door, then hooked it to the right. "When is your dad giving you your car back?"

"Pretty sure never. I'm surprised he hasn't slapped a chastity belt on me at this point. Or acquired a house arrest anklet." She stopped at her locker, turning the combination lock. "Thanks for giving me a lift."

"Would've been better had you given me road head on the way in, but, whatever..."

She threw a smirk over her shoulder. "You'll make me choke and ruin my mascara."

"I like it when you choke on it."

She shut her locker door, then leaned back against the metal. I stepped closer, bunching the material of her skirt in my hand. "Did you wear this skirt for me, baby girl?"

"What if I did?"

"Then, I'd do this." I slammed my lips over hers, gripping her hips and pushing her up the locker wall until her legs wrapped around my waist. This was a show. Me staking a final claim. "You make my dick so hard."

"What are you doing?" she breathed. "Everyone is looking." But her legs never loosened on my waist, and she made no effort to separate her lips from mine.

"No shit. That's the point, baby girl."

A whistle sounded. "Put her down," Smith blew her whistle again. "This ain't no fraternity house hot-tub jacuzzi."

My fingers dug into Drew's thighs before the whistle sounded again.

"You nasty-ass kids..."

I put Drew down, and when I turned around, Smith had her demerit pad out, scribbling away. She ripped the sheet off and handed it to me.

"Mr. Nasty." Then she filled out another form and passed it to Drew. "And Miss Nasty."

When she walked away, Drew waved the paper in my face. "You're a terrible influence."

I draped an arm over her shoulder and started toward her classroom. "Be sure to send your father my regards." I smacked her ass before she ducked through the doorway, then I went back to my locker to put away my stuff.

Wolf peeked out from behind his open locker door, nodding toward Drew's classroom. "Dude. What the hell was that?" The metal door banged closed, and he leaned a shoulder against it. "You screwed her, didn't you?"

"No."

One of his bushy brows lifted. "You jab her more than twice, *you're* fucked."

Hendrix popped around my shoulder, out of nowhere. "Twice? What the fuckity-fuck, Wolf? You don't go back for seconds." He punched Wolf's head, and Wolf socked him in the stomach.

Hendrix doubled over, coughing out, "That's as good as the Golden Rule. One and done."

I shoved him away from me. "I haven't fucked her."

Drew was so much more than a fuck.

"Because you're weak." Hendrix cackled, twisting the combination to his locker. "You've had weeks, and you haven't speared her with your Moby Dick harpoon? I would have already had her gargling my balls, then I'd have hit it and quit it."

He yanked a book out of his locker, and everything else inside came tumbling out in a cascade of papers and trash. He bent over, grabbed his textbooks, and tossed them back inside before kicking the rest of the shit to the side with his shoe.

With a shake of my head, I pushed past him.

I made it halfway down the hall before Wolf caught up to me. "That crap back in the hall was a statement, dude."

"I know. It was supposed to be."

Wolf stopped mid-stride, dropping his chin on a shake of his head. "Ah, hell. Here we go again..."

## CHAPTER 31

## DREW

"RUMOR HAS IT, Bellamy West is your boyfriend," Nora said, falling in step beside me as I cut through the crowded corridor.

"What?"

"And I've never known Bellamy to have a girlfriend."

I shook my head. "We're not...together."

Were we? No. We hadn't even had sex. And if there was one thing a guy like Bellamy would usually qualify for, it was sex with no strings. Somehow, though, I'd gotten tangled in the strings without the sex.

It had been two days since Bellamy had kissed me in the hallway, and I'd noticed a shift in the status quo of Dayton High. Gone were the vicious glares. Instead, people refused to look at me, shifting to get out of my way like one brush with me might be a death sentence.

That could only mean one thing. They thought I was his, even if I didn't.

"They're just rumors, Nora."

"Whatever you want to tell yourself."

I cut into the bathroom, saying I'd meet her in the cafeteria.

That was a mistake.

When I came out of the stall, my pulse instantly ticked up. Nikki and two of her friends were leaning against the sinks.

Nikki was Dayton through and through, and I really wasn't.

My hand slipped into my purse, fingers wrapping around the can of mace I always kept in there because...razor blades. "Are you really going to jump me in a bathroom over a guy, Nikki? Bit cliché, don't you think?" My voice sounded remarkably strong, considering the internal panic. A hundred different scenarios ran through my head, from a broken nose right through to getting shanked and bleeding out on a gross bathroom floor.

"You're nothing but a Barrington whore." A sneer pulled at her lips. "Bellamy will get bored of fucking you soon enough."

"Great. Then why are you in here?"

She took a step toward me, and all my fears were confirmed when she pulled out a small knife. Her friends moved to grab me, and I don't even know what happened next.

Blind panic. Survival instinct. Something.

I sprayed mace like it was the perfume counter at Macy's. Somewhere in my flailing around, a sharp sting sliced over my arm. I had no idea if Nikki had actually gone for me or just caught me in the shitshow of my chaos because I had my eyes closed for half of it.

Stumbling out of the bathroom, I dropped the mace back into my bag and noticed the trickle of blood creeping from the small cut left by the blade. I robotically walked to the cafeteria, grabbed a napkin, and pressed it to my bloody arm in a bit of a shock.

Nora looked at me wide-eyed when I fell onto the stool beside her. "What the hell happened?"

"Nikki happened."

"Wait. She cut you?" Diane looked horrified. It was Dayton. Even I, the girl who two months ago, was enrolled in one of the most expensive prep schools in the country, wasn't really surprised, so why was she?

"Uh, I'm not sure. There were pepper spray and flailing, but she definitely pulled a knife, like before that."

"You pepper-sprayed her?" Nora snorted. "You carry pepper spray?"

"Well, yeah, it's Dayton, Nora!"

Diane cleared her throat and nodded across the cafeteria. "Word of advice, you might want to tell Bellamy *before* he finds out."

On a glare, I peeled off the foil lid from my crappy, grape Push-Pop. "He's not my keeper. We aren't even together. Besides, I already blinded her."

She and Nora exchanged loaded glances.

"Drew," Nora inhaled a very deep breath. "Again. He doesn't date. And he's dating you, whether you realize it or not. He's not stable."

Diane nodded. "I mean, they burned this girl's car once, simply because she broke up with Hendrix and called him an idiot."

"Jesus Christ." What the hell had I gotten myself into? Oh, wait, I decided to lust after the guy who broke into my house and almost got me off with the baseball bat he used to smash the place up. Crazy, crazy, crazy. I actually feared for Nikki a little bit, and I loathed the girl.

Nora took a bite from her apple. "You need to go to Brown before he finds out. Get her kicked out."

Diane touched my hand. "Bellamy being a psycho aside, what if she'd actually stabbed you, Drew?"

"Fine. If they take my mace away, I'm going to be pissed."

So I went to Brown, mainly because I was not about getting shanked, but also because I knew, firsthand, the extremes Bellamy would go to for revenge. I didn't want him getting into trouble because Nikki was a crazy bitch.

That boy wasn't getting arrested for anyone but me.

By the end of the day, the school was rife with gossip that Nikki had been expelled.

Great. Glad it was that easy for her. Not that I was bitter or anything.

Hendrix glared at me when I walked up to detention with Bellamy.

Mrs. Smith waved me over. "Good afternoon, Miss Nasty." She passed me a clipboard and made me sign my name. "Go sit down and reflect on why the hell you let that boy stick his tongue down your throat in the middle of the hallway. And you, Mr. Nasty..."

She handed Bellamy the clipboard. "You go sit down and think about why you think it's okay to disrespect Miss Nasty like that."

He scribbled his name over the line.

"I wasn't feeling very disrespected," I said under my breath. Of course, she heard.

"Oh, you were feeling something all right." She snatched the clipboard from Bellamy, then chugged her thermos. "His arousal all pressed into your woman parts."

"Woman parts." Hendrix shoved past us on his way to the back table. "More like his Arby's sauce all up in your roast beef sandwich."

I rolled my eyes. "Do you have to call it a roast beef sandwich? The imagery is just…"

Bellamy stopped at the end of the table and whacked Hendrix in the face with his notebook.

Wolf chuckled and sank to the stool across from Bellamy. "You're gonna give him a head injury."

"He is a head injury, Wolf." Bellamy glanced at Hendrix and threw up his hands. "What do you want me to do? Punch him in the nuts next time he says shit like that?"

Hendrix glared across the table. "Did you just threaten to damage my baby batter mixer?"

"Wow. What Diane sees in you…" I mumbled.

"A nine-inch cock and a tongue that works magic. I know that's hard to imagine with Bell's one-inch Vienna sausage…" Hendrix grabbed at his crotch. "But I'm hung like a camel. Pretty sure I have a future in porn."

"Congratulations?"

"I'd call myself Kamikaze Kummer because there's no pussy I won't bomb dive."

Bellamy grabbed my hand, yanking me up from the table while he snatched his books up. "I can't deal with this neurotic shit anymore today."

"How the hell did you even become friends with Hendrix?"

"I blocked it out." He said before sinking to a stool a few tables over.

"Like a traumatic event?"

"Exactly."

The late-afternoon sun poured through the cafeteria

windows like a greenhouse, and with no air conditioning in here, the air felt stuffy and oppressive. I shrugged out of my jacket before taking a seat beside him.

"What happened to your arm?" He glanced down at the bright-blue Band-Aid across my forearm.

"Um..."

"Holy shit, Bell," Hendrix shouted.

I glanced across the cafeteria to where one of the cheerleaders was now sitting beside the idiot.

"Psycho Bitch got expelled for trying to shank Psycho Bitch Number Two!"

When I looked back at Bellamy, his jaw was tight. Eyes narrowed.

I flipped Hendrix off. "Shank makes it sound so overdramatic."

"Seriously?" Bellamy reached for my arm, and I yanked it away. "You thought you'd just not mention that?"

Years of spoiled-brat syndrome kicked in, and I bristled at the idea that I had to tell him anything. "Did I need to?"

"Don't know, Drew? Do you think you do?" He ripped off the Band-Aid, skimming a finger over the razor-thin cut.

"I handled it," I said. Not well, but still.

"And Drewbers pepper-sprayed her?" Hendrix cackled. "Sprayed her like a cat, Bell! Ole' Salami Tits got seasoned with mace."

I groaned and pointed at Bellamy. "Don't say a word."

His gaze held mine prisoner for a beat before he opened his textbook. "Next time someone does shit like that, you better tell me."

I fought the little spark of indignation that rose in me, and I should have kept my mouth shut. "Or what?"

All he did was smirk.

God, he was annoying. "Fuck you."

## CHAPTER 32

## BELLAMY

THAT EVENING, Hendrix and I crept through the dark alleyways running between the trailers until we came to Nikki's.

I dropped my backpack to the gravel, then rifled through it for the two glass bottles of gasoline and the tattered cloths.

Hendrix snatched one from my hand, immediately cramming the rag into the neck. "I'm doing this because I hate Nikki and I like burning shit, not because I like Drew."

"Whatever, man."

Was what we were about to do shit? Absolutely, just like half the crap we did. But Nikki had pulled a knife on Drew, and like hell was she getting away with that.

Hendrix took a lighter from his pocket. "Why are you doing it, Bell?"

Because I liked Drew. "Because we have a reputation to uphold, asswipe."

Hendrix struck the flint, the flicker of the flame catching the cock of his brow. "She must suck a good dick."

Sometimes I hated him.

We lit the bombs, hurling them across the trailer park before we took off running. We made it over one chain-link fence before the flash of fire lit up the night sky.

Hendrix cackled as we booked it toward Wolf's, quickly scaling the ladder that always rested against the side of his house, then rolling ourselves onto the roof.

"Burn, baby, burn." Wolf laughed from his lawn chair, taking a puff from the joint permanently attached to his lips.

I collapsed into one of the other tattered chairs while Hendrix rummaged through the mini-fridge. "Aw, man. All you have is Natty Lite. That stuff tastes like piss." He slammed the fridge door and sank to the seat beside me, cracking one open anyway.

We sat there for a moment, basking in the glow of Nikki's burning car. I could hear her screaming at the top of her lungs from here.

"It's gonna explode," Wolf said with a wicked grin. "Any minute."

Hendrix leaned back in his chair, inhaling a deep breath. "Nothing like the smell of a car bomb to make you feel alive."

And there was no doubt—never had been—we were a little screwed up.

The red and yellow flames reached over the trailers' tops, sending a spiral of gray smoke up against the dark sky.

I didn't do this for my reputation. I did it because I was pissed. Few things in life enraged me: my shithouse dad, someone screwing with my family, and evidently, now, someone messing with my girl.

Wolf sat up. His narrowed gaze stared out over the trailer park. "Oh, shit. Here she comes."

About that time, I noticed a shadow moving down the dirt path.

"Bellamy!" Nikki shouted. "I know that was you!"

She stormed up to Wolf's trailer and stopped, hands on her hips as she stared up at his roof. "I'm going to send your ass to jail. Just like she did."

Hendrix cackled, then hurled his half-full beer can over the roof, right at her. "Shut up, Pepperoni Nips. We've been sitting here, drinking. All night."

"Bullshit!"

Wolf sighed. "You got any video footage to prove it?"

A loud boom echoed through the night, the glow of fire flashing like a mini bomb.

Nikki spun around, hands on her head. "I cannot believe you, assholes!"

"Maybe it was that kid, Dickey," I said. "You know, the one whose dick you sucked to start rumors about Drew."

I glanced over the edge of the roof, and God, I wished there was more lighting because I'd love to see the look on Nikki's face right now.

"Which, by the way, thanks for all that. Had you not tried to set her up, I would have missed out on the best blow jobs I've ever had. The girl has no gag reflex."

"You are so..." An angry growl bounced off the trailers.

The electric-blue glow of a phone screen shined through the dark. This girl was really about to call the cops? Oh, no. That's not how shit worked in Dayton, and she knew it.

"Do you really wanna go down that road, Nikki?" I said, and she froze, glancing up at me.

"Snitches get stitches," Hendrix said, shooting a sinister smile at me.

"Come on, Nikki," Wolf said. "I'm sure whoever did it only meant it in fun." He bit back a laugh.

"Kinda like I'm sure you only pulled a knife on Drew for good fun, huh?"

Moments of silence passed, the soft crackle of the fire the only noise.

"You're such a loser," Nikki said, dropping her phone to her side before storming back to her trailer, ranting.

The guys barked out laughs. Hendrix grabbed another beer from the fridge then sank down beside me, glaring. "Reputation, my asshole, Bell."

"Like I said," Wolf flicked his roach over the side of the house. "One doomed motherfucker."

And maybe I was.

---

I left Wolf's in time to get home before mom had to leave for work.

As soon as I cut the engine, I could hear dad shouting. Shit breaking.

Arlo was on the front porch, ears plugged and crying.

Anger built like a ticking time bomb as I jogged up the wooden steps. I went to kneel beside him, but something loud banged inside, and the scream that came from my mom made my blood run cold.

"Stay right here, Arlo," I said already on my way through the door.

From the entrance, I could see Mom on all fours, crying and begging him to stop.

Before I could get to her, Dad took a chair to the back of her head, and she crumpled to the floor.

That rage that had always stayed below the surface, bubbling and heating, waiting to explode, erupted with the force of a millennia-old, dormant volcano. With utter destruction and fury...

The flashing lights from the ambulance bounced around the destroyed living room.

**Me: Can you come get Arlo from my house? Please. Like right now?**

I'd sent that to Drew because Nora's family wasn't at home, and I had no one else I could trust with him. And I trusted her. I fucking trusted her...

"Son, put down the phone." Jacobs's boot tapped the broken glass strewn across the floor.

Under normal circumstances, I would have sent the next text while glaring at that prick, but nothing about the situation that brought the cops to my house was normal.

A text from Drew popped up on my screen: **Yeah. Is everything okay?**

And I set the phone beside me on the couch.

One of the other officers brought Arlo back into the room and placed him beside me.

He sniffled, wiping at his tears with his sleeve before he latched onto me. "You can't take him to jail. No one else will take care of me." The pitiful sob that followed practically yanked my heart clean out of my chest.

"It's fine, buddy. They just need to ask me some questions."

The other officer glanced at me, and I could see it all over his face. His hands were tied, and he didn't want to have to do it, but they had a protocol. Domestic violence case—no conscious witnesses. I was going to jail.

He pulled Jacobs to the side and exchanged a few words

while Arlo cried on my shoulder. He'd seen shit no kid should have to see.

"Is Momma gonna be okay?"

"Yeah. She'll be fine, buddy. They just have to make her feel better for a few days."

CHAPTER 33

DREW

IT HAD BEEN FIVE MINUTES, and he hadn't answered me.

I would have left as soon as he texted me because for him to ask me to get his brother—I had no idea why he hadn't asked Nora, or Wolf, or even Hendrix, but I knew how important Arlo was to Bellamy. He wouldn't ask if he weren't desperate—but I couldn't find where my dad had hidden the car keys. I tried to call Nora, but she didn't pick up.

So, I ended up walking to the Jet Pep across from the subdivision and catching the bus before walking two blocks to Bellamy's house.

As soon as I rounded the street corner, the red and blue flashing lights came into view, and I panicked. I had no idea what went on in Bellamy's house, but whatever it was, I knew it was bad enough that Nora had to watch Arlo when Bellamy went to jail.

He didn't trust his dad with Arlo...and he texted me to please come to get him. And now the cops were there...I took off down the street, rushing past the patrol cars in his drive, and stopping when I saw the broken window in the front.

I had never been in any situation like this and had no idea what to do. Was I supposed to knock on the door or not?

I went up the steps, unable to ignore the small spots of what looked to be blood on the concrete. Then I knocked on the door, my heart banging in my chest.

It swung open to a middle-aged police officer. "Drew Morgan?"

"Yeah."

He stepped outside and quietly closed the door. Then he placed a hand on my shoulder and moved me a few feet away from the entrance. "Once you get the kid in the car, go ahead and leave. He's seen enough, and I really don't want him to see his brother carted out in cuffs."

In cuffs? Bellamy was being arrested...

"Ma'am? Did you hear me?"

"I don't...I don't have a car. I took the bus here."

"Shit..." He turned his face to the walkie-talkie on his shoulder. A beep sounded. "Can you send back-up? I need to escort a young lady and a child home."

"Ten-four, Robins."

I stared back at the flashing lights. What in the hell was going on?

"I'll take you home," the officer said. "You don't need to be walking around these streets at this time of night."

Part of me didn't want to ask, but... "What happened?"

"Domestic dispute." He glanced back at the door. "The mom got it pretty bad, but I think she'll be all right. And if I'm being honest, Dan got what he deserved."

Static crackled over his radio. And from that snippet of information, I gathered that Bellamy had beaten his dad, probably for hitting his mom. Yet, he was the one being arrested. Anger coursed through me as I thought of Bellamy being taken to jail for defending his mom. It was wrong.

"Five minutes, Robins." The officer nodded before walking back inside.

I waited outside on the step, staring at the broken glass on the driveway while a crippling sense of pity for Bellamy and his brother surged through me.

Eventually, another patrol car pulled onto the street, and Officer Robins walked out with Arlo, his face tear-stained and red, and a ratty backpack slung over his shoulders.

He sniffled when he looked up at me. "Hey, Miss Drew."

My chest squeezed when I placed my hand on his little head. "Hey, Arlo."

The cop opened the car door, and I followed Arlo into the back seat.

I really hoped my dad wasn't home to see a cop car pull up in the drive, but even if he were, surely to God, when he saw Arlo, he just wouldn't say anything.

The engine cranked, and the patrol car pulled away.

Arlo quietly cried, looking out the window at the passing streets of Dayton. He was already conditioned to think that this was normal, and that was heartbreaking. Worse, from the little I'd glimpsed of Bellamy with him, I knew he tried hard to give his little brother something better. And instead, he got this.

"Where do you live, Miss Morgan?" The officer asked.

"2112 Barrington Cove."

He rolled to a stop at the four-way.

"Barrington Cove?" He glanced over his shoulder with pinched brows. Like he didn't believe me.

"Yeah. Is...that a problem?"

"There's a bus in Barrington?"

"My father and I are having authoritative differences that involve my lack of a car."

I could only imagine what he must be thinking. A Barrington girl turning up on the bus to get a kid from a domestic dispute.

"He doesn't like the guys I date." That one statement pretty much covered it.

He pressed the gas. "Ah. Okay..."

Silence filled the car, intermittently broken by Arlo's sniffles. I rubbed his back the entire ride through Dayton.

When the patrol car swung into Barrington, the scenery changed entirely. Everything perfect and polished.

Arlo plastered his face to the window. "Are those castles?"

"Not quite."

The officer dropped us off, and thankfully, my dad wasn't back yet.

"Thank you for the ride, officer," I said.

"No problem."

"Do you know when Bellamy will be out?" I asked.

*When*, not if, because surely, they wouldn't keep a kid for defending his mom. Then again, I didn't know exactly what had happened.

"Twenty-four hours is typical." He looked at me for a moment, then gave a curt nod. "You have a good evening, miss."

"Thanks."

He drove off, and I herded Arlo toward the front door.

His eyes widened as he walked into the house, sheepishly lingering in the foyer.

What the hell did I do with a small child who had just been through things I couldn't imagine.

"You want a Push-Pop?" I asked. It was all I could think of.

"No. I'm not hungry." His bottom lip poked out, then quivered. "I don't want Bellamy to go to jail, Miss Drew. And I want my momma to be okay."

I didn't know what to do, but the second he started crying, I scooped him up and took him to the couch, holding him while his skinny shoulders shook.

"They'll be okay, Arlo. Your brother loves you. He wouldn't leave you for long." I wrapped him in a blanket, turned on the TV, and changed it from the news to *SpongeBob*.

After a few minutes, he drew in a heavy breath, then rolled out of my lap and pressed back on the sofa. "This is squishy." He bounced back again, then turned and face-planted the cushion, his troubles temporarily forgotten. "And it smells good. Are you rich, Miss Drew?"

I laughed. "My dad is."

He slowly looked up at me, and his little brows tugged together. "Is he famous?"

"No, he's just an old man who works all the time. You might meet him later." And that would be fun. "When he gets here, we should play a game?"

He nodded.

"Okay. Whatever I say, you have to pretend it's true. Then if you win, you get Push-Pops and another toy. Sound good?"

"Yeah! Another horse with a sword on its head?"

"If that's what you want."

"Yay!" He bounced on the cushions before pulling the blanket to his chin and settling in to watch *SpongeBob*.

My dad turned up a couple of hours later, stopping in the doorway and frowning when he saw me playing a board game with Arlo. "Drucella, who is that?"

"This is Arlo. Arlo, this is my dad, William."

Arlo shot up and scurried across the hardwoods, stopping abruptly in front of my Dad and giving him a rigid salute. My dad just stood there, staring down at the kid like he was some kind of alien.

"I've never met a rich person before, mister. Do you have a big room with all your money and a diving board you jump off of and swim around in it like Scrooge McDuck?"

I laughed. Hard. The look on my dad's face was priceless.

"No. I do not." Dad's narrowed gaze drifted from Arlo to me. The old man had no sense of humor. "Why is a child here?"

I pushed to my feet. "Peehead, watch TV for a minute. I need to talk to Scrooge McDuck."

Arlo hopped up onto the couch, kicking his feet before I left the room.

Dad followed me to the kitchen.

"You said you wanted me to get a job, so I'm babysitting."

"Babysitting?"

"Yeah. Nora normally looks after him, but she couldn't, so..." If only he knew Arlo was actually the little brother of the Dayton bad boy who I was hot under the collar for. And I was watching him because said bad boy had been arrested—he'd keel over.

Dad leaned against the kitchen island, loosening his tie. "He looks dirty."

"He's a kid. Newsflash, when they aren't raised like little Stepford drones, they play and get dirty."

He started toward the minibar, then stopped. "You're. Babysitting?" Like he was stunned.

"Why is this so hard to believe? Easiest money I've ever made. He eats anything sugary and watches cartoons. He's me in a small person."

With a shake of his head, he grabbed the whiskey and poured half a glass. "Well. Just. Don't let him stain the carpet."

"He's not a puppy." I rolled my eyes and got two Push-Pops from the freezer. Anyone would think the man had never been around a child.

Oh, that was right, he hadn't.

The officer said Bellamy would be in jail for twenty-four hours, and their parents were obviously both in the hospital, which meant Arlo was not leaving. So, I pulled my phone from my pocket and pretended to check it. "Look, his mom just texted and asked if I could have him for the night. She has to work a double shift." The lies fell from my lips so easily, I should probably be ashamed.

"Fine."

"I'll also need to take him to school tomorrow. Please, can I have a car?"

His eyes narrowed.

"Just for tomorrow," I added.

He folded his arms over his chest, suspicion written all over his face.

"I'm trying to be responsible. I can't get him there and myself to school on time without a car. I'll give you the keys back right after school. I promise."

He huffed out a breath, and I knew I had him. Because

this might have been the most adult thing I'd ever done in my life, taking care of a kid.

"Right after school."

"Thank you."

"And put a towel on the bed. I don't want him soiling the sheets."

"Jesus. I can't with you."

When I rounded the corner, Arlo was lingering in the hall. He turned and ran off when he saw me.

"Little eavesdropper," I said when I caught up to him in the lounge and tossed him the popsicle.

"Nuh-uh."

"Um, yes." I tickled him, and he squealed, giggling in a way I was sure these stuffy walls had never witnessed.

"What do you want to watch, Peehead? If I have to watch one more episode of *SpongeBob,* I'm tossing you in the pool."

"You have a pool?"

After fighting with Arlo about the fact that he had no swimming trunks—and I was pretty sure he was lying about being able to swim—we watched a film, and he fell asleep.

I waited until my dad retired to his room to carry Arlo's deadweight up to one of the spare rooms, then tucked him in with the unicorn I'd won him.

The idea that a stupid stuffed toy I had won the kid brought him some joy made me happy. His life was shit, and I hated it for him and Bellamy. Because Bellamy was trying his best, despite crappy circumstances.

And one night with the kid made me realize that this was a lot of responsibility for a teenager.

I dropped Arlo at school the next morning, and the entire day I was on edge, barely able to focus on anything.

I checked my phone between every class, hoping they had let Bellamy go. Partly for my sake but mostly for Arlo. He was a great kid, and I didn't mind having him, but I could only pull this off with my dad for so long. He needed his brother and some stability.

It wasn't until I was back in the car line alongside all the moms that afternoon that my phone finally beeped with a string of texts from Bellamy.

**Dickhead: Just got out.**

**Dickhead: Thanks for getting him.**

**Dickhead: On my way to get him from school.**

**Dickhead: Sorry. I couldn't text until now.**

The back door opened, and Arlo clambered in. "Hey, Miss Drew."

"Hey bud, put your belt on, okay?"

"Yeah."

**Me: It's okay. I'm here. Peehead just got in the car.**

**Dickhead: Can you meet me at the park in ten minutes? I'll grab him.**

He wanted to meet at a park. That was weird.

**Me: Sure**

"We're going to the park, Arlo. Your brother's there."

He squealed, and I pulled away, blasting rock music I was totally getting the kid into.

We'd been through half of In This Moment's latest album this morning on the way to school, and he was totally into it. Because it was way better than Bellamy's crappy rap.

As soon as I pulled up to the park, I spotted Bellamy's tall, broad frame slumped at one of the picnic tables, his feet kicked up onto the bench. His hair was messy, and even from here, he looked tired or, perhaps, just defeated.

Arlo jumped out of the car before I'd even cut the engine, and I followed at a distance as he ran up to his brother. "They didn't keep you!" he said, latching onto Bellamy's leg.

"No. Just asked me questions. Did you have fun at Drew's?"

"Yeah. She's rich. And her Dad's..." Arlo stuck out his tongue. "Yuck."

A group of screaming kids ran by, catching Arlo's attention before he ran off as I came to a stop at the end of the picnic table.

Bellamy looked at me. The tormented expression that rippled over his face caused a knot in my stomach. "Thanks again for getting him." Bellamy scrubbed over his neck. "Nora's family wasn't there, and I—"

"It's fine, Bellamy. He's a good kid."

He could barely look at me, and I could imagine he felt all kinds of shitty right now.

"You know I could have brought him to your house," I said, gesturing to the park behind us.

"Yeah. The house is still a mess."

I wanted to ask him what had happened and why he was the one who got carted to jail. But I had a feeling he wouldn't tell me anything. "Are you okay?" I asked, my voice barely above a whisper.

His gaze held mine like he was trying to read me just as hard as I was him.

"Bubba!" Arlo sprinted back over, dust kicking up behind him before he skidded to a stop.

Bellamy knelt down when Arlo reached for his face and attempted to whisper: "There's Tina. See her? In the pink cat shirt? By the big kid swings."

Bellamy glanced in the direction of the swing set, then smiled. "Yeah. You gonna talk to her, Arlo?"

Arlo's eyes grew wide. "No."

"If you like her, you gotta talk to her." The exchange was so cute, my stupid heart hiccupped.

Arlo scuffed his shoes over the pea gravel, his gaze drifting up to me. "Like you're talking to Miss Drew?"

"Yeah." Bellamy snorted a laugh. Then scruffed a hand over the kid's dark hair. "There. Now you look savage. Go tell her she's pretty."

"But...how?"

"I'll show you." Bellamy pushed off the bench, closing in on me in an instant. He grabbed my chin while I stood there, frozen, transfixed. "You're pretty." His thumb brushed across my lip. "Beautiful. Fucking stunning."

Holy shit. It should not have made me melt on the spot, but it absolutely did.

His teeth raked his lip on a smile that said he knew exactly what he was doing. "Just like that," he said, dropping his hand from my face.

I barely noticed Arlo run off.

"You're an asshole," I mumbled.

"Whatever. You liked it."

I watched Arlo skid to a stop in front of the little girl, then grab her chin, just like Bellamy had mine. Whatever the kid said made her cheeks turn pink, then she threw her arms around his neck.

"Little player in the making," Bellamy said, grinning.

"What is he, six?" The fact that I was predestined to lose to boys like this since childhood was disturbing.

"Yeah..."

"He's cute. And even my dad thought he was well behaved, which is more than he says for me, so..." Comes to something when a six-year-old is held in higher esteem than me. "If you need me to watch him again—"

He grabbed my face and dragged me in, slamming his mouth over mine while the screams of children faded into the background. His tongue parted my lips. His thumb grazed my jaw. And just when my lungs felt they might explode, he pulled away.

"You're fucking me up, baby girl." He took a slow step back, that familiar sexy smirk of his settling over his mouth. "Come on, Arlo," he shouted across the playground. "We gotta go."

I felt like I'd just been through a spin cycle as I watched him walked back to his car.

When I got home, I went straight to the freezer for a Push-Pop, noticing the pale-yellow Post-it note stuck to the fridge.

*Drucella. Emergency business meeting. Out of town for a few days. My American Express is on the counter. For food ONLY. Do not use the car. I will check the mileage. -Your father*

A few days. It was Tuesday. My birthday was this Friday. Despite being a shitty father, he'd always made an effort on my birthday, like that annual act accounted for his yearly parenting quota. He'd be back. Even he wouldn't miss my eighteenth birthday. I took my Push-Pop to the living room and sat on the sofa. In the silence of this massive house, the loneliness that constantly remained on the periphery of my life crept over me.

I tried to call Genevieve, but it went to voicemail, and so

that ebbing sense of abandonment dug its claws in further. With no car, I couldn't go see Nora. It was just me. I hated it. Hated this house, this life, my dad…

My phone beeped like Bellamy could sense my turmoil.

**Dickhead: I can't get enough of your lips.**

My heart stuttered for a split second, and a smile threatened.

**Me: Who knew you were romantic?**

I knew that comment would annoy him.

**Dickhead: I'm not.**

**Me: Uh-huh**

**Dickhead: How is my choking you romantic?**

**Me: I happen to like being choked.**

**Dickhead: No shit.**

**Dickhead: Arlo keeps coming in my room, shouting at me to tell you Hi.**

That made me smile.

**Me: He's cute. Did Peehead get a date?**

**Dickhead: I took him by the 7-11 for a Slurpee, and he got her a ring out of a gumball machine.**

**Dickhead: So much for him being a little player…**

**Me: Aw! That's so cute.**

**Me: You let him be a nice boy**

**Dickhead: Nice boys get shit on.**

**Dickhead: Shat on.**

**Dickhead: WTF ever you say. Girls take shits on them.**

I wasn't sure anymore whether Bellamy was the nice boy or not.

**Me: OMG. That's why he thinks I'm pooping on you?!**

**Dickhead: No. I'm not a nice boy. I'm an asshole**

**Me: I know.**

**Dickhead: And you like it.**

I hated that I did because if that didn't scream daddy issues, I wasn't sure what did. Bellamy left me caught between wanting something and being terrified of having it.

As I stared at our open message thread, I questioned what the hell I was doing.

We had just over a month left of school, then summer, and then college. And I was falling for a guy who played his cards so close to his chest, I had no idea what I was doing anymore.

**Dickhead: This is where you say: Yes, Bellamy. I like it...**

**Me: I like it.**

And that would undoubtedly be my downfall.

## CHAPTER 34

## BELLAMY

ARLO PUT his open palms beneath the automatic hand sanitizer pump once.

Twice.

Three times.

"That's enough, Arlo," I said, watching liquid drip from his hands to the hospital floor.

"It smells good."

I sanitized my hands, then opened the door to Mom's room.

She pushed up in the bed, smiling the second she saw us. "There are my boys."

The bruises on her face were an ugly purple, and the gash on her head had been stitched up. Gritting my teeth, I dropped my chin to my chest and stared at the hospital tile.

I hated him. I hated that he'd done this to her for most of her life.

"Momma!" Arlo ran to the bed and crawled up, snuggling in beside her. "I stayed at a castle last night."

"You did?"

"Uh-huh. Miss Drew had Push-Pops and Cokes in glass bottles. And more bedrooms than the Motel-8."

"Really?" Mom's gaze slowly lifted to me with an arch of her brow. "And who is Miss Drew?"

I rubbed a hand over the back of my neck. "This girl I'm..." I wasn't even sure what was going on between Drew and me anymore. But whatever it was, when I wasn't around her, I missed her. "I'm dating. She came and got him last night while..." You were carted off unconscious to the hospital, and I was hauled off to jail for assaulting Dad.

"Anyway."

She nodded, tugging at her hospital blanket. "That was sweet of her."

"I like her," Arlo said with a curt nod. "She's nice and smells good."

"The officers said your charges would be dropped now that I've been able to give witness and..." Her jaw tightened. Tears built in her eyes that she quickly swiped away. "I'm sorry."

"Mom, don't. You didn't do anything."

"I just..." She pulled in a ragged breath, then pressed a kiss to the top of Arlo's head. "I wish they'd let me go home today. I'm fine. Really."

They'd held her for observation since he'd given her a concussion.

"They said you can be discharged tomorrow."

"Just want to be able to bill us more," she grumbled.

I sank into the chair at her bedside, clasped my hands, and leaned over my knees, staring at the hospital tile.

Before I left the jail this morning, Officer Robins had helped me fill out a temporary restraining order—the guys at the precinct were all too aware of the shitshow that went on at my house, and I couldn't just let her stay in this mess. I couldn't let Arlo stay in it. Because what would happen when I eventually left?

I stopped by the family court and dropped off the paperwork after I picked up Arlo from the park, and part of me thought I should tell Mom, but then, I knew I needed to tell her that when Arlo wasn't around.

"Grandpa's coming up," I said.

"Yay!" Arlo clapped. "Pop-Pop's coming."

"Dad? You called him?"

"Yeah. I don't want you staying at the house alone."

Mom drew in a heavy breath.

All these years, she'd never breathed a word to him. Had made me promise I wouldn't tell because Grandpa was bat-shit crazy.

I'd listened to her back then because I was a kid, and that's what kids do—listen to their parents even when they know it's wrong.

I wasn't a kid anymore, though. And someone had to take care of her.

After we left the hospital, I swung by Home Wares and grabbed locks for both the doors, changing them before I made dinner, then made Arlo get ready for bed.

A peaceful silence hung over the house without the hum of a baseball game in the background or the constant creak of Dad's recliner. And maybe that's why Arlo snuck into my room at one in the morning. It was *too* quiet. We didn't know how to handle peace.

He crawled into my bed, tucking Spike between us on a huff. "Are they gonna get divorced?"

The chirp of crickets outside my window filled the

silence of the dark room. "Yeah."

Arlo knew Dad was mean, but he was still young.

I could clearly remember being his age and loving my Dad, even after he'd hit me. I spent years trying to figure out why I sought out his approval. Why I loved someone who hated me. I wasn't even sure when the need to love him morphed into rage-filled hate.

"Does that mean I have to go stay with him sometimes?" Arlo whispered. "Billy has to go stay with his daddy every other weekend, and I don't want to stay with Daddy without you."

I turned on the pillow to face him.

He petted over the unicorn, refusing to look at me. With a restraining order, he wouldn't get visitation, and even if he tried, there was no way in hell I'd let Dad win anything but supervised visitation. With any luck, he'd be serving a couple of years in jail anyway.

"No. You're not gonna stay with him. Don't worry about that, okay?"

He nodded, then grabbed my arm and tugged on it in a silent plea for me to let him on my chest.

I wrapped my arm around him and patted his back. "It's gonna be different from now on. I promise."

---

I put the last coat of paint on the living room wall and stepped back with a smile.

The places where I'd mudded the holes weren't even visible.

Wiping the paint over my jeans, I snagged the bucket and brush and headed onto the back porch to clean up.

I'd spent the last day patching holes and cleaning up the

shit my dad had broken in the middle of that scuffle. The coffee table broke in two when he threw me into it, but I went by the Salvation Army and found one I thought she'd like for ten bucks.

The back door banged against the side of the house when Arlo sprinted out, wielding my phone above his head. "Baby Girl's texting you!" And that was weird coming from my six-year-old brother.

**Baby Girl: When are you coming back to school?**

I stared down at the message and smiled.

**Me: Don't know yet**

**Me: Come over?**

**Baby Girl: I can't drive my car. Dad's threatening to check my mileage now.**

**Me: I'll come get you**

I just wanted to see her. Bad. It had only been a few days, but I couldn't stand it any longer.

**Baby Girl: Just come over here**

**Me: I have Arlo**

**Baby Girl: Bring him**

**Baby Girl: Don't park your car on the drive, though. My dad likes to appear like a freaking genie**

I shoved my phone into my pocket, then slung the water from the paintbrush. "You wanna go to Drew's after dinner, Arlo?"

"Yay!"

---

"She said they aren't castles, but I think she's lying." Arlo stood outside my car, hitching up his pants in the dark while he waited on me to scoot across the passenger seat.

"These aren't castles," I said.

"They look like them."

And they kind of did—at least compared to the houses in Dayton. Two and three stories. Brick. Manicured lawns.

"Why'd we have to park all the way down here?" he asked as we started up the small hill.

"Because."

"Because isn't an answer."

God, I loved him, but sometimes the kid was exhausting. "Because Scrooge McDuck doesn't want people to visit her."

"Why!"

"She's in trouble."

Arlo shook his head. "Your fault, huh?"

This one actually wasn't my fault. It was all on her and her anger, ramming a Maserati into my car…"No, it's not my fault." I gave him a playful shove, and he giggled.

"I don't think she'll poop on you."

"No?"

"Nuh-uh. She's nice. Nice girls don't poop on people."

I laughed, scrubbing the top of his head before we started up her drive, the enormous house lit up with landscape lighting. "I hope you're right, buddy."

He took off, running up the porch steps to ring the doorbell. Repeatedly.

Light cut across the porch when the door swung open. He darted inside without a hello.

"Butthead! You're supposed to say hey first," I shouted, kissing Drew on the lips as I stepped inside.

He stomped back over. "Hello, Miss Drew."

"Hey, Arlo." Drew cut into the living room, then came back with her hands behind her. "I got you presents."

Arlo jumped up and down before she gave him another unicorn toy, this one with a shiny blue horn. "Thank you."

She lifted a brow. "No, *that* one you won." Then she handed him a pair of SpongeBob swim trunks. "You can swim in the pool this time, Peehead."

He snatched the shorts, squealed, then hugged her. "I like you, Miss Drew."

"I like you, too, Arlo." She smiled before leading us through the kitchen and outside.

Arlo stopped on the porch steps and gasped. A massive unicorn float drifted across the surface of the illuminated pool.

"A horse with a horn!" he shouted, barely stopping to change his shorts.

Drew sank into a lounge chair then sat right back up when Arlo jumped in, her gaze focused on water. "He can swim, right?"

"Good enough..."

She started to push up, and I latched onto her arm.

"Yes, Drew." I almost laughed but didn't because that shit right there was chipping away at my armor. "He can swim."

"Asshole."

Yeah. This girl was doing my heart in, for sure.

I tapped her shoulder and motioned for her to scoot up. She hesitated before she shifted, allowing me to sink behind her. Her stiff body slowly relaxed against me, and I rested my chin on the top of her head.

"Where'd you get the shorts from?" There was no way the girl had a pair of kid's SpongeBob pants on standby.

"Nora and I went to Wal-E-Mart and got some, in case

he came over again. Kid gave me hell about swimming last time."

And for the first time, I thought I might understand why people fell in love. Because that…that made my chest go a little tight when nothing else ever had. "And the float?"

"That, I actually bought last summer. Dad says it's a monstrosity, so we never get it out."

I skimmed my chin over her soft hair. "It is a monstrosity…"

"Arlo doesn't think so." She nodded toward the pool.

His legs were wrapped around its neck. He fist-pumped the air and let out a war cry. "To the death, Horny Horse!" Water splashed when he kicked his feet.

"Now I'm just picturing a horse with a boner," Drew laughed.

"You're sick."

A long beat of silence stretched between us, filled with the sounds of Arlo splashing around.

She took a deep breath and turned her cheek to my chest. "Is your mom okay?" Her words were barely a whisper.

This was the crap I wasn't good with.

No one outside of the guys and Nash knew about what a shitshow my life was, and she did. There wasn't much in life I was embarrassed about. I'd grown up wearing thrift-store clothes and shoes with holes, just like most everyone in Dayton, but that shit—the crap with my dad—that wasn't someone not finishing school, not making the cut. That wasn't someone who hit the bottle a little too much or got hooked on a drug that controlled their lives. That shit wasn't just a lifetime of bad decisions; it was inherently who he was.

And now she knew that, and she was still right here.

"She comes home tomorrow," I said.

"That's good."

Minutes passed. I watched Arlo have the time of his life, playing some make-believe shit with that unicorn float.

"Are you going to get in any more trouble over it?" she asked.

"No."

Her fingers played over my arm before she let out a heavy breath. "Do you want to talk about it?" she asked.

The memory of that night snuck in, uninvited. My blood pressure immediately spiked.

Did I want to talk? Not really, but I had no idea how much she knew, and I didn't want her to think I was the kind of guy who would just beat up my old man—even if I were the kind of guy who would break into her house and destroy shit with a baseball bat.

"He deserved it, Drew. He really fucking deserved it."

She sat up and swung her legs over my thigh, then brushed her fingers over my cheek. "I don't think you'd hurt someone unless they deserved it."

I couldn't help but laugh at that shit. "I broke into your house with a baseball bat and destroyed it."

"Well, I did get you arrested. Which, by the way, I'm sorry about."

"And I'm sorry I got you fired." I swept her hair from her face. "God, that word is like thorns in my throat."

"My point is, you didn't hurt me."

"You're a girl."

"In a place like Dayton, does it matter?"

"Shit like that should always matter."

A small smile touched her lips. "See, you're like a knight in thrift-shop armor."

"Nah, baby girl. I'm a villain who just wants the princess."

"Me? Oh, no, I'm the evil queen."

I pulled her into my lap, kissing her. "Even better."

"Ewww! Why would you do that?" Arlo whined from the side of the pool. "That's the part in movies you're supposed to cover your eyes for."

"Close your eyes if you don't wanna see it." I kissed her harder. When she went to pull away, I squeezed her hips.

"We're going to scar the kid."

"He's looked at my dad's *Playboys*. He's fine."

## CHAPTER 35
## DREW

THE DATE CIRCLED on the calendar mocked me when I reached for the milk. What better way to start out my eighteenth birthday than eating cereal in the kitchen—alone?

My dad still wasn't home.

No texts or missed calls—but it was only seven.

He'd probably taken an early flight so he could be home by the time I got back from school. God, why did I care? I didn't even like the man.

The doorbell rang, and I tossed my bowl into the sink, then went to answer it.

A man with a clipboard stood on the threshold while a noisy trailer truck backed up to the drive. "Drucella Morgan?" he said, making checks on his paper.

"Yes."

"Just need you to sign." He passed the clipboard to me.

After I'd scribbled my signature over a dotted line, he passed me a set of keys, along with an envelope. Then he went to the truck and lifted the rolling door while I opened the letter:

*My Darling Daughter,*

*Happy eighteenth birthday, sweetie. I hope you like the car. Love you!*

*Bisous,*
*Irina - x*

A ramp lowered to the asphalt, and a few minutes later, a baby-pink Porsche, with a massive white bow stuck to the hood, reversed out.

The car probably cost a small fortune. In baby pink. God, I hated that color.

Gifts were how Irina showed her affection—because I'd never quite use the word love. Most kids would give their right arm for that car, but for me, it was nothing but a reminder of my absent parents. At least my mom had remembered. My dad couldn't even manage a simple message before his first meeting.

I closed the door, typed out a thank you text to my mom, then finished getting ready for school and went to wait on the porch for Nora.

Her car pulled in front of my house. I could see her sitting behind the wheel, gawking at the pink Barbie car before I reached the drive. When I got in, she let out a low whistle. "Nice car."

"Thanks. My mom sent it." I intentionally left out the "for my birthday" part. I didn't want the attention. Plus, my own father couldn't be bothered with it; why should anyone else? It was just another day anyway; it didn't matter.

The entire drive to school, I kept refreshing my phone to check for a text. And every time nothing popped up, I felt worse. I cared, and I didn't want to.

By the time we pulled up to Dayton, my mood was sour.

I swear the only thing that made this school bearable was Bellamy. Even when we were enemies, he at least made it exciting, and his absence only added to my bleak outlook today.

Come lunch, there was still no text from my dad, but at least Genevieve messaged me Happy Birthday.

I grabbed my shitty lunch and didn't even bother with a Push-Pop, because all that was left was cherry, and that was worse than grape. On a huff, I tossed my tray to the table and sank to the stool beside Nora.

"You okay?" she asked, picking over her salad. "You seem mad or something."

"I'm fine." I unwrapped my sandwich then lifted the bun to inspect the meat.

"Why do you keep staring at Hendrix, Diane?" Nora nudged me in the ribs. "She's like ogling him."

"I am not!"

Nora started grilling Diane, her questioning coming to an abrupt halt when a rainbow sherbet Push-Pop dropped in front of me.

"Happy Birthday, baby girl," Bellamy whispered in my ear, low enough no one else could have heard. His warm breath tickled my skin as his lips pressed to my throat. Every nerve ending lit up, and there it was—the real reason I missed him. He wasn't just exciting. He set my soul on fire and filled the cold void that I hadn't even realized lingered within me until him.

Before I could thank him, he was on his way back to his table.

"Aw." Diane sighed. "He gave you a Push-Pop!"

"He probably stole it from a freshman." Nora shook her head.

Probably.

My phone buzzed on the table, and a text ribbon popped up at the top of the screen.

**Dickhead: And don't think part of that gift isn't selfish. I like to watch you suck it.**

I glanced across the cafeteria. Bellamy's attention was aimed directly at me, that smirk playing over his lips. I didn't care if it was selfish. I had no idea how he knew it was my birthday, but it didn't matter. He did, and he remembered. All while, I knew he was dealing with his own problems. It made my heart do a pathetic little cough.

**Me: Thank you**

When I got home from school, a package from Genevieve waited on my porch.

I took the box inside and untied the bright-purple ribbon, pulling out a slut-red dress.

A note fluttered to the floor, Genevieve's perfect handwriting scrawled across it wishing me a happy birthday. And still not a word from my dad.

I managed to hold it together until it was nine o'clock at night, and I sat alone in the living room, staring at the text.

**Me: Hey**

**Dad: I'm at a business dinner. Is it important?**

No, apparently, I wasn't important. Not like I didn't already know that, though.

Rejection sank in deep, like a blade wedged between my ribs, stilting my breaths, and I gave in to tears. Tears that I hated to spill over him. Tears he didn't deserve.

Swallowing hard, I pulled myself together and shoved my emotions down into that dark little hole where Black Mountain had taught me to hide them.

I typed out a text to Bellamy, then stopped halfway through and deleted it.

I was down and in need. A text now would be me starting to rely on him, and that was a slippery slope I couldn't afford to go down. Not with a guy like Bellamy—not with a guy I felt like I'd already lost control with.

I was used to having no one, and it was best to keep it that way for the next few weeks until Barrington and Dayton were distant memories.

So instead of inviting him over, I poured a glass of wine, necked it, and sent a text to Nora and Diane.

**Me: Party at mine tonight. Invite everyone. Free drinks and a pool.**

Screw my dad.

# CHAPTER 36

## BELLAMY

**HENDRIX: You going?**

   **Wolf: He's going.**

She hadn't invited me. She hadn't invited anyone—Nora had. That threw me for a loop.

Nora couldn't be throwing a surprise birthday party *at* Drew's house, and there was no way her asshole dad would let this many people come over—especially not the likes of people from Dayton so... What the hell was going on?

   **Hendrix: One of you dickwads pick me up. Free drinks. I'm getting hammered. Then I'm going to be doing the hammering...**

   **Wolf: Bell's gonna be hammering Paris Hilton.**

Cars lined the street when I pulled up in front of Drew's house. Every window was lit up.

   **Me: Might. Don't know.**

I sent the text to the guys, then stuffed my phone into my pocket, shimmied over the center console, and started up her drive.

Landscape lighting gleaned over the side of a pink Porsche with a ridiculous white bow on the hood. Porsche or not, that thing was hideous, and I absolutely could not see Drew driving it.

Loud music poured through the open door, and I followed the hum of conversation into the kitchen. There were no balloons, no streamers, nothing that would indicate it was a birthday celebration.

Nora and Diane stood at the counter, taking shots while a group of football players cheered them on.

The second Nora slammed her shot glass down, her gaze locked with mine. "Oh. Yay. You came." She staggered over to me and dug a finger into my shoulder. The liquor must have been doing a number on her. "What exactly are you trying to do with my friend?" she asked.

"Your friend?"

"Yeah. My friend." She crossed her arms over her chest and popped her hip to the side. "The one you're...dating."

"Ah. *That* friend."

"Don't be you, Bellamy."

I snagged a bottle of beer from an ice bucket on the table. Some expensive shit imported from Belgium. "And what's that supposed to mean?" I said.

"Don't break her heart."

I stared at Nora for a moment. I didn't believe for one second I was in a position to break Drew's heart...

"Oh my God." She groaned. "If Drew ends up like all your other cast-offs, crying in a bathroom over your shitty ass, I will cut you myself." She gave me one final stare down, then sauntered off.

If there were girls in the Dayton restrooms shedding tears over me, that was due to their own ridiculous assumptions. Because I had never given a girl a reason to believe they meant anything.

Drew, on the other hand, was quickly becoming everything to me, and there was no way in hell I'd give her a reason to cry.

I shouldered through the crowd and outside to the deck.

One of the underclassmen hoisted himself onto the railing, butt-ass naked. His foot hit one of the concrete planters. It toppled to the pavement below and shattered before he cannonballed into the pool on a scream.

Kids from Dayton wouldn't consider something a party unless shit was broken and something had been set on fire. Drew's house was going to be trashed before the end of the night.

A chorus of cheers erupted from the side of the porch, catching my attention. People raised their cups above their heads as Drew climbed onto the patio table in a skin-tight, red dress, the low-cut neckline barely covering her nipples.

She lifted a bottle of liquor above her head while her hips moved in beat with the music. When the chorus picked up, she busted out moves that would have put a Vegas showgirl to shame.

I shifted through the crowd, anger sparking in my chest at the few guys staring a little too hard at her.

Drew shimmied to the left, and one side of the table bucked up, throwing her off, and right into the arms of a Dayton football player. I wanted to kill him. I shoved people out of the way and grabbed her arm, snatching her away from him.

"The fuck are you doing?" I said, glaring at him.

He held up his hands, waving an invisible white flag before he quickly disappeared amongst the other partygoers.

"Bellamy! You're here." Drew stroked my face with sloppy movements. She was shit-faced. On her birthday. That I had a feeling her dad had forgotten.

This probably wasn't going to end well.

"Yeah. Thanks for the invite."

"I told Nora to invite *everyone*."

"I'm not Nora's—" And I stopped before the word boyfriend came out.

"Don't be sad." She swayed on her feet, then tipped her bottle back with a slosh.

I took the liquor, holding it up to the porch light. The damn thing was almost empty. "I think you've had enough." Shaking her ass with her tits out. She'd absolutely had more than enough.

She gave me a once over while chewing at her lip. "I really haven't had enough of you." Then she grabbed my shirt and yanked me close. "Wanna come fuck me on my dad's desk?"

The idea of pounding away at her on her dad's desk would be impossible to turn down—if she weren't drunk.

She laced her fingers through mine and led me into the house, straight through the crowded kitchen and into his office.

She closed the door, and I stared at the paper-covered desk at the back of the room, my dick swelling at the idea of bending her over it.

The lock clicked. Her dress clung to every dip and curve as she crossed the room, and that bright-red lipstick just begged to be smeared. And even though I'd never been so attracted to a girl in my life, I could not screw her while she was this drunk, and if she touched me...

She moved closer. "You look hot."

"And you look drunk."

Then she shoved me hard enough that I stumbled back onto the desk. "Not that drunk," she said, placing her hands on either side of my thighs as she climbed up and straddled me.

"Drew..."

The friction of her grinding against me was too damn much to stand.

She nipped at my ear, then whispered, "I want your dick in my pussy."

Those words went straight to my dick, like an adrenaline shot, and when she fisted my hair, a switch flipped. I couldn't not touch her any longer.

I gripped her bare thighs and stood, wrapping her legs wrapping around me. The heat of her bled through my jeans, and I was two seconds away from losing the last bit of control I was somehow clinging to.

"Say it," she breathed, her lips at my throat as she tugged my hair. "Ask me if I'm wet for you."

This shit was just too much. I turned around and slammed her onto the desk. "I know you fucking are."

Papers crumpled, stacks of files toppled to the floor. And then it was nothing but hands in hair and her fingers fumbling for my belt.

My lips were on her throat, the swells of her exposed tits, any piece of bare skin I could get to. I'd wanted to bury myself in her for so damn long, but what made it worse, I wanted more than just this now. I wanted *her*.

I pulled her thong down her legs, tossing it to the side of the room as she unfastened my jeans.

"God, I fucking want you," I groaned, biting her neck.

"Yeah, you do."

Her fingers wrapped around my dick and that touch alone was almost enough to make me come. And through the lust-filled haze, my conscience ate away at me. I could not fuck her when she was this drunk.

"Do you have a condom?" she asked.

I bit back a groan as she worked her tight fist over my shaft. "I'm not fucking you when you're shitfaced."

"I'd fuck you sober, anyway."

"Doesn't matter."

She tugged my dick closer to her bare pussy, and my jaw set. This was a form of temptation akin to the inner circle of hell. And drunk, she was the devil.

"I'm not fucking you tonight, baby girl."

I slipped my hand between her legs, and holy shit, was she wet. It took all of thirty seconds before she tightened around my fingers. That was enough to send me hurtling over the edge.

I sank my teeth into her shoulder on a groan, coming in her hand. And when I pulled away, she slipped her fingers between her lips and sucked me off.

"You're seriously trying to kill me, aren't you?"

"Couldn't fuck you if I did that, could I?" She smirked, then hopped off the desk and snatched a bottle of liquor on her way out of the office.

She was absolutely going to kill me...

An hour later, she could barely walk, which was why I was carting her inebriated ass up the stairs to her room.

I closed the door, and just when I was about to put her on the bed, she swallowed. Then swallowed again, focusing on a spot on the wall.

"Are you gonna be sick?" I asked.

She nodded, and I hurried across the room to the bathroom.

"Oh..." She heaved.

"No. Wait! Wait...."

The second I placed her in front of the toilet, she puked.

"I told you, you were gonna throw up."

She lifted her middle finger and leaned farther over the bowl.

I pulled her hair away from her face to keep the vomit out of it, and she made a weak attempt to swat me away.

"Go...away."

"And leave you in here to pass out in puke? Nah..."

She groaned, threw up some more, then flushed the toilet and slumped against the tiled wall. "This is the worst birthday ever." She wiped at the mascara streaking her cheek. "And now you're watching me puke."

I scrubbed a hand over my face before dropping to the floor beside her. "It's no big deal."

"He forgot." She traced a finger along the grout in the tile, then rested her head on my shoulder, and something in my chest went tight.

"Yeah. Well, he's an asshole."

"I shouldn't even care."

"But you do. And that's fine." I knew that to be true. I hated my dad's ass, but over the years, I'd still found myself trying to make him proud. Trying to get a moment of attention. "Come on, you should go to bed."

I pushed up, helping her to her feet before I grabbed the purple toothbrush I figured was hers, pumped toothpaste on it, then passed it to her, and I left her to it.

I ran a hand through my hair while I paced in front of her bed. Pissed as hell at her dad. Angry he'd hurt her. Furious I couldn't fix it. And I'd never cared enough about anyone else outside of my mom and Arlo to ever give a shit.

My phone beeped. Then beeped again.

**Hendrix: Where are you at, dickweed?**

**Hendrix: Wolf and I made a bet you're getting your dick sucked.**

"You gave me a Push Pop."

I shoved my phone in my pocket and turned around to Drew, standing in the doorway of her bathroom. The straps of her dress hung off her shoulders, and the look on her face was pitiful.

"Yeah..."

"It's the only thing that made me happy today."

And that was sad as shit. "There's a Porsche in your drive and *my Push-Pop* made you happy. That's messed up. That Push-Pop was two bucks."

"The car's pink. My mom doesn't even know I hate pink." She pushed away from the doorframe, staggered to her bed, and collapsed on top of the covers. "But *you* know I like rainbow Push-Pops. Not grape or cherry. But rainbow."

I was pretty damn sure, her dad forgetting her birthday had to make her feel invisible. I sank to the bed beside her, rubbing a hand over her exposed back. I didn't want her to feel invisible. "I'll buy you all the rainbow Push-Pops you want, baby girl."

She looked up from the comforter and smiled.

"You gotta get out of this thing." I helped her sit up, slowly pulling her dress over her head. I skimmed my hand along her side. The way I felt with her—like something missing was right there—it was something I couldn't ignore anymore. "I really do fucking like you."

"I like you, too," she whispered.

"Good." I kissed her forehead, then pulled my shirt over

my head and tugged it over hers. "Come on," I laid back on the bed, bringing her down onto my chest.

"Thank you."

"For what?" I swept my hand through her tangled hair.

"For being nice."

"Only to you, baby girl. Only to you…"

## CHAPTER 37

## DREW

"DRUCELLA MORGAN!"

I jumped awake, then groaned, and face planted my pillow. "Go away," I mumbled into the cotton. My head felt like it was in a vice while my stomach churned, threatening to rebel.

"Get the hell out of my house!"

I bolted upright to find my dad standing in the doorway, glaring.

Panic worked its way through me when I glanced over at Bellamy, shirtless, tattooed, and with a smirk that said he didn't give a shit that he'd just been caught in my bed in nothing but his boxers.

Mortification was not the word. I was in such deep shit.

I dragged a hand through my bird's nest hair as I shoved out of bed, wearing Bellamy's shirt.

"I come home to find the house ruined. Again. And you with this...this..." My dad gave Bellamy a nasty once over, and I knew exactly what he was thinking—what he saw.

Muscles, tattoos, piercings. Bellamy had *bad* written all over him.

"This boy," he spat the word. "In your bed. Drucella, you are out of control!"

"Can you give me five minutes?" I went to the door and tried to push him out into the hall. "Then, we'll talk about it."

"I didn't raise you to act like a whore!"

He might as well have slapped me, and I didn't know what to say. He was rubbing salt in the wound he'd already inflicted by forgetting my birthday.

Dad's gaze shifted behind me. Bellamy's hand touched my waist, pulling me back so he could place himself between my father and me.

"You're a fucking asshole," he said.

I went to move, but Bellamy held me in place.

"And you, young man, are not welcome in my house. Taking advantage of my daughter..."

Two seconds ago, I was a whore...

"Just a birthday present." Bellamy laughed, his hand coming back around my waist and tugging me against his side. "Because you see, *I* didn't forget it was her birthday."

I'm sure my face turned twelve shades of red. My dad's sure did.

"Get out of my house." My father rubbed at his chest on a heavy breath. "Before I call the police!"

"Sure thing." Bellamy tugged on his jeans, zipping them as he cupped my cheek. "Get dressed. We're leaving."

"You are *not* leaving with him," my dad snapped. The anger in his voice caused me to flinch.

I knew exactly who I wanted to be around right now, and it wasn't the man who had forgotten about me and called me a whore. Consequences be damned.

I went into my closet, quickly threw on a sundress and a

pair of shoes, and came back out before they had a chance to kill each other.

Bellamy took my hand, pulling me toward the door. But my dad didn't budge.

"You asked me to leave," Bellamy said, an edge to his voice I'd never heard. He stepped forward, towering over my dad. "You gonna move or what?"

A trace of fear showed on my dad's face seconds before he backed up. Slightly.

Bellamy knocked his shoulder as he led me into the hall.

We made halfway down the hall before my dad started after us. "Drucella! You are not leaving with that reprobate!"

Bellamy turned to face him, walking backward down the hall. "I know you forgot, but she's eighteen now. She doesn't have to do shit you say." Then he flipped him off just before we started down the stairs.

Nora was right. Bellamy was awful. And I'd never wanted anyone the way I wanted him right now.

He kicked empty bottles out of the way as we headed through the foyer.

"I wanted to punch him." The door slammed behind us, his anger only growing as he dragged me toward his car. "Fucking asshole."

He opened the passenger door, then climbed over the console to the driver's side. "Fucking prick." Jamming the keys into the ignition, he glared at my house while I climbed in.

I tossed my head back against the headrest. Honestly, I was so tired of fighting my dad every step of the way. Not like I didn't know I was a nightmare child, but he didn't give a shit about me, and rejection by my own father had molded me into something bitter.

"Look at me." Bellamy grabbed my chin, forcing me to face him. "You're not a whore." Then he put the car in reverse and peeled off, leaving tread marks on my dad's precious cobblestone drive. "He shouldn't talk to you like that."

"He hates me," I said. "It's fine."

The shock had faded. When I thought about it, I wasn't really surprised my dad called me that. I'd almost become numb to his eternal disappointment.

"It's not fucking fine." Bellamy took a hard right, then floored it onto the main strip of the highway.

"It could be worse." I knew his dad was an asshole. At least mine wasn't violent.

By the time we pulled into Bellamy's house, he wasn't as tense. He shoved the key into the lock, and I turned back to stare at the empty drive.

"Is your mom here?" I asked before following him into his house.

"No. Grandpa took her and Arlo to some flea market over in Georgia yesterday." He tossed his keys onto the coffee table, then dragged a hand through his messy hair.

I watched him for a moment. No one had ever defended me or stood up for me, and they certainly hadn't put themselves between me and my father's ugly words. But Bellamy had. Whatever thread of resolve I was hanging onto, whatever excuses I had for avoiding this, evaporated.

I kissed him hard, tugging at his hair as my body bowed toward him like he owned it.

"You told my dad to fuck off."

"Yeah." He grabbed my hips. Then slammed his lips over mine in an angry kiss. "No one disrespects you."

"What if I want *you* to?" I shoved his hand between my thighs.

A smirk pulled at his lips. "I didn't get you expelled yet," he said, even though he was already lifting my skirt

"I told you our deal was off."

"So, you wanna be disrespected..." He placed a light hand on my throat, then yanked my underwear down with the other. "That's what you want, baby girl?"

Hell, yes, I did.

He shoved his fingers inside me as he backed me across the room. "Because as long as I've waited for this." His fingers went deeper. "Fucking *waited*..."

He had, and so had I.

He pulled away from me just long enough to strip out of his shirt, then he was right back on me, hands between my legs and teeth raking over my neck.

By the time he backed me into his room, he had me completely naked and my body strung tight.

My legs hit the edge of his mattress. He shoved me back, covering my body with his. Each brush of his hand over my bare skin sent the rabid need only Bellamy stirred within me spreading like wildfire.

My hands went to his zipper, tugging his jeans over his hips. When I fisted his hard dick, he groaned and reached for something on the floor. He moved back, his gaze set between my spread legs as he rolled a condom over his shaft.

"I'm gonna fuck you up so good," he said. Then he shoved my legs beside my head and slammed into me without an ounce of mercy, just like he had promised. My breath caught as he stilled, buried inside me.

"God-fucking-damn." His fingers dug into my legs in a bruising grip before his pace quickened. Every thrust hard and punishing, like he hated me and wanted me in equal measure.

I wanted more, for him to lose all control. "Thought you hated me," I said, raking my nails over his broad back.

His teeth sunk into my shoulder on a thrust that had my breath catching in my lungs. "So much."

Bellamy was everything I thought he would be and more. Brutal, raw, powerful. He made anyone before him seem tame and demure.

"Your pussy feels so good."

My head hit the headboard with each thrust. A moan slipped from my lips, and heat built within me, tightening and coiling as I fought for breath.

"Do you like the way I feel inside you?"

I grabbed his ass on a moan, pulling him deeper into me as an answer.

"Tell me how good it feels."

"So fucking good."

"It's about to feel a lot better."

He went deeper. Harder. Brushing against me with each roll of his hips until my body fell apart. Like he'd dug his way so far inside me, he was plucking apart every fiber that held me together. And when he had me gasping for my next breath, every nerve ending burning bright, his hold on my hips tightened, and he rolled over.

"Now. You get me off, baby girl."

I moved over him, my entire body sparking like a live wire.

"Faster."

He pulled and tugged at my hips, forcing me over him harder before he threw his head back on a deep groan. The faster I moved, the more unhinged he became until I felt mindless in the insanity of it.

His head jerked back on the pillow, abs tensing, grip tightening. The muscles in his shoulders strained as he let out a guttural grunt. "Shit..." His fingers flinched into my hips before he dragged me down on top of him.

"I really, *really* hate you," he said, pressing a kiss to my forehead. "Like fucking really."

I huffed a laugh. "I really hate you, too."

---

I lounged on Bellamy's bed, wearing one of his shirts. A box of half-eaten pizza sat open in front of us, and I felt a million miles away from my actual life. I'd take Bellamy's small bedroom over my dad's colossal house any day. I wanted to stay in this bed, eating greasy pizza forever.

"I wonder how much fun your asshole dad's having cleaning up that house."

"He'll pay someone to clean it." Actually, that was a lie. "Or he'll make me pay for it. He can add it to my tab."

He slid his fingers over my thigh. "You can stay here if you want. Fuck him off real good."

"What about your mom?"

"She won't care. Already texted her."

My heart fluttered pathetically. What was it about this boy? He had nothing, and yet, he kept giving me everything. "Thanks. He'll probably be leaving for work again tomorrow. He's never there."

"You could still stay..." His lips pressed to my neck. "I'll make it worth your while, baby girl. Promise."

And within a matter of moments, the pizza was on the floor, and he had me undressed and pinned beneath him.

A door banged. Followed by Arlo shouting for Bellamy. Bellamy shot out of bed, butt naked, tripping over his shoes on his way to the door to lock it. The handle rattled.

"Bubba? Why do you got the door locked?"

"I'm studying." Bellamy cocked a brow at me.

I stood up, throwing on clothes. "Is your mom here?" I whispered over the continuous rattling of the handle.

"I guess."

"Oh my God." His mom was here, and he was naked, and I was in his room, probably looking like we just went ten rounds—because we had.

I threw his shirt at him. "Put clothes on."

With a half roll of his eyes, he tossed his shirt back at me, then grabbed his jeans. "Calm down."

The handle stopped shaking. "Momma. Bubba's got a girl in his room! I hear her."

"Shit." I went to the window, trying to unfasten the latch, but it was rusted shut.

"What in the hell are you doing?"

"I don't want your mom to find me in here," I whispered, turning to look at him. "I look like a hoochy!"

"You're my girlfriend. Not a hoochy. Jesus Christ."

*Girlfriend.*

Nora said it, he'd even half said it, but this was the first time he'd said it like that. Just casually. I'd avoided discussing it, happy in my little denial because I was going to college, and I did not need to be getting into a relationship. But I wanted it now. I really did.

Then he went to his door and unlocked it. Arlo immediately opened it. His gaze drifted from me to Bellamy to the bed. "Where are your books?"

"It was...mental math," I said.

Arlo frowned, then dragged me to the hall. "You need to meet Momma."

At those words, I grew nervous. What if she didn't like me?

Bellamy took my hand from Arlo, continuing to lead me toward the kitchen.

A dark-haired woman moved around the dated, yellow cabinets. A kaleidoscope of bruises covered her face, and I swallowed around a sudden lump in my throat. I couldn't help but pity her.

When her gaze shifted to Bellamy and then me, a smile spread over her lips. "You must be Drew." She opened one of the cabinets. "It's nice to meet you. I'm Carol."

"Hi. Nice to meet you, too."

"Thank you for looking after Arlo last week. It was very kind of you." Her gaze dropped, but not before I saw the trace of shame in her eyes.

"It's no problem."

"I told her that you have a castle," Arlo said, skipping around an old dog asleep on the kitchen rug.

As if sensing her discomfort, Bellamy leaned down and kissed her cheek. "You okay, Mom?" It was sweet, completely at odds with everything he projected.

She nodded. Then rummaged through the cabinet, pulling out boxes. "Did work go okay today?"

Bellamy glanced away from me. "Yeah. It was fine."

I was pretty sure she wasn't asking her son how business was pushing dope.

"Where's Pops at?"

"He dropped us off and went to the bingo hall..."

Bellamy helped his mom fix some sandwiches. After we ate, she left to take Arlo to the library, and we went back to Bellamy's room.

I fell back onto the bed, wondering if maybe his mom did know he dealt weed. She didn't have a problem with me being locked in his room; maybe it didn't bother her. "Does your mom know what you do for money?"

"Hell no." He flopped onto the mattress beside me, grabbing a football from the floor and tossing it in the air.

"So, she thinks you have a job?"

"She thinks the guys and I mow lawns." Another toss of the ball. "For Barrington...because no one in Dayton could afford that shit."

The image of him mowing his lawn that day when I was at Nora's sprung to mind. All muscles and sweat. Hell, I'd pay him to mow my lawn. Shirtless. So would all those Barrington housewives. "I can see why that's plausible."

"And FYI, the shit money those rich assholes do pay to have their lawns mowed isn't close to enough to cover bills. Because I did try it before I started dealing."

"I'm not judging," I said quietly.

I'd seen enough of Bellamy's life now to know it was hard. There were enough people in this world making far more money than him, doing seriously immoral shit beneath the veneer of CEO or politician.

He tossed the football a few more times before flipping onto his stomach. "I don't do it because I want to, Drew. I don't wanna be that person." His brows pulled together. "People do what they have to, you know?"

"I can't pretend to understand." I stroked my thumb over his cheek.

Bellamy did some unsavory things, but the more I learned about him, the more I wasn't sure how bad he actually was. Wasn't this just survival?

"But I can see it's hard."

He nodded to his dresser. "Open the top drawer."

"Okay..." I got up and opened the drawer. An envelope

stuffed with cash was tucked in the back corner amongst a nest of socks.

"That's what pays the bills and has for the past two years. I seal it up and write our address on it and mail it to her. Because she sure as hell wouldn't take it if I tried to just hand it to her." He half-laughed. "Prays every night to bless whoever sends it. Hate to tell her the prayers don't work."

Bellamy was eighteen and bearing the weight of the world on his shoulders.

"So just... whenever your dad tries to act like he knows who I am?" Seconds of silence ticked by while Bellamy stared at the ceiling. "That's who I am. I steal, and I deal, and I fuck shit up, but that right there is why."

"Bellamy..." I walked over to the bed and crawled over him. His hands went to my waist as he looked at me. "I know who you are." I pressed a kiss to his jaw. "You're a bad boy." Another kiss. "Who's secretly good." And another. "I won't tell anyone, though, because I have a reputation, and I can't be dating good guys. I like to piss my dad off."

He smirked before I kissed his lips.

## CHAPTER 38

## BELLAMY

"NOT GOING TO CHURCH...YOU should be ashamed of yourself." Pops shook his head and closed the front door.

I looked at Drew. "He's not going to church. He's going gambling."

"I'd rather play poker than go to church," she mumbled.

Mom bustled around the corner with a full face of make-up.

Everything about her looked ten years younger because that asshole was out of the house. The restraining order was now official, and I couldn't be happier. They'd given dad a court date, although he'd gotten out on bail.

"I'm taking Arlo over to Genie's," she said, "and I'm going to stay and talk."

Because she'd never been able to just go do things on her own outside of work or grocery shopping. He wouldn't let her. She felt like she had to explain. And that made me feel like I should have beat that fucker's ass to the point of death long ago.

"Love you, baby." She leaned over the couch and kissed the top of my head.

"Love you, too."

Arlo raced into the room, exchanging some weird handshake with Drew before he followed Mom out the door.

"Hey! Butthole!" I called over the back of the couch. "Are you going to tell me bye?"

He ducked his head around the front door. "Bye, Bubba!" Then he was gone.

"I'm his favorite." Drew smirked.

"Good to know his loyalty can be bought with Push-Pops." I leaned over, sinking my hand between her thighs. "Just like this pussy."

"Rude."

"It's really not." I slammed my lips over hers, threading my fingers through her hair before I slipped my tongue between her lips. The more I was around her, the more I couldn't get enough of her.

The alarm on my phone went off, and I tossed my head back on the couch. "Shit. I gotta go do something." I pushed to my feet. "Come on."

A slow smile overtook her face. "Is it something illegal?"

This girl liked a thrill too much, and I liked that she liked it. "Of course."

We pulled up to Hendrix's house, and Drew lifted a brow as we climbed out. "Should've known."

Hendrix opened the door, took two steps out, then shook his head. "This is bullshit, Bell." He pointed at Drew. "That right there is walking, fucking bullshit."

"Shut up, Hendrix." I shoved past him into the living room and toward the back porch.

"Seriously. You seriously brought *Drucella* over here for our man shit. You disappoint me." Hendrix kicked open the screen door, mumbling under his breath as we followed him outside.

"He's prickly today," Drew whispered.

"He's always prickly."

Hendrix cut through the overgrown grass to the tarp-covered car at the back of his lot. He tossed the cover off, revealing an old Chevy Dodger with a cracked windshield and missing hood.

"What is that?" Drew lifted a brow.

Hendrix sighed. "Bell, you're dating a girl who doesn't even know what a car is."

Drew flipped him off. "That is barely a car." Then she glanced at me. "Is this stolen?"

"Yeah."

Hendrix took a pair of pliers from the toolbox, scowling at Drew. "Is that car stolen, she asked. Like we'd just have shit sitting around. God, rich girls." He moved toward the car and leaned over the engine. "Wolf and I are going to another revival this week. If you can get away from Medusa, you should come."

I had no reason to go to that crap with them. "I'm not trying to pick up girls, asshole."

"Oh." He glanced over at Drew and rolled his eyes. "That's right. You've gone all pussy and shit. Fine. We'll keep the virgins to ourselves."

"Whatever, Hendrix." I grabbed a razor blade from the kit and went to the driver's side to file off the VIN number.

Drew leaned against the side of the car. "I'm sorry. You're going to church revivals. To get laid."

"Yeah." Hendrix cackled. "I caught me two virgins with one hook."

I glanced through the windshield just as Hendrix pulled at his crotch.

"So wait. You got two virgins into a three-way?" Drew asked.

I shook my head, climbing out of the car to grab the number from the doorjamb. "Don't ask him shit about it. Just pat his back and—"

"Call me Casanova." He chucked the pliers at me. "And screw you for not wanting to know more, you dickdribble."

Drew's phone rang. Then rang again, and again.

"Irina." There was a pause before she turned away from us. "No, I am not putting you on video. Why? You wouldn't—Fine. Jesus." She glanced around before turning her back to the yard and holding her phone in front of her face.

"Where on earth are you?" A woman's voice came over the speaker.

"Out."

"Is that—are you doing charity work?"

"No! Look, can I call you later?"

"Your father tells me you've run off with a Dayton boy, a criminal. Ruined his house. He's very concerned about your well-being. You need to return home, Drucella."

Hendrix's ears perked up at that comment. He shoved away from the engine, stalking toward her. "Who's that Drewbers?"

The glare Drew leveled on him could have made hell freeze over.

"Is that him?" The woman sounded alarmed. "Are you in a ghetto?"

Drew's face went red. "Mom! Will you stop? I will call—"

Something inside of me snapped. "No. That's not him," I said, moving toward Drew. I snatched the phone from her hand. Then stared at the dark-headed woman with a face full of makeup and puffed-out cheeks. "This is him. What's up, Momma?" I lifted my chin, then swiped a hand over it.

Hendrix cackled in the background. "Yes! You just went from pussy-ass bitch to stunner, Bell."

Drew tried to snatch the phone, but I held it out of her reach. "You just called her Momma!"

The woman stared at me for a moment, then brought a glass of wine to her red lips. "*Are* you a criminal, young man?"

"Depends on what your definition of one is."

Drew jumped up and managed to grab the phone. "No, Bellamy is not a criminal. Yes, I trashed his house because I had a party because he forgot my birthday. Also, dad called me a whore. Thank you for the Porsche. I love you, and I will call you later!"

"Bisous, darling."

Then she hung up and turned on me. "You," she poked my chest, "And you!" Then she jabbed at Hendrix. "I can't."

I lifted a brow. "The ghetto…"

"She's sheltered! She lives in Saint Tropez and thinks champagne is an appropriate breakfast option."

And this was the girl I was falling for. Hard and fast, like an idiot skydiver without a parachute.

## CHAPTER 39

## DREW

A CLOUD of black exhaust coughed from the tailpipe as Bellamy drove off, and I stood on the front porch, staring at the door. My dad had called my mother, and not only did they hate each other, but he'd never admit his failings to her willingly. And that was enough to tell me whatever I was about to walk into was going to be bad.

I slowly closed the heavy wooden door. The click of the lock echoed into the tall foyer.

"Drucella. Come here."

The force of my heartbeat sent a nauseating feeling churning in my gut as I followed the sound of his voice. My dad sat at the breakfast bar, a glass of whiskey in front of him. "Hope you enjoyed yourself." He stared into the glass, swirling the whiskey before he polished it off.

"I'm sorry I had a party and the house got trashed." From the look on his face, I needed to apologize, or he might kill me. "It was my birthday."

"And, I assume that should excuse your behavior?"

"You forgot."

He pushed up, grabbed a bottle of water from the fridge

and a small paper bag from the side of the counter, then handed both to me. The fact that he totally ignored my comment made me resent him so much.

"Do us both a favor and take those." I peered inside the bag at the little white box.

"The morning after pill? Are you serious?"

"The fact that you know what that is without even looking at the packaging says it all, Drew."

A slow fire built in my chest. The way he looked at me was not much different than the way he'd looked at Bellamy. And I hated him.

I hated him for judging Bellamy. For judging me. For thinking nothing was ever good enough. All the resentment and feelings of inadequacy bubbled to the surface.

"Well, you know, I do have daddy issues. That being said, I didn't fuck Bellamy." Not on Saturday night, at least. "Despite my being a '*whore*.'"

On a heavy sigh, he swiped a hand down his face. "I shouldn't have said that."

That wasn't an apology, though.

"That boy is no good for you, Drew," he said. "Trust me on this." He moved toward me, attempting to take hold of my arms, but I backed away. "I only want what's best for you."

"Really, Dad? Because it seems like you just want to make me miserable. You put me in that school. Practically threw me to the wolves after I begged you not to. I didn't even cheat at Black Mountain." My voice cracked slightly, frustration making me emotional. "And now you're mad I'm dating a Dayton guy."

"You're *not* dating that boy!"

Defiance rose over any premise of tact. "I am. I'm eighteen. You can't stop me."

He slammed a fist over the island, the boom echoing into the tall ceilings. "He has nothing to offer you, Drew. He's Dayton. His best prospects are jail time and a string of dead-end jobs. And I'll not allow him to drag you his depth."

"What are—"

"I sent you to that school to try to teach you some discipline! To show you what life could be like if you didn't get your act together, not to wallow around in the dirt with its scum."

My temper spiked violently. "He's not scum!"

He inhaled a deep breath, closing his eyes like he was willing calm. "Give me your phone."

"What?"

"Give me your phone. Right now!"

"No!"

He practically ripped my bag from my shoulder, taking out my phone and holding it up. "I pay for this, so if I deem it fit to take it away, I will! You are not to leave the house, and you're not going to school tomorrow. Test me, and I will lock you in your room."

What the hell? "You sound insane!"

His jaw ticced. "I'm done with this conversation." He snatched his whiskey glass from the island and placed it in the sink. When he turned around, he pointed an angry finger at me. "And you're done with that boy." Then he stormed out of the kitchen. Seconds later, the door to his study slammed shut with finality.

He hadn't listened to a damn thing I'd said. He hadn't even apologized for forgetting my birthday. And now he'd taken away my phone, isolating me further in this house.

Bellamy would try to text me, and what would he think

when I didn't respond? That I was ghosting him? That I didn't like him?

The thought had my stomach twisting and knotting. I went to my room and opened my laptop, thinking I could get to him on social media, but the second I tried to pull up the sites, a message from the internet provider popped up, saying they'd been blocked.

My dad was an absolute dick, and there was nothing I could do.

## CHAPTER 40

### BELLAMY

ME: **I can still smell you on my sheets**
**Me: Taste you on my tongue...**

I was in the middle of typing out something really vulgar when a text from Drew came through.

**Baby girl: Drucella will not be seeing you anymore. - William Morgan**

Heat crept over my cheeks as I stared at my phone.

Arlo sprinted past me, pretending to fly Spike through the air.

*Drucella will not be seeing you anymore.* Because he thought he could dictate her life. Just like that. When he couldn't even be bothered to remember her birthday.

That heat bled from my face to my collar, then down to my chest as I snatched my keys from the coffee table and left.

I'd show him just how wrong he was.

By the time I parked in her dark drive, my blood was a spitting, angry cauldron.

I shifted over the console and threw open the passenger door, thumbing over my nose on my way up the sidewalk that led to the front of her house. My pulse sounded like a war drum in my ears by the time I pounded over the door. The ridiculously ornate porch light came on. Then the door opened to Drew's dad, just as pious and arrogant looking as he was the other day.

He closed the door enough that I guess he felt safe. "Drucella is not seeing you anymore."

"Bullshit."

"Young man. You need to leave. Now." He went to close the door the rest of the way, but I slapped a palm over the heavy wood, halting it.

"You may make decisions for her, but you don't make decisions for me."

Some of his color drained from his face. "I've put in for a stay-away order. If you choose to show up on my property again, I'll have you arrested."

"Like getting arrested is anything new..."

He attempted to close the door again, but I didn't budge. Drew was the best thing that had happened to me, and like hell, I was going to let this asshole rob me of the last few weeks I had with her.

"You're rich," I said. "So I'm sure you understand what determination is, which means I'm sure you'll understand me when I say, I'm determined to see your daughter." On a smirk, I removed my hand from the door, then turned my back to him and started to my car.

I hoped that asshole let that statement resonate.

The next morning, I stared at Mr. Morgan's text while I waited at Drew's locker.

That must have been the hundredth time I'd read it, and it still sent a flash of red dancing across my vision.

The halls began to thin out, the bang of locker doors fell silent just before the tardy bell rang. And Drew wasn't there.

She wasn't at lunch.

Or biology.

And when Smith didn't call her name on the roll, I knew the dick had pulled her out. He'd paid Brown to keep her in this shithole school through the theft and vandalism and drug dealing, but one look at me in her bed and he had unenrolled her.

Because her dating a guy like me was so much worse than any of those other things...

A cyclone of emotions ranging from anger to defeat swirled through my head as I crammed my books into my backpack. With a slam of my locker door, I shouldered my book bag and started toward the exit.

A light drizzle of rain fell from the overcast sky, and I ducked my head on my way through the parking lot to keep it out of my face.

"Bellamy?" Nora called my name just before I reached my car. The splash of her shoes through the puddles sounded before she stopped beside me, a frown on her face. "Did Drew get kicked out or something? She wasn't on the roll, and she's not answering my texts."

"Yeah, because her dad has her phone."

The rain began to fall a little harder. "What? Why?"

"Because he's a dick." I unlocked the passenger door, then tossed my book bag into the back seat. "He texted me last night from it. So my guess is, he took it."

She wasn't enrolled at Dayton anymore. He'd threatened to have me arrested if I showed up at the house again. And he had her phone. There was no way for me to even talk to her at this point. Unless...

"Do me a favor," I said, leaning into my car to open the glovebox. I rummaged through papers for the burner phone and its charger. "Take this to her."

I held out the device, but all Nora did was stare at it, confused.

"Dammit, Nora. He won't let me talk to her or see her. Would you please take it to her so I can at least check on her?"

Slowly, she took the phone from my hand. "So...this is your fault?"

"My fault. Her fault. What does it matter?"

On a sigh, she crammed it into her purse. She took a few steps around the back of my car before she paused. "You like her. Like you actually like her, don't you?"

"No shit."

She held my gaze for a moment. "Okay. I'll take it to her."

"Thank you."

I climbed into my car, scooted across the console, and sank behind the wheel, watching the drops of rain splash against the windshield.

I don't know what I expected to come from this thing between Drew and me anyway. We were worlds apart, and even if she *weren't* jetting off for college in New York come fall, I'd known since day one her family would never approve of me.

The people of Barrington lived in the castle on the hill, and I was nothing more than a peasant. And that shit only worked when it was a poor girl after a rich boy.

This thing with Drew was never supposed to be anything more than a little fun, a deal. A sordid exchange. She was supposed to be a one-time high—something I could easily walk away from and quit, but wasn't that how all addictions started? The thought of being without her sent a crippling sense of hopelessness creeping through me. Which meant, like all addicts searching for that high, I was probably about to do something really stupid to satisfy my craving.

## CHAPTER 41

## DREW

ONE DAY.

That was all it had taken for my dad to yank me out of Dayton and place me in the school I now wanted no part of.

I stared across the breakfast bar at my dad, the hatred inside me bubbling like lava. He looked so damn smug that I was sitting here, in the navy blazer and skirt that made up Barrington's uniform.

It was like he thought going to Barrington would fix me and cleanse me of my taint. I could see it all over his face—he thought order had been restored. But it would never be restored because I didn't fit into his uptight box, and I never would. No matter how many stuffy uniforms he forced me into. All I could think about was the fact that graduation would be in a few weeks, then it was summer, and I could... What, leave? Go to France? That was what I'd usually do. My mother was better than my father, but it was another shiny bubble of expectation. And the little pinch in my chest reminded me that I'd be half a world away from the only person who offered me a glimmer of happiness.

He slid car keys across the marble counter, a Porsche emblem on the fob. "You may have your car back."

That car? He was giving me *that* car. Like I needed to draw extra attention to myself. The Dayton trash in a baby-pink Porsche...

It seemed misery was my fate, whether I liked it or not.

When I pulled up to Barrington and parked between the Mercedes and BMWs, my stomach knotted.

Bellamy had made no secret about us, making out with me in the halls of Dayton. Rumors traveled like wildfire through small towns, and I had no doubt people in this school would see me as trash, no matter how much money I was from.

I was braced, ready for a barrage of shit. But no one gave me a second glance. No one spoke to me at all. Not even Olivia when she passed me in the hall.

It was like I didn't exist. I'd almost forgotten that this was how the rich kids got their retribution, by ostracizing. Marking someone as a leper.

And after going to a school full of car bombs and razor blades, being ignored was nothing short of a welcomed peace.

This would be easy. Keep my head down, get my exams done, and then, in a month, I would be free of this bullshit and my dad's control.

The dismissal bell rang, and I gathered my books, sprinting through the crowded halls to the exit, then hurrying across the parking lot to my car.

My dad's rules were crystal clear. School and home. Bellamy's house was twenty minutes away, but I had to risk it because, for all he knew, I'd just ghosted him.

I sped through Barrington until pristine verges dotted with colorful flower beds turned to overgrown, hard shoulders.

I wound through the rat's nest of Dayton until I pulled up outside the single-story house with Bellamy's dented car parked outside. My chest went tight as I made my way to the front porch, then knocked and waited.

Bellamy opened the door. He was like night to Barrington's bright, sunny day in his tight, black shirt and grease-stained jeans. And I was all about the darkness.

His gaze swept over the Barrington uniform, and he promptly adjusted his dick. "Barrington, huh?"

"It sucks." It had only been two days since I'd seen him, but it felt so much longer.

The second his arms came around me, it felt like all my problems disappeared.

"My dad took my phone. I wasn't ignoring you."

"I know."

I pulled back, but he didn't release me. "You know?" Realization washed over me. "Did he message you?"

"Right after I texted you about how good you taste."

Oh, my god. Groaning, I buried my face in his chest, absolutely mortified on every level.

"I wonder if he watched that video I sent you…"

An almost pleased laugh bubble from his throat. The thought of my dad, sitting at his desk, reading our dirty exchanges, watching the video of Bellamy masturbating…everything inside of me felt weak and disgusted. I wanted to throw up.

Bellamy leaned against the wooden doorframe, tracing a finger beneath the waistband of my tartan skirt. "Wanna go make a video?"

"I can't stay." I wanted to. God, I wanted to.

On a huff, he half-rolled his eyes and pushed back from the entrance. "Give me a second."

He disappeared down the hall, and I stood on his small porch, listening to the noise of cars backfiring and dogs barking.

The floor inside creaked as he rounded the couch, then stepped back through the open door. He handed me an outdated phone along with a charger. "I sent Nora over with it, but he wouldn't let her see you."

"The fact that Nora agreed to help you..." That just proved I was at a crisis point. And the fact my dad had turned her away was ridiculous. I swear the man wanted me to be every bit as bitter and lonely as him.

"You just gotta make sure to forward any texts to me," he said.

I lifted a brow. "Is this a drug dealer phone, Bellamy?"

"It's a business phone, baby girl." He swept a piece of hair behind my shoulder. "Your dad should like that."

Laughing, I grabbed the front of his shirt and pulled him closer. "I'm sure he will."

When I pressed my lips to his, it was like pure electricity, adrenaline crawling through my veins in a slow burn. Bellamy's fingers dug into my hips like he would hold me hostage if he could.

At this point, I wanted to let him. He was my escape from my shitty reality.

"How often can you sneak over here?" he asked, his lips still touching mine as a warm breeze circled around us.

"Maybe a couple of times, but he's not stupid. He's very vigilant in my imprisonment."

Bellamy's jaw set at that. "You do realize you're eighteen..."

"And completely reliant on him. My phone? He pays

for it, so he can take it. My car? He pays all the running costs. I live in his house. Even if I got a job, he'd take the money off me because I 'owe him' for my Black Mountain tuition. And my only other option? My mother, who lives in France. He has me by the balls."

And I hated it, hated that this privileged lifestyle had equated to a golden cage. I couldn't even date who I wanted.

On a heavy breath, he swept a hand through my hair, studying me. "I'll text you later."

"I give it a week, and he'll go on some business trip."

He kissed me hard like he was trying to imprint himself on me. I didn't know when I'd see him again, and that had a little knife digging in my chest. Bellamy made me feel alive and staying away from him would make my bleak life a whole lot darker.

## CHAPTER 42

## BELLAMY

THE CONCEPT of not pulling your weight was foreign in Dayton.

Growing up, we had little choice not to pitch in by either working or stealing. So the fact that Drew, at the age of eighteen, had nothing that was really hers blew my mind.

I bought my clothes. I paid for my car. My gas. My phone. And I paid my fair share of bills…

I laid in bed, more aware now than ever of just how different life for all those Barrington pricks was. They were handed everything, and it seemed that was lorded over their heads, used to control and manipulate. Setting them up to be the manipulative little shits they'd undoubtedly turn into because they had been raised to believe that money was power over everyone around you.

It had been a week since she'd shown up at my house, and thoughts of her occupied most of my waking hours.

**Me: Is he ever going to leave?**

Two days ago, her dad was supposed to leave for business. And hadn't. I didn't realize how *much* I needed her until she was gone.

**Work Phone: He needs to. I can't take much more.**

I missed her, but I couldn't tell her that, so instead, I went with:

**Me: My balls are about to rupture.**

**Work Phone: You know your right hand didn't fall off, right?**

**Me: No shit. It's the only reason I'm not dead yet.**

**Work Phone: Do you think of me?**

Of course, I do. Who else would I think of? I was hard up for the girl. She had to know that.

**Me: I go to the picture on your InstaPic page of you on some yacht in a barely there bikini and blow my load to that.**

**Me: Since you never returned my favor and sent me dirty pictures**

**Me: Selfish-ass**

**Work Phone: Well, I'd send you something to get through this difficult time, but your "business" phone doesn't have a camera…**

**Work Phone: You could always sneak through my bedroom window and take one yourself.**

Like hell I'd waste time taking a picture. I'd be buried balls deep inside of her within two minutes flat.

**Me: I'd take more than a picture…**

**Work Phone: I know you would.**

Fifteen minutes later, I parked at the country club and cut across the golf course that backed up to Drew's street. Then I climbed the wrought iron fence surrounding her back yard.

From there, I could see the silhouette of her dad's flashy car in the drive. I had no doubt the asshole actually filed for a stay-away order, and I had no doubt he'd call the police if he caught me on his property. So I just couldn't let him catch me.

Because this—this was bullshit.

I dropped to the ground and went straight to the side of the house, grabbed hold of the latticework, and scaled it, climbing over the balcony like some asshole out of Shakespeare.

Jesus, what had my life become?

Through the French doors that led into her room, I could see Drew sprawled horizontally across her bed. Her head hung off the side, and her gaze fixed on the ceiling.

I tapped on the glass, and she jumped. The moment her gaze swung to the window, she scrambled off the bed and opened the balcony door just enough to squeeze out.

"Oh my God. I was joking about sneaking in my window!" she whispered. "He'll get you arrested."

Grabbing her face, I slammed my lips to hers. The taste of her bled through my veins, relaxing my coiled muscles like a much-needed hit. When I pulled away, her fingers fisted in my shirt, and I pressed my forehead to hers. "I don't give a shit what he does."

She glanced back into her room, then over the railing. "Come on." Then she led me through her bedroom, straight into her bathroom, where she locked the door and promptly cut on the shower.

"You'd risk getting arrested for a fuck?"

Not a fuck, but for her? Yes. "I'm not getting arrested," I said.

Steam slowly billowed over the glass shower door as I slipped one strap of her tank top off her shoulder. Followed by the other.

Then I pressed my lips to her throat.

"Bellamy..."

"Drew..." My hands cupped her bare tits as I covered her mouth with mine. "Don't want to waste water, do you?"

I shoved off her shorts, then her thong.

"We cannot fuck with my dad here," she whispered, not doing a damn thing to resist me.

My fingers found their way inside her, immediately coaxing a moan.

It was absolutely messed up that I was doing this to her. In her house. With him downstairs. But screw him for being a dick.

I pushed my fingers in deeper. Then I stopped. "This sure as hell feels like we can..."

"You're an asshole," she said, gripping my wrist and forcing my hand to move again.

"That I am."

She yanked at my belt, and within seconds, she had me undressed, and I had her naked body pinned against the tile wall of her shower, head tossed back on a moan while I buried myself deep inside her.

I wanted her more than I'd wanted anything in my life.

I kissed along the column of her neck, licking at the water cascading down her body, and all I could think about was how I could hold onto this—hold onto her a little bit longer. "Don't make me go days without this again." I moved inside her.

Her breath hitched, thighs clamping around my hips.

I went at her harder until her nails embedded in my back, and I had my hand over her mouth to silence her moans.

She tightened around me, and I dropped my chin to my chest, biting back a groan as I came.

The idea that neither of us had to go without this cycled through my head. There were only three weeks until graduation. And then what...

We were on borrowed time, but that was what I'd been living on for the past few years of my life; stealing cars and dealing drugs to pay bills—there was a definite risk there. And there was a massive risk here. Each day I spent with Drew, each kiss, each fuck, would make losing her harder, but I didn't care.

She was a high, a thrill, something I needed even if I knew it would be to my own damn detriment. I was a risk-taker, and I was pretty damn sure Drew Morgan would always be my greatest risk.

She cut the shower off, then we dried each other off.

Naked, no makeup, her hair a damp, tangled mess—God, she was gorgeous. Perfect. Mine.

Mine for how much longer...

"How long were you planning to stay after graduation?" I asked, running the towel over her hair to dry it.

"I don't know. I usually go to stay with my Mom in the summer because I hate my dad. I *was* thinking I'd stick around this year."

"Why?"

"You know why."

Because of me.

I handed her the towel, and she wrapped it around her body. Three weeks until graduation. Then eight weeks until she'd be leaving for college.

"So why are you going to stay *here*." I grabbed my jeans from the floor and pulled them up. "If we can't even see each other?"

Inhaling a hard breath, she nodded. "Is this the part where we break up?"

"No. This is the part where you leave." I'd spent the last seven days away from her, and I didn't want to do that again. It was rash—absolutely—but wasn't that how Drew and I worked? On a series of rash decisions. I started into her room, heading straight for her closet.

"What?"

I grabbed one of her suitcases and started filling it with clothes.

She stepped inside the closet, gripping the towel around her chest. "And go where?"

"To my house. He doesn't want you to see me? Fuck him."

"Bellamy..." She let out a sigh. "Pretty sure your mom is not going to be okay with that."

"What if she was?" I threw a stack of jeans into her suitcase. I knew my mom, and she wouldn't care.

"If she's not. I'll get my own place. I don't give a shit. You're not staying in this house like some trapped princess locked in a tower. And if you do, I'm going to jail..."

"I..." Her eyes closed, and a moment of self-doubt crept in. Maybe she didn't feel the same way I did. "It's not as simple as that, and you know it," she said.

"No, I don't know it." I tossed more clothes in. "Because I wouldn't let someone control me like this." Another shirt landed in the suitcase.

"You have your own money, Bellamy. I'm just...some spoiled brat."

She wasn't. She was so much more than that. "Then stop being a spoiled brat, Drew."

"How?" She stared at me like I'd lost my mind, her gaze shifting from me to the suitcase I kept filling. "By moving in with you? You have to know how crazy that sounds."

"Yeah? And you're fucking crazy, so..." I zipped the suitcase and glared at her.

I sounded crazy, and I knew it, but that's what Drew did to me. Made me lunatic crazy. "And you've made me a complete psycho," I said.

A small smile touched her lips. "Believe me when I say, I'd love nothing more than to walk out of here and flip my dad off on the way out the door. But I have nothing to offer you, Bellamy."

"Oh, you've got plenty to offer me, baby girl..." I stepped toward her, grabbing her waist. "I'd have you at my beck and call." I smirked.

"You're a dick."

Everything about why I was doing this was selfish. Every damn thing. Because I wanted as much of her as I could have before she left. I wanted every damn second I could steal with her. So I pushed where I knew she'd give.

"Where's the rebel at? The girl who had me arrested and let Hendrix set her car on fire just to try and get expelled?" I yanked her close, brushing my lips to hers. "You aren't a spoiled brat, baby girl; you're a fucking nightmare. And no one locks the evil queen in the tower..."

"This is why my dad doesn't like you. You make me want to do insane things. You make me want to set fire to everything shiny and watch it burn."

"Nah. I just give you the match."

"You're absolutely insane..." Her gaze lingered on mine for a moment before she let out a breath. "Screw it." She kissed me before resting her forehead against mine. "Move in with my criminal boyfriend? Why not?"

"That's the spirit, baby girl."

"But we have to plan this out..."

And the next morning, I sat at the Jet Pep across from the entrance to Barrington Heights, waiting until her dad's Maserati zoomed past to go to her house and grab her shit.

## CHAPTER 43

## DREW

I PULLED AWAY from the bank, cutting through the rush hour traffic in the center of Barrington. Instead of turning toward Barrington prep, I headed into Dayton. To Bellamy.

This was insanity.

I'd only known Bellamy for a few weeks, and half of that time, we'd hated each other.

He'd seen me at my worst, and if anything, my worst was what he liked best. In a world where I'd always been sub-par, he made me feel like something special.

I wanted whatever this crazy, burning addiction I had for him was. I craved the way he made me feel so alive, like all my imperfections *were* perfect. I'd jump into the unknown for him, but also for me. Screw the future and the what-ifs and maybes.

This might have been a mistake but not one I would regret.

When I pulled up to Bellamy's, his car was in the drive and

the trunk was open. He stepped outside of his house and went straight to his car to haul another of my suitcases out.

I was really doing this. No going back.

I'd emptied my account before my dad could figure out what I was moving in with Bellamy and his family because I knew the second he figured it out, he'd cut me off. I was going to re-enroll in Dayton to finish school.

Holy shit. I was moving in with him...

Would his mom think I was dragging her son down? Should I have spoken to her myself and asked to stay with her? The protocol for shacking up at eighteen was a little hazy. I would pay her, though...I thumbed through the cash in the envelope, about six thousand dollars. The price of a handbag normally. Now it was the price of freedom—for a little while at least.

I stuffed the envelope inside my purse and got out of the car.

Bellamy stood at the back of his Honda, an unreadable expression on his face as he stared at the bumper. "You cannot leave that thing in my drive."

I glanced at the Porsche, then back to him. "Well, where do you want me to put it?"

"I don't know." He swiped a hand through his hair. "We'll have to get a tarp and cover it up. Someone will absolutely try to steal it."

I walked toward him. "Well, *you* would know..."

This boy was a car thief, a drug dealer, a criminal, and though I said he was no knight and I was no princess, it sure as hell felt like he was saving me.

He grabbed onto my hips, pulling me in for a kiss. "Think he's gotten the, 'you're not in school' text from Barrington yet?"

"I'm almost disappointed I didn't get to make a show of

leaving. You know I like some theatrics." I could picture my father's face when he realized I wasn't coming back.

I didn't think for a second he'd been upset at losing his daughter, just angry that he couldn't control me.

"I think we should just skip school and fuck, since no one's home. What do you think?"

I thought it was a great idea.

I'd just broken a nail on his headboard when the muffled noise of a car door closing came through the single-pane bedroom window.

Bellamy leaned over his headboard to peek through the plastic blinds. "The balls on this asshole..."

"Who is it?"

He rolled off the bed, pulling on jeans before storming into the hall. "Your dad."

Of course, he was here. The man had barely given a crap about me, but now, when I decided to pick a poor guy...now he suddenly wanted to try and parent me.

"Bellamy, do not punch him!" I called after him, hurrying to get dressed.

I pulled my shirt over my head on my way into the hall just as the lock to the front door clicked.

"You need to get the hell off my porch." The pure restraint was evident in Bellamy's tone.

"I will do no such thing. I'm here for my daughter."

The silence seemed to stretch on for minutes, but it could have only been a matter of seconds before I made it into the tiny living room.

Bellamy stood, arms crossed. Jeans not fastened. My nail marks fresh on his bare chest. My soul died a little bit at that moment.

"She's not leaving." His back muscles bunched and tensed. One wrong word from my dad and Bellamy may very well knock him out.

My father's gaze skirted over me like I was no better than one of those hookers up by the pawn shops in Dayton, and I shouldn't have cared, but it cut me to the core. "Drucella…"

"I'm not coming." I held my breath, my pulse going haywire as Bellamy's fingers threaded through mine. "I'm eighteen. I'm moving out."

My father's face turned every shade of red, then purple. "That's how you want to be? Fine." He smoothed a hand down his pressed dress shirt. "If you want to play poverty-stricken house, by all means. Play."

His gaze swung back to Bellamy, and he paused like he was about to say something. "The least you can do is wear a condom. Let's not make her momentary lapse in judgment a lifetime of punishment."

When I glanced at Bellamy, he looked like he was ready to blow. "Get the hell," he took an unsteady breath, "off my porch."

My dad gave me one last disapproving look before he turned and stormed down the drive to his car.

## CHAPTER 44

## BELLAMY

THE NEXT DAY AFTER SCHOOL, Drew went with me to pick Arlo up from the bus stop, then go meet the guys at Waffle Hut.

Arlo shot inside, hurling himself into the booth, then patting the plastic seat. "Miss Drew, you sit next to me."

Hendrix's head lifted on a glare, tracking Drew as we made our way across the restaurant. She sat beside Arlo, and I sat next to her.

"Don't, dude." Wolf shook his head at Hendrix. "Just don't."

Hendrix twisted the straw paper in his hand, then dropped it to the table. "You disgust me, Bell."

"Jesus Christ, man. Shut up." Not that I expected Hendrix to be excited about my moving Drew in. I threw an arm around Drew's shoulders, and Hendrix sank back in the seat with a snarl.

"It's bullshit, Wolf." He snatched up a menu. "And you know it."

Drew flipped him off. "You need me to buy you a tiara over there, drama queen?"

One of his eyes twitched before he looked at me. "And you chose to live with that..."

"Miss Drew's living with us?" Arlo clapped his hands. "Yay!"

"No, Arlo." Hendrix leaned across the table with a stern glare. "It's not yay. She's a succubus, and she's just sunk her claws into your brother and is dragging him down to an estrogen-riddled hell."

"Estrogen?"

"Don't listen to Hendrix, Peehead." Drew patted Arlo's head. "He's just salty because no girls like him for more than one night."

This would never end.

"Hendrix. Shut up. Drew, shut up." I grabbed a menu. "Arlo, yes, she's staying for a while."

Wolf chuckled, opening his menu and hiding his face behind it while humming the tune to "Another One Bites the Dust."

After the waitress came over and took our order, Arlo crawled over the back of the booth to go to the restroom.

Hendrix glared at Drew for a second. "So we're gonna talk business in front of her now, I guess?"

"Yeah..."

Wolf's gaze drifted to the front. "Shit..." He yanked the joint from behind his ear and crammed it into his pocket. "Cops are coming over here."

Officer Robins stopped beside our booth, a cup of coffee in his hand.

His gaze shifted from me to Hendrix to Wolf, then stopped on Drew. "Miss Morgan, right? How you doing?"

Wolf and Hendrix stared straight ahead at the wall.

"I'm good..." She glanced at me like I knew what the hell was going on. "How are you?"

Hendrix groaned, tossing his head back on the booth.

"That's good to hear. Just came in for a cup of Joe. They've got some good coffee here." He took a sip from his mug. "Just thought I would come by and check that you were okay. We've had a report down at the station that says you're a missing person..."

Jesus Christ. She was eighteen; there wasn't crap that could be done about it if she decided to leave. But since he saw her as nothing more than a possession, I guess it made sense to him.

"Oh, that's...Nope. I'm right here."

"Well, your father seems to think you're missing." Another sip of coffee. "Guess it might be those authoritative differences, huh?" His gaze strayed to me momentarily.

She actually laughed. "Let's just say they escalated."

"I see. I'll make a note when I get back to the station, ma'am. Call him and tell him you're A-Okay."

"Sure."

"All right then. You kids have a good day." Then he walked off.

Hendrix scoffed. "Miss? Ma'am? We get called assholes and little shits."

Because we were. Drew snatched her drink. "You are an asshole, Hendrix."

"This is the kinda shit I'm talking about, Bell." He balled up a napkin and lobbed it at Drew. "Getting all Chatty Kathy with the police. Calling me names. Giving me head injuries. What's next? Burning my house down and taking a shit on it?" He shook his head. "Where is the line?"

"You pissed in my car!" Drew all but shouted.

"You got him arrested!" Hendrix did shout.

Wolf barked out a laugh. "God, Zepp is missing some grade-A shit."

Arlo came back and Drew helped him over the back of the booth while I ignored the argument continuing to go back and forth, seething.

The waitress brought our food over before I finally couldn't take it any longer. Her dad thought he'd get me in trouble, and that lit my ass on fire. "Your dad just implied I kidnapped you; you realize that?"

The banter fell silent, and Drew's hand landed on my thigh. "My dad is an arrogant old man who is pissed because I'm not falling in line. He's just throwing everything and anything he can at the situation because he has no control." She squeezed. "Really, you should be flattered. You have him so on the ropes."

Flattered? Pissed was more like it.

Arlo stood up in the booth, patting Drew on the head. "Miss Drew, you wanna watch *The Good Dinosaur* with me tonight? It's sad. The dinosaur parents die."

"Well, now you just told me the ending."

He frowned. "It's not the ending. That's just the beginning."

"That's not depressing." She snorted, tugging his shirt down where it had ridden up. "Sure. You want popcorn?"

He nodded enthusiastically.

"Okay. Eat your burger before Hendrix steals it like the vulture he is."

He leaned across the table, whispering, "Arlo. Remember the bro-code. Bros before hoes."

Drew covered Arlo's ears. "Really? He is going to figure out that is not the garden variety soon."

When she released him, he glanced over at me, his little

brow creased in confusion. "*I* before *E* except after *C*, and bros before hose..."

"No! Do *not* go to school and say that crap."

Hendrix cackled like the idiot he was, and I crammed fries into my mouth.

I couldn't deal with this shit...

## CHAPTER 45

### DREW

THE REST of the week went by.

Me waking up at Bellamy's.

Us driving to school.

It became a weird kind of normal, and I felt a kind of warmth I had never experienced before in my short life. Bellamy, Arlo, their mom. It was a family—a *real* family, unlike mine.

Over the past week, I'd watched Carol hug Arlo and kiss Bellamy's cheek, and each time it made my heart squeeze, pining for something I'd never had and it was now too late for.

Bellamy had to go do some 'work,' so I'd offered to pick Arlo up from the bus stop. When he hopped into my car, he stuck out his tongue.

"Why is the stuff on your seat pink?" he asked.

"Don't judge me, kid. My mom picked it out. What music do you want?" I put the roof down, and a grin covered his face.

"The angry lady who screams."

I fist-bumped him before changing the station and putting the car into drive. "You tell your brother that rap sucks."

"No way. That'll hurt his heart, Miss Drew."

I laughed because it would. It really would.

I scruffed his hair. "We can't have that, kid."

It was a quick two-block drive back to Bellamy's house. I went to pull into the drive, then pumped the brakes when I saw a pick-up parked where I usually did.

"Daddy's here!"

Panic instantly washed over me. I pulled over at the curb, staring at the rundown truck. "What? That's your dad's car?"

He nodded, reaching for the door, but I grabbed him and pressed the button for the locks. "Let's wait here." Then I took out my phone and called Bellamy. It rang a few times, then connected.

"Hey."

"Your dad's here."

"Shit... Just stay in the car." The whine of his engine revving came through the speaker.

"When does your mom get off work?"

"Not until later."

"Should I call the police?"

"Hell, no! Pops is there, and they'll take him to jail. Just... I'll be there in ten minutes."

Why in the hell would they take him to jail? Bellamy's dad was the one with a restraining order on his ass. "Okay..." I said.

When I hung up, Arlo frowned at me. "Why can't we go inside?"

"We have to wait for Bellamy, okay?"

"Okay."

There was a beat of silence, filled only with the angry lyrics coming from the sound system.

I stared at the front of the house, wondering if his grandpa was okay. I hoped Bellamy was right, and his grandpa was crazy because, as far as I'd seen, he was just a bit kooky and redneck.

No sooner had I thought that before shouting came from the house.

A salt-and-pepper haired man, who looked an awful lot like an aged Bellamy, shot around the carport, blood trickling from his forehead. He clamored into the pickup, and Grandpa sprinted around the side of the house with a golf club raised above his head.

The truck's taillights flashed, and the engine revved. But before Bellamy's dad could back out, the old man hurled the club at his windshield. Then picked up a brick from the flower bed border and chucked that at the truck before it peeled out of the driveway.

"Pop-Pop!" Arlo cheered.

I unlocked the door, staring wide-eyed at Bellamy's batshit crazy grandpa as I got out of the car. The old man leaned over his knees on a wheeze.

"Need to smoke less, Pops."

"Aw, smoking ain't got nothing to do with this, sugar-pie." He placed a hand to his chest. "I'm just pissed that I couldn't run faster." He covered Arlo's ears with his old, weather hands. "Or I would've killed the son-of-a-bitch. Then you and me'd be going out to the woods to bury him." He spat on the ground before uncovering Arlo's ears.

Okay, he really was crazy.

Bellamy's car chugged into the driveway. When he got out, he looked pissed as hell.

"I busted the son-of-a-bitch upside the head with his own nine-iron." Grandpa grinned, placing a cigarette to his lips and lighting it. "Teach that motherfucker to come back 'round here." He hitched up his pants and took a hefty drag from his smoke.

Bellamy cast a deadpanned look in my direction. "See. No cop's gonna take a nine-iron to someone's head..."

This was so Dayton that I didn't even know where to begin.

"You think your momma would make some of her famous meatloaf?" Grandpa whacked Bellamy on the back. "Attempted murder sure can stir up an appetite."

This was insanity, and this was what I'd chosen to immerse myself in.

I guided Arlo inside, and he went right past the hole in the drywall, the upturned coffee table, and smashed picture frames. He just sat down on the couch and turned on the TV like it was any other Tuesday. And that was the point where my heart sank because the kid thought this was normal.

I knelt and started collecting broken shards of the ceramic lamp.

Bellamy came in, dragging a hand through his hair as he took a quick survey of the damage before he flipped the coffee table back over.

"Do you need to check he didn't take anything?" I asked, thinking of the envelope of cash in his dresser drawer. "Like...in your room."

"He doesn't know about that." He grabbed a shattered frame, removing the picture before he went to the kitchen to throw the broken wood and glass away.

Arlo was used to this, and so was Bellamy.

I wondered how many times Bellamy had seen this shit

when he was a little boy, but without a big brother to look out for him. I wished someone would have been there for him, but he was still the pillar holding it all up even now.

When he came back into the living room, I took him by the jaw and kissed him. I didn't want him to feel like the lone pillar.

His hand came to my waist; his forehead pressed to mine. "Don't judge me by this shit."

Cartoons hummed in the background, and I was absolutely judging him by this shit. Because as much as it may embarrass him, how he dealt with it just showed how truly good he was.

"You're so not a bad boy," I breathed.

"Don't tell me shit like that…"

"Why?" I put my lips to his ear. "Does it make you want to prove me wrong?"

His hands went to my ass. "Absolutely."

"Ewww!" Arlo shouted before tossing a throw pillow at us. "I don't like it when you do that!"

"Fine…" Bellamy huffed, threading his fingers through mine before he led me to his room.

He flipped the lock, then cocked a brow at me. "You're gonna regret telling me I wasn't bad…"

I really didn't think I would…

---

Later that evening, after we'd helped Arlo with his homework, we left to grab groceries for dinner.

Bellamy zoomed past Wal-E-Mart, and I thumbed back at the brightly lit building.

"Uh, didn't you want to go there?"

"Can't go to that one. There's another one at the other end of town."

I waited for him to explain, but, of course, he didn't. "Well, are you going to tell me why, or leave me in suspense?"

"Hendrix kept stealing random shit, and now we're banned. It wasn't even good crap. It was plungers and porcelain Santa Claus decorations."

"Is he a kleptomaniac or something?"

"No, his brother used to hit him in the head with a whiffle ball bat when we were kids." He lowered my window, a light breeze rustling through the inside of the car. "He was also the glue eater in first grade."

I snorted. "Explains a lot." I imagined the three of them as kids, probably complete little assholes.

Bellamy parked at the back of the Wal-E-Mart lot, grabbing a random cart from an empty space before we headed toward the entrance. Something beeped behind me, and I turned to see an old man in a mobility scooter, a camo baseball cap on his head and denim overalls. No shirt beneath. And the best part of it was, he was wearing pink crocs.

I moved out of the way. He winked at me as he whizzed past.

Bellamy threw a loaf of bread into the cart, then a jar of peanut butter.

I followed him around the store, watching people trudge through the aisles, looking like life had completely drained them. Children screamed, sprinting around the massive store. It was just… like nothing I'd ever seen. Because I hadn't. I hated to admit that I'd never even been in a supermarket. My mom and dad both had housekeepers who cleaned and did the food shopping. And I'd been boarding.

Bellamy chucked canned vegetables in. Vegetables in a can. I didn't even know such a thing existed.

"Do me a favor," Bellamy said, fishing a sack of coupons out of his pocket. "Tell me how much these are worth."

I frowned at the coupons. The most they were worth was fifty cents off. These couldn't amount to much more than ten bucks max. Instead of saying anything, I counted them. "Eight seventy-five."

He entered the amount on his phone, then stared at the screen. I realized he was adding it up, working out exactly how much money he had, and with each passing moment, an uncomfortable knot formed in my chest. He was dealing weed and stealing cars, risking jail, and he still had to add up fifty-cent coupons to cover groceries.

We headed to the checkout and loaded the groceries onto the conveyor belt.

"Look, just let me buy it..." I said, hoping I didn't offend him. The last thing I wanted was for him to think I pitied him. Of course, I did, but only because I cared about him. A lot.

"It's fine." He tossed a box of rainbow Push-Pops onto the checkout.

"It's the least I could do. Just..." I waved him away, taking my Amex from my purse and handing it to the cashier. He glared when I passed the coupons to the lady.

I swiped my card, and seconds later, she offered me a sympathetic smile. "I'm sorry, ma'am, your card has been declined."

Declined. *Declined!*

With a smile, I dug in my purse and handed her cash, my heart rate rising in an angry rhythm. That wasn't my dad's card. It was my mom's. That meant one thing...She was on *his* side.

The cashier passed my change across, then my receipt before wishing us a blessed day as we headed to the exit.

We silently loaded the groceries into the trunk. I couldn't believe my mom had sided with my dad. She hated him. After the groceries were tucked away, we placed the shopping cart into the corral, then went to get in the car.

Bellamy crawling across the passenger seat to the driver's side usually made me laugh, but not today.

"You okay?" he asked, backing out of the parking spot, then coming to an abrupt halt as the man in the scooter whizzed past.

"She sided with him."

"What do you mean she *sided* with him?"

The car barreled over a speed bump before he turned onto the main highway.

"My mom's cut me off, and that means she took Dad's side. And she hates him."

For Irina to agree with William, hell must have frozen over. I'd never had my parent's love, but I'd had their money, and to a degree, Irina's affection. Now I had neither.

Bellamy's phone rang. He pulled it from his pocket and stared down at the screen, swerving into another lane. "What the hell kinda number is that?"

I snatched it from him. "It's French." I didn't have my phone, but my dad had Bellamy's number...so, I answered it. "Bellamy's phone."

"Drucella." My mom's voice came over the line. "Where are you?"

"In the car."

"Are you with *him*?"

"Yes." We stopped at a red light. A massive truck pulled

up beside us, the rumble of the engine shaking Bellamy's car.

"You *moved* in with him, darling?"

"Yes!"

"Where exactly are you living? In the ghetto?"

"Oh my God. Mom!"

"Irina, darling. You'll make me feel old calling me Mom."

The light changed, and Bellamy sped off, weaving in and out of traffic. "Does she want to tell me to wear a condom, too?"

Shooting a death glare at him, I held up a hand. Now was not the time.

I argued back and forth with her for the next five minutes until we pulled up to his house.

"Mom, I have to go and get the groceries out of the car."

"Put me on video call. I want to see where you're living."

I stared at the front of the tiny house my mother in no way would approve of. She had no idea the struggles most people face. "No," I said.

"If it's acceptable, I'll reactivate your credit card."

"It's acceptable."

Silence.

Bellamy glanced at me before reaching across to open the door. "She sounds like a fucking delight."

"She's probably drunk." It was the most likely excuse I could come up with.

I climbed out of the car, rounding the back when the phone beeped with a video call request.

She would keep trying until I accepted, so I took a breath and answered.

Mom came into view, diamonds around her neck, and a half-empty glass of champagne in her hand. If I had to guess, the twinkling lights in the background was the view of Monaco from her yacht. "Well," she said. "Let's see it."

Just then, Bellamy leaned over my shoulder. "Hey, Momma. I see where my baby girl gets her good looks from." Then he kissed my cheek.

And my mom's blush matched my own like she was a freaking teenager. Oh my God.

I cleared my throat. "Just remember, not everyone lives in what looks like a five-star hotel. It doesn't mean it's not acceptable."

I went inside the house, hurrying past Carol with a wave and cutting into Bellamy's room. The last thing I wanted was for Carol to hear my mother judging the home Carol had been generous enough to invite me in to.

"This is Bellamy's room." I did a quick spin around.

It wasn't flashy, of course. It was just an old bed and a dinged-up chest of drawers. A few car and football posters.

"I am perfectly fine here. Dad got unbearable. He took my phone. Basically called me a whore. Threatened to have Bellamy arrested..."

"Your father's always been unbearable. And you are not a whore." She drained the rest of the champagne from her glass, then held it up in the air for someone to refill. "Speaking of your father, he sent me Bellamy's records—is that what you call them? Prison report card. Whatever it is..."

"Of course, he did." It didn't surprise me one bit that he'd managed to get hold of them.

"Darling, believe me, I understand the appeal of boys like that."

The bedroom door creaked open, and Bellamy stepped

in, flopping down onto his bed.

"They're dangerous and exciting. I once dated a man who had been to prison, you know? It was a rush." She fiddled with the strand of diamonds around her neck like just the thought of said man made her flustered. "But you are eighteen and beautiful and intelligent, with the whole world at your feet. If you were dating him, fine. But you *moved in with him*! That's..."

Insane? Like I didn't already know that.

She shook her head. "You have to see there's no future in this."

I wanted to walk out of the room so Bellamy couldn't hear her berating him, but I had a feeling he'd think I was hiding things from him.

"Those are dad's words, not yours."

"We'll talk about it when you get here."

Bellamy's gaze immediately locked with mine. I didn't miss the subtle clench of his jaw before he grabbed the football from the floor and started tossing it into the air. Like maybe he could ignore everything she'd said.

"I don't know what I'm doing this summer yet, Mom."

"What? You always come here." I opened my mouth to speak, but she cut me off. "Darling, you'll come to Saint Tropez for the summer. We'll drink wine and shop, and we can talk about your future."

Come to Saint Tropez and forget about him, more like. I was glad she didn't say it when he was right there, though.

"And if I don't?" I asked.

"You will, sweetie."

"Mom..."

Someone called for her in the background. "I have to go, darling."

"Are you still cutting me off?"

Her lips pressed together. "When you run out of money, come to France, and we will discuss. Bisous, darling. Bisous, Bellamy." Then she hung up.

I threw my head back against the headboard on a groan.

"What *the fuck* is a bisous?" he asked.

"It's French for kisses."

He tossed the ball into the corner of the room, then dragged me onto the bed with him. "I'll give you some fucking bisous, on your pussy..."

CHAPTER 46

BELLAMY

OVER THE PAST FEW WEEKS, living with Drew had become my new normal.

Our after-school ritual consisted of coming back to my empty house and climbing into bed, then lying here, talking before we went to pick my brother up from the bus stop. And the shittiest part about it, it was all about to come to an end.

Drew lay on my chest while I traced circles over her bare back.

We graduated in two days, and I'd ignored that fact for three whole weeks. Because graduation marked the beginning of summer, and every day closer we came to fall was one less I had with her. Come mid-August, she was off to Cornell. Thousands of miles away.

But I didn't want to think about that shit right now.

I kissed over the swell of her chest. Then sucked her nipple into my mouth.

"Insane in the Membrane" blared from my phone, but I kept working my lips down her body. The ringtone cut off, then immediately blasted again. And again. And again.

"You going to get that?" she asked.

"It's just Hendrix."

It rang again. Groaning, I snatched the phone from the nightstand and placed it to my ear. "What do you want, dipshit?"

"What took you so long? You porking Drewbers?"

"If you actually need something, you better stop with the bullshit, or I'm hanging up."

"You were supposed to be over here thirty minutes ago to help us with that Toyota Tony wanted."

"Shit..." I glanced at Drew's naked body. I'd forgotten.

"Shit is right. And while you're so busy hiding your Willie Wonka in Drew's chocolate tube, the Oompa Loompas are fucked. Oompa-Loompa-doompadee-doo. What do you get when you guzzle down jizz, getting your ballbag in a terrible tizz? What are you at getting fuckity fucked? What do you think—"

I hung up. Because as long as I had him on the line, Hendrix would sing every freaking contorted stanza of that song.

Drew fought a laugh. "You know, if he wasn't so insane, I'd actually say he's creative."

"Don't ever say that to him."

If she ever gave him something that halfway resembled a compliment, he'd be strutting around like a peacock with its tail feathers spread.

I snagged my jeans from the floor. "I've gotta go over there for like an hour. You wanna come, or you wanna stay here?"

"I'll come with you. I secretly enjoy Hendrix's weirdness." Drew scooted off the bed, my gaze trained on her ass when she bent over to grab her dress. "And no, I won't tell him that."

Hendrix poked his head up from the hood of the banged-up Toyota. His glare immediately directed to my right at Drew as we crossed the overgrown yard.

"You are a thorn in my side."

I glared at him. He still had a chip on his shoulder over the entire shitshow that went down with his brother's girlfriend. "Chill the hell out, Hendrix. She's not here to steal cars."

The smile that worked over her face resembled the one she'd get before she did something crazy—like ram a Maserati into my car. "Can I steal one with you?"

"No." Adding Drew into the mix would end up in nothing but carnage. That was for damn sure.

She lifted a brow at me. "No?"

Something whistled past us. "See! What is it with women trying to do our guy shit?" He pointed at the open hood. "This is guy stuff." Then he pointed at Drew. "Not rich-girl shit."

"I'm not a rich girl anymore."

"Oh, right. Barbie in her Barbie-pink Porsche is now a millionaire slumdog."

"That was a present from my days of wealth," she said. "I can't sell it, and I can't afford another car, so fuck off."

"You fuck off."

My jaw set. "Hendrix..."

"And I'm pretty sure anyone can steal a car," Drew continued because God knew she couldn't stop. "Doesn't require a dick. Besides, not like *I* want to *actually* steal it." She rolled her eyes. "Just go for a joyride."

Hendrix scoffed as I rounded the hood to grab a socket

wrench. "A joyride, Bell. She said a joyride! Freaking joyride," he mumbled, yanking at the spark plugs. "You already had a joyride on his dick today and made him late. That's all you get, Drewbers."

A screwdriver flew past his head. "Changed my mind, Bellamy. He's annoying as all hell."

Hendrix thumbed back at her. "Are you gonna stand for this? She threw a blunt object at me. And she's already given me one head injury when she Hulk threw me off her other car."

Shaking my head, I went to work on the engine. I couldn't deal with the two of them.

"I will never get all pussy whipped like you and Zepp." He fiddled with the plugs. "It's shameful. Like, you should have every player stripe you ever earned ripped right off your pimp suit."

Drew leaned against the side of the car, glaring at him. "Well, in your case, you must look like a damn zebra. A chlamydia-riddled zebra."

Hendrix pushed up from the engine, wiping grease over his shirt. "So you think STDs are a laughing matter, Drew?"

"You are such a drama queen."

His brow lifted. "And you're a stealer of joy."

"Not Bellamy's 'joy.'"

I rounded the corner, taking Drew by the shoulders. "Please, for the love of God, just stop talking to him. The longer you engage, the longer this takes."

The back door banged shut, and Wolf crossed the yard.

"What's up his asshole?" he asked, nodding to Hendrix, who was still standing by the front bumper, arms crossed while he glared at Drew.

"Man, just don't ask," I said. "Come help me get this

shit fixed up." I started to the car, but Drew grabbed my hand and yanked me back a step.

"You know," she trailed a finger down my stomach on a seductive grin, "if you take me to steal a car, it would really turn me on." The path of her finger moved lower, sweeping over my crotch. "I'd probably feel the urge to suck your dick while you're driving it."

Hendrix popped over the hood like a prairie dog, his finger-pointing. "That's some Medusa shit right there."

I glanced at Drew's bottom lip, gripped between her teeth. The thought of getting road head from her while I drove a stolen car down a deserted highway should not have turned me on as much as it did. "You gonna swallow?" I asked, grabbing her hips and yanking her tight against my body.

"Don't I always?" She smiled and kissed me, nipping at my lip. This girl.

"Deal."

"What?" A loud bang came from the hood when Hendrix slammed it shut. "You traitorous whore!"

"Come on, Hendrix," Wolf chuckled. "She promised him head."

"And that's an illegal move. If I had a flag right now, I'd throw it."

I rounded the car and opened the driver's side door. "Stop sulking, Hendrix."

Wolf sidled up beside me, pulling the dipstick from the oil carrier. "Tony said to drop this one off around ten." He shoved the stick back in. "Figured we could go pick up that old Mustang around midnight?"

"Yeah. That works."

A few hours later, Wolf's headlights shined over a brown Mustang parked in a vacant lot by the river.

"I think whoever owned it died," Wolf said. "It's been here for weeks."

And from the grass growing over the wheel wells, it was a likely story.

He continued driving down the dirt road, finally parking behind a tackle shop.

Drew hopped out, and I grabbed my bag before stepping into the muggy Alabama heat that enveloped me like a prickly blanket.

"You're stealing *that*," Drew asked, nodding toward the absolute piece of shit Wolf was approaching.

I shined my flashlight through the window, groaning at the grass growing from the seats.

The car looked like it hadn't been driven in years, which meant everything was most likely screwed. "Yeah," I said. "Wolf, man. Tony wanted this?"

"Yep. Gave me the directions and everything."

"God, this is gonna be a shitshow."

We got to work.

I popped the locks and climbed behind the wheel, unable to get the thing to start once I pulled off the steering column. "It's not gonna start."

Wolf walked to the middle of the dirt road, looking both ways before striding back. "I mean, this place is deserted. And Tony is giving us five grand for it. We've got time."

"Five grand? Shit." That was double what he usually gave, then again, it was a 1979 mustang, and while it was in shit condition, someone could restore it and make it worth a damn sight more than that.

Drew rested her chin on my shoulder as I worked with

the dangling wires. "Aren't you supposed to steal a working car?"

"You aren't *supposed* to steal any car..."

Her fingers played over the back of my neck. "It's kinda hot, though, seeing you get all dirty doing guy shit."

It took over an hour to get the damn thing running, but once we did, that engine purred like an angry jungle cat.

Drew attempted to pull weeds from the seat before she sat down. "This is far less exciting than I thought it would be."

"You want exciting, baby girl?" I revved the engine before fishtailing out of the overgrown lot. The car swerved across the gravel road, catching air when it hit an embankment. "Better?"

"Oh, yeah."

She reached for my belt, then pulled me out, and my foot pressed harder over the accelerator. Her warm lips wrapped around my dick, and I had to fight to not close my eyes.

"Shit, baby girl." I reached around her to shift the gear, swerving around Wolf's pickup and bypassing him.

I dropped the gear down a notch and waved, pointing at Drew's bobbing head before I sped off.

Something about the speed of the car, the headlights cutting across the dark road, the adrenaline spinning through me at the possibility of getting caught in a stolen car—it did it for me.

It wasn't two miles down the road, I had my hand gripping the back of Drew's head, the other arm stiff against the wheel and my legs stretched out, the speedometer at one-thirty, and the fire of the best orgasm of my life tearing through me at warp speed.

Drew pushed up, wiping the corners of her mouth on a smile before she fell back into her seat. "Next time, I'll let you fuck me on the hood..."

That's when I knew I was in love.

God, I was screwed.

CHAPTER 47

DREW

WE SAT at the rickety kitchen table, eating the hamburger steak and macaroni I'd helped Carol prepare. Arlo bounced up and down, humming to himself while Grandpa messed with his dentures.

Despite knowing this was temporary, I couldn't remember having ever been as happy as I had these last few weeks. Even though I was living in a small house, in the worst part of Dayton, and my father hated me. Because I no longer ate Push-Pops for dinner on my own. Carol treated me the way I wished my mom would, asking me how I was, making sure I ate. Little things like that.

I had a taste of the things money could never possibly buy.

"So, you're graduating tomorrow. That's exciting," Carol said as Bellamy took a seat next to me. My stomach knotted.

"What's graduating?" Arlo said, spearing a piece of macaroni.

"It's when you finish school," I said, forcing a smile.

"And then what?"

I didn't want to think about the "then what" because, in my case, it meant I had to move a thousand miles away. And that was the last thing I wanted to do.

"Then, you either get a job or go to college." I forced another smile, then took a sip of water while he nodded.

Carol cleared her throat. "Speaking of college. Where is Cornell, Drew?"

Grandpa reached across the table to grab a roll. "That's up there in New York, ain't it?"

"Yeah."

Carol's gaze shifted from me to Bellamy, then back. "Oh, that's nice. New York."

That same sense of loss settled into my chest every time I thought about going.

It was stupid. I was always going to Cornell. Since I had turned ten years old, it had been my dream—my planned escape.

Dayton was meant to be temporary.

Bellamy should have been temporary.

But in the little time I'd had with him, I'd felt more complete than I had in my entire life. And suddenly, New York felt like the ends of the earth, and I didn't want to escape anymore.

Carol helped herself to more macaroni. "Bellamy applied for scholarships at Alabama State, and the university down in Birmingham."

"Mom..."

"What? You're in the honor's society at school. You have a good shot at it, honey." She beamed, and I shouldn't have envied the pride she had in him.

I looked at him. "*You're* in the honor's society?" I tried not to sound too shocked, but seriously?

He angrily shoveled a piece of meat into his mouth, glaring at me as he chewed. "Don't be a dick, Drew."

"Bellamy!"

Carol gasped, Grandpa snickered, and Arlo started chanting dick over and over while I laughed.

"I didn't ask to be in it," he grumbled. "They just do that shit."

"It's not a bad thing," I said, thinking I just didn't expect it from the local drug dealer.

He cocked a brow on a smirk. "Exactly...so keep that shit to yourself."

"He'd be the first in our family to go to college. I don't know why he's so grumpy about it."

"He's grumpy about it 'cause you're making a fuss, Carol." Grandpa shook his head, then guzzled his Budweiser. "Men don't like no fuss over them."

Grandpa had decided to move in ever since Bellamy's dad had shown up. I could tell Bellamy felt better having him here, and it took some of the stress off his shoulders.

I glanced at Arlo and found him staring at me, not eating. "You okay, Peehead?"

His eyes watered, and his bottom lip poked out. "Are you moving, Miss Drew?"

I faltered, unsure what to say. I did not want to make him cry. My life was becoming increasingly conflicted. And shouldn't I be used to that by now?

"Yeah, but I'll come back and see you."

I didn't look at Bellamy. Of course, he knew I was going to Cornell, but we hadn't discussed anything, really. And while I'd moved in here on a whim, I never could have predicted just how much my little safe house would feel like home.

Arlo's frown deepened before he pushed back from the table, then took off down the hall.

The door to his room slammed closed, and Carol sighed. Bellamy stared down at his plate, obviously avoiding looking in my direction before he started to push back.

"I'll go," I said, rising to my feet and following after the little boy who had already had such a turbulent life. I knocked on his door, and when I got no answer, I pushed inside.

He was face down on his SpongeBob bed sheets, the unicorn I'd won him on the floor.

I took a seat on the edge of the bed and rubbed his back, heartbroken at his quiet sobs.

"Arlo, I promise I'll come back and see you."

At this point, I'd come and see the kid, even if Bellamy and I didn't work out.

"Every week?" His little voice nearly killed me.

"How about every month," I said. "But I'll bring you presents."

He flipped over to glare at me. "No." Then went right back to his pillow.

"And we can hang out on the holidays. Every summer and Christmas and Easter."

"Still not good enough!"

"We can FaceTime every day."

He sniffled, still refusing to turn over. "Why don't you love him no more?"

Words got stuck around a lump in my throat. Arlo thought I loved Bellamy—and didn't kids usually see everything adults refused to see? *Shit.* Was I in love with him?

It was something I wouldn't easily admit to myself because then it would mean I needed Bellamy. And I didn't want to need anyone.

What if I did love him? The boy had never said much more than he liked me and wanted to screw my brains out. But the way that he made me feel… That made me believe he loved me, even when I didn't want to. Because love was uncomfortable. It made people vulnerable. And it had the power to destroy everything.

"No, that's not it," I said. How did I explain this to a kid where he'd understand? "That school is just far away, so I can't live here."

"So, go to Bellamy's college. So you don't have to leave us."

And that thought had plagued me for the last couple of weeks as I'd filled out back up "what if" applications. I told myself it was in case Cornell got wind of my discipline record from Dayton. They'd accepted me before I had even gotten kicked out of Black Mountain, and I guessed my dad paid them to honor that offer after my expulsion. Of course, that wasn't actually the reason I filled out that application to Alabama State, but changing my chosen college for a guy I'd been dating for a couple of months… It was naïve. It was absolutely insane.

"We'll see," I said.

That made him sit up. He wiped at his nose with his sleeve. "Promise?"

Damn, the kid was killing me. "I promise I'll think about it," I said, then I kissed his forehead.

Arlo threw his arms around my neck and told me he loved me.

That was the first time I'd heard those words from another person and felt like they meant it—

And that was soul-destroying.

Later that night, I lay in Bellamy's bed, staring at the ceiling. My chest was still raw with emotions.

A sliver of light spilled into the room from the hallway when he cracked the door and crept in. "He made me read that dumb book about the snoring man ten times before he fell asleep," he said.

Even on the nights that Carol was home, Arlo insisted Bellamy be the one to read him his bedtime story. He said Bellamy did the best voices.

"He also said he needs a phone to FaceTime you if you move." He tugged his jeans off before climbing into bed. "He said you told him you might stay..." He dragged me onto his bare chest.

I rested my palm over his chest, feeling the steady beat of his heart. "The kid strong-armed me." It was half a lie. "I said I'd think about it."

We were graduating tomorrow, and as much as I was ready to be done with school and controlling adults, I wasn't ready to face the fork in the road that had magically appeared in front of me.

Bellamy exhaled, staring up at the ceiling as he swept his hand through my hair. I knew it bothered him, but he would never say anything. That wasn't how Bellamy worked.

"You know you're gonna go, Drew," he said. "Just rip off the Band-Aid and make it easier on him..."

"I feel shit for leaving him." I'd never been so torn in my life. I didn't want to leave either of them.

Bellamy reached over to the nightstand and turned off the light, and we lay there in the darkness. The only noise was his heavy breaths and the occasional sound of Scooter howling at the cop sirens in the distance.

I wondered when I left, would I eventually become

some long-forgotten girl who he had once rescued. Would time and distance make all of this seem like something he could lose?

"You know..." He exhaled, lifting my body with the hard rise of his chest. "I'm not gonna be okay with you dating other guys up there, right?"

"What?"

"Just because you move doesn't mean I'm done with you, baby girl."

My heart skipped. A pressure in my ribs eased as he answered a question I had debated in my head for the last few weeks: Would he want to stay with me?

"You'd still want to be with me when I'm halfway across the country?"

"You could be on the other side of the globe and I'd want to kill a motherfucker for *thinking* he could have you." He was a Neanderthal, but his possessiveness meant everything at that moment.

"No one else could have me." I had to say it, had to put it out there. "But, it will be shit for you."

Seconds passed where the beat of his heart against my palm quickened.

"It'll be shit either way," he said.

I imagined myself in New York. Bellamy stuck here or at college nearby. For four years.

"Eventually, you'd move on," I whispered, and that thought killed me—him with a faceless girl. Her having Arlo's love, maybe even Bellamy's. It made me feel sick.

"No. Because I fucking...." His hold on me tightened. "I like you, Drew."

"I like you, too." That wasn't even close to it, though. Because I loved him, but a guy like Bellamy....he wasn't the guy who fell in love with a hopeless girl.

And I was hopelessly in love with him.

Silence engulfed us once more. Whatever I did, it would be tough, but I felt like someone had my back for the first time in my life. Bellamy felt like gravity, keeping me in orbit.

"So, how does it feel to have spent all those years in your stupid-ass prep school just to receive a diploma from one of America's worst schools?"

"You know, I don't appreciate your negativity right now."

"Dayton graduate..." He snorted. "Do you even know the alma mater?"

"Definitely not. God, I can just imagine how awful that graduation ceremony is going to be."

"Pretty terrible." He swept a hand over my arm. "Some guy usually sells his moonshine out of the back of his truck, so half the football stadium is shitfaced by the end of it."

"Wow." I'd have skipped it if I could. Mainly because I knew no one would be there for me.

Neither my mom nor dad had even called me. I shouldn't have cared. My dad wasn't someone whose approval or pride I needed. Stuff like that shouldn't have to be earned with blood, sweat, and tears.

My fingers crept over Bellamy's chest, playing with the small crucifix at his throat.

"Is your mom going to graduation tomorrow?"

"Yeah. Why wouldn't she?"

"I don't know. Thought she might have to work."

"Nah. She put in to be off three months ago."

"Of course," I whispered, my voice wavering.

"Screw your dad, Drew," he said, sweeping a hand over my face like he knew exactly what I was thinking.

"Not like I expect anything from him at this point." It

bothered me, of course, it did. My dad's rejection was still a knife in my chest. I couldn't voice that out loud, though. "I'm his greatest disappointment, remember?"

Bellamy grabbed my face, forcing me to look at him through the dark. "You're smart and funny, and you stand up for yourself. And if he thinks anything about that's a disappointment, he can go to hell."

I didn't know what to say.

His hands knotted in my hair as he shifted his weight on top of me, peppering kisses down my throat. "You're the best person I've ever known, baby girl. So fuck him."

A lump formed in my throat, my heart squeezed. "I don't deserve you," I said.

"You're right." He pressed a soft kiss to my mouth. "You deserve better."

"I don't want better."

"Good. Now tell me you hate me."

I smiled. "I hate you. So much."

## CHAPTER 48

## BELLAMY

THE LONGER I LAID THERE, staring at the ceiling, the angrier I grew. Until the small trickle of fire seeping through my veins turned into a raging inferno. He'd hurt her, and I couldn't stand it.

By the time eleven o'clock rolled around, I'd climbed out of bed and thrown on clothes, quietly leaving the house. And now, I was pulling onto the street she used to live on, fuming.

I wanted to punch him in the face for making her feel like shit.

The motion detector flashed to life when I parked in the driveway behind his stupid Maserati.

Another light came on when I stepped onto the porch, then banged a fist over the door.

Footfalls came from inside before Mr. Morgan opened the door, still in a dress shirt and slacks. Clutching a whiskey glass in his hand like a true, arrogant prick. He stared up at me, and the urge to punch him right in the face was almost unbearable.

"You've made it apparent what you think of me," I said.

My jaw ticced. "But I'd like to make it crystal-fucking-clear what I think of you, *William*. I think you're pathetic."

He bristled, and when he went to close the door, I caught it with my hand, barging my way inside his foyer.

"I'll call the cops if you don't leave."

"I don't give a shit." My fists clenched at my side. "If that's what it takes for you to listen to me, call them. You think money and titles and boarding schools are what's important? Flashy cars and Rolexes." I flicked the face of his watch, and he stumbled back a step. "When the thing that should have more worth to you than anything is your daughter."

His expression fell, going completely blank. "My daughter was just fine until you dragged her down to your level."

I moved forward, and he moved back. "You think she was just fine when she has a father who didn't even remember her birthday? All she is, is a possession to you. Something pretty you can flaunt. Something you could brag about." I shoved at his chest, and he stumbled against the wall. "Well, fuck you!"

His mouth opened and closed like a fish out of water before he bolted toward the kitchen.

But I wasn't done. "Do you even love her? Because if you do, you sure as hell don't act like it, and it pisses me the fuck off!"

When I rounded the doorway, he was behind the kitchen island, his cell phone in one hand and a butcher knife shaking in the other. "Get out of my house!" he managed.

Drew would never admit it, but she wanted him at her graduation. For whatever reason, and this—this wasn't the way I got him there. On a deep inhale of breath, I told myself to tone it down a few notches.

"You don't want me dating her because you think I'm bad for her, right?" I slowly backed toward the doorway. "I'm not the one breaking her heart. She graduates tomorrow, from the shitass school you forced her into, and right now, she's in *my* bed, crying because she thinks you won't be there." Unable to tamp my anger, I slammed a palm over the door frame. "And you don't even deserve her tears because as far as I'm concerned, you don't deserve her. That's coming from someone who *does* fucking love her."

And with that, I stormed out.

---

Bright orange from the setting sun blanketed the sky as we sat in the football stadium for graduation. I sat two rows behind Drew, staring out across the field at the parents' side. Searching for William Morgan.

It was hard to believe that this shitshow chapter of my life was about to be over.

Around here, high school graduation was the pinnacle of a person's life. Half the student body either failed out or dropped out, so for those of us who stuck it out...

Throughout the entire ceremony, all I thought about was how, in less than three months, I'd be losing Drew. Had anyone told me at the beginning of the year that I would absolutely be pussy whipped by the most rebellious girl in Barrington, I wouldn't have believed them. But I wouldn't change it for the world, even if I did end up losing her and having my stupid heart broken.

Brown called out David Hope, then Megan Hurst, and

Zeppelin Hunt should have been in the middle of them, but he wasn't. And that was a hard pill to swallow.

When Brown called Drew's name, I stood, and so did Mom and Arlo and Pops. And, to the far side of the stadium, stood Mr. Morgan, in his suit. Hands clasped in front of him as Drew shook the principal's hand.

After the ceremony, chaos ensued. Parents and siblings flooded the field, while some kids took off toward the parking lot. I was halfway across the stadium when my phone vibrated in my pocket. I figured it was Drew asking where the hell I was, but instead of Baby Girl, the contact read: **Piece of Shit Morgan: I'd appreciate it if you'd meet me in the parking lot. I'd like to speak with you. I'm in parking spot 112. -William Morgan**

I glanced across the field to where my mom and Arlo were talking with Drew and Nora's family.

Then I ducked between the bleachers, into the dimly lit parking lot.

Every single person I passed had a stupid-ass grin on their face. And as I made my way toward that shiny Maserati, I realized for most people here tonight, all they had to look forward to after this would be a bunch of dead-end jobs, piles of delinquent notices, and a string of divorces. Because this was Dayton, and it was nothing short of quicksand, few people escaped.

Mr. Morgan pushed away from his bumper, straightening his tie before I stopped a few feet in front of him.

"You wanted to talk?" I said, keeping my distance.

"I have no doubt you love her, and I have no doubt she thinks she loves you." He dropped his chin to his chest on a hard breath. "And you may not see it—she may not see it, but I do love her very much. It's the only reason I tried so hard to be successful. And it's the only reason I don't want to see her throw her entire future away."

Throw her future away. That comment dug inside me with barbed wire hooks as people passed behind us, laughing and talking.

He pulled an envelope from his pocket, then stepped forward to hand it to me.

A letter from Alabama State College addressed to Miss Drucella A. Morgan.

"Since she was ten, she's wanted to attend Cornell," Mr. Morgan said. "She's been accepted there and to two other Ivy League schools. So tell me, young man, why she's applied to a university here?"

I stared down at the envelope, knots kinking my stomach.

"I may have been wrong with my first judgment of you, but I stand by the fact that, if she stays with you, she will ruin her entire future. And I don't mean that as a slight. It's, unfortunately, the way the world works." He smoothed a hand down his shirt. "Because what on earth could you possibly give her?"

Another jab. Another dig. The paper crumpled in my hand. I couldn't give her money or cars or Armani jeans. But if she stayed with me, I'd give her everything I had, and more than anything, I'd love her. I tossed the acceptance letter to the ground and glared at him.

What could I give her? "I'd give her everything you didn't," I said.

He held my gaze for all of five seconds before the headlights of his car flashed, and he rounded the front. "Unfortunately, the real world doesn't work like a fairy tale, young man. It runs on money and greed." And then he sank behind the wheel, slammed the door, and cranked the engine to his ridiculously expensive car that screamed for attention while I stood in the parking lot.

His taillights faded into the distance before I picked up the crumpled acceptance letter and shoved it in my pocket.

It didn't have to be one or the other. It didn't... It didn't have to be Cornell or me.

And that's what I kept telling myself as I walked back to the football field to get my girl.

## CHAPTER 49

## DREW

A WEEK LATER

THE ALABAMA HEAT clung to me the second I got out of my air-conditioned car. This heat was getting unbearable. My tank top stuck to my back anytime I was out in it, but not even the gross humidity could dim my mood because I'd just gotten a job.

Like an actual, adult job. At the mall in a cute little boutique.

Not that I didn't like just hanging out with Bellamy and the guys—even Hendrix—or Nora and Diane. But the girls had summer jobs, and the guys were always stealing and dealing.

I had enough money to get me through the summer, but I actually wanted to work. I didn't want to be some Barrington brat. It felt good to get something without my dad's help.

I tossed my car keys onto the side table by the door, the manic laughter of *SpongeBob* spilled from the TV.

"Hey, Peehead," I said when I passed Arlo on the

couch, his attention glued to the screen.

"Hey, Miss Drew. Bubba's outside."

I followed the hum of the lawnmower to the backyard, and I stood on the porch for a second, admiring how good Bellamy looked with his sweat-slicked chest, pushing the mower through the tall grass.

He caught my staring, then cut the engine on a smirk. "Why are you standing out here, staring at me like a creeper?"

"I'm perving. Not creeping. It's different."

"Fine. That's acceptable." He reached for the pull.

"I got a job," I said before he cranked it.

I expected him to smile or say congratulations or, at the very least, offer some smartass remark, but instead, all he did was stare.

"What?" I said. "Why are you looking at me like that?"

"Why did you get a job?"

"Uh, to earn money. What else am I going to do all summer?"

He swiped a hand over his chin, then gave a violent yank to the pull and cranked the mower again. He turned his back to me and cut through the yard. One simple movement that set fire to my very short fuse. What the hell was wrong with him?

I stalked after him and grabbed his arm. "Bellamy!"

"What?" He released the handle and the engine died down.

"Why are you being a dick?"

"What do you want me to say?" His jaw set as he yanked away from my hold. "Congratulations?"

So many things flew through my mind, but I settled on: "How about, just not be an asshole?"

He paced the length of one of the overgrown flower

beds, his hands behind his head. "Why did you apply to Alabama State, Drew?"

That stopped me for a minute because how did he even know about that? I hadn't even heard back from them. "I...I'm just keeping my options open."

"Options open." He half laughed. "You got into fucking Cornell, Drew. What other options do you need to keep open?"

"Just...options." Because I was torn. Because I wasn't sure that the thing I had always wanted was, in fact, what I wanted anymore.

Bellamy confused the matter far more than I'd ever like to admit.

"I don't want to talk about this." I turned and headed back to the house, fighting the tight feeling in my chest.

School was over. Summer would be over before we knew it, and I had to make a decision like, yesterday. And the rational, obvious decision was not the one I wanted to make.

Cornell was in New York, and I knew how this went. For a few months, we'd see each other, but eventually, the distance would get too hard. Missing someone all the time would get too hard.

I wasn't ready to miss him. I wasn't ready to let him go.

I was terrified of turning around one day and realizing I'd lost him while gaining, what? A degree in philosophy from Cornell. There was literally no way to make a career out of that. My half-assed, Ivy League, middle finger to my dad was starting to seem very unimportant.

Bellamy snatched hold of my wrist as I reached for the back door. "Why did you really apply to Alabama State, Drew?"

I looked at him, at the guy who suddenly felt like the

center of my world. How could he not know? "Do you really need me to say it?"

"Yes."

"Because I don't want to move a thousand miles away from you!" It felt like a gunshot, something I couldn't shove back in the barrel once it was out. But the fact that he didn't know this pissed me off.

His chin dropped on a sigh, then he pulled me tight against his sweat-slicked chest. "God, I hate you."

"This isn't complicated, Bellamy." I closed my eyes, inhaling the scent of fresh-cut grass and gasoline and sweat.

This, what we had was easy; it was pure. It was two people and a connection that some would never be lucky enough to find. It was love. And I'd forgo pretty much anything for the one thing I'd never had. Perhaps it made me a fool, but I didn't care.

"No." He took my chin in his hands. A torn expression creased his brow as his eyes searched mine. "It's stupid."

"Then, I'm stupid."

I wanted to tell him I loved him, but fear wrapped around my throat.

What if he didn't feel the same way? What if I'd inadvertently trapped him by moving in here?

It was rash, a heat of the moment decision he'd made when my dad was being an ass. He was an eighteen-year-old guy living with his girlfriend...

Maybe he wanted me to go to New York.

His thumb swept along my jaw. "You're messing up your whole life for me, baby girl."

I didn't want to talk about this anymore, didn't want to fight, and try to justify this hurricane of feelings. So instead, I kissed him.

The home goods aisle at Wal-E-Mart was crowded, thanks to a summer blowout sale. I maneuvered the shopping cart around a group of women fighting over a sequin-covered pillow as Nora scooped up a set of purple bed linens.

"When are you leaving for France?"

I looked away, feigning interest in an ugly frog lamp. "Uh, I'm not. I'm going to stay here for the summer."

"What? Why? I thought you always went to France for the summer?"

"I got a job. I can save a bit of money before I go to college."

It was a lie. I would work and put the money in that envelope to help Carol. She needed every penny, and I knew as soon as I was in college and not living with Bellamy, my mom would probably activate my credit card again.

It was the living with him part she had an issue with, not dating. Like she thought I would marry the guy tomorrow.

"You're staying for Bellamy, aren't you?"

I shrugged.

Nora sighed, then turned to face me. "I get it. You want to spend the summer with him before you go to Cornell. It's still gross because it's him. But whatever."

"Something like that," I said, drawing a line over the sequin pillow.

Nora was my only friend beside Genevieve, but Gen was going to Brown, and I'd never tell her what I was considering. I figured Nora might understand, and I needed to talk to someone who wasn't Bellamy. "I got accepted to Alabama State."

Nora's eyes narrowed as she put a toothbrush holder back. "I'm sorry. You did what?"

"I applied as a backup, you know, in case Cornell rescinded their offer after I got kicked out of my last school." Bullshit, bullshit, bullshit.

"Right...." She pushed the cart down the aisle, then stopped. "I know it's bullshit, Drew, but I don't blame you."

"What?"

She closed her eyes, sucking in a deep breath while mumbling that she couldn't believe she was saying this... "He's like, in love with you. Like big time. I don't blame you."

And that was the last thing I had expected from Nora because everyone else, including Bellamy, seemed to want me to go.

"He wants me to go to Cornell," I said.

"Doubtful."

I leaned back against one of the shelves with a groan. "I feel like I'm being stupid and naïve and completely ridiculous."

"Do you love him?"

"Yeah." And I hadn't even told him that.

"Then stay with him. You can get a degree anywhere." She turned down another aisle cram-packed with towels. "God, I hate myself for being on his side right now. He's such an asshole."

"This is a weird moment for me, too." I patted her shoulder. "I thought you'd be the first person to stick a foot up my ass and death threaten me into going to Cornell."

"He's a complete dick," she said. "But, I wish someone looked at me the way he looks at you."

By the time I walked out of the store, my mind was made up.

## CHAPTER 50

## BELLAMY

I SAT on the half-rotted picnic table in my backyard, staring at the letter in my hand that read: *We regretfully write to inform you that you were not selected for a scholarship for the upcoming academic school year.*

My leg bounced on the seat, my chest going tight as the hopes I'd had to get the hell out of here went up in a cloud of smoke. Then again, hadn't it been stupid of me to think I would?

The bang of Nash's screen door cut through the quiet afternoon.

"Hey, man." Leaves crunched on the other side of the fence, then stopped. "You still out here?"

"Yeah."

"You got any sauce?"

I balled the rejection letter in my fist and tossed it to the fire pit in the corner of the yard, telling myself I'd just have to push a little more weed, steal some extra cars, and go to the community college. Because I refused for this to be my life forever.

"Yeah, man," I said. "Give me five, and I'll be over."

I grabbed a baggie from my room, then headed back outside and climbed the fence to Nash's yard. He raised a Budweiser from his tattered lawn chair as I waded through the overgrown grass to his dilapidated porch.

"Ten bucks." I tossed the weed to him, and he handed over some cash.

"Dude, what's the sad panda face for?"

"Just same old shit." I sank into the chair beside him, trying to forget that my only options were still dealing and stealing for a short while.

"What's up with you and the pink-Porsche girl?" He jerked his chin toward my house, already pinching a bud from the bag to roll a joint. "She's like, living with you or some shit?"

"Yeah."

His brow lifted. "Why?"

"What do you mean, why?"

"Just saying, dude." He tipped his chair back, skimming his hand over the knee-high grass. "She's a rich girl."

"*Was* a rich girl..."

"What do you mean, was?"

*That* I was not going to discuss right now. "Man, just some bullshit with her parents cutting her off—"

"'Cause of you."

I swiped a hand over my face, watching the gnats dance in the late evening sunlight. When it got down to it, it was because of me. She wasn't a rich girl anymore because of me...

"Oh, shit. You're like, into her. Dude..." He whacked a hand over my back, patting me like he pitied me. "Hate to break this to you, but in a year or two, that girls going to resent your ass so much, she won't even be able to look at you. Take it from someone older, who's been there, done that, made those mistakes."

Older. He was only twenty-one. He rolled a joint and passed it my way.

I took a single toke before handing it back. Just enough for the calming buzz to start working its way through my veins. "And what the hell do you know about rich girls, Nash?" I asked.

"Rich girl. Poor girl. They're all the same when you take something away from them." He placed the paper to his lips, eyes narrowing like he was thinking. "I dated this girl a few years back. Totally into her. Fucked like rabbits. I thought I was gonna marry her or some stupid shit. She got an offer to go out to UCLA to do some theatre bullshit." Smoke billowed from his lips. "She'd always wanted to act, but when it came down to me or UCLA, she picked me. Then got pregnant. Then we broke up. And that was it. No UCLA. No chasing her dreams." He offered me the joint again, but I declined. "And guess whose fault she thinks it is?" He thumbed at his chest. "Mine. And she hates me."

"You have a kid?"

"Yeah. She won't let me see him, though."

An old engine rattled into his drive, blasting its horn. Spencer, the singer of his band, leaned through the lowered window and shouted that they needed to leave.

Nash pushed up. "I wished I'd told her to go. At least she wouldn't hate me...And I could see my kid, maybe." Then he skirted around the side of his house, leaving me alone in his yard with a very real fear. The last thing I wanted was for Drew to resent me.

I was in bed that night when she came in from her shift at the mall, scrolling my phone, comparing pictures of Cornell to Alabama State while wondering how in the hell she wasn't going to hate me if she stayed.

"Hey," she said, kicking off her tennis shoes.

"How was work?"

"Good. How was…business?"

"Shit."

She changed out of her clothes, pulling on one of my T-shirts, then crawled into bed beside me. This had become so normal—her here, with me. It had only been a matter of weeks, but every thought I had about my future revolved around Drew.

I'd stay with her no matter what. But if she ended up resenting me…

Her lips went to my neck. "Pretty sure I can improve your day." She trailed her fingers down my stomach, beneath the waist of my boxers, but I stopped her hand from dipping any lower. We couldn't keep going like this, or at least, I couldn't.

The bed creaked when she shifted onto her elbow to stare at me through the dark. "What's wrong?"

"You can't just stay here because of me."

On a sigh, she rolled to her back. "I don't want to talk about this again."

"I don't give a shit."

"God, why does it matter? I'm studying philosophy, Bellamy. It's not even a real degree. Cornell, Alabama… makes no difference aside from a piece of slightly more pretentious paper."

"That's not the point. How long have you wanted to go to Cornell, Drew?"

The hum of a motorcycle roared by outside, shaking the window. "That was before."

Before me. I bite back a sarcastic laugh. Because before me, the only lifestyle she'd known was filled with trips to Saint Tropez and Barbie-pink Porsches, and expectations of Ivy League. And she acted like that could all be disregarded.

"How long, Drew?"

"I don't know. Years."

"And how long have you wanted to go to Alabama State?"

"You want me to go to New York? Is that it?" An edge of hurt laced her voice. "Because if you don't want me around, just say it, Bellamy."

"Jesus Christ. That's not it..." I wanted her to stay for me, and I wanted her to go for her. And I couldn't have both. "I didn't get into Alabama State." I turned on the pillow to face her.

All I had to give her was love, but love didn't pay bills. It didn't buy a house or put food on the table. And the thing she couldn't possibly realize was how hard it was to come by money.

Love was easy. Money was hard.

"I'm sorry." She placed her hand on my cheek, stroking her thumb along my jaw. "You deserved to get in," she whispered.

"You need to go to Cornell. Don't just stay here because of me."

The bed shifted, and she sat up, raking both hands into her hair. "Why are you doing this?"

"Because you have no idea what you're doing—"

"I know what I'm doing. Evidently, you don't, though."

I sat up that time. If she had any idea the mental torture

I'd put myself through trying to sort through this shit. Trying to put her first instead of myself. Trying to make sure she was doing what was best for her without giving a damn about my own dumbass heart.

"Oh, you know? Do you know what it's like to be poor, Drew? Do you know what it's like to have to choose between power or water? Do you know what it's like to count pennies for gas? Because that—*that* is what you're choosing over yachts and trips and a massive house."

Her fist thumped my chest. "I'm choosing you!"

"And I'm choosing you, too." Because this sure as hell wasn't me choosing me. She was willing to sacrifice everything for me, and this was where I sacrificed for her.

"Go to Cornell, Drew."

Her jaw set. Nostrils flared. "I'm going to freaking Alabama."

"God, you are so stubborn!" I pushed off the bed, pacing the length of my small room. "And what happens if we don't work out?" I stopped to stare at her, and it looked like I'd just shot her with a poison-laced dart. "You gonna regret your decision then?" I asked.

"Why would you say that? You think we should break up?" She pushed to her knees. "If you want me to go, just say it!"

"Answer my question. If we don't work out, are you going to regret staying here?"

"Fuck you, Bellamy." She got off the bed and snatched her jeans from the floor, which I immediately yanked out of her hold.

"Answer the question." I just wanted her to look at the situation.

"I would never regret you. Clearly, we aren't on the

same page." Her pained expression swept over me. She went to move past me, but I pinned her to the wall.

"I'm not asking if you would regret *me*, dammit. I'm asking if you would regret this." I jerked a chin to my room. "The shitty-ass life you would have backed yourself into. Not going to Cornell. Not having fancy cars you can demolish anytime you feel like it because money means nothing."

She shoved against me. "Stop putting your money complex onto me, Bellamy. This is your issue, not mine."

A fire crackled to life inside me, and when she tried to break free of my hold, I only held onto her harder. "You're about to make it your issue, though. That's the fucking point!"

Seconds passed. Her eyes searching mine, the slight glimmer of tears building. "You sound like a guy who wants his girlfriend to break up with him because he's too pussy to just do it."

My face heated. "If you think for a second, I'd put your feelings over mine if I didn't want you…"

She closed her eyes, several tears breaking free before she dropped her head back to the wall. "Just stop talking."

And now I felt like shit. I just wanted to protect her, and I didn't know how the hell to do that when all I was trying to protect her from was me.

"Fine," I said. Then I slammed my lips to hers, working her thongs over her hips. By the time I had her on my bed, I was mumbling how much I didn't want her to leave.

At the end of the day, love makes a man selfish. And I was so in-fucking-love with her, I'd apparently turned into the most selfish bastard there was.

## CHAPTER 51

## DREW

THE STREETLIGHT from the window danced over Bellamy's perfect face, casting shadows over his broad shoulders as he moved over me. I clung to him like I could keep him forever if I just held on tight enough.

"You feel so damn good," he whispered into the crook of my neck, fucking me deeper. Harder.

I needed this—him—and it terrified me that I could sense him pulling away.

Rejection burrowed into me like a disease, the symptoms of which hadn't yet fully arisen. But they would. And I knew the feeling well because I'd suffered it my entire life.

What would happen if I went to Cornell?

Bellamy would stay here. We would have a long-distance relationship where we saw each other, when? Every other weekend? I knew how that went when people ran out of things to say in phone calls and life went on without the person who was so far away. I'd done it with my parents when I went to boarding school. At first, my dad called me every day and now look at us...

Bellamy would stop missing me because he'd learned to

live with my absence. I'd learn to stop missing him because it hurt too much to be away from him all the time. And our lives would drift apart. Then there was the massive elephant in the room that I liked to completely ignore, while Bellamy was now pointing at it and shouting in my face. Money.

It meant nothing to me and something to him, and I hated that. Hated that it was a factor and love wasn't enough to save us.

I loved him; of that, I was one hundred percent sure. But I wasn't sure if he loved me. Maybe that was why he wanted me to go to Cornell because deep down, he didn't feel the same.

His lips brushed my throat on a groan. Each powerful muscle tensed beneath my fingers, and I met him right there, digging my nails into his back as we both tumbled over the edge together.

He pressed one last kiss to my lips, then rolled to his back, panting.

I laid in the darkness, listening to the heavy rasp of his breaths as a plethora of thoughts flew through my mind.

He wanted me, but he also wanted me to go to New York, not to live this life with him. Back and forth, I went. It was like whiplash, and my panicked heart wouldn't seem to slow. Like it knew what was coming and bracing my body to run.

All my emotions felt like this messy, knotted ball inside me, and every doubt Bellamy had poured into my head earlier started to surface.

I waited until his breaths had evened out, until his fingers reached for me in sleep, before I got up and went to the bathroom and splashed cold water on my face, trying to calm down.

It would be fine. It would be fine.

When I slipped back into his room, the blue screen of his phone flashed and caught my attention. I glanced down at the ribbon of text still on the screen:

**Nash: Did you figure out what to do about the girl with the pink Porsche?**

**Nash: I'm telling you. Resentment is a real thing.**

Resentment? My chest tightened until I couldn't catch a good breath. Bellamy resented me... He wanted me to go. I was an issue to be fixed, something he needed a solution to. He wanted to break up. Was that why he'd started a fight tonight?

Tears pricked my eyes, and the ugly, black tendrils of rejection set in. The familiar symptoms rising like a rogue wave and drowning me in an instant. I couldn't stick around and wait for him to deal a death blow.

With tears silently streaming down my face, I forced myself not to get back in that bed, lay down, and pretend like everything would be okay. It clearly wasn't. So I got dressed, then collected my phone and purse, leaving all my other clothes behind.

I cast a glance at Bellamy, the pain in my chest digging in like claws. I wanted to kiss him, but I didn't want to deal with the mess of him watching me leave. Because I knew he wanted me. But he didn't.

It was only when I passed Arlo's ajar bedroom door that I realized I couldn't leave him without a goodbye.

I tore a page from the notepad in the kitchen and scribbled out a note:

*Peehead,*

*I have to go away for a while, and I couldn't say goodbye.*
*I'm sorry.*
*Look after your mom and be good.*
*I love you, little guy.*

*Drew*

I left it on his bedside table, taking one last glance at how peaceful he looked with his unicorn clutched to his chest. Then I placed the rest of my cash on the kitchen counter for Carol. I wouldn't need it where I was going. Money wasn't an issue there.

As soon as I pulled out of the drive, I called my mom, refusing to look in my rearview mirror at the ramshackle little house that felt more like home than anywhere else ever had.

"Darling. I'm just having my morning mimosa. It must be late there..."

"Can you get me the next flight out?" Tears blurred the road in front of me.

"Of course. Dayton straight to Marseilles, first class." She sounded far too pleased about my heartbreak. "I'll send a car to pick you up once you land."

I was running to the only place I could go, the only place I had left. Halfway across the world, and I wasn't sure it would be far enough because with each passing moment, I was cracking open, bleeding from the inside out.

For the first time, I understood why people married for money and not love.

## CHAPTER 52

## BELLAMY

SOMETHING HIT me in the face, and my eyes popped open to the early morning light.

"I don't like you!" Arlo shouted, then slammed my door.

I swatted his old, stuffed donkey from my chest to the floor. "What the..." And when I rolled over to grab onto Drew, she wasn't there.

I sat up, raking a hand through my hair just as the door swung open again.

Arlo stormed in, a SpongeBob pillow lifted over his head. "You're a butthole!" Then he lobbed the pillow at me.

I shot out of bed, snagging him by the back of his pajama top before he'd made it down the hall. "Hey, come here."

He attempted to wrestle free, but I picked him up and threw him over my shoulder.

"What's your deal?"

He pounded his tiny fists over my back. "You're a cockblock!"

Jesus...

"You didn't tell me Miss Drew had to leave!" His fist

kept slamming against me, and I just stared at the end of the hall. Leave?

Without putting him down, I went back to my room and opened the closet. Her clothes were still there. Her suitcases stacked at the top.

Then I went to the window, twisting the cord on the blinds. Her car was gone, Hendrix's tarp that usually covered it, a messy ball on my hood.

"Put me down." Arlo kicked his feet at me, and I dropped him to the bed.

She left? I glanced back through the blinds. Left for work or to grab breakfast maybe... "She probably went to get donuts or something, Arlo."

"No, she didn't. She left me a note. You didn't tell me she had to leave..." His eyes watered before he threw himself face down onto my pillow.

She'd left and gone where? Back to her dad's? I mean, Jesus Christ, we'd gotten in a fight, then fucked and made up, and she left?

A soft knock sounded on my door, and I glanced back at my mom, standing in the doorway with a handful of cash fanned out like it was poker night. "Bellamy. Why was two grand in cash on the kitchen counter?"

It was Drew. The queen of overreaction. Of course, she had left.

I swiped a hand down my face and shook my head. "Drew...I guess."

"She can't just keep giving me money, Bellamy. She's..."

"I know."

Mom glanced at Arlo, sobbing on my bed, and frowned. "Why is he crying?"

"Because she..." And what was I supposed to say—Drew left and upset Arlo even more.

She was having a Drew moment, and by the afternoon, I'd have her back over here, pinned underneath me. "Don't worry about it. It'll be fine."

Mom stood there, glancing from me to Arlo, then back.

"I promise, Mom. It's fine, she went to work and..." I was going to kill her when she came back. Leaving Arlo a note was over the top.

Mom gave a half nod, then said she was going to start breakfast. The second I heard her in the kitchen, I glanced at Arlo.

"Where's the note, buddy."

"In my room. On my dresser." His muffled sob came from the pillow.

I went to his room and grabbed the note, skimming over it. Cryptic as hell—but at least *he* got an "I love you." I stormed back to my room and shot off a text: **Seriously? Arlo's crying. WTH are you?**

*Message not delivered.*

And that—that made me chuck my phone at the wall.

---

Ten hours later, she hadn't come home.

I was shitfaced at Hendrix's house when she finally texted back.

**Baby Girl: I didn't mean to make him cry**
**Me: Where are you, Drew?**
**Baby Girl: France.**

France? My grip on my phone tightened, my heartbeat pulsing behind my eyes. That was a joke. It had to be. How long did it even take to fly across the freaking Atlantic?

**Me: You're kidding. Right?**

Minutes passed, my knee bouncing like a jackhammer.

We'd gotten in, not even in a fight. Not even a freaking fight, and she had left and *gone to France*? Not to Nora's house. Not back to her dad's or even a five-star hotel two cities over. France. Because *that* was Drew.

**Me: Seriously, Drew. France!**

**Me: You want to get all pissy at me for trying to make sure you know what the hell you're getting into with being poor**

**Me: And you just leave. And go to France**

**Me: France**

**Me: FUCKING FRANCE!!!!!**

Hendrix handed me a shot of whiskey, shaking his head. "I tried to tell you, but you wouldn't listen." He stared down at my phone, then snorted. "Never have I ever had a demon spawn Medusa fuck off to France to break up with me," He cackled, then kicked me. "Drink, you dickhead. Because that's you!"

I slammed the shot, then chucked the empty glass at him before going back to my phone. I wanted a reaction. Something because this—*this* hurt like a bitch.

I was drinking so I wouldn't cry, and my chest was all tight. All I could do was think about her because I could still smell her on my shirt. And I almost, almost told her I loved her last night because I felt that bad that she thought I would want her to leave. And then she does this...

**Me: So what, are you too pussy to break up with me, Drew? That what it is?**

**Me: Fuck off to France so you don't have to break up with me?**

**Baby Girl: I don't want you to resent me.**

Resent her? For what?

Hendrix dropped beside me on the couch, this time handing me the bottle of whiskey. "There are two ways to handle this. Listen to Sarah McLachlan and cry like a bitch or watch porn."

I glared at him.

"Wait. Pink Floyd goes with The *Wizard of Oz* so maybe..." He grabbed the remote and turned on the TV, then the stereo. "Arms of the Angel" blared through the speakers as some muscled up guy took a girl in a nurse's outfit, doggy style.

"If this isn't art," he said. "I don't know what is."

And I just stared at my phone, wishing I could hate her. But I never would.

## CHAPTER 53

## DREW

THE WARM MEDITERRANEAN breeze swept around me as I stood at the wooden door of Mom's villa. And from the smile on her completely made-up face when she answered in her silk robe, she was far too happy to have me.

She passed me her glass of wine the second I stepped inside. "You look terrible, darling."

I was broken-hearted and jet-lagged; what did she expect me to look like?

"Thanks," I said, trying not to roll my eyes.

She handed my bag off to Marco, the butler, and guided me inside. I downed my wine before I even reached the kitchen, and Mom topped me right up.

That's how that went for the rest of the evening.

I sat by the pool, on a sun lounger, next to my mom, staring out over the city that swept into the sea while I got drunk. And although she drank more than me, she didn't get drunk because the woman had a ninety-ten wine-to-blood ratio in her veins.

It was sunset when Marco came back by the pool with a

fresh bottle of wine. He filled my glass, then disappeared between the palm trees and Hibiscus.

"So, what made you decide to leave the lovely city of Dayton so suddenly?" She lifted her glass to her lips, her gaze set on the sun setting over the turquoise water.

I inhaled a ragged breath. "Bellamy and I broke up."

Kind of. I didn't really know. I just got out before he could do it.

I tipped my drink back again, hating how horribly fragile I felt right now. "Go ahead," I sighed. "Say I told you so."

"Darling..." She rubbed a hand over my arm. "Being young is difficult."

And that was a glittering piece of wisdom from Irina Morgan De Arman.

"It is when you're me." I hated that I sounded so pathetic and that I was so bitter. Bitter about my dad, my mom, my shitty yet "privileged" upbringing. My being sent to Dayton, and lastly, Bellamy.

It was all seeping into me, like thick, black tar, until each beat of my heart felt sluggish and drawing air was a chore.

"I don't want to talk about it, okay? I'm here, and I'll stay until I go to Cornell."

Just like my dad wanted, just like Bellamy wanted, because what I wanted was never a factor, and it never had been.

On a sigh, she settled back against her lounge chair. "Whatever you want, darling. Whatever makes you happy." Then she patted my hand.

"Thank you. And thank you for getting me a ticket."

"Of course, darling." Then she started talking about random crap, and for once, I appreciated her rambling on and on about herself: The new yacht her husband, Pierre, had bought, the landscaping she had ordered to be done in the lemon grove, the new purse she'd put on order. It was meaningless, with about as much depth as a puddle, but I needed that because my own shit was so deep, I would drown if I thought about it.

My phone dinged. I grabbed it from the table beside me, nearly knocking over an empty wine bottle. Then I steeled myself and opened the new message from Bellamy.

**Dickhead: Fuck you, Drewbers.**

Then a picture came through of Bellamy, passed out on Hendrix's couch.

**Dickhead: You broke his heart. Congratulations, you Medusa Whore.**

Then a picture of Hendrix shooting me a bird popped up.

I pushed up from my chair and crossed the terrace, disappearing into my bedroom. The warm breeze blew through the opened French doors, and I collapsed onto the bed, the first tears breaking free. And they kept coming. Sliding down my temples and staining the pillowcase until it was soaked.

---

It had been a week since I'd left the States. A week of non-stop shopping and champagne and parties, but it wasn't nearly enough to distract me. I was more miserable than ever because I missed him. Everything hurt.

The cherry wood deck of Pierre's yacht clicked beneath my heels as I approached the stern, my fingers wrapping around the metal railing as the breeze tousled my hair. The sun had long ago set behind the hills of Monaco, the lights of the city a speckling of stars against the dark silhouette of the night sky. The lap of waves against the hull and the tinkle of champagne flutes almost drowned out the low hum of music from the party around me.

I tipped back my glass before grabbing another from the tray of a passing waiter.

Over the last week, I'd realized that my own company was torture, and yet, I hated everyone. Short of getting drunk and crying some more, I had no bright ideas. Though truthfully, I'd mastered the art of skipping right over an emotional drunk and going straight to numb with a side of "inability to give a shit." It was the only way to avoid this hollowed-out feeling in my chest, like something vital had been stolen.

My phone beeped, and my heart stuttered, hoping it was Bellamy. He hadn't made contact since Hendrix had texted me, and that told me everything I needed to know. I wanted him to be every bit as broken and desperate as I was, to share my pain and validate it. To tell me he wanted me. Missed me. Something.

I'd fought the urge to contact him every single day, and every time that urge rose, the word resentment flashed through my mind like a neon warning sign.

I checked my phone, my heart sinking at the sight of Genevieve's name.

**Genevieve: Hey, babe. Just checking in on you.**

**Me: I'm fine.**

**Genevieve: Breakups suck. I know it doesn't seem like it right now, but it's**

**probably for the best. You'll get over it eventually. I promise. xx**

I didn't respond to that.

I held on to the notion that time would heal all wounds, but I wasn't healing; I was dying. It had only been a week, and it was the worst of my life. I just wanted to be able to stop thinking about him, stop longing for him, for a single minute.

After I drained another glass of champagne, I cut through the partygoers dressed in their expensive dresses and tuxedos. The last thing I wanted was to be around these people. Screw this. I was going to steal a bottle, go to my cabin, and drink on my own.

That was until my mother found me.

Her dress clung to her petite frame, making her look every bit the wealthy socialite she was.

"Darling." She brushed my arm, eyeing the empty glass in my hand.

My father would be disapproving, but Irina only flagged down a passing waiter, procuring me a fresh drink.

"Why aren't you mingling?" she asked, sweeping a stray piece of hair from my face.

"I don't want to mingle." I couldn't stand my mother's friends. They were always the worst.

I glanced at the dark sea beyond the railing, wishing I could jump in, just to ruin this perfect dress and wash away the curls in my hair along with the professionally applied makeup. I felt like a doll, a commodity. Shiny and fake. I hated everything about this.

"Henri Valant is here." She moved to stand beside me as she nodded toward the party. "You see the good looking one, with the dark hair? He's a European football player. Lots of money. Models for Armani, too." She shifted to face me again, lifting a brow.

And he had arrogant prick stamped on his forehead.

"Not interested, Irina."

She rolled her eyes. "You know you could come to university here."

She was trying to plan out my life for me, from a ready-made, rich boyfriend to college. Just like Dad. I wanted to scream.

"I'd love to have you here," she said.

I shouldered past her, cutting through the glass doors and into the kitchen. After I swiped a mini-bottle from the fridge, I descended the stairs to my cabin that resembled the inside of a luxury hotel suite.

My back hit the mattress, probably creasing the expensive dress my mother had picked out for me. Then I opened the champagne. Every luxury money could buy surrounded me, and never had the saying "money can't buy happiness" been more true. I was miserable. And drunk. And now I was crying. God, I was pathetic, but I wanted nothing more than for Bellamy to be here, hiding and getting drunk with me.

I all but polished off the mini-bottle, and now I was so drunk I didn't care if he hadn't contacted me. The need to speak to him, to see him, to hear his deep voice. So, I Face-Timed him, closing my eyes as the phone rang, thinking he probably wouldn't even answer.

Just when I was about to hang up, the call connected. The pixelated colors on the screen focused on Bellamy's stern face. God, he was beautiful, all ticcing jaw and blazing dark eyes.

He didn't say a word, just glared through the phone.

"You look mad." My voice hitched. Tears clogged my throat as I tipped the Champagne bottle up.

"Are you drunk?"

"Yep."

He dragged a hand over his face, resting back against his headboard. I missed him. I missed that tiny little room... "Why are you calling me, Drew?"

"Because I miss you."

Seconds passed. The hull of the boat creaked as it rocked over waves. "Then why did you leave me?" he asked.

I turned the bottle up once more, trying to chase away my heartbreak, but I couldn't. "Because I think you wanted me to."

"Jesus Christ." He shifted, a blurry vision of his bedroom coming into view for a split moment.

"I trapped you. It's okay. I should never have moved into your house—"

"Stop."

"And you're just good. You know, like a really good egg."

"Shut up, Drew. You sound...I don't even know. But not like yourself."

"I'm not," I whispered. I wasn't me without him, and could I be any more pitiful right now?

I slumped back against the pillows, feeling the weight of desolation breaking through my drunken haze. Tears broke free once more, and I closed my eyes. I had no idea if Bellamy was even still there, and I refused to look. "I need you," I whispered.

"You don't *need* anybody, Drew..." And I wished that were true. "All I wanted you to do that night was answer one question. I just wanted you to tell me you wouldn't regret it."

"You wanted me to say you were a mistake. That you weren't good enough."

"Jesus Christ." He exhaled. "I wanted you to tell me I *was* good enough, Drew."

No one could have been any better for me than him. "I saw the text from your friend. I don't want—"

"You went through my fucking phone?"

"Don't be...Screw you. No, I did not."

"Then how did you see the text?" The smug look on his face made me irate. Even from a thousand miles away.

"Because it lit up the room in the middle of the night like freaking Times Square, and I saw it pop up. I don't want you to resent me."

He wanted me to go to Cornell. He didn't want me in Alabama. And I just wanted him, anyway I could have him.

"That text wasn't about *me* resenting you. It was about you resenting me. For giving up everything." He stared through the screen. Jaw tight. "I literally want to kill you right now..."

I huffed a laugh. "What am I giving up, Bellamy? Please tell me."

His head thumped against his headboard on a groan. "Everything. Shit I can't ever give you." This boy. He had no idea. He thought this life was so damn perfect, and it wasn't.

"Do you want to know where I am right now?" I drained the last of my champagne and chucked the bottle to the floor. "I'm on my mom's yacht, in a four-thousand-dollar dress, drinking champagne, and I am fucking miserable and empty because it means nothing."

Even through my blurred vision, I could see the crease in his brow, the hurt in his eyes. "Yeah, well. You wanna know where I am right now? I'm in the bed I used to share with you. By myself because you fucking left me. Over a text, you didn't even know the context of."

Fresh tears broke free. "You know it was more than that—"

"You didn't even tell me goodbye. Give me a chance to explain anything. You just left." It was like he wasn't listening to me.

"You are so hell-bent on me going to Cornell, Bellamy, and all I want is you!"

"All you want is me, and still, you *fucking* left."

"If you wanted me the way I want you, you wouldn't—"

"Jesus Christ, Drew. I fucking love you," he shouted, anger and hurt bleeding through his voice. "And if you loved me, you wouldn't have just left like that. So don't you tell me I don't want you."

And that triggered a barrage of tears, ugly sobs that lanced through my chest like a machete. I couldn't speak, couldn't breathe, couldn't deal with anything in that moment. So I hung up. And God, I loved him. So much.

---

I woke up with a pounding headache and the echo of Bellamy's words in my mind. *I fucking love you.* Why couldn't he have said that sooner? It all felt so messy now, but I knew one thing; I loved him, and I realized how stupid I was to leave him simply because he might reject me.

It was because I loved him that he had the power to hurt me, and the second I thought there was even the slightest risk of that, I ran. But I needed him, loved him, and I would take Bellamy over this life any day.

My mother waited on the balcony, the same way she did every morning, at the head of the table, a spread of coffee and fresh fruit sprawled before her. Far more than either of us ever ate. A huge sun hat and sunglasses covered her face, jewelry dripping from her like a walking advert for Cartier.

"You look terrible," she said, thrusting a cup of coffee at me. "Sit with me."

"Thanks." I took the chair beside her, picking at a few pieces of melon.

"I'm all for staying thin, sweetie, but you need to eat more." The expression on her face was almost a frown or as close as her Botox would allow.

"I appreciate your motherly concern." I was pretty sure she just didn't want me to be ugly; after all, that was the worst thing a girl could be in her eyes.

The citrus scent wafted up from the lemon trees in the gardens below, mixing with the faint trace of the ocean that permanently lingered in the air.

"Darling, I think we need to talk."

I let out a sigh. "If this is about last night..."

"You've done nothing but get drunk since you arrived here, sweetie."

"And? You drink with breakfast, mother." I scrubbed a hand over my face. "I... I need to fly back home."

"Why?"

"You know why. The same reason I've been drunk for five days straight. I need to go back to Bellamy."

I waited for her lecture, but instead, her head tilted, eyes tracing my face with something akin to pity. "You think you love him."

"I do love him."

My mother pursed her lips, plucking her coffee mug from the table. "Love is a fantasy of young women, Drucella. And when that fantasy shatters, it will take a little piece of you with it. Save yourself the pain, my darling."

"You sound like you're talking from experience." Though as far as I knew, Irina Morgan De Arman had never loved anyone. "When I know you married for money," I said. "Three times."

There was a beat of silence where only the distant cawing of seabirds caught on the ocean breeze. My mother swallowed, tracing circles over the side of the mug. "I met your father when I was young and he had nothing."

That took me by surprise. I knew nothing about how my parents met, only how they had divorced. I'd always thought dad was from money like she was.

"I loved him deeply," she said.

"Really?"

A small smile touched her lips. "He wasn't always an asshole. Money changed him because he wanted it more than me. More than you. Became obsessed with it. I felt neglected, and I looked for that love elsewhere." Her shoulder lifted. "Though I never found it."

"Did he love you back?"

"I believe so. Until he didn't." Her gaze shifted to me. "Men are fickle creatures, Drucella. Believing anything else is simply childish. What are you going to do if you go back to this boy?"

The breeze kicked up, sending one of the table linens dancing over the patio. "I don't know."

"Is he going to college?"

"He applied to Alabama State. He didn't get the scholarship."

"So he's going to what?" Mom lifted her glass to her lips. "Work a dead-end job for the rest of his life?"

"I don't care if he does! I will still love him. You can't change it."

"Cornell is a long way from Dayton—"

"I don't want to go to Cornell. I got accepted at Alabama State."

"I see." Her lips pursed together. "I think you should go to Cornell."

"And then what? Get a degree. Forget all about Bellamy. Marry some rich guy I barely like, and do nothing with the rest of my life like you did?" It was harsh, I knew that, but I was frustrated and angry that she couldn't see, I wasn't her and I didn't want her life. I gripped the edge of the table, meeting her gaze. "I love him, Mom. Remember what that feels like for just a second. What if Dad had never stopped loving you?"

She smoothed a hand over the pristine tablecloth. "Well, things might have been different. But I don't regret it. I met Pierre..."

"You don't love Pierre. You like him, but you don't love him." I dragged a hand through my hair, angry at myself and her and the world. I wanted to reach through that cold shell of hers and make her remember this madness. I wanted her to recall what it's like to feel like another person is your source of oxygen. To have them set your soul on fire. But maybe she didn't want to remember.

"And if it doesn't work out?" she asked. "You're talking about sacrificing a very blessed future for this boy."

"But what if it does work out, Mom?" I was almost shouting because she did not get it. "What if it does?"

"Oh, Drucella." She looked out over the ocean beyond, then released a sharp breath.

A few seconds of silence passed between us before her gaze met mine. Then she swept a piece of hair behind my ear, and her fingers gently brushed my cheek. "Love is reckless, and you always were wild." The faintest smile played over her lips. "Tell me about this boy. I want every detail."

## CHAPTER 54

### BELLAMY

I STARED AT MY WALL, fighting the emotions whirling through me like an F-5 tornado.

My gaze landed on Drew's clothes still hanging in my closet, and the pain intensified. I wanted to hate her, I really did, but I couldn't. I fell back onto my bed, scrolling through the novel's worth of text messages between us because I was a masochist, apparently.

**Me: You working sucks.**

**Baby Girl: It does, but I'll suck something else later.**

I scrolled some more.

**Me: I can still taste you on my lips.**

**Baby Girl: You're such a pervert.**

**Me: Fine. I miss you.**

**Me: And the taste of you on my tongue is making it worse.**

And then, one of the last ones gutted me.

**Baby Girl: I can't wait to come home.**

**Me: I'm waiting, naked in our bed.**

She thought I resented her. Jesus. I should have just told her I loved her long before now, regardless of how terrified it made me. She *thought* I wanted to break up with her, so she went to France. Then she cried when I did tell her I loved her, and she hung up. Because that was Drew.

I rubbed at the growing tightness in my chest before I chucked my phone across the room.

I fumed for a while, blasting Linkin Park.

This was a shitshow of a mess I was going to have to try to untangle because I loved the irrational girl in a way I was sure I'd never love anyone else, and that made me fucking crazy. I knew it did.

Halfway through Linkin Park's album, Arlo came into my room with Spike clutched to his chest. He turned down the music, then crawled onto my bed. "Is tomorrow the day Daddy gets in trouble?"

Tomorrow was the court date to determine what kind of jail time he'd serve for assaulting my mom. And I had to stop myself from smiling because the son-of-a-bitch deserved it. "Yeah, buddy."

He frowned, picking over the unicorn's horn. "I don't want him to go to jail, though."

Arlo didn't understand. He'd grown up seeing the crap Dad did, thinking it was normal. It's hard for someone to digest the notion that the person who was their hero is nothing more than a villain. Because no matter how shitty their Dad is, a six-year-old can't see it.

I wrapped an arm around him and held him against my chest. "I know. But he hurt Mom, and that's not right, you know?"

"I know. But he said he was sorry."

"Yeah, and sorry isn't enough sometimes, Arlo."

He gave a curt nod. "But they'll feed him in jail and let him watch TV?"

"Yeah. They'll feed him."

"Okay."

The bang of pots and pans came from the kitchen before Grandpa shouted for Arlo to come to help him make pancakes for dinner.

Arlo's face lit up, and he pushed off the bed, sprinting out of the room so fast he dropped his stuffed animal.

I got out of bed and picked the toy up. I never thought looking at a stupid stuffed unicorn would make me want to cry.

The next day, I went with Mom to court, standing between her and Dad to make her feel safe. I hated the man and wanted to be nowhere near him. The evidence was lined up. Years of domestic violence calls to the cops, pictures of injuries, and police statements. When the judge gave him three years, I released the breath I'd been holding. While I wished it had been for longer, it was enough because it got her away from him. And that's all I could ask for.

She was quiet the entire drive home; silent tears streamed down her cheek. Even after everything, she still thought she loved him, and damn if that didn't make me livid.

"Are you okay?" I asked when I pulled into the drive. I knew she wasn't. I knew there wasn't anything I could do, but it would be shit of me not to ask.

"Yeah. I'm fine, baby." Then she painted a watery smile on her face. "Tell the boys I said hi, would you?"

"I'll stay, Mom."

"No. Pops is here. Just...go have fun with your friends.

Please." She kissed my cheek. "You deserve to have some time to yourself, Bellamy." Then she got out of the car.

I hated to leave her, but I figured maybe she needed some time alone to process everything.

**Hendrix: I'm taking a shit at the Waffle Hut.**

**Me: I don't want to see a picture of your shit.**

**Hendrix: Too late.**

A picture popped up, and I immediately deleted it before backing out of the drive.

The entire way to Waffle Hut, I played the conversation from last night over and over in my head. And I kept coming back to her saying she felt like she'd trapped me.

Trapped me.

I stopped at a red light, staring at the traffic crossing the intersection before I banged a fist over my steering wheel. Why did I have to fall for the crazy rich girl? A crazy poor girl would have gotten pissed and gone to a friend's house to bitch about it because she wouldn't be able to afford to jet off to France to sulk and drown herself in champagne on a yacht.

I parked beside Wolf's truck. Then shot off a text to Drew. I hadn't texted her last night because I figured she was still drunk, plus I was annoyed as hell. But this was getting ridiculous.

**Me: Whenever you get done pitching your fit, come home.**

**Me: I love you.**

**Me: Don't fucking cry about it.**

Hendrix and Wolf were already in a booth, and

Hendrix had the Big Slammer Meal spread out in front of him.

"Way to wait, asshole," I said, sliding into the booth.

Hendrix slurped back some of his milkshake. "I was hungry. Did you not see that shit I took? There was nothing left in there."

I snatched a menu up.

"So," he said. "I was telling Wolf, I think I could make money in amateur porn."

Of course, he did.

"This entire sappy music and porn thing has given me some ideas."

I stared across the Waffle Hut table at him. "No one wants to see your dick."

"Don't come crying to me for a job when this blows up." He pointed at his crotch.

Wolf chuckled. "I can see this shitshow now. Next thing you know, he'll be recruiting girls from revivals."

Hendrix slapped his arm on a grin. "Reading my mind, man. Reading my mind."

The bell over the door jingled. Hendrix glanced over my shoulder, the idiotic grin on his face falling to an angry frown. "Oh, hell to the fuck no!"

Wolf's gaze shifted, then he grabbed Hendrix by the shoulders and attempted to shove him out of the booth. "Let's go."

"No way. This is bullshit."

"Out, Hendrix." Wolf shoved him hard enough that he toppled to the floor.

I turned in the booth, and the site of Drew standing a few feet behind me nearly knocked the wind out of me. She looked exhausted, in a T-shirt and pair of leggings, her hair piled on top of her head in a messy bun. How in the hell...

A roller coaster of emotions rolled through me, peaking with relief and dipping down to anger.

Hendrix passed by her and shook his head, mumbling, "bullshit" beneath his breath before Wolf got him outside.

Drew walked down the aisle, then stopped at the end of the booth, hesitating. "Can I sit?"

"You haven't slept, have you?" I could tell she hadn't.

"No. The flight was shit." She slid into the booth across from me and took a deep breath like she was stealing herself.

"You gonna tell me how you knew where I was?" Though I had a really good idea...

Her lips twitched ever so slightly. "You're not the only one who can use that app."

"You aggravate the absolute shit out of me."

"You're the original stalker here, not me."

"And you're the biggest drama queen I've ever met." I reached across the table, threading my fingers through hers. Such a simple touch should not have been able to provide that kind of relief.

"I was drunk!"

I lifted a brow. "When you left for France?"

She groaned. "Will you shut up? I came to tell you something, and you're ruining it."

I fought a smile and leaned back in the booth, waving my free hand across the table to give her the floor.

"Thank you." She sucked in a breath. "I love you."

And that made me feel like the richest motherfucker in the world. "I know, baby girl." I smirked, just to be a dick. "But I'm not gonna cry about it."

"You're such a prick. I don't even know why I like you, let alone love."

I got up from the booth, sliding in beside her. "I told you

because you crave this kind of chaos." I gripped her chin and slammed my lips to hers, kissing her like my life depended on it. "You do realize you're a nightmare, though?"

"Thought you didn't want a princess?"

"Nah, I only want you."

The girl had literally put me through hell since day one, but damn, was it worth it.

## CHAPTER 55

## DREW

#### 4 DAYS LATER

I CLASPED Bellamy's hand tightly in mine as we walked up the steps to my dad's front porch.

My father opened the door, standing there in his usual immaculate suit, the lines of his face unreadable.

This was the price of my freedom this time.

My mother had paid for my ticket back and reinstated all my credit cards, she'd even agreed that she would pay my tuition for Alabama State, and the price? I had to agree to visit her three times a year, and this, dinner with my father. And that threw me for a loop.

I had no idea why she would try to rekindle our desecrated relationship.

"William." Bellamy was the first to speak, probably because I was frozen and mute.

"Bellamy. Drucella."

God, this was so awkward. I wanted to crawl into a deep hole in the ground.

"Come in," he said, stepping to the side to allow us inside.

This house felt so alien to me now, like another life that I'd watched on television rather than lived. My father showed us into the dining room with the enormous ten-seater mahogany table. A table that would never be filled.

For a second, I actually felt a trace of pity for the man. He lived in a self-made fortress of isolation with only his money for company. It was bitterly sad.

I took a seat across from Bellamy. My father remained standing at the head of the table, clutching the back of the chair. The two men could not have been any more different. My father was perfectly polished, while Bellamy was wild and rough.

"You must be wondering why I invited you both here."

"Well, I'm here because Irina told me I had to be," I said. Outside of that, I wouldn't give him a second of my time.

He nodded, the lines around his eyes sinking. "Yes, I've spoken at length with your mother, and she has shown me a few things."

With that, he took an envelope from the inside of his jacket pocket and slid it across the polished table but not to me. It stopped in front of Bellamy.

My dad cleared his throat, his attention aimed at my boyfriend. "I've thought long and hard about what you said the night you forced your way into my house." His brows tugged together as he scowled at Bellamy, who looked completely unfazed, as always.

What the hell was Dad talking about? When did Bellamy force his way in here—outside of the two times he broke in?

"And while I absolutely do not agree with your criminal history, I must believe, given the opportunity, you wouldn't be involved in the activities you currently use to provide for yourself." He swept a hand toward the letter.

Bellamy's confused gaze met mine before he grabbed the envelope and opened it. "What in the..." He shook his head, then his dark eyes met mine. "It's a scholarship. To Alabama State."

I couldn't help the little hiccup in my chest.

"I provide a scholarship every year." Dad smoothed a hand down his tie, looking distinctly uncomfortable. "This year, I'd like to extend it to you, Bellamy. As a thank you for making me realize there are some things money can't buy."

"I..." Bellamy frowned at the letter. "I can't take this."

"Bellamy..." I started.

This might be his only shot. Regardless of our relationship or the issues with my dad, he should absolutely take this. I wouldn't allow him to let pride, or loyalty to me, get in the way.

"It's in your name," Dad said, finally taking a seat. "The funds are reserved only for you. So you can either use it or let it sit there."

The three of us fell into silence for a moment.

"I hope this goes some way to making amends, Drucella. I..." He let out a hard breath. "I love you, and I've only ever wanted the best for you. After speaking to your mother, I realize I have gone about it wrong and that perhaps you value different things in your life to us."

I literally had no idea what to say. None. A lump formed in my throat. Tears stung my eyes. "I only ever wanted you to love me," I whispered.

My dad dropped his chin to his chest. "And I'm sorry I made you feel that I didn't." He pushed up from his chair. "I'll go and get dinner from the kitchen."

A man of few words and fewer emotions, but he did

love me. In a heartbeat, Bellamy was right beside me, lips brushing over my hair as he pulled me into his arms.

"This is so freaking weird," I choked, half crying and half laughing at what a mess I was. "You have to take that scholarship, Bellamy."

"Whatever you want, baby girl."

# EPILOGUE

### DREW- 4 YEARS LATER

"WET FOR ME, BABY GIRL?"

The streetlights flashed through the curtained windows of the limo as we wound through the city streets. The glow was just enough that I could make out the perfection of Bellamy's face. All dark hair and perfect jawline, a smirk that promised to make all my problems disappear—of which I had none.

"You say that to all the girls?" I asked, then felt him smirk against my skin while he worked the strap of my dress from my shoulder.

"Only you..." He pulled my panties to the side, and his finger slipped inside me. "Soaked, like always."

His teeth raked my neck, and that addictive buzz hummed through my veins the same way it always did for him. "I'm not fucking you," I teased.

"*Not* gonna fuck me, huh?" His finger worked deeper. "So what, you came all the way to France with me and hopped into the back of a limo to play a game of 'get to know you?'" His mouth moved from my throat to my breast while he pushed my skirt above my hips.

I let out a laugh that was half lost on a moan when his fingers pushed deeper.

"So what, baby girl? You wanna know my favorite color?"

"Your favorite color is black."

He glanced up, frowning. "That's not how you roleplay, Drew." Then he spread my legs and settled between them, locking eyes with me as he nipped at the inside of my thigh. "Or should I call you Genevieve?"

It had been over four years, and he still wouldn't let me live that down. "Oh, fuck you, Bellamy." I fisted his hair and yanked.

"That's more like it." His teeth sank into my skin on a groan, then his hand went for my throat. "I like it when you get all angry."

Less than five minutes later, his dress slacks were undone and he was buried inside of me.

There was something undeniable sexy about him in that tuxedo, going at me like a wild man. He might look civilized right now, but he wasn't, and there was nothing civilized about the way he fucked me. Choking and biting between whispered, dirty words.

The car rolled into the port just as that weightless feeling took hold, heating my body in a tidal wave of bliss. I had to bury my face in Bellamy's chest to silence the moans.

"Shit," he huffed, picking up his pace until he stiffened, then let out a guttural groan I knew the driver had to have heard.

"I swear to God, I could never get tired of this." He pressed a kiss to my lips, sweeping a hand over my jaw then tugging my dress back in place.

"Good." I kissed him before we stumbled out of the car onto the harbor side.

Mom's yacht was docked farther down, a floating ode to luxury and all things Bellamy and I had very little to do with these days. Even though they were at our full disposal.

I took his hand, winding my fingers through his. I needed to tell him something before we stepped on that boat and someone offered me champagne I couldn't drink. My stomach clenched with nerves, and I chewed on my bottom lip.

He turned to look at me, and his brows knitted together. "Are you going to throw up or something?" And ironically, it wasn't that far off the mark.

"I have to tell you something," I said.

His expression fell, suspicion evident in the scowl now shaping his face.

Panic settled in. "I uh..." I fidgeted with the top of my dress even though it was completely in place. "I know it's not ideal...but..." Deep breath. "I'm pregnant."

His eyes slowly widened as his gaze dropped from my face to my stomach, then back. "You're pregnant..." He swiped a hand over his jaw. "Okay. You're pregnant. Shit. Okay. So... Right."

He paced the promenade for a second, dragging his hand through his hair and mumbling to himself.

I knew what he must be thinking. We were twenty-two. This was ridiculous, but we were okay. Bellamy had just graduated with a business degree and was working for my dad, learning the company's ropes. I'd just secured a job as a social worker.

We weren't rich, but we were fine.

Although, Arlo may kill us. Last week at dinner, before we left for France, he'd made the statement that we weren't allowed to have a baby until he was grown-up, claiming he refused to share our attention. I'd just have to make the idea of him being an uncle at ten years old seem like the best thing in the world—and buy him another unicorn. Now, if Bellamy would just say something because my nerves were making me sick.

Bellamy came back over and grabbed my hand. "Okay. So, I have to ask you a question." Then he dropped to one knee on the cobblestone pathway, the lights from the boats playing over his face. "Will you marry me, baby girl?"

"Oh my God. This is so Dayton right now. You do not have to marry me just because you got me knocked-up."

"I was gonna marry you anyway." He glared up at me. "Stop ruining shit, and say you'll marry me."

I rolled my eyes. "Fine. Yes, I'll marry you, but I'm not waddling down some aisle."

He straightened and kissed me in a way that said he'd never leave me. "You want to keep it Dayton? We'll just go to the courthouse when we get back to the States." He smirked, then pressed another kiss to my lips.

I took his hand, starting toward the boat. "My dad always said you'd get me knocked up."

Good thing my dad liked him now. This was so cliché, the rich girl getting pregnant with the bad boy.

"Guess I'm just no good, huh, baby girl?"

But he was. Bellamy West was good just for me.

the end

Do you want to know what happens with Zepp and Monroe, and read more about the Dayton High Boys? Click here to read No Prince, free with Kindle Unlimited

Do you want to know more about Black Mountain and why Drew REALLY got kicked out? Read Popular. Warning, this one is a twisted, dark romance.

Want to know more about Nash and his band? Click here to read Over You, an angst-filled, second chance rock star romance. Free in Kindle Unlimited.

In the mood for a hilarious, sassy female lead? Click here for Rebel by LP Lovell. Free in Kindle Unlimited.

## MORE KU READS

### *Second Chance Romance*
The Sun - Stevie J. Cole
Over You - Stevie J. Cole
ExRated - Stevie J. Cole

### *Rockstars and Enemies to Lovers*
Over You - Stevie J. Cole
Jag - Stevie J. Cole
Stone - Stevie J. Cole
Whiskey Lullaby - Stevie J. Cole

### *Steamy*
Tiger Shark - LP Lovell
Falling in Between - Stevie J. Cole
Rebel- LP Lovell

### *Dark Romance*
The Wrong Series - Stevie J. Cole and LP Lovell
White Pawn - Stevie J. Cole
The Game - Stevie J. Cole and LP Lovell
Bad Series- Stevie J. Cole and LP Lovell
Absolution- Stevie J. Cole and LP Lovell

### *Total Tear Jerker*

The Beginning and End of Everything - Stevie J. Cole and LP Lovell

### **Other reads** *(not in KU)*

The Kiss of Death Series - LP Lovell

The Collateral Series - LP Lovell

The Touch of Death Series - LP Lovell

The Pope - LP Lovell

The Saint - LP Lovell

Darkest Before Dawn - Stevie J. Cole

### *Steamy Contemporary*

The She Who Dares Series - LP Lovell

## KEEP UP WITH RELEASES

→ Text READ to 77948 to receive new release text alerts (US only).

## ACKNOWLEDGMENTS

Thank you for reading!

Behind every book is a team of people who help bring it to life. There are so many people to thank for helping us with No Good.

**Candi Kane PR** literally has the patience of a saint, and we would be lost without her.

**Autumn Gantz** from Wordsmith Publicity and **Charlotte Johnson** do our social media and PR for us, and are both absolute gems. Thank you so much for all you do.

**Caleb and Adam**...bless you both for hand feeding us chocolate, Diet Coke, and Wine.

For this book we have to give a massive shoutout to our beta readers, **Kerry Fletcher, Author Laura Barnard** (She's hilarious. If you love rom com run and buy her books), and **Jen Lum**. This one was a tough one for you guys.

**Kerry Fletcher**. Girl, you put up with so much. You're like, part PA, part mother and part super hero. I love you!

**Lori Jackson**. Thank you for this awesome cover. It's so pretty.

**Stephie**, thank you for your ever vigilant editing.

There are so many blogs and individuals who have helped us along the way and you are all hugely appreciated.

Anyone who has ever written a review, posted a teaser, or read any of our books...Thank you. Your ongoing support means the world.

Printed in Great Britain
by Amazon